Also by Sheila Gilluly

Greenbriar Queen

The Crystal Keep

Sheila Gilluly

HEADLINE

For my brothers, Skip and Bill,
from your 'big' sister,
with love and a wink.

From the Books of the Painter . . .

In that tyme there was great clashing of wills, the Three Powers against the One, and the One relented not, but swore that alle shoulde be doomed. Thus he raged ever against the Realms of the Three, and thus he ever tried to topple them, gnawing and gnashing at the Foundations.

Now it came to pass that the One stole from his brother, the Lord Aashis, a piece of crystall of surpassing beautie. This was a piece of the firmament itself, the Skye Roof, dark and lovely the waye a summer's eve is dark and lovely. Bye his Wilde Fire, the One blasted and broke that crystall until it laye in fragments about the hem of his robe. Then he bethought him that a thing might be made of those crystall fragments that woulde turn foul alle of Lord Aashis' fair creation, alle stars, alle winds, alle waters. He pondered how this myght be accomplished.

When he had thought deeply upon it, he set about to make the Pypes, and with them he summoned Beldis, the Wolf.

Prologue

They should have left an hour ago.

Though it was barely more than four hours after noon, the spring sun was already low, its pale light nearly swallowed by the branches of the trees that sheltered the bog high on its western side. The turrets of Greenbriar Castle jutted against the northern sky only two miles distant, but that was scant comfort. The archers on its battlements might see them, but once the sun set, they would be on their own.

The two peat cutters, father and son, had lingered longer than they should have over the bricks of turf, even though the other men from the town at the foot of the Sweep had called to them to leave the rest of the stacking till the morrow. Then the others had left to their homes, and still the two had worked on. Tomorrow was the naming day of the youngest in the family, and they wanted to be able to stay home and make a holiday of it. A neighbor had promised a lamb for the boy, and all the family would walk over the hill to get it.

At last Cobb straightened painfully, put a hand to his back, and told his son, 'Good enough, Dickon. We'll do the rest day after tomorrow.' He slung his patched and grimy cloak about his shoulders and cast an eye up at the setting sun. 'Shouldn't have stayed so long, belike, but 'twill be rare nice to have the whole day to ourselves, eh?' He took the slane, the peat spade, Dickon handed up to him out of the deep turf cutting where they had been working.

'I own I won't be sorry for the rest,' his son grunted as he steadied himself on the muddy bottom of the trench. 'Seems we've been diggin' peat for a lot longer than a couple of weeks.'

'Aye, but we'll be grateful enough for it in the dead of next winter, I don't doubt. Give us your slane and get yourself up to dry ground.'

As Dickon shifted the spade, the iron blade clinked against something buried in the seeping peat under his boots. 'What's here?' he wondered.

'Some old blighter's broadsword, I'll bet,' his father said, crouching at the edge of the cutting. The bog often gave up old armaments to their slanes. Everyone knew this was where Beod Greenbriar had fought his battle with the Unnamed an age of the world ago. 'Dig her up, lad. Let's have a look at what ye've found.' Sometimes the iron was still sound enough to put to use as another kind of implement.

With a couple of swift strokes, Dickon cut a sizable wedge of peat and lifted it with his slane to the lip of the cutting. He hopped nimbly out of the trench, and both men crouched over the brick, cleaning the heavy muck away from the firm object, which grew under their hands into cylinders arranged from smallest to longest. They had dug up what looked to be an old set of pipes of the sort that shepherds sometimes played, but no shepherd's pipe was ever of darkly shining crystal and bound with gold. Cobb whistled low between his teeth. 'Now that's what I call a right handsome day's work!'

Dickon grinned and dove into the trench again, jabbing around with his spade to see whether there might be more treasure waiting to be found. Some minutes later he pitched the tool out of the digging and climbed up again. 'Not a damned thing,' he declared disgustedly, hunkering down.

His father laughed, turning the pipes this way and that. 'Well, by the Powers, boy – how much luck do you want!'

'Enough to get us that blooded ram of Corwyn's.'

The older man considered, burnishing the pipes on the hem of his cloak. 'You might have enough right here to do that.'

A wind rustled the grasses and sent a chill right through their old cloaks, and on that cold air was borne a low snarling that sounded near at hand, as near as the peat turves. Cobb cast a look over his shoulder. 'We'd best get moving. Look, it's got pretty dark. Sun's dropped behind them trees.'

'No.' Dickon gestured to the large outcropping of rock a hundred yards left of them. ' 'Tis the Wild Feller's Foot-stool that's blocked it. Place gives me the collywobbles.' Time out of mind, the local people had scared their children with the tale of how the Unnamed often sat up on the rock, observing bad boys and girls with his cold eyes. Though most of the adults professed not to be affected by the story, still they did not linger long near the dark rock, and so of course the children knew that the story was true. Now Dickon twisted his shoulders as the shadow of the Wild Feller's Footstool fell across them. 'Let's head for the bogway, Dad. It'll be safer goin'.' To facilitate movement across the bog, balks of wood had been laid down to form a solid road-way in ancient times. As the bog rose to cover the wood, more was thrown down atop it. In the shifting environment of seeping ground, thin bog grasses, and bottomless pools that could swallow a man and horse whole, the bogway was a reassuring path.

The wind lifted their hair in its icy fingers again, and Cobb shivered. Dickon was stooping to gather their spades when from the bogway there came a rhythmic thump of uneven wooden wheels over the balks and the tinny clanking of many pots. In the dusk Cobb listened tensely, then swore under his breath. 'Damn! It's a tinker! Probably Tomasheen – he was up to the town earlier.' The traveling tinsmiths were notorious thieves and ruffians, exactly the sort of wild man one didn't want to meet in the bog with night coming on and a valuable set of gold-bound pipes.

'Give them here!' Dickon whispered hoarsely, and his father thrust the pipes into the younger man's hands. Quickly Dickon set them down and toppled a couple of peats over them. In the twilight, they should be hidden enough.

The tinker chirruped his horse to a stop and peered. 'Who's out so late?' They could see his hand drop to his dagger hilt.

'Two that know you, Tomasheen. Go on about your business,' Cobb answered coldly. They had missed a fat hen after the tinker's last visit.

'Ah, Masters Cobb and Dickon, I'll be bound.' His hand took up the reins again. Dickon relaxed a little, but at this distance they could not see the expression beneath the stringy black hair, so he still gripped his slane. 'Why, you should be warm beside a fire, lads. 'Tis a wild place to be from moonrise to sunrise.'

'It affects you not,' Dickon answered surlily, reaching down for their lunch basket.

From the tinker came his peculiar grunting laugh, and the peat cutters could almost see his yellow teeth bared in their customary snarl. 'Not many things would argue right-of-way with a tinker.'

'Not many would live if they did,' Dickon muttered, and his father grasped his arm warningly.

Cobb raised his voice. 'Good evening to you, Tomasheen. May yer way be straight.' The rest of the ritual farewell added 'back to our door,' but most folk prudently omitted that part when speaking to a tinker.

The cart did not move. 'I was wondering if ye'd like a lift back to town. I could spend another day there.'

'He knows!' Dickon whispered, but Cobb merely tightened his grip on his son's arm. 'Thanks, no,' he answered firmly.

In the long moment of silence that followed, Cobb knew the tinker had read his thought: if they accepted a ride, they would be responsible for inviting the tinker to take sup with them. The peat cutter could picture his wife's face if they walked through the door with Tomasheen at their heels.

'So be it,' Tomasheen said icily. 'Die in a bog hole then, ye ugly son of a whore!' He slapped the reins across his horse's rump and the wagon started forward.

'Shut yer rotten face!' Dickon yelled back, wresting free of his father's restraining arm and flourishing his slane.

The tinker threw back over his shoulder, 'Aye, well, fact is, puppy, I made the trip this way oncet just about . . .' He paused to reckon Dickon's probable age. '. . . twenty years ago, and the wenches were just as welcomin' then!' He laughed again.

Even in the dark shadow that had overspread the bog, Cobb could see the flush that raged in his son's face. 'Ignore the old bastard. The pox has gone to his head,' he said loudly enough to carry to the tinker above the clanking. Dropping his voice, he reminded Dickon, 'The pipes!'

With a visible effort, the young man restrained himself from running after the cart to thrash the tinker, and bent once more to collect their basket. When the cart had thumped far enough away, he cut through the bricks of peat under which he had hidden the crystal-and-gold treasure.

Cobb put a hand to his back and tried to twist out the rick that was starting there as he grew chilled. 'Let's go, lad,' he urged.

Dickon began flinging turves aside. 'I can't find the damn things!'

His father crouched to help him.

Tomasheen had heard it in their voices: they had found something in the bog they did not want him to know about, something of value. He reined in gently, and the obedient horse drew to a halt. 'Stay awhile, Molly,' he murmured, and she turned an ear back to him as he swung down from the high seat.

The tinker went back down the bogway, soft-footed in his worn boots. With his hood cast over his head and his cloak drawn about his chin, he could not have been seen much beyond a man-length. When he judged he was near enough to the place, he struck off across the bog, going carefully with his tinker's land-sense guiding his feet. Behind a tussock that rose up suddenly he could hear ragged breathing and a hissed curse. '. . . lost them!'

Cobb's voice was deeper and a little calmer. 'We've just misplaced the things in the dark is all. We'll come out here again at first light – let's away home. Yer mother'll be worryin'. Come on.'

Dickon cursed again, but it was a quiet and resigned sound, and then there came a clank of slanes being knocked together to dislodge the heavy peat. Tomasheen smiled. There won't be anything to find in the morning, whoreson! he thought gleefully.

On the night wind came the too-near howl of a wolf.

The two farmers went suddenly silent, and even the tinker felt his nape prickle. He heard them hastily gather their things and thud away, striking off for the bog road, using their spades as walking sticks to probe each step before putting a foot wrong.

The tinker listened carefully and heard when they stepped onto the wooden bogway, Cobb saying something quiet to console his son. Tomasheen smiled again, then quick as a weasel went around the tall clump of bog grass and stopped where they had been digging. Mostly by touch, he probed the cold turves, peering to see a glint of metal. He hoped it might be coin they had uncovered and lost.

He shifted position slightly, working more toward the dark bulk of the Wild Feller's Footstool. His toe nudged something solid beneath the pile of turves. Tomasheen thrust his hand into the peat and came up with smooth cylinders that his fingers quickly identified as a set of pipes. He frowned and brought them almost to his nose to see better. That was when he discovered the gold. The tinker's thin lips parted, and he began to breathe a little quicker. No wonder they'd been so bloody hasty to get rid of him!

He examined his treasure, buffing its dark glass length on his cloak. Like most other tinkers, Tomasheen appreciated a fine set of pipes, and like most others, he could play, though he wasn't as accomplished as some. He cast a glance at the bogway, found the mouthpiece ends by touch, and fitted the pipes to his lips. He blew softly.

There was no sound.

Frowning, he did it again, putting a little more wind behind it. Again, there was no sound. Then it came to him that the things had been buried in bog for who knew how long, so of course they would be blocked. One long finger-nail dug at the end of the pipes, but he could not scratch anything loose, so he tucked them into his belt and rose.

There was snarling suddenly – much too close. Even as he began to run, he cast a look back. At that moment Molly gave a shrill whinny.

'That damned tinker's about!' came Dickon's angry cry. Even over his own splashing footsteps, Tomasheen could hear the thudding down the bogway. Cobb and his son were coming back after him, guessing that he had crept in behind them.

'Wolf!' he shouted in warning, but they must have ignored him, because he still heard the footsteps converging on his own. Suddenly he caught the glint of their upraised slanes.

He ran full-tilt into a low snag of gorse and slammed to the seeping ground. He had fumbled the dagger from his belt and risen to his knee when the wolf leaped over him.

Cobb must have seen it, for he cried out and jumped off the bogway into the beast's path to save Dickon. But the young man had seen it too, and he was at his father's side, grounding the butt of his slane as though it were a boar spear. The wolf closed the last few yards at a dead run. Up over their rude weapons the beast sprang and bore them both to the ground, while Tomasheen lay still as a log and tried to gasp air back into his lungs.

Dickon threw up his arms to shield his neck, and the inch-and-a-half-long claws raked his gut, spilling bowel into the heather. Dazedly he tried to gather himself with his muddy hands.

The beast landed lightly and instantly whirled to leap again, going this time for the older man's neck. With desperate strength, Cobb thrust the wooden handle of the spade crosswise into the jaws and tried to twist the beast's head back. But the flying claws furrowed his chest, and the massive jaws gnashed through the ash handle as if it had been a twig. Though he tried to pull his dagger from the sheath at his belt, he was no match for the wolf. It buried its fangs in his throat and ripped until the hot blood fountained.

Dickon had crabbed away. The wolf licked its chops, turned from Cobb's body, and began to stalk him. Pace by exaggerated pace it crept toward him, unnaturally toying with the whimpering morsel. The young farmer dragged himself in an extremity of pain, his stare locked on the uncanny flash of blue that shone from the beast's eyes. He was too far in shock to know how close he was to the edge of the turf digging. He hunched, got an elbow under his body, and shinned backward – over the edge. There was a brief cry and then silence.

The wolf walked to the lip of the digging and stood staring down. After a moment, it licked its muzzle. Its face held an expression that in a hearth-hound would have been a grin.

Tomasheen got his feet under him and ran as he had never run before.

Lazily almost, the wolf padded after him.

'Tinker.'

Tomasheen heard himself called. His desperate eye swept what he could see of the bogway, hoping to find a late hunter with a spear – a long one. He opened his mouth to gasp a call.

'You, there. Tomasheen.'

The dry voice was behind him. But the wolf is behind me, his confused mind whispered.

'Yes, it is I. You might stop running like an overgrown hare. It makes me hungry.' There was a suggestion of a smile in the words.

The tinker leaped up onto the bogway and raced for his wagon. Stay, Molly girl, he thought desperately.

'She will,' the voice told him. 'I won't let her bolt.'

He risked a look to the side. The wolf was pacing him easily. In his terror, the tinker was sure he saw the beast's eyes flash bright sapphire for a moment. Tomasheen gathered his remaining strength and flung himself up onto his wagon on the side away from the creature and crashed his way along the rail until he could slide onto the seat. Scrabbling for the reins, he found his voice. 'Gi'up!' he shouted to Molly. But she was frozen, staring at the wolf as if she had been turned to stone. 'Gi'up, damn you!' he raged and slapped the reins across her gray rump.

'That will do you no good. She's much more frightened of me than of you.' The wolf sank casually to its haunches and regarded him.

Its eyes *are* blue, the frantic man thought irrationally. He had lost his dagger, but he rose on his seat and shouted savagely, 'Get away, you!'

The wolf laughed, its tongue lolling.

That sardonic laugh hit Tomasheen like a spray off a cold waterfall, and he grew suddenly quiet, scowling. 'By the Powers, if I had a knife . . .'

'You'd miss.'

'Don't you hurt Molly.'

'I am not hungry for horseflesh, Tomasheen.'

The tinker lifted his head. 'Go back to your haunting, demon, and bother me no more.'

'Haunting? You think me a ghost? I am quite real, I assure you.'

Tomasheen stared down at it. If you're real, you're the biggest son of a whoring wolf I've ever seen, he thought.

The fangs bared in a lupine grin.

The tinker shivered and was angry at his fear. 'If you're going to kill me, beast, do it!'

'Oh, no, my friend. You and I and the Pipes have much work to do for the master.'

Tomasheen sank down on his seat suddenly and felt the black crystal pipes pressing into his midsection. He brought them out. 'These?'

The wolf nodded.

'What kind of work? What master?' His face hardened. 'Us tinkers don't have any masters!'

The blue eyes sparkled. 'You know what master.'

The tinker's flesh crawled, and the pipes were cold in his hand.

'As for the work . . . let us just say you will enjoy seeing all your enemies, everyone who's ever given you a harsh word or worse, get their proper rebuke. Won't you, Tomasheen?'

Tomasheen would. 'Like those two back there?'

'Indeed.'

The wolf knew when the bargain was struck. It rose and as it did so seemed to flow into the shape of a man, lean and dark-haired. The blue eyes met Tomasheen's newly terrified gaze, and the thin red lips parted. 'Oh, come. You were half expecting it, weren't you?'

The tinker nodded jerkily.

'I want to move the meat back to the digging it and its cub

made. It will rain later, and the mess will be hidden from a casual eye by morning.'

Tomasheen swallowed. 'Who are you?'

The dark stranger pondered. 'Beldis was the last name they gave me,' he said as though to himself, 'but I suppose that won't do nowadays.' He thought for a moment more, while the tinker sat rigid and tried not to hear the deep rumble like a suppressed snarl that came from him. The Wolf suddenly grinned up. 'Badulf. That's what you can call me,' he said. 'We'll scare children from here to the three seas!'

Tomasheeen tried a shaky smile, but when the Wolf god beckoned him down to help move the bodies, the tinker blanched again in the darkness. 'All my enemies, you said?'

Badulf laughed slyly. 'And not a few of mine! The Pipes will play much mischief, my friend!'

The tinker put them on the seat. 'These called you from –'

'From my sleep. Yes. Awakened and refreshed me. You finally have an instrument worthy of your talent, Tomasheen.'

The tinker looked into the blue eyes. He nodded shortly and slipped down to the wooden roadway. I'll get a spear somewhere and hide it in the wagon, he was thinking, and then when he's killed most of them . . .

What a specimen, Badulf was thinking. Couldn't you find me someone more suited to the task, master?

Dark laughter floated to him out of the ground, out of the bare branches of the trees, out of the dark spaces between the stars.

'Soon, my Wolf, soon,' the dark whisperer assured him.

The corpses were dumped into the turf digging, and the tinker's wagon rolled away into the darkness. By midnight it was raining heavily, and Badulf stopped Tomasheen with a word, swinging down from the high seat. He resumed his natural form and loped alongside the tin-plated wheels for a while. When next the tinker thought to look for him, the dark, blue-eyed shape was nowhere to be seen.

It was not until he recognized a lightning-blasted tree that Tomasheen realized this was the lane to a farm where he had once been caught red-handed with a fine fat lamb under his arm. The farmer had beaten him senseless, the tinker recalled with sudden dread.

Then with growing satisfaction, he knew the Wolf must be hungry again.

PART 1
Storm Warnings

Chapter One

The news was brought to the queen on the Sweep, where she walked with the young Lordling.

'Mumma, birds in my woods,' he was saying, chubby finger pointing at the flash of white and emerald that marked the flight of a Binoyr.

'They are not your woods, you silly old Gerrit,' she answered, for they had played this game many times before. 'They are named for Uncle.'

'No,' he said positively, having newly learned the power of the word.

'Yes,' she countered as she always did, and smiled at the presumption of the little tyrant.

He tugged her to a stop and bent to pick up a bright red leaf. While he tried unsuccessfully to stick it to his nose, she looked around for Captain Peewit Brickleburr, who with his men would be on guard somewhere near. A drowsy mid-summer breeze rustled through the trees, and there were companionable twitters all around. Here and there amid the oaks and beeches were sprinkled straight-limbed young trees with bright red foliage and pearled berries, and as the queen's eyes rested on one such, she smiled.

Ariadne remembered little of her battle with the Immortal Tydranth, Lord of the Wild Fire, but sometimes she dreamed of ice and snow, and a black fissure opening in the very Sweep where she stood now. The crevasse had snaked away, certain doom unless the queen acted quickly. She could still see in her mind's eye the smooth surface of a stone with tiny lines like trees running through it, and a gray-eyed boy's grin. Without knowing why, she had hurled the stone into the darkness and there had sprung good green grass and a forest of tiny saplings to seal the victory of the Greenbriar Queen against Tydranth that day.

Now, though only five years had passed, the trees of Gerrit's Wood had already grown to their young maturity, and their dappled shade was welcome. Often when Ariadne had leisure from the press of affairs inside the castle walls, she walked here. It was almost as refreshing as being in Yoriand beyond the mountains.

One of the Binoyr, its white body and emerald tail feathers glossy against the leaves, alighted in the birch over her head and began to sing. Ariadne scooped up Gerrit in an extravagance of relaxed good humor. He let out a surprised squawk, then hugged her neck delightedly. They were discussing the possibility of having honey cakes for supper when the queen happened to look over the top of her son's curly head toward the castle's main gate. While Gerrit prattled on, she watched the First Watchman, Kursh Korimson, come toward her, and she knew by the look on the dwarf's face that the news wasn't good.

Peewit silently came from the woods to stand beside her. 'There's been another,' he said, voicing her own thought. The rest of the bodyguard was standing back out of earshot, but even so, Ariadne motioned to the captain to withdraw them. Whatever the grim dwarf had to say would be for her ears only.

Kursh had caught sight of them now. He came purposefully across the cropped turf, wiping sweat from his brow where it was creased by the band of his eyepatch. Gerrit squirmed, and when Ariadne put him down, the boy ran with a yell toward the First Watchman. Korimson absently swung the child to his shoulders and steadied him there with one hand while he brought the other to his chest in the Greenbriar salute.

The queen nodded acknowledgment and asked quietly, 'What is it?'

Being no courtier, he answered her plainly. 'Three more, my queen. On the Willowsrill road near the Hurdles. Sometime last night.' His mustache was bristling, and Ariadne could see that he was holding his anger in check at the cost of a bitten tongue. The Hurdles was only ten miles or so upriver, and the troops from the castle patrolled the road. There had already been talk in the taverns about why the queen's men couldn't even protect innocent folk. Now there would be fresh fuel to the fire.

Peewit sighed. 'Were they –?' Mindful of the child, he stopped. When the dwarf nodded curtly, the captain shook his head and muttered.

Ariadne knew what they meant. In the months since Spring Court, more than two score people had died, victims of wolf attack. Such things had not been unknown in Ilyria; one or two solitary shepherds or charcoal burners were found each winter. But never before had people been attacked in the summer, when there was plenty of easier game, and never before had a single beast been responsible for so many deaths. The queen's

huntsmen had grown quite familiar with the huge footprint.
Now the wolf had killed again only ten miles away. That was
last night, the queen thought. By now it could be . . .

Ariadne became aware that Peewit and Kursh were waiting
for her reaction. 'I'll want to talk to the patrol that found them.
How many others know?'

The dwarf's bushy eyebrows climbed. 'The rumor is already
down to the pantry, my queen. The men were seen when they
rode in, of course, and it showed in their faces. And then there
were all the people coming in from upriver this morning for the
festival; many of them passed by the place.' He winced as
Gerrit suddenly drummed his feet and yelled for his 'horse' to
gallop. He shook his head. 'There's no way to keep it quiet.'

The queen's lips thinned and she snapped, 'Gerrit, be still!'
The boy's first surprise dissolved a quivering chin. Immediately she patted his foot. 'I'm sorry, sweet. Mumma isn't angry
at you. But sit still now and don't be kicking Master Kursh like
that.'

'My horse!'

She reached to lay a finger across his lips. 'If you spur your
horse that way when you are grown, you should hurt it. Nothing that lives is for hurting, my wee knight. Hush now. You may
play later.' She let her gaze fall to the First Watchman. 'Fidelis
is examining the bodies as usual?'

'Aye, my queen. He said he will have a report for you by
evening.'

Ariadne nodded and glanced thoughtfully at Peewit.

'I shall summon the commanders, Your Majesty,' he
answered, understanding perfectly, as he usually did.

The queen leaned back in her chair and gave them all a sweeping look. She did it to give herself time to think, but nevertheless
she was aware of the effect of that cool, summing gaze on the
men who stood before her. She had chosen to review the commanders in the smaller audience room rather than in Rose Hall
because the servingfolk were scurrying about in there, trying
to get the impressive chamber ready for the festivities of her
Crowning Day feast on the morrow. But the commanders did
not know what was in her mind, and saw only that there was a
royal dressing-down to come and that the queen was angry
enough to slight protocol this way. That in itself would snap
them to attention, she thought grimly. They were good men,
however. She was reminded of that when, despite their collective feeling of guilt, not one of them dropped his eyes to avoid
hers. Quite a few reddened, but none flinched. She returned
her scrutiny to the bent head of the man who knelt on one knee
before her.

'Well, Bryce, we've mucked up wonderfully well, haven't

we?' She saw his sudden exhalation of breath at her
surprisingly mild tone, and how he swallowed before he looked
up at her.

Quietly the young commander said, 'We rode all night, Your
Majesty. It was not until we were on our way back here before
dawn that we found them.'

'But you had checked their camp earlier, correct? Surely you
would have noticed if all was not well.'

Bryce nodded. 'Yes, Your Majesty. When we stopped to
speak with them just after moonrise, they offered us tea. Later,
when we rode back that way after checking the camping
parties farther up by the Hurdles, the carters' fire had burned
low and they were asleep around it. We heard the snores.'

'And yet, within a few hours, the wolf had attacked and
killed them all with nary a scream escaping to waken any of the
other campers? It strains belief, commander.'

In the face of her impatience, there was little that the young
officer could say. She was not at all surprised when Captain
Peewit interjected, 'It does strain belief, my lady. Or would, if it
were the first time we had heard a similar tale. But as all of us
are aware, the pattern here is exactly the same as all the
others.'

There was a collective held breath in the room. The queen
tapped one tapered fingernail against the arm of the chair and
frowned. 'I am aware of the pattern, captain. We added these
nightly patrols precisely to avoid a recurrence of it. They obviously have not worked. Now I would like to hear your next-best
plans.' She swept them all again. 'Well, gentlemen?'

Out of the corner of her eye she had been watching Kursh
chew his mustache and tug at his eyepatch. She judged he was
ready to pop, and when he pushed past Peewit to stand in front
of her, she knew what was coming. He sketched a gesture of
homage, and she nodded that he might speak.

'Begging pardon, my queen, but there's one thing we all know
has to be done.'

The tension stretched. In the back ranks, someone craned for
a better look, and his sword clanged against one of the stone
pillars. The sound seemed to echo, though this was probably an
illusion. The queen said, 'Be good enough to explain yourself,
First Watchman.'

'Not one of the forty-odd victims has been a Barrener, yet in
each case there have been Barreners nearby. We know that,
because our lads have questioned them. It sounds to me rather
like those scum have got some big wolf they've brought down
out of their mountains, and they're loosing it on our folk as
sacrifices!'

There was a rumble of approval that someone had finally
said it, and Kursh pulled at his eyepatch.

Ariadne silenced them with a look. 'What do you propose?'

'Round them up.'

'What then?'

'Send them all back to their miserable mountains.'

'And if they will not go?'

He hesitated only a moment. 'They will. With the right persuasion.'

It was out at last. This had been brewing for months, and not in Kursh's mind alone.

Ariadne answered steadily, 'No. Not that way. Not ever.' She raised a hand to forestall the dwarf's protest. 'We have not a shred of evidence that your guess is correct. And even if it were, not all of the Barreners are members of the Wolf Cult. You would cut off the arm because the finger has a splinter.' He glowered but said nothing. 'Kursh, most of the Barreners are decent enough folk, or can be if we give them the chance. Their ways are strange to us, that is all. No doubt ours are to them. In time, we will understand each other better, and then Ilyria will be the stronger for having their loyalty.' The dwarf's face had gone stiff and cold, and beside him Peewit's jaw was clenched. She knew that to have their long faithfulness answered this way must wound them both, but if she did not get this clear with the leaders of her army now, there would be a bloodbath.

She continued, 'I know what you are thinking – that you can never forgive them for what they did to all you held dear. But I do not have your memories, for which I am thankful. I can forgive, and I must. I will have a strong, peaceful kingdom to give to my son.' She looked from Kursh to Peewit and then to the others. 'You will all help me, I know.'

She raised her chin. 'Now, this is what we will do about these attacks. Patrols will be doubled immediately. Draw every master huntsman from every manor in the kingdom and set them under our Master Forester. They will be organized by him into tracking teams. Cameron, are you getting this?' She paused to glance at the official scribe. At his busy nod, the queen continued, 'All traffic along the River Road is hereby restricted.' She waited out the surprised murmur. 'From now on, everyone travels only by boat. I know, I know – the merchants will howl that the freight rates will break their purses! Therefore, we hereby suspend our customary tolls until the wolf is killed and it is safe for our subjects to use the road as they have been wont to do.'

This brought one or two approving nods. The queen's generosity would make it easier to enforce the edict.

Ariadne smoothed a wrinkle in her gown and caught Kursh's eye. 'Last, we shall ask for volunteers from among the First Watch to be sent out as our eyes and ears to collect information on the doings of the Wolf Cult. It will pay us to make no mistake in this business – either way.' The dwarf's shoulders straightened, and he nodded briefly. 'We leave the selection and briefing of these spies in the capable hands of the captain and the First Watchman.'

Peewit saluted. 'We shall have the list for your approval before lamplighting, Majesty.'

She nodded and rose. 'Let us see to the slaying of this beast with all dispatch, gentlemen. The folk depend upon the protection of your good swords. Do not fail them again.' The queen descended her throne, and as one, her commanders saluted.

Not bad, Ariadne thought. I expected more grumbling.

The cooling breeze brought the excited voices of the crowd already gathering on the Sweep below the castle, and as she took a breath of fresh evening air on the balcony of her solar, Ariadne wondered if her policy on the Barreners would cost her the friendship of the gruff dwarf and the perceptive Littleman. They had come so far together. . . .

She was in the midst of a forest fire when she heard a discreet cough behind her. 'What is it, Meara?' she asked without turning.

'Beggin' your pardon, my lady, but there's a messenger come with a letter for you from Covencroft.'

Alphonse, she thought, and turned with a smile. Meara dropped a curtsy and handed her a slim packet bound with ribbons and sealed elaborately with wax. Ariadne laughed aloud at the sight of the gaudy thing, and Meara joined her. 'What in the world?' the queen wondered.

'It's another puzzle, my lady, I'll be bound. Master Wizard knows how they tickle you so. Go ahead – try to open it!'

Well, now, Alphonse, out to test me again, are you? the queen thought with relish. We'll see about that!

She took hold of one end of the tangle of ribbon and tugged experimentally. As she had expected, it did not loosen. It was as if some invisible glue held the knot. Next she tried the wax seal, but it did not yield to her fingernail as a normal one would have. Knowing from past experience that a knife would be equally useless, she looked at Meara. 'Hmm.'

'You might try the edges, my lady. Like last time.' The waitingwoman's eyes were shining with fun. The wizard's letters were rare enough to be a delectable curiosity.

So Ariadne carefully felt along the edges of the parchment for the telltale notch that she had taken three days to find last time. But there was no notch on this one. 'Hmm,' the queen said again. 'It was a candle flame the time before that, wasn't it?'

'It was. Shall I fetch a light?'

The queen frowned. 'No. He never repeats, anyway. This is a

new one, I'll be bound.' She thought for a moment and then brought one end of the ribbon over to touch the seal. Nothing happened. ' 'Twas just an idea,' she muttered. Absently she carried the letter into the royal apartment and sat down in one of the chairs before the unlit fireplace. Shortly, she had tried untying the knots, starting each time with a different one; slipping the seal off the paper altogether; prizing the individual sheets apart from the edges; holding the thing to a flame until it singed and she concluded that he had not, indeed, repeated that trick; tapping the packet in every kind of rhythm she could think of; and coaxing it in all her nicest tones to open, dammit.

But it did not open, and the afternoon shadows crept closer to her chair. Finally she flung the letter down impatiently. 'Well, that's enough of that. On the day before Crowning Feast, I can spare no more time on a jest.' Despite her words, she was keenly disappointed. If Alphonse had sent a letter, then it must mean that he would not be there tomorrow. She had been so sure he would come this time. Meara read the sudden pall over her mistress's mood and tactfully decided to tend to the tea things. She asked the queen's leave and turned toward the door.

Beside Ariadne's chair, one of the ribbons waved gracefully into the air and began to untie itself. Meara had stepped back to the side table to get the tea tray. The ribbon collapsed limply upon the packet. Ariadne looked quickly to see if Meara had noticed, but she was only clucking to herself.

A moment later, when the waitingwoman had pulled the door closed behind her, the queen smiled delightedly as the packet untied and unstuck itself and lay waiting for her to read the wizard's message.

Lady Queen,
If you are reading this, you are alone. It wasn't a puzzle this time but a necessity – Meara is a worthy woman, but some things are not to be shared. I will be there by Crowning Day and we shall have time to talk in full, but for now let me caution you to be very careful about how – or if – you use the Crystal until we talk. There are strange things afoot.
                              Affectionately,
                              Alphonse

Ariadne stared at the note. There was no trace of a smile in her now. She had expected another apology for his poor correspondence, another regretful refusal of her invitation to visit. In the five years of her reign, he had never come back to Greenbriar. From Master Chiswic, head of the Meld of Wizards, she knew that Alphonse had voluntarily put himself deep into the training that he would have had as an adept, but had bypassed when he became the Unmaker.

Now he would come, but not just to share in the feast and talk over old times. Now he would come because he had something to tell her, something she was fairly sure she would rather not hear. The queen's hands were cold, and she chafed them absently.

The doorlatch rattled, and Meara swept through with the tea tray. Before Ariadne even grasped what was happening, the ribbons threw themselves across the page and began to pull tight. The queen barely got her fingers out of the way. She hurriedly flipped the packet onto the rug and tried not to look at it as Meara set down the tray. The waitingwoman was intent on the china, and did not look up as she reported, 'My lord consort's home, lady. I heard his party come into the hall as I was fetching this.'

Ariadne sneaked a glance: the wax was sealed. 'Did my husband have a successful hunt?'

The woman leaned to hand her the cup. Her voice dropped to a conspiratorial whisper. 'Not a thing. The poor deer are safe for another day.' She had no fear that the queen might take this for effrontery. Neither of them could see the sport in hunting.

Ariadne absorbed the news with only a corner of her mind, sipping the fragrant brew. While Meara made up the fire, the queen's hand went to the Crystal of Healing on its golden chain about her neck and remained there.

Turning to attend to the lamplighting at last, Meara stooped to pick up the wizard's letter and lay it on the stool. She tapped it with one finger. 'That one's a real puzzle, and no mistake, my lady.'

Ariadne agreed.

Peewit Brickleburr, the Captain of the First Watch, opened his eyes and cursed under his breath as the knocking sounded at his door. He swung his feet down from the footstool and tightened his belt as he went across to open it. Outside he found young Jamison.

The orderly drew himself to respectful attention and saluted. When the Littleman answered it, Jamison held out a packet. 'Letter for you, sir. From Covencroft. Just came in.'

The superscription was Alphonse's. Peewit looked up at the human. 'Was there one for Her Majesty as well?'

'Indeed there was, sir. As usual.'

'Good enough, Jamison. Thank you.' Brickleburr made to shut the door.

'Pardon, captain, but the First Watchman is late for your meeting. Shall I fetch him?'

The rumor about the new spy group must already be out,

Peewit thought. 'I asked him not to put your name on the list, Jami. I think you'll be of much more service to the kingdom right here.'

The young man hesitated a moment. 'I could do the job, sir.'

'I have no doubt at all of that.' The captain nodded back down the corridor. 'Do fetch the First Watchman. Only don't make it sound like an order, please.'

A carefully muted grin tugged at the orderly's lightly mustached lips. He saluted once more and turned smartly down the hall. Peewit closed the door thoughtfully. Why had Alphonse sent a letter if he intended to come himself? The last the Littleman had heard from the wizard a month ago, Alphonse planned to arrive by Crowning Day. A change in plans?

He carried the letter over to the hanging lamp. Though it was sealed only with wax, the packet was designed to challenge. Brickleburr ran through a string of standard opening gambits and, when none of them worked, settled into his reading chair with some satisfaction. The game he played with the wizard was one of the few amusements he allowed himself, for it tied him to the special gifts of his kindred. Each of the wizard's seals was a puzzle, and puzzles of all kinds intrigued the Hearthfolk, Peewit's people, called by others the Littlemen.

First he gave his attention to the lettering which had been pressed into the wax. To his surprise and delight, it was a few words from a verse that had come down through the ages in Littleman lore, purportedly from Comfrey Lichen himself. Fair enough, Peewit thought; the key is Littleman, then. Now how did young Master Freckles pick that up? He frowned in concentration and delicately smoothed over the wax letters until he had a clear field. He chose one possible countersign and, with a stylus, pressed it into the seal.

Nothing happened, though that wasn't too surprising. It was, after all, only his first effort. For nearly half an hour, he played the puzzle, but it did not yield to his guesses. Impatiently he sat back and rubbed his eyes while he considered the problem carefully. The breeze coming in through his window had grown chilly, and he rose to shut it for the night. A tiny speck of flitting light caught his eye, and as his night vision cleared he saw that the evening was full of fireflies. The sight of that starry multitude made him achingly sad, for the fireflies were a special care of his kindred. Tales said that Littleman villages were lit by firefly street-lamps, but Peewit had no idea whether it was true, for he had never been to his ancestral home and could never go there. Such was the doom of the Pledged, the one Littleman out of all who was vowed from Comfrey Lichen's time to serve the Greenbriar monarch, forsaking his own people.

For a moment the captain watched the weave of lights. Then,

never one to feel sorry for himself, Peewit drew a breath and leaned on the sill, extending one hand. Softly, almost soundlessly, he began to whistle. The air was an ancient one, and the fireflies had heard it before. Within a minute of measured heartbeats, a cloud of them had gathered outside the window, and he invited one or two to light on his palm. He whistled a slightly different melody, explaining what he wanted so they would not be frightened of the lamp. They followed him inside. The letter lay on the table with the phrase he believed was the trigger already scratched into the wax. The tiny gems of light flew to it and danced their dance above it.

With a crackle of paper, the seal opened and the letter stretched out like a cat.

The Littleman laughed, carried his friends to the window on his sleeve, and bid them good night. Then he settled himself once more and began to read.

When the loud rap came at the door, Peewit started and came back from where the wizard's letter had taken him. He was surprised to find that the fire needed wood. How long had he been sitting? The queen would be waiting!

He yanked open the door, expecting to see a royal page summoning him, but instead Kursh stood clutching a paper. It would be the list of proposed spies. The Littleman ran a hand through his curly salt-and-pepper hair and motioned the dwarf in. Hurriedly he retrieved his uniform tunic from the chair back. 'We'd better get moving.'

Kursh sat stiffly down at the table. 'That's my best advice,' he said, tapping the list of names with one blunt finger. 'Had a fine time trying to get around to ask all of them too. They all said yes.' The Littleman was scanning the lines. 'None are married or betrothed.'

Peewit looked at him sharply, thought about it, and nodded. 'Right. Good thinking.' Under his breath he added, 'Until now, I hadn't realized how dangerous this assignment could be.' When he met Kursh's gaze again, he noticed the dwarf was studiously avoiding the open letter lying on the table near his elbow. He turned it so Kursh could read. 'From Alphonse.' He hoped his voice did not betray how the wizard's news had shaken him.

But Kursh merely glanced at the paper and looked away, while his hand went to settle the eyepatch. 'What's the news? You look like you've been hit with a mace.'

The captain finished buttoning his uniform. 'Read it.'

The dwarf thrust his chair back and stood. 'I haven't got time to read a sodding letter! What does it *say*?' he rasped.

Peewit gave him a searching look, noticing only then what he would have seen immediately had he not been so preoccupied.

Beneath his beard, Kursh was pale. His bristling eyebrows were drawn down so far that his one good eye peered out from a cavern. 'It's another headache, isn't it? That's why you were late.'

The dwarf waved a hand impatiently. 'Never mind my bloody head. What does the boy wizard have to say?'

'You should see Fidelis.' He cut off Kursh's angry retort, and answered, 'The Meld is certain that the Unnamed is preparing to attack us again.'

The two old comrades stared at each other until Peewit reached to extinguish the lamp. As Kursh walked heavily to the door, the Littleman glanced out the window. There were no fireflies outside now.

Chapter Two

The royal consort lifted his right heel from the basin of warm water and gingerly examined a blister. 'Damn boots,' he grumbled. 'Next time I wear a new pair of boots to go hunting, remind me about this.' He carefully dried the offending foot on a thick towel.

Ariadne, busily checking over her raiment for the next day's public appearance (though she knew that Meara would have everything ready, as usual), passed behind his chair and bent to plant a kiss on the back of his neck. 'Poor dear,' she teased into the pleasing scent of his hair. 'Shall I feed you some Elixir and make it all better?'

'You could be a little more sympathetic.' His voice told her that he was playing it up for her benefit. She patted his shoulder and continued on to her dressing table. He shifted in his chair. 'I presume I'll be able to get in line with the rest of the needy supplicants for the Healing tomorrow, at least?'

Ariadne laughed and began to unpin her hair. 'Really, Sal – you'd think you were at the gates of Ritnym's Realm!' She gave him a grimace in the mirror. 'You are the grumblingest old bear I know!'

Ka-Salin came to encircle her waist from behind and rest his chin on top of her head. 'But the best-looking,' he drawled and grinned like a cat in a creamery.

The queen elbowed him in the ribs, but looking at him in the mirror, she had to agree. By the Powers, she thought once again, how did you get so lucky, Robin my girl?

The prince consort was unquestionably a fine figure of a man. Ka-Salin, fourth son of the King of Shimarron, was slender but well-knit and tall, with the easy grace of the superb horseman. He had thick hair so absolutely black that its highlights were midnight-blue, and his eyes were bluer than any mountain lake.

Ariadne reached up to trace the line of his narrow mustache, trimmed and waxed in the Shimarrat manner, and her hand drifted to the jewel he wore in his right ear. 'That's a new one,' she murmured.

Ka-Salin kissed her palm. 'Yes. Do you like it?'

'Very much. It makes you look . . . disreputable.'

The consort growled amorously. 'Marvelous.'

She smiled, but pushed him away. 'I've too much to do!'

'My dear, you know that between them, Meara and Rhys-Davies could run the whole show. Why flutter on so?'

The queen drew the boar-bristle brush through her hair. 'It's just that I want everything to go smoothly.'

He took the brush out of her hand. 'It will. It always does. Your people love you, my queen.'

A perverse imp caught her tongue, and she heard herself say, 'They love to get their hurts healed, that's what they love.'

'And why should they not? Who better to give your worship to than Ritnym's Daughter?'

She flinched away from him. 'Sal. It's bad enough to hear that nickname from the common folk, who don't know any better. I don't need to hear it from you!'

The consort quietly put the brush on the dressing table and went back to the crackling fireplace. He picked up a silver ewer and goblet. 'Wine? It would relax you.'

The queen tried to gather up the shards of their broken mood. 'Yes. Thank you.' She walked to him. 'I'm sorry, dear. I didn't mean to snap at you that way.' Her eyes brushed the letter from Alphonse still lying on the small tea table. 'I've a lot on my mind, that's all.'

'Oh, I know. It's a bugger being royal.' He sat down in one of the carved cherrywood chairs and drank deeply of his own goblet.

I deserved that, Ariadne thought ruefully. 'It is,' she agreed, gathering her skirts and taking the other chair. Womanwise, she asked, 'Do you remember my first Crowning Day? I was so glad your father sent you as his ambassador.' Her eyes twinkled. 'Though I remember thinking that you looked a bit of a rogue.'

'An altogether startling perception. You knew me well, even then,' Ka-Salin answered. He sipped his wine and smiled at a memory. 'Remember that fellow who knocked me on my head in the lists that afternoon? The one from Westphalia? What a mountain he was!'

The queen shared his reminiscent laugh. 'The Knight of the Open Hand did us a great service, love. If you hadn't gotten your brains scrambled that way, you would have ridden home the next day and we should never have gotten to know one another.'

The consort twined his fingers with hers. 'I've often wondered whether my father paid the fellow to do it. If so,' his blue eyes lighted mischievously, 'it was the only good thing the old boy ever did for me!'

Ariadne managed her most demure voice. 'He did me no disservice, either.'

Ka-Salin leaned to kiss her. There was a knock at the chamber door. Ariadne called, 'Yes, Meara?'

The carved portal swung inward just far enough for the waiting woman to stick her lace-capped head in. 'Pardon, my lady, my lord, but the captain and the First Watchman are here with Master Fidelis.'

'Good. Show them to the library, please. Oh, and Meara, has my son gone to bed yet?'

'He has, my lady. I just spoke with Cele. She tucked him in early tonight so he wouldn't miss his nap so much tomorrow. Shall I have her rouse him?'

'No. It can wait until morning, I suppose. I just wanted to go over his part with him to be sure he's got it.'

Meara chuckled. 'I think you needn't have any fear on that account, my lady. The Lordling's been reciting his little speech to anyone who will listen for three days now. And his bow! He's a proper little gentleman, he is.'

The consort suggested mildly, 'Your mistress will be wanting her tea presently. You have it ready, of course.' In the Shimarrat court of his father, servants were not so familiar. It was not that Ka-Salin did not like Meara; he just thought she took too many liberties.

A bright spot of color appeared in each soft cheek, and Meara bobbed her head. 'Aye, my lord.' More quietly, she asked, 'Shall I serve you in the library, my lady?'

'Thank you, Meara. That would be nice. No doubt the gentlemen will appreciate a soothing cup, too. It's been a long day for all of us.' This last was directed at her husband.

Meara bobbed again, and closed the door softly. Ariadne said, 'She is a chatterbox, but she means only the best.'

'Mistress Gossip,' Ka-Salin grunted as he fitted a soft pair of house slippers onto his sore feet. He rose and stretched. 'Well, I'm off to my chess game.' He bent to kiss her, picked up the silver flagon, and limped out.

When the door had closed behind him, Ariadne sat looking into the dancing flames, knowing that it was not chess but dice that drew him. She wondered idly what excuses the other gentlemen involved made to their wives. Ah, well. Men would be men.

Abruptly she remembered why the Littleman and the dwarf were waiting for her, and on the heels of that thought followed an echo of Alphonse's cryptic letter. How could she not use the Crystal until she had talked to him? The Ritual of the Rose was the main event of Crowning Day! She shook her head and went to meet the leaders of the First Watch.

Going through into the antechamber, the queen took in the scene at a glance, even as she nodded to acknowledge the obeisances of her ladies-in-waiting and pages. Two members of the First Watch were on guard at the outer door that led into the broad corridor, where petitioners would doubtless be hoping for a word with Her Majesty before the evening was done. A minstrel was seated in the middle of the ladies' group, and he had risen to make a graceful and highly theatric bow. She resisted an impulse to grin, and said, 'Please continue. I heard you, Festil – you are in fine voice tonight.'

He straightened the ribbons on his lute and glowed. 'May I have the inestimable honor of playing for Your Majesty on this, the eve of Ilyria's greatest celebration? I have made a new song specially for the festivities.'

'Ah, alas, I shall not have the pleasure of hearing it this evening,' the queen replied, twitting him only a little, for despite his foppish mannerisms, he was a wonderful musician. 'But that will give me much to look forward to on the morrow.'

Festil cast his eyes down. 'Your Majesty is much too kind.'

'Not at all. Pray excuse me, all of you.' She paced nearly the length of the antechamber and stopped to let one of the young pages open the library door for her. Inside the softly lighted room, Meara was pouring the tea, and Peewit stood on a chair, examining a leather-bound tome from one of the shelves. At the long polished table, Kursh sat with his head sunk on his chest, apparently asleep, and Fidelis was staring off into space.

At the sound of the door, the captain got down from the chair and came to respectful attention, and the other two got to their feet. They saluted. Meara filled the last cup.

'Be easy,' Ariadne invited them, and took the cup Meara handed her.

'Our apologies for being late, Your Majesty,' Peewit said, and pulled the list of names from his tunic.

The queen waved one hand. 'No matter. I had other business myself, and I know you have had quite a lot to do to get things in order for tomorrow.' She took the list and gestured that they should sit. Meara curtsied herself out of the room. Ariadne scanned the names, her eyes stopping at one, but she asked only, 'You've spoken with them all? They understand what they are to do?'

'Kursh briefed them, my lady.'

The dwarf nodded. 'They're good men. They should do well.'

He did not meet her eyes, and Ariadne assumed that this was because he was still angry over the way she had not taken his suggestion about the Barreners. 'I am confident they will, Kursh.' She blew on her tea. 'About this afternoon – I hope you know that I value your counsel.' Her soft tone made it an apology.

Korimson looked up then, and she was struck by how tired he seemed. The dwarf had not been young when she had first met him five years before, but in the last months he had gone much grayer. 'Oh, aye.' He made a vague gesture. 'I go on too much, anyway.' He looked down at the fragile china cup cradled in one large hand. 'I just hope we don't all live to regret showing them mercy, my lady. They're a treacherous lot.'

She was not inclined to argue further that night. Catching Peewit's eye, she changed the subject. 'I had a letter from Alphonse today. He's coming tomorrow!'

The Littleman saw no reason to alarm her with his own news from the wizard, so he let a smile answer her. 'It will be nice to see everyone again, won't it?'

'That's the only saving grace of the whole, long affair,' the queen agreed.

While she was still smiling, Peewit said, 'I would like to go out as one of the spies, my lady.'

The queen set down her cup and looked at him with surprise, as Kursh frowned and Fidelis leaned to look past him. 'What?' she asked.

The Littleman sipped his tea. 'You must admit, I am probably the most suited person in all of Ilyria for the job. It would be much safer for me than for any one of the men whose names we've suggested.'

Ariadne realized even as he was still speaking that he was right. Because he was a Littleman, Peewit could pass through most places without anyone's ever realizing that he was there. She did not know exactly how the power worked, and when she had questioned Peewit about it once, he had answered only that it was no sort of magic, but only an extraordinary talent for being still. Whatever the truth of the matter, the ability of Littlemen to disappear was known to every child in Ilyria from bedtime stories. 'But I need you here!' she heard herself saying while these thoughts flashed through her mind.

'Oh, I would go out only for a few days at a time. We could put the story about that because of the wolf attacks, I am inspecting all of our posts.'

Before the queen could answer, Kursh cut in. 'Someone should go with you. Your precious spell won't be any protection against a sword.'

'It isn't a spell,' the Littleman explained patiently, 'and going with me would just put one of the other men in danger.'

'I wasn't thinking of one of the other men. I was thinking of me,' the dwarf said flatly.

'Obviously, you can't both go,' Fidelis said. They looked to the queen.

Ariadne nodded. 'But you won't leave until after tomorrow,' she ordered.

The captain answered, 'None of the men will. We've already given instructions that they mingle with the crowd on the Sweep. Maybe one of them will overhear something.'

'Very well,' she assented. 'But do be careful!'

He grinned. 'When am I ever not?'

She could have named a few times, but she did not, merely shaking her head. The lightness that he had attempted to inject dissipated when she finally nodded to the chief physician. 'You look worn, Fidelis. The examination was as bad as the others, I am guessing.'

The wiry doctor folded his hands on the table. 'Bad enough, my lady. There is nothing new. Throats ripped, fang and claw marks. No sign of chains or shackles on the victims.'

The Littleman broke the silence. 'Well, tomorrow will be a long day. I suggest Her Majesty rest.' The Watchmen rose to take their leave.

The Littleman was out the door first, followed by Fidelis. Kursh stopped with his hand on the knob to look back at Ariadne. 'About this spying mission. You really ought to stop Brickleburr, my lady. He's no cadet anymore to be playing at will-o'-the-wisp with a bunch of murdering Barr – scum.'

'Kursh, you know that he intends to do this anyway. Should I make him disobey an order?'

He frowned and sighed. 'I wouldn't fancy trying to clap him in irons down in the dungeon.'

She laughed lightly and bid him good night.

This was the worst one yet, the dwarf admitted to himself as he made his way back to his room down the hall and around a corner from the captain's chamber. They had just bid each other good night and Peewit had urged him again to consult Fidelis about the headaches. But he couldn't do that, Kursh knew – not tonight and not tomorrow and not for the days after that, either. There was always too much to do. Besides, you didn't ask a question when you really didn't want the answer. He could deal with the pain. It was the sound in his ears that really bothered him. That's what seemed to start each one of the beastly things off.

It's just the heat, he told himself. There's a storm brewing. It makes my head ache.

The corner in the hallway seemed far away, but he finally turned it and was out of sight of the sentry stationed near the captain's door. Kursh put out a hand to the stone wall and, closing his one good eye against the torchlight, guided himself to his own door. No orderly waited outside it; the dwarf had never seen any reason to have one, and tonight he was especially glad not to have to deal with some young whippersnapper who would insist on helping him off with his boots, as if he couldn't manage it himself.

He closed the door behind him and opened his eye in the soothing darkness. Ignoring the cold hearth, he went to the window and thrust open the shutters to peer up at the night sky. He expected to see clouds brewing, but instead chips of crystal glowed on a field of black velvet. The night couldn't have been clearer. 'Impossible,' he muttered. He craned to check as much of the horizon as he could, but there were no clouds racing the stars, no rising wind, no heat lightning – no sign of any storm.

He was forced to conclude that the headache was something else. Just for a moment he pressed his forehead to the cool stone casement. When he looked out again, though, his shoulders were squared and his beard bristled. Damn it all, then. He'd drown the rotten thing in flotjin. He reached to swing the wooden shutter closed but froze with his hand on the latch, for across the heavens streaked a fireball, and it left a trail of sparks behind it. In an instant the shooting star had fallen down the sky in the direction of the sea and nothing was left of it, but a suggestion of starsmoke streaming.

A peaceful smile which none of the squires under his tutelage would have recognized spread across the dwarf's face. Among humans the fireball might be considered an ill omen, but to the dwarves no sight was more blessed, for it meant Aashis of the Winds was blowing crystal.

Far out in the sea rose the cliffs of Jarlshof, island kingdom of the dwarves, the place of their beginning. From the first, circumscribed as they were by wind and water and open sky, they knew more of the ways of Aashis than did any of the other kindreds, and it was to the Lord of the Winds that they gave offering for full nets and calm seas and the boon of dying on land. And it was the Power himself who had given them crystal to make their hearts strong and to be their servant.

This was the way of it, as the dwarvish bards told the story Aashnasse, the Festival of the Wind:

Far back in time, farther than the ocean is deep, there was a dwarf. Olin was this one's name, and his father's father's before him. He was a delver, and deep were his diggings, but never could he find what he was after, and never could he rest until he found it. 'What do you seek?' his father asked him, and Olin did not answer, for he did not know. And, 'What do you seek?' his goodwife asked him. 'Why is ours the only boat unpainted? Why don't you fish?' But Olin did not answer, for he did not know. And, 'What do you seek?' his boy asked him. 'Why do we hunger? Father, why don't my bones grow?' But Olin did not answer.

Instead he grew wrathful and silent and took himself away from them, and he climbed up, he climbed up the long face of Barak-Gambrel, to the top of Morning Greeter Mountain. And there he sat him down. 'Well, I am here,' he said to the Wind. 'What do you want of me?'

Now, assuredly this was not the way to ask, but he had climbed a long way. And the Wind answered, 'What do you seek?'

Olin bethought himself. 'A strong son,' he said.

'Your son is strong,' the Wind told him.

'But he does not grow,' Olin argued.

'Open your eyes,' the Wind told him, and blew him back down the long face of Barak-Gambrel, and Olin tumbled to a stop in his own dooryard, much bruised and broken and with the breath knocked from him. His son picked him up and bore him on his own back into the house, and held him while the woman took Olin's broken bones and set them. Then Olinson took the boat and fished while his father watched from a bench in the dooryard. Olinson caught much and salted some so they ate well that winter.

And that was how Olin learned that he had a strong son.

When the spring brought the new grass up and the ewes dropped their lambs, Olin climbed up, he climbed up the long face of Barak-Gambrel, to the top of Morning Greeter Mountain. He stood with his face to the warming breeze. 'I am here,' he said to the Wind. 'What do you want of me?'

'What do you seek?' the Wind answered.

Olin pondered. 'A wife who is not a shrew.'

'Your wife is not a shrew,' the Wind told him.

'But she nags,' Olin argued.

'Open your ears,' the Wind told him, and blew him back down the long face of Barak-Gambrel, and Olin rolled through the door of his house. His wife turned from the hearth, where she simmered seaweed to collect the tiny shrimp that hid in it. And, seeing that Olin had been up the mountain again and would not be strong for work for many days, she shook her head and handed him the ladle to stir the pot. She put the baby on his knee and the next smallest she tied to his back, and a caldron of soiled clothing soaking she set by his foot. 'Here,' she said. 'The cold water will help your bruised hands.' Out she went, whacking the bushes to drive the sheep before her to high pasture. Night came and she did not come back, and morning came and she did not return, for she had gone to the high pastures and would not be back until snow fell. And the baby cried and the little one howled, and the clothes rotted in their tub. The shrimp weren't good, either.

And that was how Olin learned that his wife was not a shrew.

Hardly had the goodwife returned in the fall and byred the sheep than Olin climbed up, he climbed up the long face of Barak-Gambrel, to the top of Morning Greeter Mountain. And he made himself small before the Wind and lay on his belly and clung to the stone. 'Well, I am here,' he sighed. 'What do you want with me?'

'What do you seek?' the Wind answered.

Olin answered. 'To know what you want of me.'

And the Wind soughed and laughed as it does in the belly of a sail. 'Now we can talk,' Aashis said.

And that was how Olin of the dwarves learned of the Power of the Wind, and of waters, clouds, starshine and moonshine, and many related things. When they were done talking, Lord Aashis sent Olin into the delvings he had made, and Olin brought out the first crystal, and there on Barak-Gambrel, on the top of Morning Greeter Mountain, the Lord Aashis showed him how to blow it.

Now Olin climbed back down and returned to his strong son and his wife who was not a shrew, and he showed others how to work with the crystal, for such had been the Lord Aashis's direction. And the people prospered, for now they need fear storms no longer and the wind and water were their friends.

Olin also prospered, but he never climbed Barak-Gambrel again. And we do not climb it, either.

That is what the bards told.

It had all happened a thousand lifetimes ago, of course, and Aashis no longer spoke to the descendants of Olin except in the way of signs and portents as other Powers spoke to other kindreds. Some of the dwarves had long since left Jarlshof to trade and then settle in foreign kingdoms, as had Ochram, who joined forces with Beod Greenbriar in the first war against the Unnamed. Since those days, there had always been dwarves in the service of Ilyria. Regrettably, some others had even fallen under evil influence and lived among the Barreners, forswearing their ancestral allegiance to the Three Powers and following instead the fierce worship of the Wolf. But these were few, and not all were to be blamed for it, having been captured and enslaved generations ago.

In one respect, however, the dwarves had not changed since Olin's day: they still shaped the crystal. Dwarvish craftsmanship had found a multitude of designs and uses for Aashis' gift, ranging from goblets and decanters and marvelously faceted lamps down to fishnet floats and water jugs. But these were only apprentice pieces and commercial baubles. The highest art of crystal-blowing was now found only in a few of the oldest families, and even then the talent often skipped a generation. For the real gift, the original gift, was to form crystal into Weatherglass.

Worth a king's treasury – worth a small king's life – Weatherglass was coveted by other folk because with one of the smallish spheres, a person could 'see' weather to come. Its value in commerce, especially for commerce dependent on open waterways, was immeasurable, and for good harvests Weatherglass was even more critical. Wars had been fought over it.

Anyone who looked into a Weatherglass could see storms brewing or fine days ahead, but Weatherglass in the hands of a dwarf could even moderate weather a little, though nothing that went on two legs could ever control Lord Aashis's Realm. It was handy in a fishing boat, though, and all dwarven mariners carried one of the globes with them. Among the dwarves on Jarlshof, price was no matter: the crystal was shared with all equally, as was seemly for a Power's gift.

Seeing that fireball streak across the night above Ilyria had given Kursh a steady keel once more. A headache was a headache. There were more important things.

He really did wonder, though, about the storm that did not show in the sky but that he felt on his skin. In his long life of service to the Ilyrian throne, the First Watchman had acquired few personal possessions, and most of these he had left behind at his tavern in Swiftwater Shallows when he and the other surviving members of the old First Watch had set out on the road to rescue a princess five years ago. On his occasional leaves from duty, he went back to the Skull and Sword and played at tavernkeeper again in a desultory sort of way. But for the most part, the place was run by Kathy and her parents; they collected the tariffs and sent part of them on to Kursh, and in return kept most of the lucrative trade for themselves. Now, what Kursh owned of any value traveled with him. There was a small carved chest with brass strapping set up against the wall opposite the fireplace. He took the key from the pouch at his belt, felt for the padlock, and opened it.

It had been long since he had used his Weatherglass. He had only occasionally peeked to see what the weather would be when there was a barge coming upriver with his ale shipments. Generally he could rely on his own inbred dwarvish weather-sense for day-to-day living. Now, as he took the velvet wrapping off, the smooth globe felt cool to the touch, and as he got heavily to his feet and carried it to the window, he took pleasure in that flawless curve under his hand. When he held the Weatherglass close to his eye and peered through it at the nighttime sky, there was not enough light to tell him anything, though he thought the Glass was foggy somehow.

Sighing, he set it down on the rough woolen coverlet of his cot while he reluctantly lit a candle. As he had expected, the light sent a spear of pain into his eye, and he winced away from it. After a moment, he was able to bear it and reached for the Weatherglass again. Holding it at arm's length in front of the candle, he peered into the heart of the sphere. He saw nothing at first except a magnified candle's flame. Just as he had concluded that clear weather was the forecast, the Weatherglass abruptly darkened and miniature rolling clouds were captured in its curving panorama. Flickers of lightning he could see, and the clouds torn to shreds: there must be high wind behind those streaming wraiths. Bad, Kursh thought. This is going to be bad. He lowered the Glass, believing he had seen all the forecast, but then he realized that water sloshed in the bottom of the globe . . .

no, it was waves, waves crashing and building and crashing again, and the tide rising higher than any tide he had ever seen or heard of and so high that it crested in the clouds themselves and through it all stars shooting, falling down the sky, streaking through the ether leaving their hissing tears in long trails behind them and the wind blowing him flat against the stone and then he was tumbling over and over and his fingernails clawing at streaming wet rock and there was no hold, no hold at all, and he hurtled into space without bottom. . . .

He snorted and came awake staring. Miraculously, he had not dropped the Weatherglass, which was now clear and normal in every respect. His heart thudded hollow in his barrel chest, and his breath came as short as if he had just fended off an ambush in a dark night. 'Great,' he said aloud. 'Not bad enough to have headaches that would stun a bloody ox, now I've got fits, too!' The words were angry enough, but he heard the break in his own voice and was suddenly enraged at his infirmity. Without thinking, he drew back his arm and – stopped. By the Wind, he had nearly smashed a Weatherglass!

His rage cooled in a sudden shower of fear, and he gingerly carried the thing back to the trunk and locked it away. Tired beyond his ability to fight it, Kursh blew out the candle and fell onto his cot. He drew the blanket up to his chin and closed his eye against the pain.

Late that night Ariadne slipped through the secret passageway that led from a door hidden behind a tapestry in the royal bed-chamber down a twisting flight of steps to end finally behind another portal, locked from the inside. This she opened into a servants' corridor giving access to the kitchen. She probably would never have found it on her own, but Peewit had known it was there. When she had naively burbled that it must have been convenient for the servants to bring up meals to the royal suite that way in the old days, the captain of her First Watch had patiently explained that it was actually an escape route if she should ever need one. The probability that an attacking force would seal off the kitchen area was remote, and the kitchen had access to the cellar, which gave onto the royal family's private stable. He had arched an eyebrow at her, and she had nodded that she understood. An escape route, not a tea deliveryway.

Tonight, she was not escaping from anything except her body-guard, the gaggle of court ladies asleep in their cushions around the hearth of the antechamber, and the snores of Ka-Salin, who, as usual, had come back late and soggy with wine. Unable to sleep, she suddenly hadn't been able to lie still another moment.

She did not walk the floors often, but she had learned that on

those rare nights when she did, fresh air helped. So tonight she
headed for Rose Hall and the great windows which looked out
over the Sweep. Besides, she wanted a peek at the decorations
for tomorrow's festival.

She peered around the corner that led from the kitchen to the
broad corridor of the Greenbriar fresco. There was no one in
sight. She liked skulking around her own castle at night. It was
irresponsible, of course, and Peewit would have apoplexy if he
found out, but still, it was the nearest thing she had to freedom.
Already she felt better, breathing deep of the night air flowing in
through the open window arches, but she walked just a little
faster when she passed the place where Rasullis had kissed her
and reminded her that she was a slave.

Cautiously, she crept near the end of the hall and sneaked a
look out into the frescoed corridor that was the impressive entry
to Rose Hall. The torches burned brightly here, but there were
no sentries outside the massive carved doors of the hall. She
frowned. There should have been.

The queen stepped out into the broad corridor. A sound
from the balustraded stairway to her left drew her attention,
and she ducked back from sight, but quickly realized that
the sentries must be stationed down on the next landing.
There was a ribbon stretched across the top of the staircase.
Entry to the hall had apparently been sealed. She grinned
suddenly. Her chamberlain, the ever-practical Rhys-Davies,
must have decided that someone might track in the odd speck
of dust and ruin the queen's entire day tomorrow. Sweet old
dear.

Smiling, she turned right and walked toward the carved
doors. He probably had had them sealed, too. She could just
imagine his reaction if he discovered the ribbon broken in the
morning! Trying to tiptoe, she suddenly caught her heel in the
trailing edge of her robe. She thrust out a hand to catch herself
and leaned for a moment on the wall as she disentangled her
slipper. Whether there was something odd to the touch or
whether she caught sight of something out of the corner of her
eye, she was drawn to stare at the mural.

The torchlight behind her made the Briar seem to shimmer
slightly, as though in some soft summer breeze. The crowning
roses were of clearest robin's-egg blue with a reverse of deepest
teal – looking just like the real roses she would see again
tomorrow when she worked the Crystal of Healing and affirmed
herself and her heirs as rulers – and servants – of Ilyria
forever. The clear washed blue of the painted sky was exactly
the weather promised for morning, and the grass was so thick and
green it could have been the Sweep itself. Struck by a sudden
thought, she backed off a few paces, and then a few more, to get
a better look at the whole picture. By the Powers! It was the

Sweep! There was Willowsrill faint in the background behind the Rose, and there were hills across it, just as there should have been. By the Powers! she thought again. Why have I never noticed that before?

A breeze puffed from the open window arches behind her, and the torches flickered again. In that wavering light, the startled hare that crouched in the lower right corner of the picture raised its forepaws nervously to its chin, and the thrush forever flying in the blue sky near the ceiling beams turned its head to look at her and its beak opened like a fledgling's in a noiseless peep. Then the torches steadied, and the picture was just a picture again.

She shook her head to clear it, thinking that she must be much sleepier than she had known, but Ariadne had experienced great power before and she had been tired, and she knew the difference between the two. 'Strange things afoot,' Alphonse had written. Strange things. The Greenbriar Queen became aware that she was holding her breath and that her hands had gone cold. Suddenly, waxing in the light of the torches as though someone had struck a flint, there was a sparkle near the border closest to the hall doors. She took a few hesitant steps.

There, at the remotest edge of the mural, chips of diamond caught the torchlight and refracted it in brilliant rays that illumined puffy sunrise clouds. When she peered through the beams, Ariadne saw in the diamonds a tower that rose against the pale lilac-and-carnation sky. But no, she thought with the part of her mind that was not entranced, there is no such part of the picture! What do I see? She closed her eyes tightly, and when she opened them again, the diamonds were gone, and with them the sunrise. There was only the border design of twisted vine and flower, as there had always been, except that in the light blue sky showing in places through the vine, there was the barest outline of a tower.

In the next moment she was backing away. One of the torches on the opposite wall suddenly bubbled with pitch, and the snapping made her look around. There, flitting in through the window and headed straight for death in the flame, was one of the most brilliantly colored butterflies Ariadne had ever seen. Before she had time to wonder what the thing was doing flying around at night, she had darted forward and gently caught it in her cupped hands. Through the bars of her fingers, she saw the silken scarlet, gold, and indigo of the creature's wings. Very carefully she leaned toward the window and opened her hands.

The insect remained on her palm, slowly fanning its wings and questing toward her with its antennae. It seemed to be watching her. She heard a voice, which she scarcely recognized as her own, say, 'I have seen. Go now, little one.' A moment more the butterfly lingered, and then it flew out into the black sack of night.

A wave of dizziness swept over her, and she clung to the sill until it passed. In a minute or two she was able to walk, and then the queen fled back through the empty corridors and passageways of her sleeping castle to the sanctuary of her velvet-counterpaned bed.

Chapter Three

The First Watchman carefully combed his mustache, straightened the quartered emerald-and-gold tunic of his dress uniform, and clipped the brass badge that marked his rank high on his left shoulder. He picked up his pitted battle-ax and thrust it through his wide leather belt. Carrying his helm and gauntlets, he headed for the door, but stopped with his hand on the latch. He hesitated a moment, and then went to the chest where he kept his Weatherglass. In the act of drawing the key from the pouch at his belt, he shook his head. He felt perfectly fine this morning. No need to check. Time was a-wasting and Peewit would be waiting for him. It would soon be the hour to accompany the royal retinue down to the Sweep for the ceremony.

He tugged at his beard, sighed, and gave in to his impulse to open up the trunk. Drawing the Weatherglass from its protective cloth, Kursh carried it over to his window. When he swung the shutter aside, bright sunlight streamed in, and he held the Glass up until it was bathed in the radiance. The azure sky magnified in the sphere's perfect curve, and a few light clouds floated serenely above the Willowsrill Valley. The dwarf relaxed and lowered the Weatherglass, craning to peer down over the battlements. He had been awakened early by the rise and fall, like surf, of the multitude of voices out there.

From his vantage, the green swell of the hill on which Greenbriar Castle sat appeared nearly covered with peddlers' carts and tents, and the makeshift stage of a wandering troupe of players. A flash off burnished metal marked the easy canter of the guards who kept the queen's peace up and down the broad road leading from the palace gate to the river landing. The light breeze carried away the thin fog of cooking fires and wrapped the pennons flying from the battlements about their standards.

But the most striking thing was the solid line of folk which wound from Queen's Gate all the way back down the paved road to the Willowsrill. All of them awaited their Healing. Kursh had been one of the officers riding up and down that line for the first

couple of years, and he could still feel the quiet, tense hope from
the litters and carts.

Memory took him back even further, to a snow-covered Sweep
thawing in sudden springtime, and the woman who lay pale and
unmoving against the new grass. The Greenbriar which had
bloomed near her head had smelled so sweet. . . .

A few muted trumpet notes from the keep above as the
musicians made ready for the fanfare recalled the dwarf, and
he made haste to collect his gear and get himself out the door.

A young man in the plain but decent tunic and breeches of a
tradesman sniffed the toothsome smell of frying dough-boys and
made his way through the throng until he stood before the
bubbling caldron. 'Good morning to ye, mother,' he said, already
digging in his pouch for the copper.

The stout woman turned from the tripod, slotted wooden
spoon poised to lift out one of the frying pastries for the
customer. 'And to yeself, lad.' Her keen glance took in the coin,
and she deftly scooped out a sizzling doughboy for him. 'Honey
or jam?'

'Honey.'

She drizzled the sweet amber over the pastry and handed it to
him. The coin disappeared into some fold of her skirt. She looked
him up and down. 'Ye don't be lookin' as though ye've come
for the Healin',' she ventured, and at his laugh her own grin
widened. 'Ah, I thought not, healthy-lookin' lad like you. What's
yer trade, then?'

'Cooper,' he answered around a mouthful of the savory fried
dough, and added for good measure, 'Dad and me have our
wagon up yonder.' He indicated some vague point farther up the
hill with his elbow. She nodded, pulling off bits of raw dough
from the bowl at her feet and tossing them into the fry vat. He
swallowed and licked his fingers. 'Have ye family come for the
Healin', mother?' he asked politely.

'Do indeed. A while back, me husband tipped one of these –'
she indicated the bubbling oil pot with a wave of the spoon – 'and
it caught his hand, poor soul. Oh, 'twas a mess,' she said through
the young man's exclamation of horrified sympathy. 'And now
he can't get the fist open, y'know.' The young cooper looked as
though he was regretting having eaten the doughboy, and it
would be bad for business if he lost it right there and then, so she
finished briskly, 'so we're hopin' Her Majesty's Healin' will help
him.'

He looked down at his own honey-daubed hand, and then his
eyes came up and he said in a curiously direct way, 'It will,
mother. I warrant it will.'

'Aye, well, I hope so, I hope so.' She looked away and turned a
couple of the doughboys in the caldron. 'It's a great hardship to

him,' she murmured. When the young man said nothing to this, she turned her head. He was moving away, walking quickly and purposefully up the hill, and she watched him go. A small voice piped, 'A jam one, if ye please, missus,' and she reached into the pot to pull out the one the child wanted.

As he threaded his way toward the castle walls, Jak Cooper wiped his hands on his tunic and wondered how there would ever be enough Elixir to take care of all the people like the woman's husband. He shook his head slightly and resumed his watchful scan of the crowd. He and the other spies had dispersed from the castle itself toward dawn to be already among the throngs as daylight came and people started to stir about. Since then, he had seen Mat once and twice passed Lyle. He did not believe anyone could have guessed they knew each other.

He wondered if the others had noticed anyone suspicious in the press of people, and whether Robin up there in the high keep was worried about a possible Barrener assassin springing suddenly from a sick man's litter. It was hard to think that his sister might be in danger and that he could not be at her right hand to help guard her, but he had asked the First Watchman for this assignment and he would not allow himself to think they might fail.

When Jak had first come to Greenbriar from the farm at Wolf's Glen, in all that first flush of discovery that their own Robin was Queen of Ilyria, he had reported to the new-created Squiremaster. The First Watchman had watched him step forward when it was his turn. 'Name?' the clerk had asked.

'I'm Jaki, the queen's brother,' he had replied with a fifteen-year-old's brash assurance.

The clerk had looked up from his table, and Jak had felt good until the uniformed dwarf folded his arms and said conversationally, 'If you were Jaki, the queen's brother, then you'd be King of Ilyria; and if you claimed to be King of Ilyria, I would have to kill you, of course.' Jak still remembered how the one eye had impaled him.

'Y-yes, sir,' he had stammered. 'I mean, no, sir, I'm not –' He gulped and dropped his eyes to the carefully grave clerk. 'Jaki Cooper, sir,' he amended. 'Jaki Cooper of Wolf's Glen.'

'Cooper, J.,' the clerk pronounced as he entered it in the scroll. The First Watchman had brought a hand up to smooth his mustache. 'You're a quick study, Cadet Cooper,' he had observed dryly. But it was not until years later – after he had won his commission and played dice against the dwarf – that Jak had learned about Kursh's sense of humor.

Now, he was Yeoman Cooper. And he was still the queen's brother. Trying to lose, for once, his military posture, Jak meandered on, scanning faces, picking up fragments of conversation.

*   *   *

Last night's vision of the diamond tower in the fresco had faded to a dream. With her mind full of the ceremony she would soon perform, the queen was listening for a page, a Watchman, someone, to announce that a wizard was come from Covencroft for private audience with Her Majesty. Come on, Alphonse, get here, she thought. I have to go out there soon. Strange things afoot. . . .

Meara had awakened her early, before dawn, and the queen was already up, bathed, and having her hair dressed by the time her husband wandered into the small adjoining chamber to bid her good morning.

'How do I look?' The prince consort had stopped in the doorway for her inspection. As befitted the Greenbriar Queen's husband on this most significant of days, Ka-Salin was attired in royal splendor. Over his fine white silk shirt, his turquoise doublet was laced across his chest with silver braid, and the jacket had deeply slashed sleeves lined with silver. His breeches were white, also, and he held over his arm a cloak of silver metallic cloth, lined with teal silk, and heavily encrusted with lapis lazuli formed in the Rose motif. A teal velvet hat was tilted rakishly over one eye, and a single emerald tail feather trailed jauntily over his collar. He had worn the emerald earring, too, Ariadne noted; it was a private sign between them: she had given it to him as a wedding gift. She smiled to let him know that she had seen his gesture of support, and then her look went to his boots.

He held up one hand, though she had said nothing. 'I know, I know. But it's these or go barefoot.'

The queen raised her brows, but nodded. Meara stepped back then. 'There now, my lady. You're all tucked up.' Ariadne stood and turned to the mirror for one last inspection. In sharp contrast to Ka-Salin's royal appearance – and even to the cloth-of-gold tunic and short emerald cloak that Gerrit would wear – the queen herself was dressed simply. By choice which had now solidified into ceremony, Ariadne wore the same gown in which she had first come to do battle with Tydranth and reclaim her kingdom five years ago. The soft turquoise wool gathered at her waist and draped gracefully to the ground, while the teardrop-shaped neckline stood up a bit to frame her face. The sleeves tapered to a point over the backs of her hands. With this dress, she wore the leaf-green cloak she had been given in Ritnym's Realm, and the finely wrought girdle of golden roses that she had found hanging with the gown on a hook in her Aparting on Covencroft. Over the years since then, the pulls and tears in the dress from the long journey had been skillfully mended, and a few alterations to let out some seams made the gown fit nearly as well as it had. Still, it was perhaps the least-ornamented piece in her wardrobe. Ariadne wisely chose to let the ceremony which defined her as queen speak for itself to her people. There were other times to display herself in court finery.

As she gave a final pat to her hair and lifted the Greenbriar crown from the pillow that Meara held, the page posted at the outer door opened it to admit Cele, the royal nurse, with the Lordling Gerrit. Ariadne settled the crown on her head and glanced in the mirror at her son. He looked sleepy, but at least he wasn't fussing – yet. The thin gold circlet had slipped down on his smooth forehead, though.

She turned from the mirror and reached to straighten his little crown. 'And how are you this morning, Lordling Gerrit of Ilyria?'

'Fine. I had honey cakes for breakfast,' he told her smugly.

'Aren't you the lucky one, though? Meara made me eat porridge.'

'And not enough of that,' Meara muttered as she arranged the folds of the queen's cloak.

A discreet tap came at the door of the royal apartment, and the page opened it. Over the hubbub that came in from the antechamber, Ariadne heard Rhys-Davies's lugubrious voice. 'Come in,' she called.

The tall old man stooped under the lintel, and gave a stiff bow. 'At your Majesty's pleasure we shall be ready to begin.'

Ariadne hesitated, but it was time, and the wizard had not come. 'Very well, my lord Waterford. You may announce me,' she answered formally, giving him the title his family had held for generations until the Bastard's interregnum. When the queen had reestablished a royal court in Ilyria, her First Watch had found the old man keeping an inn in the Eastmeath, near the shore. Under the Barrener King, Rhys-Davies had lost his landholdings, of course, but he had also been made to witness the executions of his wife, his three sons, and his five grandchildren. Then the Black-and-Reds had speared him and left him for dead. Loyal men had found him and taken him to a hidden Retreat. The Lord of Waterford had survived, but like so many others, there was little he could do except watch in helpless fury as the Ilyria he loved crumbled under the Barrener assault.

Ariadne's appointment of him as her chamberlain was met with universal approval. In the years of her reign, she had come to be very fond of the quietly fussy elderly gentleman who administered her castle with such grace.

Rhys-Davies bowed again. 'I shall be honored to announce you, Your Majesty.' He went out, and the noise from the antechamber hushed expectantly.

Ariadne stooped to Gerrit. 'Give Mumma a kiss?' He did, enthusiastically.

Ka-Salin murmured in her ear, 'May I give her one, too?' Without waiting for an answer, he brushed her cheek. 'Remember:

when you feel dizzy, you're to let me help, all right?' A year ago, she had all but fallen before he'd caught her.

'I will,' she promised and took his arm and Gerrit's hand. She listened for Rhys-Davies to finish proclaiming her names, titles, and lineage, and on his last word stepped through the door.

The assembled nobles and their ladies rippled like a high-grown meadow in the wind, and their bows carried the royal train out into the main corridor, where the First Watch in full dress uniform swung into step behind her. Captain Peewit and First Watchman Kursh led the procession, the Littleman with his ceremonial blade drawn and laid at rest across his forearm, and the dwarf with his pitted battle-ax riding on his shoulder. This was for show, of course; Kursh's throwing knife remained concealed in its forearm sheath, and Peewit had another secreted in his boot.

Fidelis waited at the foot of the broad staircase just inside the keep itself. He carried a small golden chest and bowed low as the queen's party descended the marble steps. Ariadne nodded a greeting, and he joined the procession. They crossed the wide paved courtyard and followed the broad avenue that went down to Queen's Gate, the main entrance in the strong encircling wall. There, Sergeant Major William Quint waited with a special ceremonial detail to signal the trumpeters high on the battlements and swing open the iron-bound gates.

The fanfare pierced the bright morning, and Queen Ariadne went forth to her people. A tumultuous shout went up as she was sighted. Peewit and Kursh led her to the place her Watch had cordoned off. Her ornately carved and gilded throne had been carried out here from Rose Hall, and by it stood the prince consort's seat, and a smaller one for the Lordling. There was also a table with linen and water set ready, and a tall gilded pole anchored firmly in the earth. Over the place her Greenbriar standard waved. Ariadne sat, and the crowd hushed. Peewit and Kursh took up guard positions to left and right, and Fidelis approached to kneel before her.

'All hail, Your Majesty. May the blessings of Ritnym, Lady of the Earth, forever attend thee,' Fidelis began the ritual.

'And through me, my people,' the queen answered. 'As it has been since Beod's time, so it is now. Let those in need of Healing take heart, for the Power is among us.' She held up the Crystal.

'My allegiance I swear, and let my life be forfeit if I be not true,' the physician pledged.

'I receive thy allegiance with honor. Arise, and let us begin.'

While Fidelis set the gold chest on the table beside the queen's throne and took out the polished silver dagger, Ariadne stood up and removed her crown. Gerrit stepped up to her, bearing a scarlet pillow with gold tassels nearly as tall as he was. The queen looked down at her son, so solemn in his best clothes. His circlet had slipped again. Slowly and very clearly, Ariadne said, 'Receive this crown, symbol of my sovereignty, and do thou hold it in honor until I resume it.' She placed the crown, glowing with amethysts, emeralds, garnets, and inlaid copper roses, on the cushion.

At her nod, Gerrit proclaimed in a singsong chant, 'I, Gerrit Greenbriar, thy heir and loyal subject, do avow that no dishonor shall come to thy crown whilst in my care.' Very carefully, he bowed.

Amazing, Ariadne thought, and suppressed an impulse to hug him.

When the Lordling had returned to his place beside his father, four young girls came forward from the crowd, bearing a garland of woven flowers. Dropping pretty curtsies, they stood elbow to elbow, as though needing each other for support. Ariadne smiled kindly and waved them forward. The one who had been chosen for the honor of placing the flower crown upon the queen's head took a couple of steps up to her, clutched the garland – and froze there. Ariadne saw immediately. She stooped to the girl, placed both her hands over the small cold ones, and guided the crown to her head. The girl's color came back in a rosy wave and she whispered, ' 'Scuse, m'lady.'

As though she had been the only one to hear, Ariadne whispered back, ' 'Tis nothing, dear. I muddle things meself sometimes. Thank ye for the flowers.'

The girl smiled shyly, and with her friends, retreated back to the crowd only a little quicker than was seemly.

The queen straightened and glanced at Fidelis. At his slight nod that he was ready, she unclasped the golden chain about her neck and slid the Crystal of Healing off it. For a moment she held it up to the crowd, so that the morning sun streamed through it. There was a sound like a sigh from many throats, though realistically only the ones standing closest could possibly have seen the Crystal at all.

Then the queen aimed the Crystal at a smooth slab of marble which had been inlaid in the turf for the ceremony, and dropped the shining thing.

The Crystal shattered, as it would for no one but the rightful ruler of Ilyria, and the small wizened seeds inside rolled among the glittering fragments. The first step of the Ritual of the Rose was complete.

Ariadne watched while Fidelis carefully collected the seeds and transferred them to a small patch of closely shaven turf at the base of the gilded pole. The physician stood, took the silver dagger from the table, and again knelt before the queen. 'I await thy pleasure, Your Majesty.'

Captain Peewit moved to stand directly behind him, and laid his naked blade against the physician's neck. There had been much joking about this during rehearsals, but there was no joking now: Fidelis would soon shed the queen's blood, and the penalty for that, had the queen cared to enforce it, was death.

Ariadne took a moment to compose herself, checked to be sure that Ka-Salin screened Gerrit's view, and then extended her wrist. Fidelis folded the sleeve back, tucked a linen cuff around the turquoise material to protect it, and quickly nicked open a vein. Crimson spurted to stain the velvet turf. Fidelis handed the dagger back over his shoulder to Peewit and rose to guide the queen's hand nearer the pole so that her blood bathed the seeds. The prince consort unobtrusively stepped closer to be ready to support her if she should need it. All eyes in the group under the waving Greenbriar standard were fastened on the base of the pole.

Ariadne stood unmoving, feeling herself go cold while dizziness narrowed her vision until it was as if she looked down a long tunnel. She was vaguely conscious of a murmur far away, and as she looked out into the crowd she watched people's mouths stretch wide without comprehending that they cheered. Very slowly her gaze fell to Peewit, who was beaming up at her, and then Kursh's bearded face swam into view. The dwarf suddenly grimaced and raised one gauntleted hand to his ear as though it pained him.

Abruptly through the faintness she heard Fidelis gasp, and the sound was so compelling that she swung her heavy head to see what was the matter. At first she saw only the Greenbriar, twined about the pole, green against the gold. Already the Rose was budded, the top blossoms starting to spiral open. Then Fidelis stooped lower and she saw what had dismayed him. The lower branchlets were wilting, though her blood still pattered down to feed the Greenbriar.

What's this? the queen asked inside her own head, but she was powerless in the trance to say it aloud. This had never happened before. The blood of Beod's descendant fed the Rose, the Rose grew, blossomed, and set hips. From the hips was made the Elixir. There was never any variation in the Ritual. What's wrong? the queen thought again.

She thought there was an echo until she realized she was hearing Peewit ask the same thing. Fidelis shook his head helplessly and looked up at her. 'I'm sorry, Your Majesty – I'm going to have to make you bleed more.'

She swayed, but managed to nod. She knew Ka-Salin took her other arm but could not feel it, nor did she feel the second cut that Fidelis made. The throne was suddenly under her, but she did not know when she had sat down.

There was mist over the Sweep now, and only individual faces came through it. The little flower girl looked scared. Was it Jak back there behind her? Gerrit peered over a crown too big for

him. Kursh was a peculiar shade of gray with his eye squeezed
shut.

A man who cradled a mottled fist shiny with scar tissue edged
up to stare at the Greenbriar and then at the queen. He looked at
the Rose failing and realized what it meant, and the queen
turned her head from his naked distress. The Rose had fallen
away from the supporting pole to hang limply in the slight
breeze. Even to Ariadne in her trance it was obvious that the
Greenbriar would not bloom.

For a moment she heard again the unearthly laughter of
Tydranth and smelled the stench of a land dying under plague
and ice. Anger flared in the queen's heart, and she closed her
hand into a fist as if to grip the Crystal in the same way she had
then. Crimson pumped from her veins.

The Greenbriar lifted its leaves and again climbed toward the
sun. Its buds burst into huge blossoms, velvety and two-toned,
robin's-egg blue and teal. One by one, the blooms showered
petals down on the upturned faces of Fidelis and Peewit, and
then red-orange hips swelled on the Briar and the queen fainted.

She tasted brandywine, and warmth flooded down into her cold
feet and hands. The sharp throbbing in her wrist dulled to a
lesser hurt, and sound came back. They must have given her a
sip of Elixir in the wine, she thought. Fidelis was asking whether
she could hear him, and a small, insistent voice kept repeating,
'Mumma. Mumma, wake up.' Closer, so that she could feel his
breath as he whispered loudly, 'I have to give your crown back
now, Mumma!'

The queen began to laugh and opened her eyes. Gerrit had
climbed up on her lap, hauling with him the pillow and crown.
She gently put him down and said in a low voice, 'Well, then,
Master Greenbriar, we had better get on with it, hadn't we?'
The Elixir gave her a wonderful sense of well-being, and she
winked smoothly at the concerned Fidelis as she stood, raised
the crown in the sight of the people, and put it on.

The glad cheering drowned out the fanfare from the battlements, and she asked, 'The Elixir is ready?'

Fidelis answered, 'Yes, Your Majesty,' and indicated the
green glass jugs lined up on the table. He held out a shimmering
blue bottle. 'This is the full-strength Elixir. Your Majesty, what
happened?'

'I am sure I don't know. Tell the others to await my summons
later. We all need to talk about this. For now, begin the distribu-
tion, please.' As he bowed and began handing the jugs to the
officers of the First Watch to take around to all those desiring
Healing, Ariadne, attended by her husband and son and the
captain, walked toward the place where the most gravely ill
awaited her.

Each of the hurt or sick had someone to receive the sip of undiluted Elixir which the queen poured into the offered tin or wooden cup. At the first Crowning Day celebration Ariadne had fed the Healing solution to each of the most gravely ill herself, and she had still been working far into the night. Since then, the ceremony had been redesigned to speed the Healing in this way. Within a couple of hours, all those who had come today for the Healing would have tasted Elixir.

For some time the queen moved up and down the rows of litters, pouring out her Healing for the people until there were no more supplicants waiting there, although more were still lined along the road, patiently holding their places until the soldiers with the green jugs reached them. Among these, one group was being closely guarded by mounted Watchmen. Some Barreners had come for the Healing. A grizzled Watchman marched past them with his refilled container of Elixir, but showed no interest in the wary looks that followed him. Ariadne frowned.

Gesturing to Peewit, she veered for the place and called to the officer she did not recognize, 'Watchman!'

He looked back over his shoulder, and when he saw who it was, shifted the jug to salute. 'At your orders, Your Majesty.'

She left him at rigid attention, and walked to the Barreners. The four young men in their rough clothing bowed, after some hesitation. Peewit made a hand sign to the Watchmen guarding the group: Alert. There was an older man lying propped up on a pallet. His eyes were open but dull with pain, and there was sweat on his brow. The queen spoke to him. 'Blessings, sir. What is your ailment?'

His breathing was ragged, and he gasped as one of the young men leaned to uncover his legs. The young man – his son, Ariadne now perceived – said, 'We are woodcutters. A fortnight ago my father's ax haft broke as we were chopping down a tree; the ax head flew back and got his leg, as you see. We've tried to clean out the dead place, but it just spreads.' He fell silent. Now that it had come to it, he could not ask for help, and there woke a smoldering in his eyes as his look went to the Watchman who had ignored them.

The queen reached to touch his arm, and then she turned to the grizzled Watchman. Quietly she said, 'There are folk in need of Healing here, sirrah. You will pour for them.'

When the soldier stared, Peewit rested his hand on the hilt of his short sword. The other Watchman darkened, but turned abruptly and began filling the Barrener's cup. The woodchopper's son swallowed and nodded his thanks. Ariadne smiled.

As the royal party walked on, the captain lingered a moment to order the soldier, 'You will report to me at the end of this watch.'

'Yes, sir.' The man kept his eyes carefully on the liquid he poured out, and wisely none of the Barreners said anything.

Peewit caught up with the queen. 'My apologies, my lady. He will be disciplined, of course.'

Ariadne looked down at him briefly. 'The Healing is for all.'

'Yes, I know.'

The prince consort, walking behind his wife and son, glanced sharply at the Littleman. 'Is it thus you answer your queen?'

Ariadne stopped and restrained Gerrit from running off into the crowd where a juggler amused the bystanders. She laid a hand on Ka-Salin's arm. 'If it hadn't been for Peewit, I would not be here to wrong him today, my lord.' She sighed and lifted her chin. 'Let us enjoy the celebration, shall we?'

Even as she let the young Lordling pull her toward the juggler, however, she was wondering what had happened during the ritual. The Elixir had certainly performed its usual wonder: all about her, sick people were rushing to and fro in the crowd, seeking relatives and friends to share the relief and joy. As the Healing took effect on more and more of them, the festival got underway in earnest, as there was no longer any need to feel a little ashamed of being frivolous in the face of so many suffering. Still, the sight of the Briar wilting had shaken her inwardly, and now she wished she could slip away up to the castle and talk it over with Peewit, Kursh, and Fidelis. Of all the thousands of folk around her, only they would understand her fear. Only they had been with her from the very first time she had used the Crystal. Those three, and one other out here on the Sweep. She gazed up the hillside to the spot beneath the castle walls. There was a marble plinth set there now, to mark the place where Captain Tristan Faring had been buried.

Peewit noticed the direction of her gaze and said under the cheers for the entertainer, 'He could juggle, did you know that?'

The queen came back to find him looking up at her as though he had read her thoughts. 'You jest.'

He shook his head. 'No, really. Tristan was actually quite good. Only he used to do it with daggers. You needn't shake your head, my lady, for it's a fact. Ask Kursh.'

'You'll forgive me if I cannot quite see Tristan in particolor doublet amusing you fellows in barracks of an evening.'

He chuckled. 'Actually it was for the king, your father, and only when we were all pretty much in our cups.' Grinning, he added, 'He only missed once, that I recall. Put it right through Kursh's leather bottle of flotjin.'

At the queen's laughter, several heads turned, and she was forced to toss her handkerchief to the juggler as a token, because they all thought her quite taken with his act. They moved off again through the crowd.

As they paused before the puppet show, a ripple went through the throng and people began to point down toward the river. 'What is it?' Ariadne asked.

Some of the Watchmen gathered quickly and made a way for her through the press of people back out to the road. She looked down the long slope to the Willowsrill and saw what the stir had been about: tying up at the landing was a vessel with a sail of many-colored stripes. A barque had arrived from Covencroft.

In a few minutes Alphonse came galloping up the road, escorted by some of her officers. His ginger hair glinted in the sun as he swung down from the saddle, and she saw that he had grown a beard, a light one, trimmed in a point. The young wizard had grown into his hands and feet, and there was an easy assurance of power about him. His blue eyes sparkled. 'Greetings, lady queen! My felicitations on your Crowning Day!' The Serpent of the Meld tattoo around his neck rippled as he bowed, and his garnet-colored surcoat was deep wine in a sunlit glass.

The queen shook her head at him. 'You've nearly managed to miss the whole thing!'

A shadow crossed his face. 'I know. Forgive me.' He nodded to Ka-Salin. 'Greetings, my lord consort. I regret we've not met before.'

The prince nodded back and took his wife's arm. 'But your fame has preceded you, Master Wizard. Welcome back to Greenbriar.'

'Thank you, sir. I am glad to be here.' Courtesies of rank dispensed with, Alphonse grinned down at Peewit. 'How are the fireflies hereabouts?'

The Littleman made an offhand gesture. 'Just fine,' he answered, and then, thinking of the wizard's news in that letter, he sobered.

The redhead saw it, and his own gaze lifted to scan the crowd. 'I hope I'll have the honor of meeting the Lordling.'

Ariadne motioned. 'He's there, with Kursh. I fear the puppet show is far more entertaining than the arrival of a barque from Covencroft!' She laughed.

'No doubt,' he agreed. 'Kursh and Peewit. William Quint still serves you, I presume?'

The captain answered, 'He's on duty at the gate.'

'Ah, of course. Where else would the sergeant major be?' He finished his look around, and when he spoke to the queen his voice went quiet. 'I thought I might find Imris here ahead of me.'

She frowned. 'I was expecting to see him with you.'

He nodded. 'We had intended to travel together, but yesterday afternoon when I sailed across from Covencroft to pick him up, he did not meet me on the shore. Thinking that he might have grown tired of waiting for me and gone back up to work, I went to Aspenglade, but did not find him, and then to the nursery of the leafkins, but he was not there, either.' He had pitched his voice low enough that none of the guard detail could hear him. 'As I say, I had hoped to find that he had come on ahead of me, though what vessel could be faster than a Meld barque, I don't know.' Alphonse ran a hand through his hair.

Ka-Salin asked, 'Was anything amiss in Yoriand?'

He hesitated. 'It had rained heavily the day before, so I could find no tracks. The trees looked well. For someone who must work alone, he has kept things remarkably tended.'

The prince consort lifted one shoulder in a slight shrug. 'Then he must have gotten another, slower boat. Or perhaps he has business elsewhere.' Ariadne was staring at the wizard, and the captain was studying the ground. 'Well, I mean, he must be all right. After all, what could harm him in Yoriand? The enchanted forest would protect him!'

The queen and the Littleman, knowing by hard experience how fragile that wondrous forest could be, exchanged a look. Ariadne said, 'He must be off tending other trees somewhere, maybe even somewhere in Yoriand itself. He just didn't hear you call, Alphonse.'

The wizard sighed and said heavily, 'No, I don't think so.'

'Why not?' Peewit asked.

The blue eyes met his. 'Because I found his harp on the grass beneath Nilarion.' He paused and looked at the queen. 'All of its strings are broken.'

Chapter Four

The bees hummed over the sweet phlox and pungent rosemary in the queen's private garden, and the afternoon sun drew out one or two tiny lizards to bask on the terra-cotta tiles of the walk where Ariadne and Alphonse strolled. Anyone watching might have thought them merely passing a quiet interlude in the day's activities before the feasting that would begin in a few hours.

The queen and the wizard paused beside the sundial, and Alphonse unobtrusively scanned the boxwood perimeter, where the First Watch – almost hidden in the greenery – made certain that the queen's privacy would not be disturbed. 'And how did you revive it when it began to fail?' he asked.

The queen drew a finger along the bronze hour marker. 'Fidelis made a second cut.'

His face, which until then had shown thoughtful concentration, became concerned as he glanced at her sharply. 'You shouldn't be out in this sun! Are you sure you're feeling well enough to wait for Peewit and Kursh like this?'

Ariadne smiled at his change in tone, her eyes lingering on a pair of butterflies flitting over the tansy before she looked up at him. 'Careful, Master Wizard – you're starting to sound like Meara!'

He snorted, but the red rose in his face. 'Sorry –' he started to say.

The queen giggled delightedly. 'Alphonse, you still blush! Oh, I am so relieved! I thought with all your wizardly studies you might have gotten unbearably stuffy!'

Now he grew positively crimson, and he made a business of turning to scan the hedges again. Ruefully he muttered, 'Usually I can control it, but you caught me off guard.'

'I'm glad.' She patted his arm. 'I wouldn't have been sure it was really you, otherwise.'

He gave her a puzzled look. 'Am I so changed? Oh, the beard, you mean.' He shrugged. 'I was in solitude for some time, and it grew out. When I rejoined the Meld, I found I rather liked it.'

'I do, too.' She invited him with a gesture to walk again, and after a moment asked, 'Have these years – your training – been difficult for you?'

Alphonse noted the way the sun brought out the honey high-lights in her hair. From safe inside his own mind he whispered, Very difficult, but it was not the training that made them so. Aloud he said only, 'Some of it was hard, yes. But I have learned much. Mostly about myself, and about how much I do not know.'

She was looking down, seemingly studying the pattern of the tiles as they walked. At his words, she nodded. 'That is always the hardest thing, isn't it?'

'A school at which we've both been scholars, I expect.'

She favored him with a warm smile. 'I expect.'

They walked on, through the trim shrubbery and careless sprays of flowers. 'Gerrit seems a sturdy, bright little fellow,' he remarked.

'Thank you. I must apologize for the way he acted, though. He's cranky today with all the excitement.' She frowned. 'That's no excuse, of course.'

He stopped in the walkway and cocked an eyebrow. 'Well, come – would you want to miss the best part of the puppet show just to meet some old friend of your mother's?'

'That's still no excuse for setting up such a howl, and I do apologize for it.'

Alphonse lifted one shoulder in a shrug. 'If you insist.' A look of surprise flitted across her face, and he wondered how long it had been since the queen had found occasion to apologize to anyone. To change the subject, he said, 'Ka-Salin seems a good man.'

The queen's face relaxed into a smile, and she reached to pick a snapdragon. 'Not bad. For a prince,' she agreed. 'While you are here, I hope you two can fit in a few games of chess.'

'I'd like that,' he answered absently, and looked around as there was a rustle behind them.

A black-and-white pied cat stepped daintily out on the path and meowed quietly. The wizard stooped to lift her. 'Well, Peewit finally found you in the baggage and let you out, did he?'

The queen walked back the few steps. 'She's yours?' She reached to stroke the purring animal.

'I'm not sure who owns whom. But this is Patience, a queen among cats.' He told the cat very seriously, 'Patience, this is Ariadne, a queen among women. You two should get on well together.'

Ariadne laughed. At the sound, the cat looked up at her and opened both eyes wide. She saw that it was blind in one eye, a milky film spreading over the green iris. The queen scratched under the uplifted chin, and Patience leaned into her hand, demanding more.

The wizard gave the cat a final pat. 'That's enough of that. Go

catch a mouse or something.' He put her down on the ground.
She twined about his feet. 'She minds well, too,' he told Ariadne
and bowed the queen toward a stone bench set under the shade
of a birch tree.

Ariadne sat and arranged her skirts. Patience hopped up
beside her, and the queen rubbed her ears and looked up at
Alphonse. She could wait for Kursh and Peewit no longer; the
question had been gnawing. 'What do you think is wrong with
my Crystal?'

He folded his arms and shook his head slightly. 'I'm not sure
anything is wrong with it.'

'But I just told you –'

'That the Rose began to wilt. Yes. But it revived, and the Elixir
certainly does not seem to have been affected: it worked exactly
as it ought.'

The queen frowned. 'But the Rose has never wilted before in
the middle of a ritual.'

'Yes, it has.' The blue eyes were steady on her. 'Though I
don't suppose you remember it, the Rose wilted the very first
time you used the Crystal. At Covencroft.'

She had a vague memory of a shimmering funeral pall cast
over the bed, Imris with a harp in his hand and a thrush's
feather resting over his heart, a Rose twined about the bed-
stead. 'I remember, a little. Fidelis tried to stop the bleeding,
before any of us realized, and Master Chiswic told him to let go
of my hand, so that my blood would feed the Rose.' At his nod,
she objected, 'But Alphonse, today Fidelis wasn't trying to stop
the bleeding! There was no reason for the Greenbriar to fail!'
Her agitation communicated itself to the cat, which pawed
lightly at her sleeve.

The wizard shrugged and looked up through the leaves. 'Still,
all I am saying is that we must not jump to any false conclusions
just because the ritual did not go precisely according to plan.'

He was surprised when the queen rose quickly and angrily
told him, 'Just exactly what village idiot do you think you are
dealing with, Master Wizard? You send me a warning not to use
the Crystal until we talk because "there are strange things
afoot," and then when I do and it nearly fails, you try to tell me
nothing is wrong! If I had a taste for mummery, I'd be down on
the Sweep watching the actors make fools of themselves!'

Her gray eyes had darkened to pewter, and as Alphonse
looked into them he perceived that it was not anger alone but
fear that brought the outburst. His own answering irritation
cooled, and he bowed slightly. 'I do not mock you, Ariadne.' He
straightened and added quietly, 'I would not.' When she turned
away, rubbing at the bandage on her wrist, he went on. 'I sent
the message to you because we of the Meld recently began to
perceive a slight, subtle change in some of the Song. Because we

were not sure what it meant, we thought it best to try to restrict the use of other powers besides our own until we had a chance for more study. Your Crystal is one of the more powerful objects we know of that lie outside our control, so I was asked by my brethren to write to you.'

The queen listened, and the leaves made a dappled pattern on her turquoise gown. The sunlight caught the Greenbriar Crown now and again as the breeze stirred. An amethyst winked, and Alphonse was reminded sharply of his master, Llodin, and of the price the old wizard had paid to bring her to her throne.

Her voice brought him back to the present. 'Has anything ever disturbed the Song except some wickedness on the part of the Unnamed?'

Reluctantly, he answered, 'No.'

'Ah.' She walked a little way up the path and faced away from him. After a moment she asked, 'Why didn't you tell me?'

'I did not want to frighten you.'

The silence stretched between them. Away out in the garden the wizard could hear a robin's call. Ariadne finally said, 'And now Imris is missing.'

'I hope that has nothing to do with the Unnamed,' Alphonse said quickly.

She turned then. 'But you believe that it does.' It was not a question. 'I presume that Nilarion is being guarded now by some of the Meld?'

He was nettled. 'Of course! Do you think I'd have left Yoriand if I had thought the danger was immediate?'

Ariadne nodded approval and even managed a small smile. 'Do be sure not to use that tone of voice in front of the others or I'll have to let Kursh box your ears.'

He did not smile. 'And now what village idiot do you think you're talking to?'

Peewit, who had flicked from shrub to shrub and crept up on them unnoticed (just to get himself a bit in practice for his spying mission), shook his head. He had heard the undercurrent in their voices, and his Littleman intuition told him that Alphonse felt something rather more than friendship for the queen, and that she might be aware of it. When he stepped out onto the paved walk, only the cat seemed to notice. Patience jumped down from the bench and trotted to meet him. The Littleman took in the situation at a glance: the queen stood with her chin jutting defiantly, and the wizard was redder than the scarlet sage that marched along the border of the path. Blast you two tallfolk, Peewit thought. Say what you mean and mean what you say. He gave a hail, and they both looked up. As he came closer, the captain saluted. 'Your garden smells like summer itself, Your Majesty.'

She ignored this and said in the cold voice which sometimes was her way, 'We have waited upon you, Fidelis, and the First Watchman. Are they not with you?'

Obviously not, the Littleman wanted to say, but he replied mildly, 'I am certain they will be along as soon as their duties permit, Your Majesty. You did say to be as discreet as possible.'

'I had not thought it would take all afternoon to be discreet.'

Absolutely straight-faced, he answered, 'It could take years for Kursh to be discreet.'

The wizard laughed. The queen seemed inclined to stay angry, but a smile got away from her before she could stop it. 'It could,' she admitted. She patted Alphonse's arm in passing and went to sit down again. Ariadne sighed and looked around at the garden. 'I would for all the world we could skip the feast tonight and take ourselves to Yoriand for a picnic.'

Peewit breathed a mental sigh of relief as Alphonse made himself comfortable leaning up against the birch. 'We'll have to do it someday,' the wizard said. 'Have you been back there since you became queen?' When she shook her head, he told her, 'You must visit! Imris has the new crop of leafkins coming along beautifully, and the whole place has been replanted with the saplings your foresters sent. The growth is young yet, of course, but still, if you did not know that there had been a fire, you would see little sign to tell you. The Eldest has done quite a remarkable job.'

Captain Brickleburr listened, and the fact that neither the queen nor the wizard mentioned the Eldest's disappearance again told him more than he wanted to know about what they feared. Powers protect us, he thought. You cannot leave us to Tydranth. Not again.

A noise from across the garden at the gate made him turn, and through the spires of delphinium he saw Kursh come through. The dwarf stopped and looked around for the royal party. Peewit sketched a bow in the direction of the queen, who had not noticed, and went to meet his second-in-command. 'What kept you?' he asked as he came close enough. 'Where's Fidelis?'

The dwarf stuck his hands in his belt. 'One of the acrobats fell off his stilts. The good doctor is tending him.' He rocked back on his heels and regarded the Littleman benevolently.

Peewit began to say, 'Well, let's get a move on,' but he had not gotten three words out of his mouth before he caught a strong whiff of flotjin. 'Kursh!' He was appalled.

'What?'

'You've been drinking! On duty!' In all the years he had known the dwarf, Kursh's judgment of time and place to indulge had never lapsed. 'First Watchman, you have an audience with the queen, by the Powers!' He began to get angry.

'Relax, lad. I took just a nip.'

'It doesn't smell like just a nip!' the captain told him furiously. He whirled and stepped in among the plantings, looking for a particular patch, and when he found it, he picked a few sprigs. 'Chew this,' he ordered and thrust the peppermint into Kursh's hands. 'Be quick about it!'

The dwarf took some and genially pulled it through his teeth.

'What is wrong with you?' Peewit whispered hoarsely, and cast a glance over his shoulder to where the queen and the wizard waited. They were both looking in his direction. The captain gave a half-wave in reply and grasped the front of the dwarf's tunic. 'You will come to attention, First Watchman!'

The dwarf slowly straightened, and gravely removed the Littleman's hand from his chest. 'Be easy, lad, be easy. I've never disgraced this uniform yet.'

'What possessed you?' Peewit was nearly beside himself.

The one eye met his own. 'It's the only thing that eases this damned headache, all right? 'Twas either take a cup, or take a flying leap from the nearest battlement. Which would ye rather have me do?' He spat the peppermint into the boxwood hedge and gave a tug at his eyepatch. 'Let's go.'

'When Fidelis is done with the acrobat, you're next,' the captain swore.

'Aye,' the dwarf muttered. 'I can't stand your nattering anymore.' They fell into step and walked toward the birch tree.

Patience sat in the middle of the path, unblinking as she watched them approach. She rose and padded toward them with her ears pricked at Peewit's low murmur, but when Kursh was a few feet from her, she suddenly laid both ears flat and arched. Her fur stood all on end and she minced sideways toward him, a yowl rising in her throat. The dwarf spared her a mumble: 'Whoa, now, kitty – I'm no mouse for you to be looking that way at me.' He stepped carefully around her and saluted. Patience lashed her tail and slunk away to the side to circle around behind the queen's bench. From under its safe vantage, she turned slitted eyes on the First Watchman.

Alphonse was looking from the cat to the dwarf, and a line furrowed his brow, but he made a slight hand sign and Patience sank back on her haunches and ran her tongue over her whiskers.

The queen seemed not to have noticed. She looked from one to the other of her men. 'Fidelis?' she asked.

The captain answered, 'Is tending an injured acrobat, Your Majesty. He will be here as soon as may be.'

She nodded and looked to Alphonse to begin, but before he could say anything, Kursh asked, 'Where is Imris, Master Freckles?'

The wizard and the Littleman both winced, but for different reasons. 'No one has called me that for a long time, Kursh,' the redheaded man said. 'As for the Eldest, I do not know where he is.'

The blunt First Watchman demanded, 'Then why aren't you looking for him?'

Queen Ariadne leaped to her feet. 'Because he desired to have speech with me as quickly as might be, First Watchman. Guard your tongue until you know the rest!'

Kursh, who did know the rest – and had known it via Alphonse's letter before the queen had – brought his fist to his chest and held the salute. 'Beg pardon, my queen. But I am worried about him, and young Master Fr – Master Alphonse, here, has ways of looking not open to the rest of us.'

The wizard sighed. 'I did not say I had not looked for him, Kursh. I said I did not know where he is.'

Ariadne said more quietly, 'And we are all worried about him.'

'Yes. Well.' The dwarf rubbed briefly at his temple. Then his eye came up to the queen. 'I'd suggest we send out Riders, then.' The royal couriers were the fastest horsemen in the kingdom, and knew all of the roads and by-ways. If Imris was alone and afoot, they might be the quickest means of finding him. Presuming, of course, that he had left Yoriand of his own will. But none of them had ever known him to go anywhere without his harp.

Alphonse was saying as much, when Peewit suddenly cut across his words. 'No, not Riders. By the Powers, why didn't I think of this before?' When they all looked at him, he said, 'Not Riders. Send the Binoyr!'

'How?' the queen demanded. 'How could we make the birds understand what we wanted them to do?'

'Don't look to me!' the wizard protested. 'I know the ways of many living things, but the Binoyr are unique, and I have never heard that any but a Yoriandir can communicate with them.'

'You could try,' Kursh rumbled.

'No,' Peewit said again. He went to stand before the queen. 'You, my lady. You are the Chosen of the Binoyr. They would understand you, if anyone.'

She nodded thoughtfully. 'I will try it.' When the dwarf turned to escort her out to the Sweep there and then, she restrained him. 'Wait a bit, Kursh. Let some of the people leave. I would do this with as little fuss as possible, and we don't want a crowd trying to follow us into Gerrit's Wood. That would only give fright to the birds, and they might fly away.' He grunted assent and smoothed his mustaches. She fingered the bandage on her wrist and glanced at Alphonse. 'Meanwhile, there is something else. The Meld has reason to believe that the Unnamed is gathering power again.'

Both Watchmen had known this from Peewit's letter, but they did a creditable bit of acting. Kursh cocked one bushy eyebrow at Alphonse. 'Another renegade wizard? I thought Rasullis was supposed to have been the only one.'

The redhead's garnet robe stirred gently in the breeze, and a wine-colored spark glowed from the ring he wore. 'He was the only one, and there will never be another.' There was a close feeling in the air suddenly, as of that puff of wind that comes right before the first crack of lightning. 'The fault is not the Meld's this time.'

Peewit asked quietly, 'Then how will the Unnamed attack us?'

The wizard held Kursh's gaze a moment longer and let the aura of his Warding wane until there was no hint of it in the light summer wind. 'The Barreners, I think.'

There was silence as all of them took this in, and then Kursh looked up at the queen. Calmly, almost gently, he said, 'I told you they were murdering scum.'

In the shuttered room Fidelis brought the candle flame nearer, and the pupil of the eye contracted sharply. He did it again to be sure, before blowing out the light and gesturing for Peewit to open the shutters once more. 'All right,' the physician murmured. 'Nothing wrong there.' He studied the dwarf for a moment. 'How long have you been having them?'

'Since last winter or thereabouts,' Kursh answered reluctantly.

Peewit stared. 'You never told me that!'

'What was there to tell? A headache isn't something you'd ordinarily report to your commanding officer. Besides, I don't get them often.'

'You had one last night,' the Littleman objected.

'So maybe this is the same one, and it only went away for a little while this morning.' The dwarf pressed the heels of his hands to his throbbing temples.

'Does that help?' Fidelis asked clinically.

'Nothing does.' A quick glance at Peewit. 'Except that flotjin will dull it.'

'But that's worn off now, hasn't it?'

'Aye. For true.'

The doctor got up from his stool and stepped around behind Kursh. The dwarf started to turn his head, and Fidelis said, 'No, stay as you are. I want to trace your neck bones.' He pressed the dwarf's head forward.

Kursh submitted grudgingly. 'I didn't fall from my horse, if that's what you're thinking.'

'We obviously don't know what you did right now. Why not let

me find out, hmm?' His probing touch found nothing out of place.
'Lift your head, please.' Kursh did, and the healer's hands found
the pulses in his neck. Attentively he studied the regular beat.

Peewit was standing with arms folded on his chest and a
serious expression. Over the dwarf's head Fidelis caught his
eye and shook his head, shrugging. He moved his hands up to
Kursh's temples and sought the pulse points there. 'Hmm.'

'What?' the dwarf rasped.

'Nothing. Just something a little odd. I was expecting to find
the blood vessels swollen and pounding abnormally, but they
seem fine.' He frowned and moved to sit opposite the dwarf
again. 'Have you had any trouble with your ears? Difficulty
hearing? Aching?'

'Not trouble, but now that you mention it, I get a –' Kursh
could not find the words for the sensation, so he impatiently
finished, ' – a rushing, I guess you'd call it. A loud whistle of
some kind. It happens right before I get the headache.'

Fidelis nodded slightly. 'That gives us something to go on.' He
thought a moment. 'I'd like to see the bad eye, Kursh.'

The dwarf stiffened, but such was the old trust between them
that he only asked, 'Must you?'

'It may tell me something.' The physician glanced at Peewit.

'No need for him to leave, Fidelis,' Kursh said. 'Peewit's seen
it. Who do you think it was that took care of it all the long way to
Covencroft? I couldn't do a thing for myself, and Tristan had no
use of his hands. Peewit can stay.' He referred to the desperate
flight from the last suicidal stand against the Bastard and the
Fallen when they had come to take the Greenbriar throne by
force. It had been in that battle that Kursh had lost his eye to a
Barrener sword.

'As you wish,' Fidelis agreed as Kursh pulled the eyepatch off
over his head.

The wizard healers at Covencroft had done a good job of
closing the ugly wound, the doctor saw. The deep seam ran from
the bridge of the dwarf's broad nose to his cheekbone: not the
cleft that a full swordstroke would have left, but rather a jagged
scratch from a flicking point. The eye itself had been destroyed,
of course, and the lacerated flesh sewn shut over the socket. It
was a grim scar, but long since healed. There appeared to be no
new infection in it now. 'You've had no seepage from it?'

Kursh shook his head. 'Never.' He held up the leather patch.
'All right?'

Fidelis nodded. He said nothing more while Kursh adjusted it,
but he could feel the question from both his patient and the
Littleman. When the dwarf's good eye met his own, he said
quietly, 'I don't know, Kursh. I can find nothing wrong with you,
yet you obviously are suffering. The only conclusion I can come
to is that you either have some deep infection in your ears, or

. . .' He stopped, knowing he did not have to spell it out for the dwarf.

Kursh's eye narrowed, but he nodded. 'That's what I thought, too.' He swallowed, and one hand came up to stroke his mustache. 'Well, then, that's that.' His shoulders squared. 'Thanks, Fidelis. I appreciate that ye didn't beat about the bush.'

But Peewit put a restraining hand on his arm when the dwarf would have risen to his feet. 'Wait. Just because Fidelis can't find the reason for your ailment doesn't mean he can't cure it. Right?' He lifted his eyebrows at the doctor, and Fidelis understood.

Getting up from his stool, he went to the table where his medical kit was unpacked. He turned with a small blue bottle in his hand. 'A drop or two of Elixir in water should give you relief. Peewit, pour out a cup from the pitcher there, would you?'

Kursh jumped to his feet, scowling. 'No, by the Powers!' He glared at them fiercely. 'Ye don't waste Ritnym's Gift on a bloody headache!'

'Why not?' the physician asked. 'The Healing is for all who need it.'

'Damn it, next you'll be using it once a month on every woman in the castle.' Kursh had flushed dangerously red, and now he suddenly went pale and squeezed his eye shut.

Peewit got to him just as Fidelis did, and they eased him to the chair. The captain brought up the only argument likely to convince him. 'Kursh, you can't serve the queen in this condition. You must take the Healing.'

Painfully, Korimson nodded. Fidelis measured the dose into the cupful of water and pressed it into his hand. The dwarf drank it down.

For a few moments he sat with his head sunk on his chest, then he slowly straightened and sighed.

Eagerly Peewit said, 'You see? The Lady's Gift is for all!' Beside him, Fidelis was smiling.

Kursh looked from one to the other of them. 'I guess it is.' He got up. 'I have a mind to take a nap – I couldn't sleep much last night. I'll see you both in a while.' They were all to meet the queen and Alphonse out in Gerrit's Wood before the feast began.

'Rest is the best thing right now,' Fidelis agreed.

Peewit ran a hand through his curly hair. 'Well, I'm off to take care of a little disciplinary matter. Sleep tight!' he teased the dwarf, and Kursh grunted something as they parted at the door.

In his own chamber a few moments later, the dwarf went straight to the mantel over his fireplace, took down the leather bottle, and poured a brimming cupful. Angrily he tossed it down and slammed the bottle back on the shelf. Then he grasped the

mantel and waited for the liquor to work. He had not the heart to
tell his friends, but the Elixir had had no effect on the pounding
in his head. No effect at all.

The mellow light of the summer evening had stretched long tree
shadows down the crest of the Sweep by the time the queen was
able to escape her duties long enough to come to Gerrit's Wood.
Fidelis, Peewit, and Kursh were already waiting, and Alphonse
came striding up the hill from the quieting festival – with
Patience trotting at his heels – just as she met them under the
wood's border.

Without speaking, the five passed into the deeper shadow
until the trees closed about them and they were safe from
prying eyes. Ariadne stopped, anxiously searching the treetops. 'I haven't much time – I hope they'll come to me right
away.' She glanced down as the cat brushed her skirts.
'Alphonse, you might have left the cat. She'll scare the
birds.'

'I think not,' the wizard answered easily. 'Patience doesn't go
in much for hunting, and the Binoyr will sense that.' He went on
a little way, craning to check through the wood. The pied cat
circled Peewit's legs, but jumped away stiff-legged as Kursh
moved up beside him.

'I don't see them,' the dwarf commented, scanning the leafy
canopy.

'Ssh,' Fidelis cautioned. 'I think I hear them away off over
there.' He pointed northward, away from the castle.

They all listened. True enough, the distinctive fluting notes
could be distinguished amid the busy multitude of birdcalls.
Ariadne walked in that direction, and the others followed a few
paces behind, so that the Binoyr would approach her.

The grass beneath the trees allowed easy passage, and they
emerged into a small open place. The pair of Binoyr were
swooping through the golden shaft of light that pierced the
glade, calling to each other. One of the birds alighted in a broad
oak, and its mate soon followed. They perched, heads cocked,
watching the queen's approach. Her Watchmen and the wizard
let her go forward alone.

Ariadne drew the light cloak around her shoulders and
walked to the base of the oak. Above her the sleek white-bodied
birds arched their necks and preened, combing their emerald
tail feathers. She regarded them for a moment. 'The Eldest is
missing,' she murmured. 'Can you understand that, I wonder?'
If they did, the Binoyr gave no sign, fluttering their feathers to
get comfortable for the night. 'Find him,' the queen pleaded. 'Go
home to Yoriand, go wherever you must, but find him!' Her own
low voice sounded pitiful in her ears. The birds were cooing
sleepily now. Desperately, Ariadne tried the only thing she

could think of. If the Yoriandirkin communicated with the birds by 'sending' thoughts, maybe she could reach them that way.

She closed her eyes in concentration and tried. But when she admitted defeat a few moments later, the Binoyr were still roosting quietly and the light was beginning to fade to dusk. 'I really wish you'd go,' she murmured. As she turned, one of the birds untucked its head from its wing and sang briefly before settling down once more.

'Eat a bug,' the queen muttered, and stalked back to the small group waiting for her.

Chapter Five

Patience sighed and worked her claws in the fine carpet underneath the table. A thread of wool frayed in a most satisfactory way. She played with it a bit, but rapidly lost interest. It was far too noisy here for any civilized rest, and it had been long minutes since anything dropped from a surreptitious hand to appease her. Sitting up, she glanced round. The booted and sandaled feet of the queen's guests were, frankly, uninteresting – but at least none of them were moving toward her in an unfriendly way. She had long since sent the prince consort's whippet squealing to its kennel to nurse its wounded muzzle, and now the spot under the raised head table was hers by virtue of conquest.

It was, however, a disappointing victory. Patience groomed her whiskers, and when she was quite awake she discovered that she was hungry for more than the crumb or two that He had thought to drop for her. She regarded the elegantly shod feet before her, and then delicately reached out to grab the wizard's toe. However, since Alphonse wore high laced sandals tonight rather than his customary soft doeskin boots, the reaction was not exactly what she had anticipated. She heard a stifled gasp, and then the thump of a heavy goblet being set down on the table above. A hand snaked under the damask tablecloth and a garnet-ringed finger shot her an angry command: 'You, Mistress Mousechaser! Out!'

She thought a retort: 'I do not chase mice. The poor things are so frightable.'

The finger pointed implacably.

She sneezed upon his foot, slid between the gilded throne and the wizard's chair, and emerged behind the head table. The Littleman was there on his raised step, keeping guard over the queen, and she sent a purr his way. But then she found the dwarf also on honor guard, and her ears flattened. There was wrongness there. She would not go past him.

Patience whisked back under the high table and ran lightly along its length. She bounced down the steps from the dais to the floor of Rose Hall and trotted toward the great doors at the other end. Near one of the large friava braziers, she stopped in midstride, one forepaw upraised. Something smelled awfully good. Her nose wrinkled, and she followed the scent. At one of the trestle tables several gallants in velvet and satin were vying for the attentions of the same lady, and the lady was waving a graceful little gold dagger with a sliver of pungent Lipopo cheese stuck on it. Patience's whiskers twitched, and she padded closer.

'Oh, come, my lady June!' one of the gentlemen was saying as he deftly deboned half a capon, and offered her a choice of dark meat or white. She chose white, and nodded that he might lay it on her platter. He licked the wine sauce from his fingers and continued, 'It is no secret that Her Majesty prefers her sister's counsel to all others'. So what do you think of my suit?'

Lady June Cooper, the queen's foster sister, cocked her head and regarded the cleft in Hilliard neBlackmore's chin. 'Why, I think yer suit has much merit, Hilly. After all, we can't be havin' these Barreners puttin' on any airs. Fancy, one o' thim thinkin' he can claim yer huntin' manor that way!'

Patience watched the sliver of Lipopo disappear between two red lips. She sat down to wait for the next one.

Another gentleman attired in the emerald-and-teal of the Queen's Second Watch stretched his booted feet comfortably out into the aisle and straightened the chain across his doublet that marked his noble rank. 'I don't see what all the fuss is about, neBlackmore. If the bas – excuse me, Lady June – if this Barrener,' he spat the word, 'is causing trouble . . .' He waved airily. 'Take care of it!'

There was an appreciative ripple of laughter around the table. The black-and-white pied cat stared unwinking at the lady.

neBlackmore laughed too and reached to tear a chunk of bread from one of the loaves on the table. 'Ah, but things are not so simple as they used to be, as your lordship has good reason to know.' He smiled slyly, and again there was laughter. Lieutenant Rigald Barrie, Count Nevelston, darkened, but smiled ruefully and lifted his hands in a helpless gesture. Just within this past year, one of his holdings had been appropriated by the Crown and turned over to a Barrener on the strength of some ridiculous claim that the fellow had brought before the queen's court.

Lady June delicately wiped wine gravy from her lips and put a consoling hand on Barrie's arm, smiling. She caught sight of Patience. 'Oh, look! Kitty's come to spy on you wicked fellas! My sister must have sent her!' She lifted her cup of wine.

The gentlemen exchanged glances uncomfortably. One of them flung a strip of chicken to the floor. 'Take it and begone, cat,' he muttered.

Patience thought: 'Cheese, fool, cheese. What would I want with a poor dead chicken?'

But there was no Lipopo forthcoming, and when one of Barrie's booted feet crept toward her, Patience sneezed on it and stalked away. When she was nearly to the large open hearth at the end of the hall, a greyhound rose to come galumphing toward her, but she froze it with a stare and passed by under its nose. She was out of temper with humans and their stupid hounds.

As she walked out of Rose Hall into the broad corridor, she knew she was getting closer to the source of all the wonderful smells. When a turquoise-liveried boy swept past her with a huge empty platter, she followed him through the mural corridor and down the passageway to the kitchen. She hesitated at the double doors, but slipped into the firelit room. Here was a bustle worse than the hall itself! Prudently she stayed near the wall and crept onto the bottom shelf of a large rack of crockery. But even here, she wasn't safe, for two large red hands grabbed for a deep bowl and she had to move. She followed the wall to a smaller adjoining room, where it was quieter and not as hot. This looked promising.

The floor was spotted with flour, and much of the space was taken up by a heavy table topped with marble. A dwarven woman wrinkled her brow as she carefully placed bits of honeyed fruit to decorate the large cake. Another woman, on whom Patience could smell the queen's perfume, sat at the table, sipping at a small glass of brandy. 'I tell ye, Thyla, if yer interested, ye should say somethin'! How's the poor fella to know, if ye don't?' the perfumed one said.

Thyla looked over the top of the cake. 'Meara, y'know if ye were in my shoes, ye wouldn't be so bold.' She reached for a bowl of whipped sweet cream and began spooning it over the cake.

'Well, by the Powers, if yer goin' to get Master Kursh's attention, yer goin' to have to knock 'im over the head with yer rollin' pin!'

Patience quietly walked nearer, sniffing at the cream.

Thyla was laughing, and now she winked at Meara. 'I thought maybe my special blueberry muffins. The First Watchman has been known to eat a whole panful by himself!'

'Well, there.' Meara lifted her glass in a toast. 'When are ye goin' to do it?'

Patience licked her whiskers and went forward a step.

Thyla frowned. 'I don't know. He doesn't seem much interested in his vittles lately – didn't eat enough to keep a bird alive when he was down to supper before the banquet. And I'd saved out a whole half-capon for him special, too.' She scraped the bowl thoughtfully. 'Didn't eat last night, either.'

Meara helped herself to a bit of fruit peel. 'Maybe he's just off his feed a bit.'

The dwarven woman snorted. 'Ever known a dwarf who couldn't eat?' When the queen's waitingwoman smiled around the sticky fruit, Thyla shook her head. 'He doesn't look good. After I'm done here, I'll make him a posset.'

'You'll never get medicine into Master Kursh,' Meara warned.

Thyla arched an eyebrow. 'That's why it won't taste like medicine,' she said. She ran a finger around the rim of the bowl and licked off the sweet cream.

Patience meowed.

Meara and Thyla both turned to look. The dwarven woman jumped in front of the table and made a warding-off gesture. 'Don't you jump up here, kitty!'

Patience regarded her, and sat very still. She meowed again, softly.

'Are you hungry?' Thyla dropped her arms. 'All right, you can have some, but mind you don't go after the cake or my broom will be after you.' She picked up the bowl and scraped the leavings into a saucer.

Noble woman, Patience thought, and stepped daintily nearer.

While Thyla set the saucer down, Meara finished off her brandy. 'I heard tell that the wizard brought his cat with him.'

Patience raised her head from lapping and gave the waiting-woman a look. It was the other way around, dear lady. She resumed licking at the cream, and Thyla's hand smoothed her fur. 'You're a pretty one, aren't ye?' the woman crooned.

Ordinarily, Patience did not like being talked to in that tone, as if she were some kitten, but she was disposed to forgive someone who had given her such excellent cream.

Thyla gave her a final pat and straightened, wiping her hands on her apron, and then tugged at the knot behind her back. 'Well, I'm going out to the hall,' she proclaimed. 'I want to get a good standing-place before Master Imris starts in singing.'

Meara looked at her with surprise. 'Ye haven't heard the news, then?'

The dwarven woman worked at the knot and glanced up. 'How would I hear any news, stuck in here all day?'

'Master Imris didn't come!'

'No! Why, he hasn't missed a Crowning Day since the first one, bless him!'

Meara straightened her cap and said confidentially, 'I hear it's worse than that: I hear he's missin'!'

Thyla stared, holding the flour-daubed apron in one hand. 'What do you mean, missin'?'

'Just that. Gone. Master Wizard went away acrost to Yoriand looking for him, and he never found him. They was supposed to come together on that great boat, y'know.'

The bakeress suddenly glanced at the open archway to the kitchen and put a finger to her lips. 'Tea, later?'

Meara nodded. 'If I can get away.'

'I can't believe it,' Thyla said in a low voice, referring to the Eldest's disappearance.

'Well, it's true.' Meara threw a look over her shoulder at the doorway, and leaned closer to her friend. 'And the queen is some worried about it, let me tell you!'

Thyla whistled under her breath and went to call the serving-men to take the cake out to the hall.

Neither of the women noticed Patience slip out, soft-footed and full of cream.

The pied cat returned to the mural corridor and hesitated, looking to her right through the huge open doors of the great hall. It was so noisy in there, and now a chorus of lutes had struck up, making things worse. She swung toward the staircase. Grass under her feet – that was what she wanted right now.

Patience trotted down the marble steps, startling several Watchmen on duty at the foot of the staircase, and crossed the broad lobby to emerge into the courtyard before the keep. She crossed the paved yard and followed the road down toward Queen's Gate. It had been swung to and barred for the night, of course, but there was just room underneath for the cat to squeeze through. The officer stationed there with his men laughed to see her go. 'Damn cat! Did you see that?' he said over his shoulder to his sergeant, and the other replied, 'I'd like to be able to get out that way to see my old lady!' There were guffaws. Patience cast a withering look back at the gate, but she was at last out in the summer-smelling turf.

She twitched her nose, which tickled with the scent of clover, and struck out from the road into the field. Shortly, she came upon a place where many feet had trodden down the grass. She approached the tall gold pole curiously. The Briar had shriveled after the ritual, as was usual, and it had been carefully taken up by the roots and burned in a seemly way. Now there was nothing left but the pole that had been its support. As Patience went nearer, she felt a delightful sense of comfort come up through her pink pads. It put her in mind of a patch of catnip Alphonse had planted for her once. Eagerly she scratched at the turf until the smell overwhelmed her and she sank to her belly in delight, and then flipped over on her back, paws dangling in midair ridiculously. She worked her fur into the turf and then lay still. The Sweep was canopied with stars, and her milky eye seemed to catch their distant glow. She sighed with content.

A moment later a swift torch of pale silver arced across the constellations. Patience narrowed her good eye to a slit, leaped upright, and sprang for the grass. Only when she was safely

buried in the longer growth beyond the trampled area did she
look up again.

The shooting star's trail still hung against the heavens, but it
wasn't the streak of light that had unnerved her: it was the
music, and the sharp crack of shattering glass that was woven
through it.

Vaguely, far on the edge of sound, Patience could just hear a
thread of song. Not the song of night wind over blowing meadow.
Not the song of pine trees on the heights. Not the ocean's music
or even the Song of the Wizards. All these she had heard before.

This was a song she had never heard, and it raised her fur and
pierced her ears momentarily. A yowl almost escaped her
drawn-back lips, but she shook herself instead and waited until
the star-trail faded, then ran for the woods.

Passing from tree trunk to tree trunk, she made her way
deeper into Gerrit's Wood without stopping. She startled a chip-
munk, which raced up into the nearest tree, but she ignored it
and went on until she reached an open glade. They were still
here, roosting in the oak. She walked to a spot beneath the
branch and sat down to catch her breath. 'You there, birds,' she
thought.

One of the Binoyr rustled in its sleep, but did not waken.

Impatiently, she repeated, '*Birds!*'

This time both of the Binoyr untucked their heads in a flurry of
white feathers. Dazedly they stared down at the black-and-
white cat.

'Your master. Where is he?'

The Binoyr looked at each other and sidled closer together on
their branch.

Moronic, Patience thought. She could suddenly taste feathers
in her throat, and she washed her face to get rid of the impulse. 'I
have not come to hurt you,' she thought at the staring birds. 'But
I must know where the Eldest is, for I have heard something I do
not understand.'

They sat a little straighter at that. One cocked its head. 'And
so have we. Before the leaves came, we heard it,' one of them
told her, and she caught a hint of condescension in its tone.

'You need not play hoity-toity with me,' she snapped. 'I am as
old in the land as you.'

'Truly,' the Binoyr agreed more respectfully.

Patience twitched just the end of her tail to let them know she
had not forgotten it. 'Why have you not flown to find your
master?'

'The Chosen is here.'

'And you may not leave her, is that it?'

The white-and-emerald bird dipped its bill. 'Even so,' it
confirmed.

Patience rose and began to pace. The birds watched her every

move with their bright eyes. She stopped. 'Have you sent your
thought to find him?' she asked.

The birds sat very still, and after a moment one said, 'We
tried.'

Patience's eyes narrowed to slits. 'What do you mean, you
tried?'

'The Eldest hath not answered. We thought perhaps he heard
us not, and so we sent our concern to him by Nilarion's Children.'

The pied cat scratched her ear. 'He is not in Yoriand, you
know. My human did not find him.'

At this, the Binoyr ruffled up their feathers, and one flew
about the glade distractedly. The other looked down at the cat.
'Dost know where he is?'

'No, you foolish hatchling! If I knew, I would get my human to
go after him!'

The other bird lighted in the tree once more. 'Perhaps . . .
perhaps the Eldest hath heard the strange music, too,' it suggested.

Patience pricked her ears, and licked her lips uncomfortably.
'Let us hope not,' she breathed. The Binoyr sat huddled on their
branch, and she left them to watch out the night together.

This time when she passed under Queen's Gate, neither the
officer nor the sergeant even noticed, and she trotted quickly
toward the keep, casting uncomfortable glances up at the
stars.

She loped up the marble stairs, in and out of the torch-light as
she passed the landings. Patience slipped by several groups of
people taking the air in the mural corridor, but stopped short
when she was nearly to the great doors of Rose Hall. There, in
the angle of the fresco and the gilt-rubbed portal, Kursh and the
Jarlshof ambassador were talking. She would wait until they
moved away. The cat sat down with her back against the
mural's border and watched the two with narrowed eyes.

Kursh was looking at the floor, apparently studying the
pattern in the marble. 'When did it happen, Nissen?'

Nissen Olafson smoothed his white beard. 'A fortnight ago.'

The First Watchman nodded and cleared his throat. 'It must
have come on suddenly.'

The other dwarf stuck his thumbs in his golden belt, and his
broad face showed pity. 'Actually no, Kursh. He had been ailing
for some time.'

Korimson looked up quickly, and his good eye began to blaze.
'My father was sick, and my dimwit of a brother hadn't the
decency to let me know?'

Ambassador Olafson said quietly, 'It wasn't Trondur; your
brother wanted to call you home. It was Korim himself who
forbade it.' When Kursh looked away, he added sympathetically,

'Your father was a good dwarf, but once his mind was set . . .'
He let the thought trail off.

'Ye need not tell me that, old friend,' the First Watchman
murmured. He turned his face to the corner and said nothing
more for long moments. Nissen Olafson waited with him, pretending for other eyes to be rearranging the folds of his crimson
velvet tunic. Finally Kursh nodded at some private thought and
said, 'I always knew he would never forgive me.'

There really was no answer to that, so the ambassador folded
his arms on his chest and regarded Kursh. 'Still, you are head of
the family now and ought to come home.'

Korimson snorted. 'I was disowned, Nissen.' He met the
other's look and said with grim humor, 'When Korim curses you,
you stayed cursed!'

'Korim is gone. Your brother asked me to tell you this: like it or
not, you and he are two heads of the same ax, and like it or not,
you are all that is left.' He paused and then added, 'I am
instructed by the Guild to convey to you their greetings, and to
let you know that you will be welcome to take Korim's place in
our deliberations.'

Kursh tugged at his eyepatch. 'I seek no power, Nissen. I am a
soldier, not a ruler.'

'Here you are a soldier. But you were not always one.' The
ambassador touched the flat crystal pendant that he wore about
his neck.

Korimson noted the gesture. 'Right. Once I was the son of a
Glassmaker.' His voice hardened. 'But that was long ago. Now I
am First Watchman to the Queen of Ilyria, and I am content with
that.'

'Are you?' the other asked quietly. He raised a hand as
Kursh's brows drew down. 'I know you never made your masterpiece because of the trouble, but you were one of the most gifted
prentices the Guild had ever trained! Haven't you ever wanted
to reclaim your rightful place, to do that which your family has
done since Olin's time? Kursh, you have the power to be a
Weatherglass maker – everyone recognizes that. Even Korim
knew it. Why do you think he was so wroth when –' He would not
say the painful thing, but went on, 'He knew what would be lost
if he sent you away.'

'Aye. But he did it.'

'Yes. Yes, he did. And I cannot say that he was wrong or right.
I know what I would have done, but I was not Korim.' He tried to
wave away the whole memory. 'But it is over now. Come home!
Take your place!'

Looking into Nissen's pleading eyes, Kursh thought of the
waves he had seen crashing in his Weatherglass just the night
before, and of the storm he felt rising. He thought of Jarlshof and
its folk, and the way the leaping logs sizzled on the great hearth

of his father's house while the snow sifted down in the winter. Then he glanced through the open doors into Rose Hall to where the queen danced with the prince consort, her jonquil gown bright against Ka-Salin's midnight-blue jacket. When he spoke, Nissen knew that he had lost him. 'I swore an Oath here,' Kursh said. 'Here will I stay until I die.'

The ambassador clasped his arm briefly. 'Then may the years of your service be long.' He sighed. 'I brought you a few trifles – my man will have delivered them to your room by now. Enjoy the nudlspritz. Lara made it especially for you.'

The First Watchman smiled. 'My respects to your goodwife.'

'And there's a small keg, of course.'

'Good. I was nearly out of flotjin.'

'Well, I should be getting back in there. I want to speak with the Westphalian ambassador before we all go out to the battlements for the fireworks.' Nissen hesitated. 'If I don't see you again before I leave in the morning, do think about what I've said.'

Kursh told him, 'There's nothing to think about. Done is done.' He held out a hand. 'Fare thee well. Safe voyage home.' When the other grasped it, he added, 'Keep an eye on the Glass, Nissen. Storms can blow up quickly this time of year. Tell the Guild I said that.'

Olafson was puzzled but nodded. Kursh watched him go back into the crowded hall and disappear among the swirling dancers. The First Watchman stood for some moments with his head bowed, and his hand came up slowly to thumb his temple. He slowly headed up the corridor that ran along the side of Rose Hall toward the stairway to the upper floors.

Patience sat quietly, looking after him. Then the thought of the music she had heard came back to her, and she made her way into the hall to find Alphonse. But when, after dodging the flying feet of the dancers, she finally rubbed up against the wizard's leg, he merely looked down and warned. 'You're going to be stepped on.'

She raised her head to him and thought: 'The Birds don't know where the Eldest is, either.'

But at the same moment, Queen Ariadne took his arm to let him lead her back to her high seat to hear and judge Festil's song, and Alphonse walked away from the cat. Patience flicked her tail and stalked away.

She took the nearest way out of the crowded room, and found herself in the corridor down which she had watched the dwarf walk a few minutes earlier. Some of the waitingmen lounged here, their service done until later, when it came time to bank the hearths and carry out whatever food and drink remained. Patience passed among them and took the stairway up.

Her wizard had been given a room near the royal apartment,

and she was thinking longingly of the thick, cedar-smelling blanket on the bed when she trotted up the lamplit hallway. But Alphonse had forgotten to leave the door open a crack, as he normally did at home, and much to Patience's disgust, she could not get into the room. She meowed, but no one came, and then she scratched at the door, but that brought no running feet, either. The whole castle was down at the feast, it seemed.

Morosely, she wandered away to prowl out a place to nap until the wizard came. One door a little farther up the hall was partly open. There was a Watchman standing guard outside it. Patience walked toward him curiously. The fellow was bored and lonely and stooped to pet and talk to her. She allowed it while she looked inside.

The soft glow of a lamp gave a faint illumination to the rocking horse with its plume of real horsehair and its saddle of red leather trimmed in silver. She slipped under the Watchman's hand and went in. He made to follow her, and the door squeaked as he pushed it wider.

Cele, the royal nursemaid, looked up from stitching on one of the Lordling's little shirts and put a finger to her lips with a frown. Then, seeing the cat, she smiled. 'It's all right, I think,' she whispered to the man. 'This is the wizard's cat.'

'Well, don't let her scratch him,' he warned and went back out.

Cele paused before taking another stitch. 'She won't do that,' she said, as much to the cat as to herself.

Patience looked at the woman, and then went to rub against her slippered foot and purr. Cele picked her up and set her on her lap, but the cat hopped back down and went toward the low bed placed along the wall under the window. Through the glass, she could see the stars winking. She leaped lightly to the foot of the bed, curled up, and let the boy's breathing lull her to sleep.

The strains of dancing music came faintly even out to the Sweep, and the weary figure leaned for a moment on the marble plinth that marked Tristan Faring's grave, listening. His dark eyes swept over the many lighted windows of Greenbriar Castle, and he could see the men on the battlements bending and straightening as they made ready the fire rockets. He sighed, patted the stone marker, and walked slowly toward the gate.

'Halt! Who goes there?' the challenge rang out from the guardpost above the ironbound portal.

The figure stopped where he was, palms up in a gesture of peace. 'A friend,' he answered in a low rasping voice.

'The gate is closed for the night, friend. You must return in the morning.'

'No. I think not.'

There was indifference in the voice that answered, 'Suit yourself, but you'll not get in tonight.'

The stranger gazed up at the guardhouse. 'Take me to the queen, please.'

A loud guffaw came from the guard. 'You haven't got all your lamps lit if you think I'd –'

'Take me to the queen, fellow. She will not thank you for keeping me waiting on her doorstep. I have come a long way through great peril, and I am very tired.' His hood was cast about his face, but a lock of silver hair had swung forward into his eyes, and he brushed it back impatiently. He added, 'I will give you a token to take to her.'

There was no reply, but he could hear a low-voiced conference going on behind the arrow slits. 'Very well. Stand as you are. Make no move toward your bow.'

'It is unstrung,' the stranger answered mildly.

In a moment the small postern door opened and one of the guards stepped through. The stranger waited quietly for him to approach. When the fellow drew his sword and stopped a few paces away, the silver-haired figure said, 'I must reach into the pouch at my belt to get the token.' The soldier nodded, and alertly moved out of the direct firing line from the guardhouse.

The stranger awkwardly opened the pouch with one hand and extracted something small, which he held up between thumb and forefinger. 'Give this to Her Majesty with my respects and tell her that while I am glad to find her men vigilant, still I would rather not stand out here all night.'

So bright was the moon's radiance that he could see the angry gleam of the soldier's eyes behind his helm. 'I will tell her, sir, but you must not be surprised if the Queen of Ilyria does not do your bidding.' The stranger gave over the token, and the guard looked incredulous. 'A feather? You want me to give the queen a feather?'

The stranger nodded solemnly.

The sword tip wavered, and the soldier backed away warily, holding the feather up. 'Stay then. I will bring Her Majesty's reply.'

When the postern had closed behind the soldier, the stranger muttered under his breath, 'Hurry up, for pity's sake.' He drew his cloak about him and sighed again.

The queen leaned over her silver goblet to say something to the prince consort, and he smiled, raising her hand to his lips and kissing it. It was very warm in the hall, and Ariadne sat back in her gilded chair and fanned herself. The musicians were giving the dancers a chance to rest and catch their breath, and just now a trio of boy violinists were struggling manfully with a motet too big for them. Serving-maids wove gracefully among the thirsty crowd, refilling wineglasses and ale tankards.

Captain Peewit Brickleburr was at his post on the dais behind the queen at the head table. The palace carpenters had built a special elevated step for him behind the queen's chair, and though he had been the subject of some good-natured teasing at the time, Peewit was glad to be able to see over the head table. The Captain of the Watch would have looked ridiculous staring at the hem of the fine damask tablecloth. The Littleman almost grinned at the thought, but recollected himself in time and kept the decorum expected of a fellow on honor guard.

He glanced over to his left at Kursh. The dwarf had been gone from the hall for some time, but that was permitted on such a long watch. Korimson appeared rock-solid, his hand casually on the sheath of the ax hanging at his belt. His good eye was on the side away from Peewit, so he was unaware of the Littleman's look. *I'm glad that business with the headaches is over with,* the captain thought.

He returned his attention to the music, but a wrong note nearly made him wince, and he found his mind drifting again. The thought occurred to him that sometime, at one of these affairs, he might forget himself and show these tallfolk what stillness really looked like. Wouldn't that make a stir, if the queen's Littleman should suddenly vanish! Behind his eyes, Brickleburr smiled and a merry urge rose within him, but he put it regretfully away. Even if one were Pledged to serve the Ilyrian throne, one should be able to be oneself every now and again. If any other Littleman had been in this hall tonight, he'd have gone still long since and would now be filching ladies' lace handkerchiefs to stuff into the pockets of the wrong unsuspecting gentlemen. That would be a right good jest! He'd make sure that Thyla's bit of a lace cap wound up in Kursh's pocket, and the queen's in Alphonse's . . . !

Mentally he came to and sucked in his breath. *Straighten up, Brickleburr,* he told himself sternly. *You've no business thinking that way, though the queen does look surpassing beautiful.* She wore yellow, the clear hue of jonquils in the spring. An edging of lace worked with gold thread and seed pearls trimmed the scooped neckline, and the same intricate needlework adorned the sleeves. The whole of the skirt was covered with a filmy overkirtle of net embroidered with more gold and pearls. The state crown had been replaced by a less ornate gold circlet set with a single cunningly wrought gold Rose. Though she had cast it back from her shoulders for now in the heat of the crowded hall, a velvet cloak of sugared violet would top the gown when she led the others to the battlements to watch the fireworks shortly. Now, as she leaned again to Ka-Salin, the light of the honey-scented candles in their crystal candelabra caught

the gold threads of her costume and she was momentarily
clothed in a web of sparkling light.

The prince consort's padded silk doublet, exactly the color of
his eyes, caught the sheen of light from the candles also. If he
was uncomfortable in the heat, he gave no sign of it; even his fine
linen ruff was still starched. Velvet breeches in dark navy and
polished black boots completed his attire. He wore a sapphire in
his ear and the silver circlet to which he was entitled by birth
and marriage both. A modest-sized badge with the quartered
dragon rampant and griffin couchant arms of the royal house of
Shimarron was embroidered on the left breast of his jacket.
Only by the very faintest tremor of his hand did Ka-Salin betray
that he had been drinking steadily since the Ritual of the Rose.
The queen had given a hand sign early in the dinner that his wine
should be well watered, and her own as well. He had accepted
the tacit rebuke gracefully, as always. Now he nodded and
smiled to encourage the young violinists, and kept time with a
silver spoon.

Peewit smothered a sigh and shifted his weight again. His feet
ached, and he was reflecting that he really was getting too old
for this sort of duty when over the heads of the crowd, he caught
a hand sign from one of the Watchmen stationed at the doors to
the Hall: Problem.

Beside him, Peewit was aware that Kursh had come to the
alert. The Littleman signed back: Where?

The gate. A traveler demands admittance. Refused.
Demanded to see Her Majesty. Refused. Sends a token. Shall I
bring it?

Peewit and Kursh glanced at each other. The queen turned
her head slightly and pitched her voice carefully to blend in with
the noise of the hall. 'What is it, captain?'

Not for the first time, the Littleman marveled at how well she
kept track of myriad things happening around her. He stepped
forward to her elbow. 'Your Majesty, the sergeant says someone
is at the gate. Naturally, the guards would not open it so late at
night. Then the fellow demanded that one of them bring you a
token.' Tactfully he omitted the impertinent demand for an
audience.

'Have the sergeant bring it here.'

Peewit bowed and signaled the man forward.

As the sergeant came up past the knots of laughing men and
women, no one paid him any attention. Alphonse, who sat on the
queen's right in the place of honor, had heard the exchange
between Ariadne and the Littleman. Now the queen said to him,
'Could it be Imris?'

Watching the sergeant pass by the upper hearth, the wizard
was extending his Warding to check for danger. He shook his
head slightly. 'Imris could call you from there,' he pointed out.

'He would have no need to send a token, even if the guards did not recognize him, which is unlikely in itself.'

Peewit went down to the floor of the hall to receive the token, and Kursh took his place behind the queen's chair, ready to drop his throwing knife from its forearm sheath if necessary. Whatever the sergeant was bringing, it was too small to be seen from the table.

Captain Brickleburr held out his hand. The sergeant sketched a salute and then laid a spotted thrush's feather across his palm.

In his surprise, Peewit did what he had long feared to do: he went still and vanished. Almost immediately, though, he recalled himself and flickered back. The Watchman was staring down at him, open-mouthed. Brickleburr met his eyes and told him, 'I didn't do that.'

The sergeant shut his mouth. 'Right, sir,' he managed, but Peewit was already up the steps to the dais.

Ignoring protocol, the Littleman raced behind the disconcerted dignitaries at the head table. A grin broke across his face like a sunbeam as he drew himself tall between the queen and the wizard and held up the feather before their startled eyes. 'He's here!' he exulted. 'He's come!'

Chapter Six

The word spread like wildfire, of course, and by the time the Eldest of Yoriand was escorted into the hall, the place was buzzing. The excited speculation died to a murmur when the azure-cloaked figure appeared at the doorway and came slowly forward with his honor guard. The three boy musicians stared in awe at the legendary bard, and others in the crowd made him reverences. Imris acknowledged these, but kept his eyes fixed on the high raised table.

Ariadne rose and did him the honor – sovereign to sovereign – of awaiting him standing. Alphonse had already left his place and gone down the steps. The queen was smiling, and she called, 'Welcome, Eldest! Now we shall be merry indeed!'

As the Yoriandir came into the brighter light near the upper end of Rose Hall, Ariadne thought at first that her eyes had deceived her. The last time she had seen Imris, on Crowning Day a year ago, his hair had been the same flaxen color as when she first met him. Now as the torchlight shone on him, she saw that the hair which showed under his hood – which he had not doffed as court etiquette demanded – had turned completely silver. He looked all at once so much like his uncle, the last Eldest of Yoriand, that she caught her breath and hoped her face did not betray her.

The Yoriandir's beech-green skin was yellowed by the light. He stopped before the high table and made a half-bow. There was a murmur at that: some had expected a deeper obeisance, for he was, technically, still a member of the First Watch. Ka-Salin frowned openly.

Imris straightened, brought his right fist to his chest, and let it fall in a brief salute. Quietly he said, 'Hail, my queen. I am sorry to be so tardy.'

Ariadne had been surprised at his bow, but she was shocked at his voice. Imris's mellow tones had filled this hall many times, but now she could barely hear him, and his voice was flat with weariness and as hoarse as if he had a winter cold. Confused, she answered, 'No apology is owed, Eldest. We are glad to see

you at any time you may grace our hall. We regret the over-
zealousness of our guards at the gate; they should have admitted
you immediately, of course.'

'They did not know me. There is no blame to them.'

By now the queen was alarmed, and she glanced at Alphonse.
The wizard was moving forward to greet their friend. She
beckoned a page and a servingman. 'Fetch a chair, and lay out
dinner for the Eldest.'

But Imris called more strongly, 'Thank you, my queen, but I
would rather a chance to rest a bit before I sup, if you would
allow it.' His fir-green eyes fell to the wizard, now within a pace,
and he whispered desperately, 'Alphonse, get me out of here!'

The wizard took hold of his arm. 'Imris, what is the matter
with you?' he murmured. The Yoriandir tried to shake him off,
and the throat of his azure cloak fell open a little. The Eldest
suppressed a gasp and clutched for the edge of the wool with one
green-stained hand, while his eyes closed.

The wizard thought past his own shock and turned to the
queen. 'I will attend the Eldest, Your Majesty. Perhaps you
would be good enough to let the captain or the First Watchman
accompany us to the chamber you have lent me. The Eldest is
anxious to greet all his old friends, particularly Master Fidelis.'

She understood immediately. 'Both the captain and the First
Watchman have our leave to make the Eldest welcome. Page,
fetch Master Fidelis to the guest rooms.' She had gone pale, but
did not otherwise let on that anything was amiss. Isolated by the
duties yet to perform that night, she ordered, 'Let Master Imris
be well served, for we are surpassing fond of him.'

At that, the Yoriandir lifted his head. A smile flickered over
his face. 'Thank you, my queen.' With Alphonse close by, he
bowed again stiffly, and left the hall by the nearest door.

Ariadne gave Peewit a look. She did not need to tell him to find
out and report to her. The Littleman and the dwarf saluted and
went down the steps. The queen did not let herself follow them
out with her eyes. Instead she dropped a hand to her husband's
arm, and with the other hand signaled the musicians to strike up
a dance. She looked down at Ka-Salin. 'The fireworks should
almost be ready. Help me keep people occupied until then.'

The prince consort rose, straightened his doublet, took a sip
from his goblet, and led her to the floor. As they came down the
steps from the dais, the queen saw a bright green drop that stood
out against the cinnamon marble tile like a green leaf on a pile of
fallen autumn rusty ones. Her lips parted, but she said nothing.

The tambours beat a merry counterpoint to the pipes, but
Ariadne felt each shiver of the bells like a screech along her
nerves.

The wooden door of the wizard's chamber slammed open and

bounced off the stone wall as Kursh and Alphonse half-carried, half-dragged the Yoriandir through and struggled toward the bed with him. Peewit followed and closed the door. 'Gently, friends, gently!' Imris was protesting. 'I will be well enough if only Kursh will not grasp so tightly!'

'Hush yourself,' the dwarf rasped. 'Ye shouldn't be talking.'

They got the green-skinned figure to the edge of the bed, and he sank gratefully into the pillows, saying mildly, 'Kursh, I have walked all the way from Yoriand this way. A little talk can do no more harm, I think.'

The captain stooped to the fireplace and hesitated. The basket near the hearth was filled with split kindling, and a log was laid ready across the andirons. He bit his lip, for the sight of burning wood might hurt the tree-tender more than his wounds. But there was no help for it: the night had chilled, and the injured Yoriandir must be kept warm. He stuffed a handful of dry tinder under the log, reached for the flint and iron on the mantel above, and struck a spark into the fireplace. Over his shoulder he said, 'Why the blazes didn't you identify yourself at the gate? We could have had Fidelis waiting for you!'

The Yoriandir caught Kursh's broad hand as the dwarf began to pull away the cloak. 'It will have to be soaked,' he told the dwarf in an aside. To Peewit he answered, 'And what would have been the effect if it were known that the Eldest of Yoriand had arrived at Queen Ariadne's gates with the wounds of a wolf attack upon him, eh? Everyone downstairs seemed to be having a wonderful time without that news.'

'Idiot,' Korimson muttered, pulling a blanket over the Yoriandir and motioning to Peewit to warm the winter stone in the hearth.

Brickleburr dusted his hands together. 'I am sorry about the fire, Imris. There is no friava here, though the queen made sure that the hearths in the hall and in your room were burning it.'

The Yoriandir smiled a little. 'That was thoughtful,' he murmured, but then he winced, and they could see his pain was growing now that he was safe and beginning to be warm.

There was a tap at the door, and Peewit went thankfully to open it for the physician. Fidelis came in with a broad grin, prepared to greet an old friend, but sobered instantly when he saw the Yoriandir in the bed. Fortunately, he had made it his practice for many years never to go anywhere without his medical kit, and now he unslung the bag and cast it upon the rug as he bent to put a hand against the green brow.

'Well met,' Imris sighed.

'I should say so,' the doctor frowned.

'It's his throat and hand,' Kursh informed him. 'He got tangled up with a wolf.'

'Powers protect us!' Fidelis gently put aside the Yoriandir's restraining hand and began to ease the cloak away. The silver torque that marked Imris's kingship of the Yoriandirkin gleamed in the firelight, and the doctor reached behind his neck to ease it apart. When the necklace sprang open, the Yoriandir bit back a cry and had to grasp Fidelis' arm. The physician gave him a moment to master the pain, for the torque had been stuck with dried blood to the lacerated and swollen flesh, and even the small tug had reopened the wounds.

Peewit had already realized that they would need water, probably a lot of it, and he had poured what was in the pitcher on the small table into the earthenware washbasin. Now he slipped out the door, jug in hand. Kursh dunked the linen towel in the basin and handed it dripping to the doctor. Fidelis began to wash away the green blood. The Yoriandir gasped and shuddered at the cold water. 'The torque undoubtedly saved your life,' Fidelis said, 'acting as an armored collar.'

Imris's good hand was clenched on the blanket. He swallowed painfully. 'I know. I could hear the beast's fangs click against it.'

The physician tried to distract him. 'We have looked for your arrival all day. The queen was sorry that you missed the festival.'

'Why? Was Festil so terrible?' the bard managed to force past his clenched teeth.

Fidelis laughed, and Kursh assured the Yoriandir, 'Worse than that, even. And his special offering must have had twenty verses.' The dwarf shook his head and smoothed his beard. 'Some songs should be allowed to die.'

Alphonse contributed, 'I found your harp, Eldest, and brought it in my baggage. Please, please, ask Festil for the loan of harpstrings. You would spare us all.'

The bard closed his eyes and smiled a little. 'I think I shan't be playing or singing for some time.'

'The Elixir will put you right in a wink,' Fidelis assured him. 'I just want to know the extent of your injuries so that I'll know what proportion of it to mix for you. And I think it would be well if you talked no more until we have you healed.'

'I told him that,' Kursh rumbled, but by now the physician had the azure wool of the cloak soaked free of Imris' throat and had pitched the linen towel into the basin. He cast it back. Beneath the cloak, the white tunic was shredded from under the Yoriandir's left arm to just above his waist. Old blood the color of dead moss crusted the garment, and fresh green was seeping through it. Imris's arm showed deep scoring, and his hand was a mess. How he had walked so far, the Powers alone knew. Fidelis's face showed only professional calm, and the dwarf had seen too many wounds in his long life to react outwardly, but both of them realized immediately that the Yoriandir had lost a lot of blood. Alphonse looked once, and then stared out the window.

The door swung open, and Peewit hauled a brimming bucket

over to the bed. Matter-of-factly he regarded Imris. 'The beast got you a good one, didn't he?'

'He bears my arrow for his pains.'

'Well done!' the captain exclaimed. 'No one else has ever even seen the thing, much less gotten off a shot at it!'

Kursh grunted and dropped his hidden dagger into his hand as Fidelis reached for his bag to get a knife. The doctor accepted the dwarf's instead and quickly cut away the ruined tunic.

The flesh beneath was slashed to the rib bones. The doctor stilled. Peewit dug in the bag and silently handed him the small blue bottle, and Alphonse took the wooden cup from the table and passed it across the bed.

'Elixir?' the Yoriandir questioned.

The healer told him, 'You may refuse it, but I will warn you that the alternative is a long and painful session with needle and thread. And then there will be infection.'

'I have no wish to refuse the Healing, I assure you,' Imris said. His eyes followed expectantly as Fidelis poured a few drops into the cup and added some water.

'Blessings,' the doctor said, and put the Elixir to the bard's lips. Imris drained the cup and lay back in the pillows.

His breathing eased almost immediately, and those who watched could see relaxation come upon him. He sighed with relief. 'It tastes like Sileaught!'

As the ripped flesh knitted before their eyes and the swelling of his throat began to reduce, Kursh was thinking, Why didn't it work for me? Perhaps a headache isn't important enough, after all? . . . Perhaps I'm not important enough. He looked down at his boots.

The Yoriandir licked his lips and said, 'I am so sleepy.'

The doctor and the Littleman exchanged a glance, thinking of the peculiar way the Greenbriar had wilted that morning. Usually people who received the Healing potion experienced an upsurge of well-being and good spirits, and wanted to be out of their beds to celebrate even before the Elixir had run its full course. Fidelis said thoughtfully, 'You went long before treatment. You probably do need to rest.'

The captain straightened. 'I should be getting down to tell Her Majesty that you are well now. Go ahead and sleep. Don't mind the fireworks; they'll be going off anytime.'

Fidelis rose and gathered up his kit, and Peewit put the stool back. That left Kursh standing at the foot of the bed. Imris's fir-green eyes caught his, and the dwarf searched for something to say, but he had never been good at that sort of thing, so he just gave the tree-tender a nod and said directly, 'I'm glad you're here.'

A smile touched the weary eyes. 'I was wishing the whole time that your ax were beside me.'

The First Watchman stroked his beard. 'You'd have got off

lighter, for true,' he rasped with what sounded like overweening pride, but was only the truth. 'And I own, I'd like to get a chance at the beast. That damned thing has caused a good deal of woe roundabouts of late.'

Imris paled and licked his lips. 'Believe me, my friend, you do not want to find this wolf. It is like no other!' His face twisted.

Fidelis put a hand to his shoulder and warned the rest of them with a glance. 'Enough talk. Put it from your mind – you are safe now.' Peewit surreptitiously poked Kursh as the dwarf seemed about to say more.

But Alphonse stooped over the bed, suddenly alert, 'Why, Imris? Why is it not the same?'

The Yoriandir king drew a shuddering breath at the memory, and his hand clutched the blanket. 'Because it is far bigger than any such animal I have ever heard of, even in tales, and because –' He swallowed hard. 'Alphonse, its eyes are sapphires!'

The wizard's brow drew into a line, and the doctor, trying for a rational tone, said, 'It was night, Imris. In the moonlight you were mistaken.'

'I had a close enough look at it,' he said grimly. 'That is how my harp was broken. The wolf sprang upon me as I played 'neath Nilarion, and I had to use my harp to smash it as it charged, else I would not have been able to reach for my bow.' The others could feel the creature's hot breath on their own necks, and Peewit shuddered. The Yoriandir looked up at the young wizard. 'Sapphires,' he repeated strongly.

Kursh's hand rested on the haft of the ax in his belt, and in his gruff voice there was no trace of fear. 'At least this description will give our hunters a definite beast to track. We'll not have to muck about killing every wolf in Ilyria.' He gave another nod. 'Ye did well, Imris. You'd best make a song about it quick, though, before Festil gets wind of the whole thing, or ye'll find yourself the hero of a long, long saga.'

The Yoriandir gave a rueful smile, and Peewit chuckled, and the chill that had brushed them all evaporated. It was a beast: it could be killed, given time and enough good hunters.

Fidelis began to speak, but suddenly there was a windy shriek, a loud boom, and the room flared with light. 'The fireworks!' Peewit exclaimed. Realizing that the queen would be out on the battlements, they knew there was no point in seeking her out for a while with a report on Imris, so they all settled to watch the special display that marked the queen's Crowning Day.

Alphonse moved the shutter aside, and they looked out at the crimson-and-amber starbursts, memory taking each of them back to the first Crowning Day, a time of vows fulfilled and rich promise for the future in the young woman they had helped to her throne. A reminiscent smile came to Peewit's face as he remembered how he had touched off the fire rockets that night.

The air was sharp with the acrid smoke of the burned powder. One after the other, the rockets leaped into the black sky and destroyed themselves in glittering showers of amethyst and gold, emerald and silver. Punctuated by the booms that rolled away over Willowsrill, they could hear the approving cheers of the crowd out on the Sweep.

After a time, the last heavy volley was fired from the roof above their heads, and the finale exploded with so many colored lights that the sky itself was obscured. Alphonse's eyes smarted and he groped for the shutter to keep out the worst of the smoke, but Peewit suddenly gasped, and at the same moment Kursh yelled hoarsely, 'The star! The star! Get it!'

The wizard threw them one puzzled look over his shoulder, and then Fidelis seized his cloak and pointed out the window. Beyond the rocket bursts, a bright red-orange disc no bigger than a dinnerplate hung steady in the sky over Willowsrill. In the time it took the young wizard's eyes to focus, the disc swelled to the size of a horseman's shield, and then it was as big as a millwheel.

The dwarf pressed his hands to his ears and doubled over with pain. '*Fight it!*' he bellowed in a voice that could have carried over a battlefield.

Alphonse stared into the smoky fog and saw Ariadne with her violet cloak whipping to shreds in the wind, and a huge dark hand that reached out across the stars to menace her. Of its own volition, his ring hand shot up and the wizard threw his Fire at the unearthly disc.

Garnet speared through the smoke and blew aside the last few harmless bits of the fireworks. On it streamed, up and across Willowsrill and to the foothills beyond, and there the wizard's Fire met the flaming disc in a shock that set the hilltops blazing and flattened hayfields for miles around.

Alphonse could hear screams of terror from those below him on the battlements and somewhere glass breaking from the titanic concussion wave, but he focused his will and resolutely destroyed the chunks of meteor streaking now across the lowlands. A few of the smaller fragments got past his Warding and these he drove hissing into the broad river, but he did not see one last cinder from the falling star until it was too late. When he was aware of it, he instinctively threw his Warding about Ariadne.

The hurtling thing struck the battlement wall just below where the queen was tackled to the stone walkway for her protection by an officer of her Second Watch. There was a sound like the inside of a thunderbolt, and then rock falling, and then ... silence.

Which was shattered by a keening, hysterical scream from

one of the women and a male voice, rough with fear, which shouted at her. Peewit vaulted the bed and raced out the door. Fidelis was quickly after him, and Kursh pulled himself up from his hands and knees, shook his head once, and followed.

The wizard and the Yoriandir both seemed momentarily frozen, but then Imris threw back his covers and they leaped for the door together.

Farther down the hall in the royal nursery, a very frightened little boy and a cat with her fur standing on end huddled together under the low bed.

PART 2

Starsmoke Streaming

Chapter Seven

The Littleman thrust his way against the tide of nobles and their ladies who flooded down the stone steps that descended from the battlement platform to the courtyard. Many of the women were still crying in the aftermath of fear, and some of the gentlemen were shaky on their feet. The wooden handrail that had been erected on the outer edge of the stairs for that night sagged dangerously, and the captain yelled at the soldiers among the crowd to keep the people away from it. He himself went on toward the top.

When he gained the stone walkway he dodged the stragglers and darted on, nearly catching his foot in one of the broad cracks that webbed the platform. Up ahead there was a knot of people in the uniform of the Second Watch. He did not see a lemon gown, and he cursed as he ran toward them. 'Hai, you, Balthazar!' he shouted. 'Where is my lady?'

The officer on the edge of the crowd threw him a salute as the captain skidded to a halt and began to shove men aside. They made way for him.

Ariadne's voice assured him, 'I am well enough, captain.' He got past the last tallfolk and saw that she was crouched over a still form shrouded in a Watchman's cloak. Below the hem, a pair of shiny boots gave back the moonlight. There were fragments of stone and mortar littered all about.

Peewit said to the man next to him, 'Who was it?'

It was the queen who answered, 'Rigald Barrie, Count Nevelston.' Her head went down and she said in a muffled voice, 'My sister thought him handsome.' Silently the captain offered his hand, and after a moment she rose. Her hair straggled out from under the crown and blew about her face as she stood looking down. 'Take him up, some of you, and bear him with all honor to the hall of mourning. We will bury him tomorrow near Captain Faring and my father.' An officer saluted and gestured to the men of his squad. The queen touched his arm and added, 'And don't let Junie see him.'

She looked about. 'Was anyone else hurt?'

Heads shook, and one soldier answered, 'No, Your Majesty. The explosion did little damage, except for here.'

The queen nodded, and her gaze returned to the covered body at her feet. Peewit realized that the men were uncomfortably waiting for her to leave the platform before they moved Nevelston's corpse. Tactfully he suggested, 'There is no more to be done here, Your Majesty. Let us go down now.'

She drew a breath. 'Yes, Peewit, I suppose that would be best.' Suddenly she looked up at one of the windows in the keep, and there was a note of fear in her voice as she asked, 'Was there any damage up there?'

The captain knew where she was looking and answered, 'I have not checked on the Lordling, my lady, but we were just down the hall and there was no damage where we were. I will send some-one immediately.' When he looked around for an officer to send, he realized that Fidelis and Kursh were standing at the edge of the crowd behind him.

'I'll go,' the First Watchman told him before he could say anything, and Kursh turned and made his way back across the cracked stonework. He met Alphonse and Imris just coming up, said something brief to them, and disappeared down the steps. The Yoriandir and the wizard came forward, Imris wearing the wizard's wine-colored cloak.

Fidelis had gone to the queen's side. 'You're certain that you are unhurt, Majesty?'

She nodded wearily. 'Let's away before anything else comes out of the sky.' At this, there were several wary glances up. She allowed Peewit to lead her toward the stairway. Imris and Alphonse drew aside to let her by, but she stopped and put a hand on the Yoriandir's arm. 'You didn't get much of a rest, did you?'

Imris smiled and put his green hand over hers for a moment before she looked to the wizard standing next to him. 'I felt your Warding. You and young Barrie saved my life tonight. If there is anything within my power that you would accept as a reward, name it.'

Alphonse answered lightly, 'A picnic in Yoriand, if the Eldest will allow it.'

Imris blinked, 'Of course.'

The queen almost smiled. 'I shall look forward to hearing Evensong again at Aspenglade.' The brief light went out of her eyes, 'For now, will you come talk with me?'

The wizard said, 'Of course, lady queen. I want to look around out here for a little, and then we will attend you. But only briefly. You should sleep.'

Her gray eyes widened. 'Sleep!' Her glance took in the shat-tered section of battlement and the shrouded form. 'I think not,

Master Wizard!' She rustled away, a ripped section of net overskirt trailing.

Several of the Second Watch peered over the handrail to be sure she had cleared the courtyard before they tended to their grisly task. Alphonse walked up the platform a little way. An officer stood there, and the wizard asked, 'The prince consort was not here?'

The bearded man shook his head. 'My lord prefers not to climb to high places, sir. He watches from the royal apartment.'

Alphonse nodded and moved to the Sweep side of the battlement, just at the place where they had taken the body away. He would be obliged to climb up on the chest-high wall to be able to peer down at the outside of it where the meteor fragment had impacted. The wizard acted on the thought, grasping one of the capstones and hauling himself up. He had one knee over and was swinging his weight to sit astride the wall when the stone under his hands shifted sickeningly and he lost his balance.

Luckily the Yoriandir had seen, and grasped his foot to pull him back. Alphonse regained his balance and carefully inched away from the loose stone. He was shaking and had to swallow a sour taste in his throat, but he said, 'I still want to look. Hold on.' Using the Yoriandir for a counter-balance he leaned out and looked down along the surface of the wall. 'By the Powers!'

'What is it?' Imris demanded as the bearded officer hurried toward them with an oath.

'It's still burning!' Fascinated, the wizard leaned further. 'Well, no, not burning,' he amended. 'But it's embedded in the wall and it's glowing.'

Carefully the officer did not touch either of them. 'Sir, would you come right down from there?' It was a command if Alphonse had ever heard one. 'I'd not like to try to explain to the queen if you went ass-over-teacup down to the Sweep.'

The wizard straightened and nearly laughed, but remembered that a man had died. 'All right, lieutenant. Stand clear.' The officer backed up and the young redhead swung down from the wall with the help of Imris' steadying hand.

The Second Watchman cleared his throat. 'Sir, some of the men have been wondering . . . that was your light that came from yonder window?' He indicated the room high above. When Alphonse nodded, the lieutenant narrowed his brows. 'Then what was the other light, the big one over Willowsrill?'

The young wizard clapped him on the shoulder. 'You've been witness to a very rare event, lieutenant. That was a shooting star.' He looked out over the silvered Sweep and across the broad band of the river to the thin line of brushfires creeping down the far hills, and he knew that there had been shepherds there. In a low voice, he added, 'Usually they land far away from where folk live.'

'I hope I never see another that close up,' the soldier said fervently. He nodded to the wizard and the Yoriandir, and went to follow his crew down the stairway.

Imris's fir-green eyes were black in the night. He listened to be sure all the men were gone. 'It's a strange star that falls right at the feet of the queen.'

'Yes.' The wizard idly traced one of the cracks in the stone-work, frowning thoughtfully. He tilted his head back to study the winking stars, and suddenly found himself wondering what might be in the black ether between those tiny silver candles.

Ariadne motioned Cele and the others back and gathered her ruined skirts. When she knelt on the sheepskin rug and peered under the bed, four eyes close together stared back at her. 'Mumma's here, love,' she told the larger pair. 'You can come out now. Come on,' she coaxed. Gerrit wriggled into his mother's arms, sobbing anew as soon as he felt safe. Patience crept out slow-motion, stopping to look warily around at each step. Her fur still stood up, and she flicked her tail nervously. 'Yes, it was loud, wasn't it?' Ariadne was agreeing to Gerrit's cries while she rocked him. She put a hand down to pet the cat, and Patience relaxed a little. 'Do you know what it was?'

'No-o,' the boy gulped.

'It was a star, Gerrit!' She held him off a little and put on a beguiling voice. 'A star came right down to join in our fireworks!'

He sniffed. 'Really?'

She nodded. 'Really.'

'It went *boom*!' The Lordling flung his arms wide to show how big the noise was.

'Oh, yes, indeedy. It was a grand *boom*!' Her hands were still cold from the near miss of that *boom*! and she warmed them by hugging her son.

' 'Deedy,' he echoed and started a giggle that ended in a yawn. He leaned against her.

'I think a certain little someone should go back to Blanket Fair.' This was the term Nelia, her foster mother, had always used when she put them to bed in the loft under the thatch. She helped Gerrit crawl back beneath the warm covers.

'Mumma, stay.' He was still whimpery when it came to the thought that she would leave.

'Cele will be here, love, and I'll be right down the hall. I have some work to do, and I must be about it. You'll be fine. No more fireworks – I promise.' She kissed him and drew the covers to his ears. He peered over the silk-bound edge of the blanket, and she had a sudden inspiration. 'Would you like the Eldest to sing you a bedtime song?'

He nodded eagerly.

The queen turned to the Yoriandir, who was standing with the others by the door and did not notice his sudden tension. 'Would you, Imris? Please?'

There was silence for a moment while the Watchmen and the wizard looked at the silver-haired bard, and when it became apparent that Imris, though exhausted, would acquiesce, Kursh suddenly said, 'The Eldest has had a long journey, my queen. I'll sit with the little master for a while.' One of the First Watchman's responsibilities was the bodyguard detail for the Greenbriar heir, and the child was nearly as familiar with the gruff dwarf as with his nurse.

The queen was somewhat puzzled, but there were too many more important things pressing to give much thought to this. 'Thank you, Master Kursh.'

He saluted as she went out calling good night to the boy and blowing a kiss. The dwarf walked toward the bed, but Patience was still on the sheepskin rug, and she stared and lashed her tail as he approached. He stopped. 'Go on with Alphonse,' he told her. 'Go on, kitty – shoo.'

Cele took up her sewing once more. 'She's been here most of the evening, Master Kursh. She seems to have taken quite a shine to the Lordling. I doubt she'll leave now.'

'I don't care about that. She's welcome to stay if Gerrit likes her. I just don't want him to get scratched.'

Cele looked over the top of her needle. 'Looks like you're the one about to get scratched. I don't think I'd go any closer.'

Gerrit rose up on an elbow and peered over the edge of the bed. 'Here, kitty. You can sleep with me.' He patted the blanket.

Patience turned her good eye up at him and hopped up onto the bed. She turned a circle once and curled against the boy's shoulder, watching Kursh all the while. Gerrit patted her. 'Look, Master Kursh,' he said. 'Kitty has only one eye, too – just like you!'

The dwarf drew up a stool and sat down. 'Just like me,' he agreed.

'Was she in the war, too?' Gerrit had heard all about the big war in which his grandfather had died. To him, it was all of a piece with stories about ogres and goblins and clever young lads who outsmarted them.

'Only with a tom,' the First Watchman muttered, and then he told the boy, 'No, I doubt she was around then. The war was a long time ago.'

Cele said from the door, 'I'll be out for a bit, Master Kursh.'

He nodded that he had heard and then told Gerrit, 'Pull that blanket up, young fellow. We'll have no sick soldiers here.'

The boy did as he was bidden and snuggled down comfortably. 'Sing me a song?'

The dwarf snorted. 'If I sang, little one, somebody would think we were killing the cat in here.'

Patience gave him an unfriendly look, but Gerrit giggled. 'I want you to sing!'

'I do not jest,' the dwarf protested. 'I can't carry a note in a bucket. Have ye ever heard me sing?' His dwarvish accent grew stronger, as it usually did when he was teasing the boy. He knew Gerrit was tickled by the sound of it.

'No,' the Lordling laughed, and the soldier saw that if they went on this way, Gerrit would soon get himself too giddy to go to sleep. He looked around and seized on an inspiration.

Retrieving a little wooden pipe from atop the trunk of toys that stood up against the wall, the dwarf said, 'I could play you a song, though. Would that do?' Luckily, the boy nodded. 'Lie back, then, and listen. This is a song that I learned when I was no bigger than you.' He fitted his broad fingers to the holes and frowned. 'If I can remember how to play one of these da – one of these things,' he caught himself in time. 'Let's see . . .' Tentatively he played a few notes, licked his lips, and began to pipe.

It began as a sprightly little tune, a fishermen's jig, such as one might whistle while he mended net. That was where Kursh had heard it first. But then it slowed and became a meditative, wandering melody punctuated every few measures by a sharp note like a gull's. Gerrit was heavy-eyed when the dwarf took the pipe from his lips.

The boy said muzzily, 'That's a pretty song. Does it have any words?'

'No,' Kursh answered. 'No words. But it's called "The Brother's Lament." ' He did not tell the child that he had just made it up.

Gerrit frowned a little and sank his hand in Patience's fur. 'I wish I had a brother.'

'No, you don't. They wet the bed.'

The Lordling considered this. 'Do you have any brothers?'

Kursh fingered the pipe, but did not play it. 'I had three,' he said softly. He sighed. 'Now I have one.'

'What happened to the other ones?'

The dwarf saw it all again in his mind, but cut the memory short. 'It was a long time ago, my lord. Go to sleep now. I'll play some more.' The boy let his eyes close all the way, and the First Watchman tried to explain it all through the pipe, but Korim was gone and there was no one else to hear.

After a while, the child slept. The dwarf's knees popped as he got stiffly up and went out the door. He did not even scold Cele and the Watchman when he passed them outside, though it was obvious that they had been together.

Ariadne was sitting in one of the cherrywood chairs before the

fire, where a birch log curled and blackened. She had put aside
her ruined gown and allowed Meara to help her into a soft,
warm woolen robe and slippers. They had discovered several
purpling bruises, and these had been treated with salve, but
nothing had helped the shaking until she went out to the other
room and Fidelis served her some brandy-laced tea. The tremor
in her hands had been so bad that Alphonse had had to hold the
cup for her. 'Sorry,' she apologized. 'I've never nearly been hit
by a star before.' She wrapped her hands around the hot cup,
and all of a sudden tears were brimming and she put a hand to
her mouth to stifle the sound of her crying. 'Poor Barrie! His
head!' Meara rescued the cup, and the doctor held her other
hand and made sympathetic murmurs.

The wizard wished he dared touch her, but he did not, so he
drew up the other chair and sat close beside the queen. 'He
went quickly, Ariadne. He never knew.' She nodded wordlessly
and took the linen Peewit handed her to wipe her eyes. Alphonse
was suddenly unreasoningly angry at the prince consort for
leaving her at a time like this. What the hell kind of oaf
was Ka-Salin anyway, not to see through the brave act she
had put on for him? A few minutes of solicitude, a glance around
at all of them and a comment that he didn't want to interrupt
a council, and then the cursed whoreson had left to a bloody
chess game! The wizard was staring at the fire, and a flare
of garnet scooted up the chimney. He drew a deep breath and
realized he was starting to sound like Kursh! He snorted at
himself.

'Are you laughing at me?'

He looked up, startled, and met her quicksilver eyes over the
handkerchief. 'What? No! Why by Nilarion Earth Pillar would I
be laughing at you? Of course not.' But there was a singular
woundedness in those eyes, and before he could stop himself, he
took her cold hand in both his warm ones. 'I was swearing at
myself, and it suddenly occurred to me how much of Master
Kursh had rubbed off.'

Now she nodded and wiped her red nose. 'Thank the Powers
for Kursh – I can always tell how badly I've mucked things up
by how blunt he gets.' She gave a last dab at her eyes. 'Why
were you cursing yourself, Alphonse?'

The blush started at the back of his neck, but he controlled it,
and in the shadows she could not see it. 'Because I need it every
once in a while,' he answered. 'It clears my head.'

She took back her hand and lifted the cup from the tray
Meara held. 'Ah, part of your wizard training, no doubt,'
she teased. She sipped the brandy and tea, composed once
more.

'An essential exercise,' he played along. 'Done thrice daily:
before breakfast, in early afternoon after chimera-roasting

spells, and again at night before weaving moonbeams. It's only
for advanced levels, though. Much too dangerous for beginning
adepts.'

That drew a smile from her.

He was congratulating himself on relieving her mood when
Ariadne set down her cup with a click and demanded quietly,
'All right, gentlemen. You have mollycoddled me enough and I
thank you for it. Now. What happened to Imris?'

The doctor looked to the wizard, and Alphonse told her.

The queen closed her eyes. 'We could have lost him just that
quickly, and never known till someone visited Yoriand to find
him.' Sighing, she opened her eyes again. 'Well, he is here now,
thank the Powers, and we shall keep better watch over
Nilarion's Keeper.' Her tone was pointed as she said to the
wizard, 'Shan't we?'

'I have Warded him, lady queen.'

She smiled, and they talked by mutual consent then of other
things until Meara's repeated throat-clearings informed the
men that it was time the queen retired for the night. Fidelis
agreed and rose. Alphonse, who would have liked to talk much
longer with Ariadne, hid his chagrin, and they bid the queen
good sleep.

Outside the doctor caught Alphonse's sleeve. 'A word
with you?'

The young redhead looked worried. 'What is it?' he asked
quietly, nodding good night to the chamberlain who escorted
them to the antechamber door. 'Is she more hurt than she would
say?'

'Oh no. It's nothing like that,' Fidelis assured him. 'It's
just something I've found in the library that I think you might
look at.'

The wizard relaxed and smiled. 'You like old scrolls so much,
you must have the makings of a wizard!' This was an old joke
between them. In the past five years, Alphonse had learned of
the healer's passion for antique artifacts and manuscripts.
Often Fidelis would send a copy of something intriguing to
Covencroft for further study. The wizards were tolerant of the
amateur, for the doctor would have cut off his hand rather than
misuse a thing of power, and they knew it.

But Fidelis had not grinned at the jibe this time. He merely
looked around briefly before saying, 'No, really, it is important,
and I need your help with it, for the script is ancient and I am
having trouble with the translation.'

Caught by his mood of secrecy, the young wizard raised one
eyebrow. 'It sounds serious.'

The wiry physician raised his eyes to Alphonse. 'It is. Too
serious to start now and have to leave. I must still do rounds in
the hospital, and then I have the duty tonight. Can you meet me

in the scriptorium tomorrow, say after the funeral for young Nevelston?'

'Certainly.'

Fidelis seemed satisfied. 'Good. See you then.' And he tapped the wizard's arm and sped away, apparently late for his patients.

Alphonse frowned after him, and wondered if the strain of examining so many wolf-mauled bodies was getting to the chief physician.

Chapter Eight

'Where will you go?' Alphonse asked.

Peewit rolled an extra shirt and tucked it into his pack. 'Across Willowsrill, I think. Maybe up around the Gap.'

The wizard drummed his fingers on the tabletop in the captain's quarters. 'Right up to the Barreners' doorstep,' he muttered.

The Littleman looked back over his shoulder. 'Of course. We must know what's brewing up in those mountains, and there's only one way to find out.' He opened the trunk at the foot of his bed and took out a small covered jar and several things that looked in the lamplight like scraggly pelts. These he stowed carefully in the pack and began pulling the laces tight.

'You'll go disguised?'

'Of course,' the captain answered again. He looked up from his packing to catch the wizard's shake of the head. 'I'll put it on after I'm well away from here, though. It wouldn't do to go riding out the front gate that way.' Alphonse plainly didn't think much of the idea. 'How else would I explain my height?'

Reluctantly, the wizard agreed that it was probably best. 'But, still, 'Wit – it's too damned dangerous for the Captain of the Queen's Watch.'

The Littleman rubbed his nose. 'It's too dangerous for anybody but the Captain of the Queen's Watch.' He left the packing and came to the table, where he picked up his pipe and began filling it. 'I could never ask someone else to do it, Alphonse.' Lighting a splinter from the lamp, he got his smoke going, watching the young wizard. He blew a smoke ring and said quietly, 'Actually, I'm much more worried about the danger here than any I'll face up in the foothills.'

Alphonse looked up. 'I'll stay with her until you get back.'

The Littleman nodded. 'It will take more than Kursh's kind of protection to keep her safe, I think.'

'And Gerrit also.'

Peewit looked momentarily stunned, but then he murmured, 'I

should have thought of that.' He looked down at the glowing bits of tobacco in the bowl of his clay pipe. 'This is wretched. Worse than the first time we fought the Unnamed, even. At least back then we did not know at first that it was the Lord of the Wild Fire who was behind it all. Fighting Rasullis and the Bastard was far easier.'

'You had a clear road back then,' Alphonse pointed out. 'You were trying to restore the throne. But now, we know that a blow is coming, yet we do not know how to fight it. No wonder we're all a little afraid.'

'I am a great deal more than "a little" afraid,' Peewit said. When the redhead said nothing, the Littleman blew another smoke ring and stifled a yawn. 'Sorry, but this old Teazle has had a long day.'

'I've bent your ear too long, anyway.' The wizard rose and stretched. He stood looking down at the Littleman. 'You will be careful, won't you, 'Wit? I'd have no one to play puzzles against if anything happened to you.' His attempt to treat the matter lightly failed.

Peewit smiled anyway. 'I'll be careful.'

But when Alphonse had gone, the Littleman blew out the lamp and sat in the firelit room, smoking and thinking, and the gist of his thoughts was that if the Unnamed was threatened by the power of Ariadne and of Imris, then how much more of a target would be the one wizard who could hear all of the Song at once? The Captain of the First Watch tried to imagine how one could protect a wizard, but the fire burned down to ash and he came to no answer.

The morning sun sponged up the previous night's dew and left the leaves clinging damply together. By the time the watch changed on the castle keep at eight, the air had already grown drowsily warm, and the stable boys stripped down to their trews and led the horses down to shade for the day along the riverbank. They went out of the stronghold by way of Armorer's Gate, though, which pierced the southern wall at the end of the blacksmiths' lane; Queen's Gate was blocked by the funeral procession for Rigald Barrie.

Kursh stood next to Peewit before the ranks of Greenbriar men who had come to honor the young Count Nevelston. They were both in dress uniform once more, quartered emerald-and-gold surcoats, but in place of the green cloaks normally worn with the uniform, they wore black ones. These drew the heat, and everyone in the silent and unmoving ranks would be relieved to finish and get back into the cooler stone interior of the castle.

Korimson himself had known Barrie only a little. The Second Watch, in which the count had been an officer, was a separate unit with its own command structure, though Peewit was captain over all and the First Watch was senior in authority. Still, there was no doubt that the young man had given his life in the line of duty, and it was only proper that the First Watch turn out to pay its respects. The dwarf felt sweat run down his forehead along the strap of his eyepatch, and he restrained an urge to wipe it away. Just then, there was a slight creak of leather and he glanced beyond Peewit to the commander of the Second Watch. Kelvin Miller, who wore the badge of the Second Watchman, had shifted uncomfortably, and sweat shone beneath the sparse hairs on the crown of his head. The slightest of smiles bunched the muscles of Kursh's cheek: old Kel was going to have a sunburn on his topknot.

The Retreat Masters were nearly done with the service, and soon it would be time for Peewit to escort the queen forward to cast the first earth on the plain wooden coffin. Kursh let his mind drift to the man who lay buried under the marble plinth nearby.

Tristan Faring had been gone for nearly five years, but the dwarf could still see him clearly: black hair brushed at the temples with gray, keen hazel eyes, the ever-present gauntlets to hide the scarred hands, the shining blade etched with the Briar that had been his pride and joy.

A bead of sweat ran into Kursh's eye, and suddenly that blade flashed before him, catching the waning light of a fading day long ago . . . there was a sound of hooves down the Sweep and the clash of arms somewhere near while a harp played sweet above the horses' screams . . . beneath the iron helm, the hazel eyes swung to him . . . Tristan's voice, strained with exhaustion, commanded, 'Kursh, protect her!' And then the battlement wall blew apart and Korimson gasped and fell back a step, dashing the sweat from his eye.

His heart thumped and he caught his breath, darting a look about and only then realizing his movement had not been noticed in the general stir as the procession formed to follow the queen up to the graveside. He swallowed thickly. Kursh had been prepared for his headaches to continue, but he had not thought his illness would come to this. Kelvin Miller passed behind him, saying in a low voice. 'Hot day, First Watchman. Be glad to get hold of a mug after this.'

Korimson grunted a confused agreement and fell in behind him. When he threw his handful of dirt on the coffin, his glance went to the marble plinth, and he fought down a shudder. He had an almost overwhelming impulse to draw Peewit aside and blurt out that the Elixir had not worked, but then Brickleburr's fist was at his chest in the Greenbriar salute and he was leading three hundred men in the Oath by which Rigald Barrie had died:

'Heart, mind, and spirit hers.
Hand, eye, and body hers.
My blood for the Blood,
Now and forever.'

As one, three hundred swords swept out and clattered against shields in the fighting man's traditional sign of approval and respect. And so they sent the young officer of the Second Watch on his way to Ritnym's Realm.

Somehow, repeating the Oath again had calmed Kursh, and now, though he could see Tristan's shade no longer, he told him, Of course I'll protect her. Go back to sleep.

When the ranks broke up into knots of barracks mates headed for their breakfast and the nobles had gone back inside Queen's Gate, he signaled Peewit by hand code that he would join him shortly. Then he stayed the gravediggers and spent a moment more by the grave. He could hear the tinkling of bells as a flock of sheep grazed on the hillside behind him, and faint shouts from the river, where the stable boys punctuated their chores with some noisy fun in the water. He snapped a salute which the gravediggers assumed was for Barrie, turned on his heel, and walked down along the battlement wall in the direction of Armorers' Gate. Peewit planned to leave by that way as soon as he could change out of his uniform, and Kursh wanted a few words with him before he left on this ridiculous spy mission of his.

Behind him he heard the spades spilling dirt onto the coffin, and he hoped none of the oafs was careless enough to knock a chip out of the plinth. Unclasping his cloak as he trod across the springy turf, Kursh paused just beyond the end of the gravesite.

The chief of engineers had waited for the funeral to be over before he walked out from the castle with several assistants to examine the previous night's damage to the outer battlement. Now he chewed a blade of grass and ran his eye over the wall. He glanced down as the First Watchman came up and nodded civilly. 'Morning, sir.'

'You're at it early, Harry. Bloody mess, isn't it?'

The engineer shifted the piece of grass and said around it, 'It is that. But not as bad as it could have been. If the thing had hit a little farther to the right, it would have opened all the old stress fractures.' He referred to the patched cracks which had been left after the Bastard's troops had rebuilt the wall. 'But I think we're all right on that score – it's mainly the surface dressing of stone and a couple of medium-sized cracks.' He nodded to himself. 'We'll have repairs made in no time, once we get that big fragment of star out of the wall.'

Kursh shifted his helm to the other arm. The morning sun glared off the surface of the battlement, and high up, near the arrow slits at the top, a crack about a handspan wide ran roughly vertically through the heat-blackened stone. In the middle of the dark place the sun reflected off the remnant of the falling star. Korimson's eye was drawn to this. His hand dropped to his side.

'Looks like a kind of dark window, doesn't it?' the engineer remarked. 'Glassy.'

'Crystal,' the dwarf murmured.

'Hm?'

Kursh licked his lips and realized that Harry was leaning slightly down to catch what he'd said. 'Yes. Glass. D'ye think ye'll get it out of the wall today?'

The engineer spat the piece of grass out and grinned. 'By the Three, I'd have some hell of a team if I could!' He cleared his throat as the dwarf did not laugh. 'No, sir, not today. You can see where it's fused to the stone; we'll have to chip it out. And then, of course, we'll need to hire a team of masons to mend the stonework – we'll have to strip off the outer paving, you see.' He flushed under the dwarf's gaze.

Kursh was not aware of the engineer's discomfort. He nodded absently. 'When your men take it down, be very careful. It might be ...' Harry was staring down at him now, frowning. The dwarf changed what he had been going to say: no sense starting a panic. 'It's a star, after all.' Which was not true, but seemed to satisfy the engineer, who straightened and nodded.

'I understand, sir. Her Majesty will want it kept for display, no doubt.'

Kursh thought not, but he said, 'No doubt.' Then he left the engineer sketching rigging with a piece of chalk on a slate, and made his way along the wall and around the turret toward Armorers' Gate.

Peewit whistled softly between his teeth as he strapped his bedroll to the saddle, and his pony pricked its ears and looked back over its shoulder at him. The Littleman grinned. 'My whistling bothering you already, old friend?' The sturdy little bay twitched a fly off its neck and sighed. Brickleburr tied the last knot and tugged at the girth to check its snugness.

Jamison strode into the stableyard with a dripping water-skin. 'Here you go, sir.'

'Thanks, Jami,' Brickleburr began lashing it in front of his saddle. 'I'd rather have wine, but Snort here doesn't care for the stuff.' The young orderly laughed and patted the black mane. 'Now, I've left the duty roster with the First Watchman, so that's all taken care of, and remember that he rises an hour before I do, so he'll be wanting to give you his orders for the day a little earlier.'

'I'll manage, sir.'

The boy sounded doubtful. Peewit hid a smile and adjusted a stirrup.

There was the squeak of a gate, and then Kursh came around the corner of the tack shed. Jamison stiffened to attention and saluted. The dwarf's brows drew down as if a little puzzled at this show, but he answered the salute as he came across the yard. He surveyed the pony's gear. 'Almost ready, eh?'

'Just done now, in fact.'

Kursh frowned. 'Where's your sword?'

Peewit tugged at a strap. 'Upstairs.'

'You bloody little –' He broke off. Jamison stared straight ahead and pretended not to have heard. Kursh blew an impatient sigh. 'Captain, sir, don't you think that's just a bit dotty?'

Brickleburr grinned. 'Maybe I should take an ax.' Because of the orderly, he did not say that such a weapon would fit his disguise, but Kursh knew what he meant.

The stolid First Watchman replied, 'Maybe you should.'

'Well, I've got a hatchet, anyway.'

'Fat lot of good that will do if –'

Peewit was standing on a mounting block, and he looked across the saddle at the dwarf. 'Nothing is going to happen. I'll be back in a few days.' He met Kursh's eye, and the dwarf looked down and tugged at the patch. Neither of them spoke.

Jamison belatedly realized that both senior officers wanted to have further speech and were waiting for him to leave. Flustered, he gave a half-bow. 'Excuse me, sirs.' To the captain he said, 'Safe journey, sir. We'll look for you shortly.'

'Have a big, soft pillow ready. I've not done much riding lately and this trip is going to be a long one.'

The young man wiped the smile off his face when the dwarf glanced at him, saluted the captain, and told the First Watchman, 'I'll await your orders in the guardroom, sir,' Kursh grunted something and watched him go.

The Littleman gathered the reins in his hand. 'Kursh.' When the dwarf looked at him, Peewit said quietly, 'I'm sorry about your father.'

Korimson stiffened with surprise and then slowly patted the pony. 'You spoke with Nissen Olafson?'

Peewit nodded. 'About another matter. He happened to mention that he'd brought you bad news.' He hesitated and ran his hand down the pony's neck. 'The ambassador says you are the head of the family now.'

'That's no matter.' Kursh began to check over the girth strap on his side of the pony.

The Littleman had never known much about why Kursh had left Jarlshof – the dwarf had made it clear that it was none of anyone's business – but he had once gotten Kursh to say that his father had forbidden him to return home. Now he guessed that there was sorrow behind the abrupt words. He ventured, 'You haven't shaved your beard off.' Once before, Kursh had honored the dead in that dwarvish fashion.

The First Watchman straightened and said flatly, 'No.' He frowned. 'Now, if that's all, I've got something you should know before you go riding up to visit the Barrens.'

Peewit accepted that he would not discuss the matter any further, and the Littleman heart of him was sick, for his people held family bonds more dear than roomfuls of rubies. He swung into the saddle. 'What is it?'

'That star that nearly fell on the queen last night – have you seen it?'

'I glanced up during the funeral.' The Littleman reined in Snort, who wanted to get going. 'What about it?'

'It wasn't a star at all, Peewit.' The dwarf's broad hand hooked in the pony's bridle to hold him, and he stared up at Brickleburr. 'It was a piece of firmament.'

'What?'

'I was just out looking at it. It's black crystal.'

There was silence in the stableyard, for they both knew that only the firmament, the Sky Roof, was black crystal.

The arch of the sky was breaking.

Peewit swallowed. 'I've got to go see what those damned Barreners are up to. Tell Alphonse.'

The dwarf nodded and took his hand from the bridle. 'Be bloody careful of yourself, Brickleburr.'

'I will. Guard the queen and Gerrit!' He pulled Snort around and touched a heel to the pony's flank. As he trotted out of the stableyard he called, 'And take care of yourself!'

'Oh, aye,' the dwarf agreed. He waved the Littleman gone. When he could no longer hear the clop of the pony's hooves, he muttered, 'I hope to hell the boy wizard has Warded him.'

He threw the damp black cloak over his shoulder, hefted his helmet, and walked slowly up to the keep.

Chapter Nine

By the time the sun had traveled a little past its zenith, Peewit was drawn off the road, well back in the screening woods, unpacking one small bag. Snort pulled at a shrub, unhappy because there was no grass under the trees.

'Quit trampling around like that,' the Littleman muttered to him. 'You sound like a whole deer herd. You'll have a hunter down our necks quicker than you can eat a carrot.' Brickleburr set a piece of polished tin up against a rock and peered into it for a moment. Then he unstoppered a jar and began to dab pine gum around his jawline. Working quickly before this dried, he took a hank of the long, uncombed black wool and carefully made himself a beard. A few moments later, a rather short dwarf with bushy eyebrows and wild beard frowned critically at his reflection. He turned his head from side to side to see as much as he could. No glue showed, and the image was true enough. A lot of dwarves were a little unkempt. He jammed a hat on his head and repacked the bag.

He had already changed, so he was no longer wearing the clothes in which he'd ridden out of the castle. Those were stowed at the bottom of his pack, and now he wore a rough linsey-woolsey shirt and dark breeches, with a stained leather vest and high boots. He remembered at the last moment to work some dirt into his hands.

He resettled his baggage and led the pony to the road. The sun was still high, and he reckoned that he had plenty of time to make it to Waysmeet, the town where the road from Willowsrill met the main track up into the foothills. There was an inn there and it might be a good place to pick up a bit of gossip.

The air was warm as he jogged along, but it was shady under the trees. He was glad of that, because the pine tar was uncomfortable enough anyway. His backside wasn't feeling any too good, either. To keep his spirits up, he began to whistle. Snort pricked his ears and shook his mane.

It wasn't until a few minutes later when the Littleman absently swatted at a buzzing near his ear that he realized honeybees were zipping around his head. He'd been whistling the Calling song! 'Oh, good grief!' He reined in the pony immediately. 'I'm sorry to have taken you from your business, friends. I must have been thinking of something else.' He began whistling the Thanks and Farewell tune, and the furry gold workers circled him once more and lifted in a light cloud to skim the treetops. Peewit watched them go. Just for a moment he had an urge to recall them, whistle the Home and Hearth song, and let the bees lead him home. He knew from his father's lore that it was the only way to find his kin, but for the Pledged there was an injunction that went with the learning: never, until the end, to use that one song. He swallowed and fought down the ache that came upon him more and more as he got older. For an instant, he wondered who they would send in his place as the Pledged when it was time. Did the lad know what he faced? He nudged Snort to a walk and went on, dreaming.

By midafternoon he was climbing the first of the low, rolling hills that marked the beginning of the rise in the Willowsrill Valley. Behind him now were the flat bottomlands with their rich pasturage and farms, and ahead were the jagged peaks and rough screes of the Barrens, the rampart of mountains that formed Ilyria's eastern wall. From where he was now the road led up through the corrugated hills, circled the shoulder of the nearest peak, and became a narrow track through the Gap, a wild pass in a high valley. Beyond that was Barrener territory. He had never been there.

He was thinking of a priest-seer somewhere up in those mountains calling down the destructive force of the Unnamed when he trotted around a bend and found himself sharing the road with a couple of wagons that seemed to have children hanging all over them. The rumbling of the wooden cart wheels must have masked the sound of Snort's dainty hooves on the grass track, and it was a moment before one little fellow tagging along after the last cart caught sight of the stranger. The boy brushed a wild shock of hair out of his eyes and then darted forward to say something to the man who drove the ox team.

Peewit guided his pony beside the cart, meeting the frank stares of the children with a friendly grin. He touched his hat and nodded to the older girl and the woman who rode in the bottom of the wagon. The man glanced over at him. The Littleman said, 'Afternoon. Warm enough, isn't it?'

The man grunted something and clucked to his team. By now, the family in the cart up ahead was aware of Peewit's presence, and he half-waved to them. 'Quite a crowd,' he commented. 'Are ye coming from the fair?'

At this, the man gave him an unfriendly look. His wife (Peewit presumed) drew her light shawl across her face and scolded the children in a hiss for staring. They lowered their eyes guiltily.

What's this? the Littleman wondered. Do I look that odd? They act afraid. Then, suddenly, he understood that the potter was afraid of being robbed. He scratched carefully at the fake beard and cleared his throat. 'Say, I was wondering – would you mind if I rode behind you a ways, but within eyesight?' He lowered his voice and said confidentially, 'Fact is, I've been looking back over me shoulder ever since I left Greenbriar. What with this wolf, I'd feel better if there were other people about.'

Now the husband studied him. He must have concluded that the 'dwarf' was probably harmless (or maybe he just wanted to keep an eye on the stranger), for he nodded. 'All right. A fellow don't know who to trust nowadays, but I reckon yer alone, right enough. Where ye headed?'

'Waysmeet tonight.' Farther than that, Peewit did not volunteer.

'All right,' the man said again. 'Us too.' He shifted the heavy rope reins to one hand and held out his other. 'Liam Potter.'

'Petyr Patursson,' the Littleman lied. They shook hands. One of the boys reached from the cart to touch the pony's nose, and Snort ducked his head to be patted.

The potter indicated the forward wagon. 'That's me brother, Kip, and his family.'

Peewit nodded toward the bed of the cart. 'Looks like you had a successful trip.'

Liam Potter smiled broadly. 'Sold out. All our stuff was bought out by the second afternoon. It's amazing what them lowlanders will pay for a good turned pot or a pitcher.' His wife unobtrusively jabbed him in the back, and he recollected that he shouldn't be discussing with a stranger the profits he had stowed under the double floor of the wagon. He straightened on the wooden seat and cast a critical eye over the 'dwarf.' 'Were you at the fair, then? I don't remember seeing you.'

Peewit had his story prepared. 'I was there, indeed. In fact, I'm sure I saw your stall. Over by that grove, weren't you? Gerrit's Wood?'

'Right agin it,' Potter confirmed.

'I thought so.' Peewit had, in fact, glimpsed the large display of clayware during the preparations for the Ritual of the Rose. 'I had a notion to buy one of your bowls for my wife, but I've a long distance to go before I get back home and I was afraid I'd break it.'

Potter twitched his whip over the oxen rumps. 'Where do you hail from, Master Dwarf?'

'The Southmark. But I thought since I was already at Greenbriar, I might as well go a bit farther and visit my brother at High Heath.' This was a village near the opening of the Gap. He knew there was quite a population of dwarves there, and figured it would explain his journey to the curious. 'We don't get to see each other often, and there's a new little lad in the family, so this seemed a good time.'

'Ah, Tychanor's Blessing be with yer family, then.' Children were especially blessed by the gentle Lord of the Warm Fire, and a sign of his approval.

''Ye've the Fire's blessing yourself, it looks like,' Peewit answered, with a wry glance at the two wagons full of boys and girls.

Liam laughed. 'Aye, we do, and grateful for it. Do you have family?' he asked politely.

Brickleburr felt a poignant sense of loss – he must be the only Littleman who did not! –but he lied smoothly, 'Two. A son and daughter. But they're both grown and have families of their own.'

The boy who had patted the pony leaned to put his hand on the smooth nose. 'What's your pony's name?' he piped.

'I call him Snort.'

'How come?' the youngster wanted to know.

The pony flared his nostrils and blew a loud sneeze into the brown hand, which was quickly snatched back. 'That's why,' Peewit told him serenely. The boy let out a surprised whoop and then began to laugh. He leaned dangerously to try it again.

His father took hold of the back of his little leather breeches with one big hand and lifted him back down to the floor of the wagon. 'That's enough. Leave Master Patursson's wee horse alone, now, or ye'll be walking with yer brothers.'

'Aw, Dad.' But the boy quieted at his mother's look, and he contented himself with picking a long sliver out of the battered side of the wagon and glancing up every now and again at the pony's pricked ears.

They climbed a long rise at the slow pace of the oxen, and the wagon up ahead suddenly stopped at the crest. Peewit thought at first that Potter's brother was waiting for them to catch up in order to have conversation with him and find out who the stranger was, but as they drew closer he could see the worried look that Potter's brother turned on them, and then the man beckoned urgently. 'Liam, hurry up!' he shouted back to the second wagon.

Without looking at Peewit, the potter whipped up his oxen. When they were right behind the forward cart, he flung the rope reins to his wife and jumped down from the seat to stride forward up the last of the hill. 'What's the matter, Kip?'

Kip Potter was mustached and stringy and, just now, very concerned. He had turned on his seat to watch them come up. 'Look.' He pointed down the other side of the hill with his whip.

As Peewit swung down from Snort and led him forward, he heard Liam's curse and when he stopped beside the man, he saw what had caused it.

The road wound like a ribbon down this hill and across the valley to the next height. In his wanderings after the Bastard had usurped the Ilyrian throne, the Littleman had passed through that valley more than once, and he remembered it as a fertile corrie cupped in the palm of the hills. There had been farmsteads and sheep and the mauve blush of heather. Now it was black, and his immediate thought was that he had seen a land burned to the roots like this before. It had made him sick then and it made him sick now.

Alphonse's Fire and the shooting star must have met right over this spot.

Liam was running his hand through his hair while he stared across the valley. 'Ned Weaver's house is gone.' His voice sounded more puzzled than shocked. The children stood in the cart beside him, round-eyed, and the youngest girl began to whimper.

Peewit said quietly, 'A suggestion, Master Potter. I'll ride on ahead and check whether there be any folk down yonder who may need help.' Both men's eyes swung to him, and he knew he did not need to make it plainer: he would go down to be sure that no bodies lay in open view of the children and women as they passed by.

Kip Potter nodded. 'Aye, Master Dwarf, that would be the best way. We'll come on slow. If ye should find something, give us a yell.'

The Littleman scrambled back into the saddle and urged Snort past the cart. He took the downward slope carefully, but where the road evened out a bit he touched a heel to the pony's side, and Snort, who was nervous at the smell of burning, jumped to a gallop.

They need not have feared what the children might see. When Peewit drew up before the tumbled stones that had been the weaver's cottage, he saw that not only had the timbers and thatch burned, but the concussion of star meeting wizard's fire had blown down the very rock walls. He slid from the saddle and walked slowly about the place. It was behind the byre that he found the charred body with its throat ripped out. The captain felt an urge to heave, but swallowed his sickness and looked again to be absolutely certain. Whether it had happened before or after the fire made little difference: the wolf had been here. Peewit went grimly out front, hauled himself into his saddle, and waved the carts forward.

He said nothing of the body, but even so it was a subdued group that rode on toward Waysmeet, and even when – after cresting two more hills – no more burned and flattened fields met them, they did not talk much. One by one the children hoisted themselves onto the tailgate of the wagon to watch the suddenly unfamiliar scenery pass slowly by.

They came down a long slope into Waysmeet just at supper-time. Though the long light of the summer evening still lay ahead for some hours, the town gates were being shut and chained. Liam stood in his wagon and gave a hail. Kip added his voice, and the gatekeeper shaded his eyes with his hand and held the gate for them. 'Ye've just made it,' he called as the ox carts rumbled up. 'Another few minutes and it would have needed a vote of the town council to let you in.' Then he caught sight of Peewit, and the friendly look he had given the Potters vanished. 'Here, now, Liam – who's this that's traveling with you?'

Liam anwered, 'Master Petyr Patursson. He's all right, Andy. I'll vouch for him.'

The Littleman said quickly, 'I don't want to be any trouble to you, Master Potter.'

'No trouble,' Kip cut in. To the gatekeeper, he said in a low voice, 'We've just come from Ned Weaver's.'

'Aye, wasn't that an awful thing?' the man answered in the same tone while he undid the padlock and swung the gate wide so that they could pass through. ' 'Twas that great light in the sky last night that did it. Young Tim Fuller was up on the hills with his pa's flock and he saw it happen. Got himself burned, and he's deaf as a doorpost. The hired men have just brought him in for Biddy Chandler to tend. Poor lad's havin' a bad time.'

Elixir, Peewit thought. 'Would there be a Retreat anywhere about?' he asked. 'The Retreat Masters might be able to help him.' He knew that Riders had been dispatched with vials of the precious healing fluid to Retreats after the ceremony yesterday. Each Retreat had its physician, and these had all been trained by Fidelis in the use of the Elixir. If they could get the burned shepherd boy to a Retreat, his suffering would be eased.

The gatekeeper's expression became wary. 'We don't have much to do with the Retreat Masters up here. The Barreners live close, and if we had a Retreat near us, the mountain men would make it hot for us. We try to get by as peaceable as we can with them. You'll save yeself a peck of trouble by not bringing up Retreats or Retreat Masters again, Master Dwarf.'

'I'll remember that,' Peewit replied evenly.

The man scratched at his beard. ' 'Sides which, what have the Powers done for us lately? When Aashis starts lettin' his stars fall on yer head, yer not disposed to be givin' thanks for it.'

Liam cleared his throat and flicked his whip to start the team rolling again. As he passed the gatekeeper, he looked down on him for a moment from the high seat. 'It ain't you that was hurt, Andy. It ain't for you to say naught about Lord Aashis or his stars. Belt up in front of me kids.'

The gatekeeper darkened and said, 'Oh, get on along with ye!' He closed the gate impatiently, and they could hear him threading the chain through the bars again as they passed down the main street of the village.

Liam Potter glanced over at the 'Dwarf.' 'Don't think bad of Andy. His woman was taken in the plague five years ago, and since then . . .' He lifted one shoulder in a shrug.

'We all lost people in the plague,' the captain said, looking straight ahead. The thought came unbidden to his mind: And likely to lose them again if the damn Barreners aren't stopped. He reached to pat Snort's sweaty neck. 'I feel bad for the shepherd boy, is all. I went deaf for a while myself.'

'Ah. Well, Biddy Chandler's pretty good at healin' folks. Still, it'll be rough for the boy, I don't doubt. Yer legs are no good to ye if ye can't hear the wolf comin'.'

Peewit gave him a surprised look, but then realized that he and Liam were thinking of two different wolves.

They drew up shortly before a rambling two-story inn. The yard was jammed with wagons and carts of every description, and they knew even before a groom came trotting over to tell them that the accommodations were full. Liam turned to call to Kip, 'If this is full, the Gorse Bush will be, too.' Both of the town's inns would be bursting with travelers coming home from the Crowning Day festival. 'What do you say to heading over to the common and camping there tonight? We'd still be inside the town walls, and the weather looks to be clear.'

'Good enough,' Kip called back. 'I just want a stout gate betwixt me and . . . harm.' He said no more before the wide-eared children.

Liam said to Peewit, 'Will ye stay with us, Master Patursson?'

'I will, and give you thanks for it. But I'll be no bother to you for provisions – I've got my own – and I'd like to stand you and Kip to a beer for speaking on my behalf to the guard at the gate.'

'That sounds good. We'll pitch camp and get some supper, and then we can walk over to the Gorse or back here to the Bog Oak, whichever you want.'

'Maybe both.' The Littleman summoned a grin. 'It's been a long ride.'

Potter chuckled and turned his team back into the street with some difficulty. They plodded on toward the town's common. On every side wives leaned from upper windows to call children home to supper, and other wayfarers like themselves hastened toward whatever accommodations they could find. They passed several parties of Barreners in the crowded street, distinguished by their long diamond-patterned hoods, and Peewit noted that everyone was studiously careful not to give or take offense. The border people walked a very fine line.

Near the common, they rode past one house set back a little from the street. There were some people gathered at the sagging fence, and at Peewit's inquiring look, Liam volunteered, 'Biddy

Chandler's.' When one of the men looked up as they rumbled by, Potter called, 'How's the dwarf boy?'

'Don't know. The old lady won't let anybody but his ma and pa get near the place. But I guess that's proper.'

'Well, if you see his dad, tell him a stranger wishes his boy well.'

The man nodded. Peewit leaned to catch hold of the nose ring of the ox nearest him and led the team around a bend in the street. They emerged onto the common and found it already thronged with camping families. The Littleman led the two carts down the narrow lane that had been left free, and finally they found a space big enough for both wagons. As quickly as might be, the biggest pair of children had fetched water and the men had built a fire. By the time the sky purpled with dusk, supper was done and the littlest already put to sleep in the flat wagon beds. Liam and Kip left their wives to get the others comfortable in their bedrolls, and steered Peewit through the falling dark to the Gorse.

Just before they stepped into the circle of lamplight outside the tavern door, the Littleman patted his fake beard firmly and felt beneath the cloth of his sleeve for the reassuring dagger in its spring-action sheath that Kursh had lent him.

Kip was holding the door for him. The captain drew the brim of his hat down over his eyes and stepped into the malt-smelling smoke.

Later, Peewit slipped through the silent wagons and around the snoring bedrolls strewn about the common without awakening anyone. He had gone still just as a precaution in case any light sleeper was disturbed, and now he went quickly down the lane and came to the sagging fence. There was a candle or lamp turned low within Biddy Chandler's house; its light came dimly through the horn window to pick out the speedwell and comfrey in her garden. The Littleman hesitated at the gate, but reckoned if he took it slowly, any creak might be lost in the breeze that had come up with nightfall. He went in.

Stepping carefully, he drew close to the window, hoping to see in, but the horn was well fitted and the chinks around the window frame were caulked with clay. He could hear no sound, except a dog's chain down the road somewhere. He crept around the corner of the house, narrowly missing a collision with the rain barrel. Foxglove stood tall against this wall, and he was careful not to break any of the stalks. He must have crushed a patch of parsley underfoot, though; he could smell it in the darkness. There was no window on this side. Peewit made his way to the back of the house.

Here the healing woman had her kitchen garden. Brickleburr stepped over cabbages and around leeks, and made for the half-door, which stood open in the summer night. The candleglow grew stronger as he got closer, and he was mindful that even though he had gone still, he might cast a faint shadow. All night while he had traded beers with the Potters and listened to the local gossip, he had had a nagging feeling – an intuition – that he had to see the young dwarven shepherd somehow.

Just as he was nearly to the doorway, he and a yellow-striped cat startled each other. The cat leaped away into the darkness, and Peewit leaned on the rough plaster wall, his heart thumping. When he calmed, he stood on tiptoe and peeked over the half-door.

By the light of a single fat candle in a saucer on the table, he saw a smallish room, furnished simply, but very clean. The hearth was swept and there was a low fire burning, with a teakettle purring on its hook. The bed was a plain cot, but it had a neat coverlet mounded over the boy, who was apparently asleep; the captain could see his even breathing and the edge of a cold compress dampening the black hair. A chair was set snug to the hearth, and in this the old woman sat, draped in a blanket. She also was asleep. A man and a woman – Peewit guessed them to be Tim Fuller's parents – were stretched out on the floor, wrapped in a good rug of sheepskin. Fuller snored and his wife's eyes were closed. Brickleburr eased back down to lean against the wall once more and think, All right, clever fellow. What now? He looked around at the garden rustling in the wind and sighed.

A soft voice above him said, 'Come in, Master Littleman, and welcome be. My hearth is honored by your presence.'

Peewit suppressed a gasp and looked up. Biddy Chandler's thin old face wore a most knowing expression, and the confused Littleman thought to himself, She can't see me – I'm still!

'Ah, now I've gone and scared ye. Beg pardon. Please don't take it hard and go away. It's been long since I've had a Teazle under me roof, and 'twould be a pleasure to share a bit o' cake and a hot cuppa with ye, if yer a mind to.'

Peewit swallowed and allowed himself to flicker back into sight. She smiled luminously and opened the door for him.

As he went past her, he whispered, 'How about them?'

'The lad's deaf as a post, poor heart, and I give his folks a bit of a posset to make 'em sleep. They was wore out with watchin' by the boy.' She waved him to the chair, but he went to stand looking down at the boy.

'Is he badly burned?'

'Naught to matter. Singed, ye might say. It's his ears that got the worst of it. He'll not hear the whippoorwills again, I fear.' She was arranging two small tea bowls on the scarred table.

Peewit pulled a stool closer and sat down as she wrapped the hem of her skirt around the iron handle of the kettle and poured for them both. He met her amused eyes over the top of the seedcake. Biddy Chandler said gently, 'The beard must be fair scratchin' yer face off. Why don't ye take it off for now and I'll give ye a bit o' salve to soothe yer chin.'

The Captain of the First Watch had not felt like this since he was very young. Sheepishly, he carefully peeled the wool away. 'It's a disguise,' he mumbled.

'Oh, aye. I guessed as much when I seen ye peekin' over me door. I says to myself, What's a Teazle goin' about dressed up like a dwarf for? And then I knew who ye must be.' She cocked her head. 'What's Queen Ariadne's Teazle doin' coming through people's gardens up here in Waysmeet?'

The Littleman coughed. 'Well I – um . . .'

The white-haired woman snapped her fingers. 'That star! Ooh, Sarai, yer going' soft in yer wits – ye should have seen that right off! The queen wants to know about that star!'

She had gotten it too quickly for Peewit's comfort. He probed, 'How did you see me, grandmother? Normally, people can't.'

Biddy Chandler smiled as she cut him a generous chunk of cake. 'Normally, people don't know how to look, do they?'

He had no idea. She seemed to know more about his kin than he did. Sipping his tea, he waited until she had served him and sat down herself. 'Have you . . . seen many Littlefolk?'

'Just one. Aye, just one.' She dripped some honey into her tea and offered him the pot. He shook his head. 'She was my friend, Tansy Mossflower was. She came to my hearth spring and fall for many a year.' The old woman lifted her tea bowl and sniffed the steam. 'I've outlived her now, I guess.' She took a sip.

The Littleman pondered this, and wondered whether any of his people were still here, near Waysmeet.

Biddy Chandler said softly, 'She told me about ye, Master Brickleburr.' When his eyes flew to her seamed face, she nodded. 'About the Pledged, and how ye can't ever go home because ye've killed, even though 'twas done in the service of the Greenbriar.'

Peewit swallowed. 'They . . . remember me?'

She blew on the tea. 'Of course. How not? The Teazles always know all of their own.'

Her words gave him a peculiar glow of comfort.

'That's brought a grin to yer face. Ye look much more Teazly when yer smilin',' she told him. Biddy Chandler got up to fetch a small blue pot from the mantel over the fireplace. 'Here. Dab a bit o' this on where the pine gum has burned ye.'

Gratefully, he did so. The stinging eased immediately. While the old woman cleaned up the crumbs of cake, Peewit went over to the boy once more. Over his shoulder he whispered, 'Has he said anything about last night?'

She flipped the last few bits of cake from her apron into the hearth and replied, 'From what I can understand, he saw a terrible big light come from yonder over the mountains, streakin' in over toward the valley. Then another light – a purplish one – come from the valley to meet it and the whole thing blew up and knocked the lad flat. He remembers lyin' there, starin' up, and then next he knew he woke up and was tryin' to get here to the town when the other men found him.'

It was just as Peewit had thought. He frowned. 'He saw nothing else?'

'Like what?'

He ran a hand through his curly hair. 'Like a giant wolf?'

Her white braids, neatly bound about her head, caught the candlelight as she shook her head definitely. 'Didn't say.'

The Littleman looked up at her. 'Grandmother Chandler, I need to wake him up. Would you mind?'

For answer she stooped over the bed and placed a gentle hand on the boy's cheek. When Tim made no movement, she removed the compress from his forehead and touched his eyelid lightly. His eyes fluttered open, and he stared up at her groggily. She smiled reassuringly and pointed to Peewit. The shepherd boy turned his head gingerly to see what she had pointed at. He frowned and squinted as if trying to decide whether this was a human boy or an adult dwarf kneeling by the bedside.

Peewit backed up a step so that the lad could see him full-length.

The dry lips opened. 'Wha –? Who are ye?'

Talk would be senseless. Instead, Peewit disappeared and then flickered back into view. The old woman giggled. 'Now ye'll have him thinkin' he's daft!'

Tim Fuller's eyes were round over the coverlet. 'A Teazle!' he breathed.

The captain nodded and smiled.

The boy glanced at Biddy Chandler. 'I'm not dreamin'?' At her shake of the head, he fixed his eyes again on Peewit. 'Do that again!' His voice was stronger.

The Littleman did.

'By the Powers, it's true, then!' Tim laughed a little. 'I figured it for a kid's story.' He suddenly winced and put a hand to his head. The old woman dipped the compress into a bowl of cool water, wrung it, and placed it back on his forehead. From under the edge of it, he regarded Peewit. 'Well, now I've seen it all,' he marveled.

The Littleman had been wondering how he could ask his question. He pantomimed writing and pointed to the boy, raising one eyebrow.

Tim snorted. 'I can make my mark, but what other use would I have for it?'

Peewit bit his lip. After a moment, he pointed again to the boy

and then to himself, to indicate that he was now playing Tim.
Biddy Chandler perched on the end of the bed to watch.

The night had been huge with stars – Peewit swept one arm
across the ceiling to show how big that starry darkness had
been. He was Tim, leaning on his crook, and looking up to watch
the sky-pictures change as the slow night wore on. Away down
the slope of the hill was the flock, down there where Mum and
Dad slept now.

Suddenly, fear. Peewit showed that, his mouth falling open
and an unmistakably terrified expression on his face. He flung
up a hand, pointing up over the crest of the hill behind him. He
shaded his eyes from the unnatural light, falling back a step and
turning his head.

Now – another light! He followed its trail across the sky,
wide-eyed. The lights met over his head, and he squeezed his
eyes shut and clapped his hands over his ears, mouth wide open
in a soundless yell. An invisible hand seemed to pick him up and
throw him to the floor, hard. He lay there, spread-eagled
and staring.

Tim eased himself to the edge of the bed and looked down. The
Littleman looked back at him. 'Ye've got it. 'Twas just the way it
happened,' the boy said wearily and rolled onto his back once
more, holding his head. Peewit snapped his fingers to attract
Tim's attention, snorted with derision at himself, and jumped to
his feet.

He touched the boy's arm, and when he had the lad's attention
once more, he pointed from himself to the floor to show that he
was still Tim, and still lying there. Then the Littleman went
toward the far wall, into the shadows away from the candle.
Suddenly he turned, becoming somehow heavier and harsher.
He tossed the tail of an imaginary hood over his shoulder and
drew in the air the diamond pattern.

'I didn't see any Barreners that night, Master Teazle.'

Peewit sighed, and his head dropped. He came slowly toward
the bed. He had been sure there must have been a Barrener
priest nearby.

'Ye've got it just the way it was, though, except for that last
bit. And except for the music, o' course.' The boy pressed the
compress to his head.

Peewit grabbed his wrist and said, 'What music?'

Tim must have read his lips. 'Right before the first light, I
heard music. There was a piper and his dog up on the ridge.' He
did not notice how Peewit went suddenly motionless. The boy
was musing to himself. ' 'Twas an odd song, though. Like this.'
Tim pursed his lips and began to whistle, but his deafness must
have thrown his pitch off. The tune wandered high and low,
grating on their ears. Biddy Chandler shook her head and looked
away.

Peewit suddenly felt his breath squeezed from his chest, and he could not get it back. His eyes went wide, and sweat broke out on his brow. Instinctively, he fell across the bed and clapped a hand over the startled boy's mouth. 'Don't!' the Littleman begged hoarsely. Tim and the old woman stared.

Brickleburr drew deep breaths and after a moment straightened. He swallowed hard and wiped a hand across his eyes. 'Powers protect us!'

Biddy Chandler put out a hand to him. 'What's the matter?'

'That song.' He shook his head. 'I don't know what it is, but don't ever let it cross your lips again,' he told the boy. Seeing that Tim did not understand, the Littleman put a finger to his lips. 'Ssh!'

'The music? You don't want me to whistle it?'

Peewit shook his head vigorously.

'It gave ye quite a turn, didn't it?' the boy asked.

The Littleman nodded once, grimly. He put a hand to his chest and drew it suddenly into a fist to show what it had felt like.

Tim's expression cleared. 'All right, I'll not do it again.' Peewit signed his thanks. 'D'ye think it had something to do with that light?'

No, but it may have a deal to do with the wolf, the Littleman thought. To the boy he shrugged.

The old woman asked quietly, 'D'ye think 'twas the music that made him deaf?'

Peewit's eyes flicked to hers, and considering his own experience with it, he answered, 'Yes.'

Shrewdly, she guessed, 'Our young queen be fightin' the Wild Feller again, isn't she?' Wordlessly, Peewit nodded once more.

'Ah,' was all she said. Then, 'You'll be on yer way back to tell her about the odd music?'

'Not quite yet. I'm going up to the Gap first.' He turned to the table to pick up the sticky wool of his disguise. He did not put the beard on yet, however.

When he turned again, she was standing, twisting her hands uncertainly. After a moment she said, 'Ye'll be needin' some seedcake for yer journey, then.' She bustled to get it.

Peewit extended his hand to shake Tim Fuller's. 'You've been a great help.' He gave the boy a friendly nod and a wink. Biddy Chandler put the bit of cake into his hand, wrapped in a kerchief. 'Thank you, grandmother.'

'Do be sure ye come back, Master Brickleburr.'

'I will.' He waved to Tim and went out. When he got to the cabbages he stepped carefully over them once more and looked back. She was standing in the doorway.

Peewit put his head to one side and began to whistle. In moments her garden was sparkling with fireflies. Smiling, he made her a courtier's bow and left that homey house forever.

Chapter Ten

In the blue hour before dawn, Kursh roused out of a sound sleep. Pain pressed somewhere in his head, throbbing like the tremolo of a piccolo pipe. He groaned quietly and lay still, as he had learned to do over the past months, for sometimes the ache would dull a little and then he could get up and make himself ready for work. Opening his one eye slightly to gauge the time by the degree of light in the room, he saw the walls begin to slide.

He gasped and clutched the edges of his bed as the mortared boulders sagged and ran like a mudslide. The ceiling timbers snarled across his bed like roots gone wild. Even while a part of his pain-wrapped mind insisted that he must have a high fever, he fought desperately against the grasping roots, wresting back the one that entwined his feet. He flung himself over the edge of the bed and grabbed for his ax, which stood always near to hand. Snarling filled his ears, and fangs caught his nightshirt and began to drag him across the stone flags of his floor. He flailed and caught the handle of his ax. When he twisted to hack at the thing, he saw glinting sapphire eyes. With his last strength he brought the ax crashing down on the wolf's head.

His blade sliced through bedclothes and straw mattress and shattered the slate floor tile beneath. Sparks struck off the iron ax head, and for an instant there was a miniature starfall. A straw caught fire and flared briefly, but died.

The dwarf panted, and sweat dripped off his large nose. He swallowed and licked his lips, then looked down dazedly at the handle that had stung his hands. A bruised nerve in his right palm sent a splinter of pain up to his armpit. Automatically, he put the weapon down and spat into his palms, rubbing them together. He was still trying to focus on the rock walls of his small chamber, which were just where they should be. His look traveled to the ruined cot, and one large hand went out to touch and be sure. A throb behind his eyes made him wince, and he pressed both hands to his ears and eased himself to the stool.

I wasn't dreaming, he told himself; I was awake and the fit came upon me anyway. And then he thought, I can't go on like this.

He took the double-headed ax onto his lap and inspected the weapon. Miraculously, though he had expected to find the haft cracked from the force of his blow, the wood was still sound; the handle hadn't even loosened from the forged head. Kursh smiled a little. It was a good ax – always had been. He ran a blunt finger along one blade and found it sound, so he flipped the weapon over and inspected the other. In the gray half-light he could see the chip taken out of the iron, but his fingers told him there was also a sizable crack. After a moment, he patted the ax and stood it carefully by the bed.

Despite the throbbing that the movement caused, he got up and went to the uniform he had left neatly folded on top of his brassbound chest. Slowly he got dressed. The dagger in its sheath was the last thing, and he carried it over to the small writing table that Jamison had brought in for him yesterday. Lighting the candle, Korimson sat down to write out his orders for the day. All the while his pen scratched across the paper, he was weighing what he should do.

On the one hand, it would be a foul thing to be derelict in his duty, and he was acting commander while Peewit was away. But on the other hand, it would be all over by the time the Littleman got home, and that would spare Brickleburr something . . .

By the time he was sprinkling fine sand over his signature and pressing the blotter over the page, his mind was made up. He folded the paper and left it for young Jamison. Kursh was about to get up when he hesitated and then drew a second sheet toward him. The headache was so bad that he had to keep one hand pressed to his temple as he wrote:

'Dear Captain.'

After a moment, he crossed that out and wrote:

Dear Peewit,
The Weatherglass is yours. I hope you see lots of sunny days in it. The Sword and Skull goes to Kathy and her parents: tell them to be sure to order more Nabilia wine before winter when the roads are closed. Please get my ax fixed and give it to Jak Cooper – I think he has the makings of an axman and I'd like to keep the weapon in service to the Queen. My respects to Her Majesty. I regret that I can do nothing to help fight the Unnamed, but it seems I do not have the time. Say to Imris that I hope he feels better soon. Tell Freckles that my brother Trondur will try to teach him glass-blowing if he ever gets tired of being a wizard.

Take care of yourself, Brickleburr – may the winds of Aashis blow soft upon your life.

He signed it and then recollected something else:

P.S. At the bottom of this trunk, you'll find a brooch with a
ruby. It was Orin's. I'd like Gerrit to have it. It should make
a nice pommel stone for his sword when he comes of age.

The dwarf sanded and blotted the note carefully and blew out
the candle. He put the letter inside the trunk for Peewit to find,
then took up the dagger.

Thyla walked briskly up the hall past the captain's quarters
and was relieved that she did not have to risk the teasing of the
young officer who would have been on duty outside the Littleman's door if Master Brickleburr had been home. A bit of the
homespun napkin that wrapped the muffins she carried had
come untucked, and she folded it down again to keep the warmth
in. Muffins were no good if they didn't steam when you split
them; she believed that firmly.

Cradled against her bosom she also carried a covered tankard
containing good strong starflower tea – the soothing herb was
fresh, too; she had bought it off a footman in the Ambassador's
retinue. She had laced it with just a drop of flotjin, figuring that
otherwise the First Watchman wouldn't drink it. Ale was his
usual breakfast beverage.

Now if this doesn't put the appetite back in him, I don't know
what will, she thought. Starflower's sovereign for all kinds of ills.

She came to the corner of the corridor and peeked around it.
Good, his door was still shut and there was no light from under it.
He was still abed.

Just for a moment she wondered what she would do if he came
out and found her there, but then she put her shoulders back and
marched up to his door. Quietly she set the basket of muffins
down, settled the napkin, and put the tankard on the floor. As
she straightened, she knocked firmly on the oak planks, then her
courage wavered and she scampered back down the hall and
whisked around the corner. She didn't stop running until she
came to the top of the stairway, and there she paused to catch
her breath and giggle a little to herself before she straightened her cap and went back downstairs to work.

When the loud knock came at the door, Kursh started, and the
dagger tip he held poised against the pulse in his throat jumped
and nicked his chin. Jamison! Dammit! Couldn't a fellow even
have half a moment's peace to kill himself decently around this
bloody damn place?

He flung the dagger end over end at the door and it stuck deep
in the wood, quivering. Jamming a thumb against the shallow
cut, he stomped toward the door, intending to blast that little
whoreson from his polished boots to the top of his neatly combed
head. Ignoring the thundering pain (and the quiet relief that

lurked somewhere back in his mind), the First Watchman
yanked the door open and sucked in a breath to tell the orderly
exactly what he thought of him.

There was no one there.

So big a breath had to go somewhere. 'Jamison, you little
squirt, get back here!' he roared. There was no answer. Kursh
growled a curse, and started to close the door. In the dim light he
saw a covered basket and a tankard, and thought, What the
bloody hell?

Stooping carefully so his head wouldn't split open, he lifted a
corner of the napkin. The unmistakable aroma of freshly baked
blueberry muffins tickled his nose with thoughts of sun and
picnics on the high heath of Jarlshof. Thyla, he realized; she
had been knocking. He picked up the basket and tankard and
thumbed the top of the mug up. Steam wafted up, threaded with
some scent he could not identify at first. He hesitated, then took
a sip. Starflower tea. By the Powers, how long had it been since
his young wife had dosed him with starflower tea that first
winter that they were at Swiftwater Shallows? His cold had
cleared right up, too, he remembered. He took another sip.
Unexpectedly he found that even though his headache still made
the rising light of the new sun hard to bear, he was a bit hungry.
He thought about Thyla and what she would think if they found
him covered with blood, and the basket of muffins untouched on
the writing table.

That wouldn't do at all. If a fellow was going to kill himself, he
ought to take care not to hurt anyone else in the process. And if
he wasn't going to kill himself, at least not now, not this morning,
then . . . probably he ought to try to eat something.

When Jamison did knock at the door some time later and the
gruff voice called for him to come in, the young orderly found the
First Watchman up and dressed and having his breakfast. The
dwarf was sitting at his writing desk and had his booted feet
propped up comfortably on his bed. He waved Jamison in,
silently handed him the day's orders, and then plucked a blueberry muffin from a covered basket on the desk. 'Eat, lad,' he
told the orderly. 'Ye could stand fattening up.'

Jamison obediently bit into the muffin as he let himself out.
When he had shut the door behind himself, he leaned against the
wall and let out his held breath, shaking his head. He did not
understand senior officers, and probably never would.

The new sun touched the small terrace set within the boxwood
hedge at the far end of the garden. Alphonse was aware of it on
the edge of his floating consciousness, but he did not open his
eyes. He was concentrating on extending his reception outward,
testing fragments of the Wind's Song for incursions by the Wild
Fire. Since last he had checked at the Meld Meet three days ago,

much more of the Wind Warding had been affected. The Unnamed was gathering power at all speed. The Wizard of the Three frowned and began to work on improving his control.

He felt a light breeze stir along his skin and flutter the silk meditation robe he wore, but there was no rustle from the hedge around him. He smiled slightly: his local control was good this morning. He deepened his trance with a quick sequence of breaths and settled to the delicate business of summoning the energy of the Song.

The redheaded man had tried to meditate in his room this morning, but he was restless and knew he needed some fresh air, so he had made his way through the sleeping hallways and come out to the queen's garden. There had been no guard posted, since Her Majesty was not present, so he had made no explanations. He didn't think Ariadne would mind, though.

As his thoughts drifted to the queen, he knew that his concentration suddenly wavered, and he was angry with himself. Back to business, he told himself firmly, and fought himself back to the control point. If Tydranth were going to attack in Aashis's Realm, then the Wizard of the Three had better be as ready as he could to counter the blow. He gathered random threads of Song and began to weave a Warding to guard Ariadne from the winds and waters and stars gone wild.

He felt the cold, moist fog grow around him, a soft and bracing air that smelled of rainwater and clean greenery. The wizard eased a wind into the mixture, and now – though he did not look to see – he knew that the mist would be circling about him, blown by a salt wind in miniature. He felt in his mind for the smell of ocean breakers and let that be taken into the Warding, as well. So far, so good. Now the more difficult ingredients.

Alphonse summoned the glow of stars and the face of the moon. These he threaded through the Warding, tucking the ends carefully so the spell would not come undone. Then, for good measure, he added the black-barred orange of a butterfly's wing. The Warding was made. The only remaining thing was to place it about Ariadne without her knowing. Even in the trance, he frowned. That would not be easy, she was so attuned by her own Greenbriar power.

His thoughts resumed the restless circle that had kept him awake most of the night, and he wondered whether, if he had spoken up years ago instead of burying himself at Covencroft, things might be different. Would she even have taken the suit of a seventeen-year-old boy seriously? The twenty-one-year-old man thought not. He noticed in the trance that the sea breeze freshened noticeably at his agitation, and he carefully damped it down again. No need to start a storm about it.

That was almost exactly what Chiswic had said the day he had come upon the younger wizard trying to practice this very meditation four years ago. It was the afternoon the news came that the Ilyrian queen was betrothed to the Shimarrat prince. Alphonse had ground his teeth and retreated to a place on the far side of the extinct volcanic cone where he often went to be alone. The old man had come after him.

Chiswic had come down into the dell, picking his way carefully and using his staff as a walking stick. For a moment, the freckle-faced youth was ashamed that his mentor had struggled all the way up the mountain to console him, but then the anger surfaced. He looked up and said coldly, 'You should have sent one of the adepts. It isn't as though I were going to turn him into a toad or something.'

The old wizard eased himself to the top of a boulder. 'I wasn't sure,' he panted. 'Besides, I haven't been up this way in quite a while. I'd forgotten how quiet it is. You can't even hear the ocean from up here.'

'Yes. It's quiet.' Pointedly, he said no more.

Neither did Chiswic.

A little nonplussed, he returned to his meditation. Maybe the old man would take the hint, and go back down to get his mid-afternoon bowl of clear soup. But his inner mind was too wild to permit any kind of control, and before he knew it, he had hurled a lightning bolt streaking out over the ocean. The clap of thunder shattered any semblance of trance, and he sighed and opened his eyes.

The old wizard met his look. 'You don't have to make a storm about it. All the fishermen from here to Jarlshof are cursing you right now, because you've scared off their catch.' The black eyes were amused.

'Too bad,' Alphonse said sullenly.

Chiswic laced his fingers about his staff and regarded the redhead. 'Yes, it is. But not for them.' When the boy raised his head, the old man said gently, 'And not for you, either.' He paused. 'It is too bad for Ariadne.'

'Why? She's marrying a prince, after all. How bad can that be?'

'Would you want to be forced to marry someone you hardly knew, much less loved, just because he had a suitable lineage and no other prospect was available? Be a little gentler in your judgment of the young queen. The imperative to pass on her Greenbriar power to an heir is a force she could scarcely hold off much longer. She must take a husband, and the sooner the better – as I am sure her councillors have told her.'

The young wizard looked away. 'She could have chosen anyone. He didn't have to be a prince.'

'Did he not? Alphonse, this is a royal marriage. A queen cannot marry where her heart wills. She must marry where her judgment tells her she can make the best political match. In this case, Ka-Salin will bring with him a stable border with

Shimarrat, which is actually a much stronger country than Ilyria. Ariadne is wise to avoid future trouble this way.'

Alphonse felt his cheeks flame. I could have brought her more impressive gifts, he thought.

'No, you couldn't have. The gifts you have are not for the giving away. You have your destiny, Ariadne has hers.' The musical voice softened. 'And that destiny is not going to be easy for either of you, I think. Maybe you can help each other with your burdens, as good friends must.'

The boy swallowed. 'I don't see how. If she marries him, I can't go back there. I just couldn't get that close to her again and not . . . say something.'

Chiswic had studied him for a time. Then, using his staff, the old man had pulled himself to his feet. 'Maybe you had better stay here and practice making storms, then. I'll leave you to your meditation, Master Freckles. For the sake of the fishermen, do be sure to cast a minor Warding to bring the fish back to the surface when you are finished.'

Sitting in the Queen's garden with the cold mist dewing his hair, Alphonse could still hear the tapping of the old man's staff as Chiswic had climbed slowly out of the dell.

In the next moment, he realized that the tapping was actually coming from someplace nearby, and that he was not alone in the garden. Startled, he wondered in his trance how he would put the Warding on Ariadne now, and opened his eyes. He saw the spell take effect. The mist gathered into a tight little cloud and rolled away above the shrub roses. He had sent it to find Ariadne, and he knew what would happen when the cloud reached the queen. He jumped up.

But he was already too late. As he chased the Warding cloud down the brick path through the rosemary bushes, he saw it hover for a moment, then let go with a brief but soaking shower on the woman who knelt to weed the lavender.

The queen's head jerked up. Springing to her feet and already turning to find the gardener who was so careless with the water bucket, she bellowed, 'Hey!'

Alphonse skidded to a stop. 'I –'

'Did you see what lame-brained fool threw that?' she demanded, angrily wiping her face on the sleeve of her work dress. Her eyes flashed as she tried to see past him to some fleeing figure going up the path toward the gate.

'What? No, listen –'

'Do not excuse him! If so much water had hit my seedlings, they'd have drowned!' Her hair dripped, and now there was a streak of mud across her forehead where she had swiped to clear her eyes.

The wizard tried manfully to hold back his laugh, and managed to sputter, 'I'm sorry – I was working on a meditation,'

before the humor of the situation overcame him. 'You're
soaked!' he gasped between guffaws.

Ariadne glared at him and paused as she flapped her apron to
shed some droplets. Then her eyes narrowed as she realized she
had been a victim of wizardry. She looked as though she ran
through the first four things that came to mind before she could
find something to say that wasn't obscene. 'You freckle-faced,
red-headed –'

He impersonated Festil the singer's extravagant bow. 'Don't
feed me to the buzzards, O Queen, I beg you!' But he was still
grinning broadly, and his plea did not have quite the force it
could have.

Ariadne considered kicking him, but his eyes were sparkling
with fun. 'I ought to send you down to the laundry. They could
use the help,' she muttered, wringing out the hem of her dress.
That set him off again, and she said tartly, 'You could at least
make a Fire. It's cold!'

He bit his lips and managed to suppress any further out-
breaks. Gravely, he held up his ring, and the garnet fire sparked
and cast a warming glow on the queen. Shortly, she was toasting
her hands to it and then turning to catch it on her back. The
wine-colored light turned her skin rosy, and there was just a hint
of steam – or of mist – about her shoulders. The rough old work
dress began to dry nicely.

'Mmm,' she murmured. 'You could have made it warm water,
you know.'

'I didn't realize you were out here. When I came out an hour
ago, I was alone. I am sorry,' he thought it diplomatic to add.

She tilted her head toward the warmth and patted her hair,
wondering whether to unbraid it and let it dry better. 'Do you
often practice your spells so early in the morning?'

Only when I can't sleep for thinking of you, he thought. 'It's a
good time for me. My head seems clearer, somehow, and that is
good for meditation.' He brought up the warm breeze a little to
wrap her. 'What about you, lady? Haven't you gardeners to keep
your flowers for you?'

She frowned. 'It wouldn't be my garden if the gardeners took
care of it.'

'Oh.'

'The plants know.'

He was about to laugh again when he recollected that it was
the Greenbriar Queen who was saying this. It was plausible that
her power did affect plants somehow. He put the idea away to
bring out and look at again later. 'Do you often work out here
alone?'

'Not as much as I'd like.' She surveyed the dewy plants. 'It
could all use a good going-over. Someday I'll get the time.'

'It looks beautiful to me.'

Ariadne smiled and redid her hairpins.

The wizard realized that she was dry now and extinguished his Fire.

Nodding her thanks, the queen picked up her trowel and absently cleaned the mud off the handle. 'Alphonse,' she asked, 'do you put much stock in dreams?'

He was instantly alert, but answered lightly, 'Only if I haven't eaten spiced pork for dinner.'

She knelt again to her weeding, and he joined her, awkwardly pulling clumps of clover. 'Careful of the thyme, there,' she cautioned, and then said, 'I had the most horrid dream last night. It woke me up, and I couldn't get back to sleep.' She half shrugged. 'So I thought I might as well be doing something worthwhile.'

'What did you dream?'

'Well . . .' Ariadne glanced at the red-bearded face intent on pulling weeds. 'I dreamed I was back in Ritnym's Realm.' At his startled look, she hastened, 'Not in Ritnym's Realm exactly – at the landing where we first found Gerrit. You remember the bedchamber, and then we were waiting for the barge? Well, I was there, and I remember that I wanted the barge to come so that I could cross, but for some reason it wouldn't. I waited and waited but it never came.' She fell silent.

The wizard said carefully, 'That does not seem so horrid.'

'No, it doesn't, just telling about it, But I felt . . . I don't know . . . terrified.' She stabbed a thick dandelion root. 'You know how feelings can be so strong in dreams sometimes and then when you wake up, you can't remember what it was that you were so afraid of?' At his murmur of assent, the queen sat back on her heels. 'What do you think it means?'

'Probably only that you were tired with all of the preparations for yesterday's activities, and then the star on top of everything else last night. I don't wonder that you had a nightmare.'

Relief flickered over her features. 'So you don't think it was a vision?'

'If it was,' he told her, 'you'll have the same dream again.'

'There's a cheerful thought.'

'Didn't have spiced pork last night at the banquet, did you?' he asked dryly. He answered her laugh with a grin, but he felt in his bones that it had been a vision, and probably a true one.

She was still for a moment. 'Actually it wasn't the first odd dream I've had of late.'

He knew by her tone that this one had disturbed her more. 'Tell me about it,' he suggested.

'Well, it wasn't a dream exactly.' A quick look. 'I was awake at the time.'

'A vision then. Why is it so hard to say?'

'Because normal folk don't have them. Only seers and Retreat Masters sometimes and . . .'

'Wizards.' There was a smile behind his eyes, but he did not let the queen see it. 'I understand. Go on, please.'

'On the night before last, I couldn't sleep, so I went down for a peek at the decorations, and as I passed the fresco it seemed to me that something was shining there. A tower, made of diamonds.'

His face was serious. 'The Crystal Keep,' he murmured. At her frown, he explained, 'The stronghold of Aashis on earth. 'Twas crystal, not diamond, that you saw, lady queen.' He carefully weeded around a rock. 'Did you see anything else?'

'A butterfly,' she answered promptly. 'It flew in through a window.'

'At night?'

Ariadne aimed her trowel at a weed, avoiding his quick glance. 'I know. That is why, when I remembered later, I concluded I must have been sleepwalking after all and dreamed the whole thing.' She threw down the tool. 'There's certainly no Crystal Keep in the painting now!'

The wizard regarded her thoughtfully. Ritnym's Realm she had dreamed of, and then Aashis's. The Powers were calling the Greenbriar Queen again as they had five years ago. But what action did the Immortals want her to take? By mistake he pulled up one of her newly transplanted slips of creeping laurel, and she shooed him from her garden to go find some breakfast.

He glanced back as he pulled the gate shut behind him. In the new light just beginning to slant across the blooms, the queen was limned in a fine mist. Satisfied, he let the Warding set, and the mist prismed the sun for a moment into a brilliant rainbow that outlined the kneeling figure. Before she could become aware of it, it was gone.

Alphonse nodded to the Watchman on duty and went musingly to get bannock from the kitchen. He must remember a saucer of milk for a certain black-and-white cat, too. She had not forgiven him for forgetting to leave the door open yet.

Alphonse picked up his knight and took Ka-Salin's sanctuary. The consort winced before he caught himself and tried to cover by stroking his waxed mustache. The wizard hid a smile. 'Your move, my lord.'

Ka-Salin pondered. His hand found the silver winecup on the stool next to him, and he sipped as he regarded the finely carved and painted armies on the inlaid board. Less than one turn of the hourglass into the game, his options were severely limited. After hesitating, he moved a councillor.

Whatever game the prince was playing nights when he made himself scarce from the royal apartment, it wasn't chess, Alphonse had found. The wizard had had to work not to beat him in the first four moves. Now he decided that enough was enough.

He moved his queen. 'Check.'

Ka-Salin's right brow drew up, then he smiled ruefully and shook his head. 'I yield.' He glanced up at the wizard and muttered, 'I should have done it an hour ago and spared us both!' He leaned back in his chair and began to laugh.

Alphonse chuckled. 'Another game?'

'Oh, no! I've no taste for torture!' He shook his head again and swallowed some wine.

The wizard poured himself another cup of tea. 'When we ride out on the hunt, Your Highness will have your revenge: my poor horsemanship will be shown up for all to see.'

Ka-Salin met Alphonse's eyes directly. 'You need not stand on court manners, Master Wizard, to spare my feelings. Just do me one favor: don't tell her how miserably I play chess. I'd like to keep some pride, if I may.'

Alphonse blew on his tea, 'All right.' The prince was obviously expecting a question, but the wizard would not ask. In the silence of the sun-filled royal apartment, they could hear the tapping of the stonemasons' hammers as work began on the battlement wall outside. Momentarily, the young wizard wondered how Peewit was doing on his solitary ride into the hills.

Ka-Salin cleared his throat and picked up the wooden queen. He placed the piece on the central square of the board, and said, 'I play dice. It gives her an excuse not to have me hanging about when she has ruling to attend to.' One corner of his mouth drew down. 'I am not much welcome in Ilyrian council meetings.' He sighed. 'So I tell her I am playing chess, though I can't stand the bloody game. She thinks I'm happily engaged in mock battles with armies that do not die. A gentleman's pastime.' He raised his cup and looked over the rim at the wizard. 'I would help her if she would let me. Will you tell me why the Eldest was late, and why my wife cried in her sleep?'

Alphonse was uncomfortable. It was obvious that Ariadne must have reasons of her own for not confiding in her consort. 'If she wanted you to know, my lord, doubtless she would have told you. Therefore, I will not cross her wishes in the matter. As to the crying, I can only guess that she was dreaming of the falling star,' he lied. 'She was frightened badly.'

'I know. She was still shaking when we lay together last night.'

The redheaded wizard controlled the flush that prickled at the back of his neck and tried to drive the unbidden image from his mind. He asked, more sharply than he had intended, 'Why were you not out there with her to watch the fireworks?' He was half hoping that the consort's story would not jibe with what the officer had told him last night.

'You sound as if you wish I had been the one who got his head smashed instead of young Nevelston.'

The Wizard of the Three realized that he needed to run

through a meditation to get himself under better control. 'I am sorry, sir. But there was a strangeness about that star last night, and I thought it odd that you were not present at a court function.'

Ka-Salin took a swallow of wine. 'Very well. Then know that I cannot abide heights.' His jaw tightened. 'It isn't cowardice. I survived an assassination attempt one of my brothers set on me. The killer tried to throw me off a turret platform.' His mountain-pool eyes had darkened. 'I was ten years old.' He sat back in his chair and raised the goblet again. 'Now, what other questions do you have, Master Wizard?'

Do you love her? Alphonse wanted to ask.

When the wizard hesitated, the consort tossed off the rest of the wine. Alphonse had realized by this point that Ariadne's husband had a problem with drink, but he was still surprised when Ka-Salin thrust back his chair and stood abruptly. 'Am I loyal to the Greenbriar Crown, because I am Shimarrat? Do you know what it's like to be the fourth son of a king who only needs one?' A bitter smile dragged down a corner of his mouth. 'I harbor no illusions: I am little more than the royal stud, but that is more than I would have in my own right in Shimarron. Yes, I am loyal to my queen.' He crossed his arms on his chest. 'Do I resent the fact that I will never be a king? Perhaps, but that is an accident of birth, and I am not such a fool as to believe that the Ilyrian court would accept me as Ariadne's full partner, even if she would.' His gaze went stone-hard. 'Last, do I harbor any ill will toward my son?' He stared at the wizard. 'No, by all the Realms. If you had a child, you would know.'

Alphonse stood slowly. 'Sir, I do not doubt you, and I am glad that we are both so concerned for the queen. I think she will need all our help in the days ahead.' He paused. 'There is danger, as you have gathered.'

Ka-Salin studied him. 'From the Barreners?'

'I fear that may be part of it.'

The prince nodded. 'Then I hope she'll let me lead a regiment against them.'

I wish it were that easy, the wizard thought. Knowing it would never happen that way, he said, 'I will fight at your right hand, if you will allow it.'

They shook on it. Ka-Salin turned to pour more wine, this time for both of them, and only then did Alphonse notice that the wooden queen had been knocked sprawling. A chill bunched his shoulder blades. He tried to tell himself he was behaving like a village weirding-woman, but he could not shake the image of a queen in robes of royal scarlet lying facedown upon a battlefield.

The prince consort turned with two silver goblets and held one out, smiling. 'To the queen's men.'

Chapter Eleven

The wizard, carefully balancing the saucer, nudged open his door. From the wide windowsill, Patience opened her one eye and watched him. The tip of her tail began to twitch.

When the black-and-white cat did not make a move to get the cream, Alphonse sighed. 'Oh, come. It was a banquet, by the Powers. You cannot still be angry that I didn't hear you amidst all that commotion.'

Patience closed her eye. 'It was important. You should have listened.'

'Well, I know the news about Imris now – he was attacked by the wolf.' He set the saucer down with enough of a click to tell her that he did not care for her snit, then joined her at the window.

The cat stretched and sat up. 'I suppose you also know why the star fell last night.' She began to wash her face to tell him that she did not care for his lame apologies.

The Serpent of the Meld tattoo around his throat rippled as he turned his head. Their eyes were on a level. 'Do you?'

'Asked you first.'

The wizard put one finger on her pink nose. 'I haven't time for this, little miss.' There was a spark in his blue eyes. He hated to be twitted, and Patience knew it.

She curled one paw about his finger, extended her claws until they just prickled the skin, and stared at him.

'Oh, all right! I am sorry about last night! There. Are you satisfied?'

'You would do well to remember that the woman is not the only queen here.'

'Yes, I know. And when we get home, I'll make it up to you. Now, what have you found out?' he insisted.

But Patience interrupted, 'How? How will you make it up to me?' She let go of his finger and pricked her ears.

He went scarlet, but replied evenly, 'Would a quarter wheel of Lipopo do?'

'That and what else?'

'That and I won't curse you with a plague of fleas, you little –'

Wisely, she began to purr. There was no sense in tempting his real anger: he had been doing so well on his control meditations lately. 'I have heard the arch of the sky cracking and a Song I do not know,' she told him.

Alphonse frowned, 'What?'

Her green eye widened. 'Last night I was looking at the stars and I heard it. I thought at first it was wind through a hollow reed. He did this once before, you know.'

'Who?' the wizard demanded.

'The evil one from long ago who bruised the face of the moon so that we can still see the marks,' she told him and licked the tip of her nose worriedly. 'It is old lore. Surely you must know of it.'

'The Unnamed has attacked the Realm of the Wind before?' His blue eyes blazing with urgency, Alphonse leaned to her. 'Patience, do you know how the other Three Powers stopped him?'

The cat narrowed her eye to a slit. 'Wait a little. I will look in my memories.'

The wizard was quiet while she looked down the long tunnel of her matriarchal line. After some moments, she turned her head to look at him. 'None of mine was present, but I can see a shining stone and a vine creeping.'

'The Greenbriar?'

'No. Much smaller and white-flowered.'

He pondered briefly. The shining stone could be a piece of firmament, and the vine . . .? He shook his head impatiently and began to drum his fingers on the sill.

Patience slapped a paw down playfully on his hand. Alphonse absently rubbed her ears, and she purred. The queen of cats suggested, 'Perhaps you should call to Master Chiswic to see if he knows anything of this.'

'I could do that,' he murmured absently, and lifted her down from the sill to set her near the cream saucer. 'I should wait until evening, though.' If he sent a Warding to the other wizard while Chiswic was awake, the old man would insist on carrying his share of the energy drain, and as he was already somewhat frail, Alphonse did not want to subject him to it. But in his sleep, in a dream, Chiswic would be a passive recipient, and the young wizard could do all the work. He nodded to himself: tonight, then.

The cat looked up from lapping. 'It's too bad you humans must write everything down to remember it; it is so much more convenient to carry one's memories in whiskers and paws.'

He smiled and wandered back to the open window. Leaning on the wooden framing timber, he stared across Willowsrill to the jagged Barrens. 'I wonder how Peewit is doing.'

'Very well, I should think. Master Hearthman knows much

about getting from here to there and back again without getting his tail stepped on.' Patience began to clean her whiskers.

'Still, it isn't a good place for him to be. Alone.'

'Neither is this.'

His thought went to Ariadne. 'No. I suppose not,' he said to himself.

The black-and-white cat rubbed a damp paw over her face and watched him. She knew his sudden silences.

The wizard sighed and swung away from the window. 'Well, I was supposed to meet Fidelis in the library, and also Kursh sent his orderly with a message to see him, so I guess I had better go. You'll find something to do, eh?' He stooped to pat her.

She stretched, fore and aft. 'The little prince will want rescuing from his nurse's company by now, I think. We played catch-the-butterfly this morning, and the woman was all in a dither that he would take a fall. Ridiculous.'

'You like Gerrit, do you?'

Patience bent her head, seeming to regard the sunbeam that warmed her toes on the stone floor. 'That kitten needs looking after,' she told the wizard soberly.

'Yes,' he agreed. 'And you are the one to do it.'

She looked up at him. 'That is just what I thought.'

He hid a grin at her self-important tone, and swung the door open for both of them.

The cat did not move, however. 'Be careful of yourself. The dwarf makes my fur stand up.'

Alphonse smiled. 'Oh, he is a good enough old fellow. You need not fear Kursh.'

'I do not fear him,' she shoved at him impatiently, but he was grinning, so she flicked her tail and sneezed on his doeskin boot as she walked past him out into the corridor. Looking back, she thought loudly, 'Don't forget to leave the door open.'

When the wizard did not find the doctor in the library and went to the hospital wing looking for him, the attendant at the door informed him that two more victims of the wolf had been brought in not long before and the chief physician was even then examining the bodies. Or what was left of them, the man said, eyes sliding sideways. Alphonse gathered there wasn't much. He did not envy Fidelis his grim task.

The orderly watched the wizard go back across the courtyard, then went back inside, 'I told the wizard that you would see him later, master.'

Fidelis focused, 'Thank you, Mat.' Neither of them looked at the nearly decapitated corpse on the stone table. It had been one of the hunters sent out after the beast. His partner's remains lay down in the cool dungeon with a couple of apprentices to keep the rats off until Fidelis could make his examination. As he had with all the victims, the doctor had looked for evidence that the victim had been tied or in chains before his death, for the Barreners usually presented the sacrifice to their god that way.

Fidelis excused Mat with a nod, calling after him, 'Have them bring in the second one.' He had a feeling he wouldn't find any clue on the second corpse, either.

But he was wrong.

It had been overlooked when the assistants had cut away the blood-soaked clothing because it looked exactly like another claw mark, and the corpse was crosshatched with them. But this was just along the outside of the right foot, and Fidelis bent thoughtfully, wondering why there was only one wound. Probing carefully, he extracted a long thin sliver of metal from the cut. He dunked it quickly into a bucket of water to clean it and held it up again. Experimentally he reached to touch it, and it bent easily.

Not iron, then, the physician thought. Now how by the Powers did a hunter pick up a piece of tin in his foot?

Normally the practice yard was filled with the clang of metal on metal, but the drill today was hand-to-hand combat. In the middle of the bare ground, two sweating boys circled each other warily, blunted daggers weaving before each other's eyes. Around them the other members of the senior squires' class watched critically.

From the shade of the open equipment shed, Squiremaster Kursh muttered to the master-at-arms, 'Dammit, if I've told that young Smithson once, I've told him a hundred times – never let an opponent inside your sword foot.'

'Aye. Fisher will have him in a moment,' Kelvin Miller agreed behind his gauntlet. Almost on his words, one of the squires feinted suddenly, drew his opponent off-balance, and tripped the hapless boy. Smithson stared up from the ground at the dagger poised above him. But after a moment, Fisher moved back to let the younger boy regain his feet.

Kursh bristled. 'Fisher, what the hell are ye doin'?' he roared and stomped out onto the exercise field. The boys made way for him as Smithson scrambled up, red-faced.

Rory Fisher mopped his sweaty face on the sleeve of his shirt. 'Well, it seemed the fair thing to do, sir,' he panted. 'He'd obviously lost the bout already, so I thought I'd give him a chance.'

One icy eye fixed on him. All the silent boys were very glad it had not been their misfortune to incur the dwarf's wrath. In the shed, old Kelvin Miller smiled a little. Unless he missed his guess, there was a show coming.

Kursh finally said slowly, 'Which would you rather be, Fisher: a live knave, or a dead jackass?'

Rory nodded, but had the courage to say, 'I understand,

master, but this is practice and I didn't think Smitty was about to kill me.' He smiled, and there were nervous laughs here and there in the crowd as he shrugged apologetically.

Kursh marked it, and knew he had found the leader in this class that he and Miller had been grooming for three years. Courage and poise Rory Fisher had, and both those were good. But he had flippancy, too (as most boys did), and under certain circumstances that could be very bad. Korimson knew it was time for what he and Kelvin had come to call the Lesson. He looked around at the widening grins, and dropped his second-best dagger from its forearm sheath into his hand, wondering in that moment where Peewit was with his best dagger. Kursh held the well-honed blade up before Fisher's eyes and let his expression set stone-hard.

The laughter died.

The young squire frowned uncertainly.

Korimson said very quietly, 'Not everyone is as easy to take as Smithson.' When Rory flushed, the dwarf slowly motioned for the blunted dagger, and the boy handed it to him. Then Kursh gave him his own sharp one. By the look on his face, Fisher was beginning to guess what would happen next.

On cue, Kelvin Miller hastened across the yard. With just the right mixture of worry and respect for rank in his voice, he thrust a brawny arm between the two and pushed the boy back. 'Excuse me, sir,' he said to Kursh, 'but don't ye think we might be done for the day?' Over the years, they had gotten the dialogue down pat.

'I do not. Stand aside,' the dwarf rasped, his eye fixed on Fisher.

'But, sir –'

'Stand aside, and that's an order!'

Miller's jaw worked, but he moved out of the way and motioned the rest of the boys back. They retreated to a safe distance in absolute silence.

'Now,' Kursh said to the boy, 'if you do not stop me, I will hurt you. That's all the warning you'll get. Guard yourself.' He dropped into a fighting crouch.

Young Fisher clutched the dagger in his hand, but did not move. He tried to make a joke of it. 'I'm sorry for saying what I did, sir. I'll polish armor from now until snowfall, if you like.'

Kursh made a lightning feint to the right that drew the boy's startled eyes and with his open hand buffeted the side of Rory's head. The scarred old practice helm rang, and the boy fell away a few paces. 'I don't like,' the dwarf grated, and closed again.

Fisher got his guard up in remarkably short order this time, the Squiremaster noted, and they circled while Kursh gave him time to think about it. A little sooner than the dwarf had expected, the boy lunged in under his purposely loose guard.

Well done, Kursh told him silently, but he let nothing show in his face as he parried the blow easily.

Rory had accepted that this was to be a real fight; Korimson could see that in his eyes, but the boy would not be taking seriously his own misgiving that the Squiremaster might actually hurt him. It was time to disabuse him of that notion.

He ducked, drew the strike, and scratched the dull dagger point the length of the boy's forearm.

The squire gasped, more from surprise than from pain, and fell back. Kursh saw him glance once at the shallow cut, and then Fisher's head was up and his jaw was set. He did not pause to wipe away the trickling blood, but grimly circled to the right – Kursh's blind side. Good boy, the First Watchman thought, and gave ground.

On the fringe of the crowd, Kelvin Miller got ready to grab the boy if this got out of hand, but Kursh made a slight sign with his free hand and the other officer relaxed just a bit.

Rory feinted toward the dwarf's blind eye, and Kursh automatically set a defense there before he realized that the boy had switched dagger hands and was coming in from the left. His thick fist shot out and knocked the blade aside, but not before he felt a sting in his biceps. You bloody little whoreson, he thought with pleased surprise, where did ye learn that one? He almost grinned but controlled it.

Miller was biting his gauntlet, and Kursh had to sign to him again not to interfere. He turned his full attention to the boy. Fisher was hanging back now, waiting for his master to take the offensive. Kursh waited him out. Two could play the patience game. As he had expected, young Fisher did not want to chance a sudden move from the dwarf. Korimson read his eyes and saw it coming.

When Rory shot out a foot to trip the dwarf, Kursh sidestepped neatly and the boy was left with his unprotected side exposed. The Squiremaster grasped his outflung arm and closed. With perfect control, he froze both of them in place with his dagger nicking Rory's left side, just under the armpit, scant inches of iron from the boy's heart.

He let the realization hit before he asked formally, 'Do you yield?'

For a moment he thought Fisher would say no, but then the boy's head dropped. 'I do.'

'Good lad,' the dwarf said approvingly, and released him for the last thing. Had the lesson been learned? To test, he turned his back to Fisher and waved the rest of the boys forward. 'Now, that should make clear that you can never trust –' Miller's hand chopped downward.

Kursh dove away to his left, whirled, and knocked the boy down with one open-handed cuff. Rory Fisher had been going for his master's unprotected back.

As the boy lay stunned, the dwarf quickly collected his own sharp dagger from where it had fallen. Now he was armed with two. As Fisher's eyes cleared, he beheld the Squiremaster looking down at him with an unreadable expression.

Miller stroked his mustache and smiled openly. The rest of the squires were spellbound, staring.

The color had drained from Rory's face. Now he wasn't sure what Kursh would do. The dwarf made a swift motion and sent daggers one after the other to thrum in the wooden shed door. Young Fisher did not follow them with his eyes. The silence stretched.

Finally the boy licked his lips. 'Two falls out of three, sir?' he managed to croak.

The dwarf began to laugh, quietly at first and then with gusto. 'Excellent!' he roared and pulled the relieved squire to his feet. He slapped Rory on the back. 'Master Miller! A cool beer for Mr. Fisher here! We're done for the day, boys. Let's get out of this sun!' Amid the released babble of young voices, he told Fisher seriously, 'Ye did well, lad, but don't ever make that mistake again – your eyes gave you away.'

'I'll remember that, sir. Thanks for not killing me.'

The dwarf laughed again and gave him a shove toward his admiring classmates. The boys goggled at the long cut on his forearm that would surely make a scar, but Fisher didn't swagger a bit, the two senior officers were pleased to see. They followed a little way behind after Kursh had retrieved his dagger.

Korimson fingered the scratch on his arm. 'D'ye think he'd have killed me, Kel?'

'Oh, no, Kursh, I'm sure not. He worships you, as all the lads do.'

The dwarf snorted, and the two of them laughed a little as they went through the echoing cool of the armory. Korimson told him, 'Next year it's your turn to do the Lesson.'

'I don't do it nearly as well as you. When you give them that look there at the beginning it could freeze the balls off –'

Jamison was saluting at the inner door of the chamber. The senior officers exchanged an exasperated look. Kursh returned the salute. 'What?' he barked.

'Beg pardon, sirs, but Master Wizard waits in your chamber, First Watchman. You did say you wanted to see him.'

'I've said a lot of things in my time that I regretted,' Kursh muttered. Beside him, Kel took a sudden fit of coughing. The dwarf raised his voice. 'Very well, yeoman.'

'You're bleeding, sir. Shall I fetch the doctor?'

'When I want Fidelis, I know where to find him. You could fetch me a pint, though. Bring it to my room. Bring one for the wizard, too. He must be grown-up enough by now to drink the stuff.'

Jamison blinked. 'Very good, sir.' He saluted and left hastily.

'Do they get younger every year?' the dwarf wondered aloud to his second-in-command.

Kel Miller only laughed and shook his head. 'See you at supper,' he said as they parted.

Kursh made his way upstairs to his chamber, swinging his arm in a wide circle so that it wouldn't stiffen up, and snapping off a brisk salute when he passed two men off-duty. It wasn't until he was climbing the long flight that the dizziness hit him. He shook his head, but that was a mistake, and he braced his backside against the cool stone wall and leaned on his knees, head down. The dizziness passed, but the headache was back, then he realized with a shock that he had felt pretty well all day until now. The queer sensation in his ears felt like a whole hornet's nest buzzing, and he dug his blunt fingers into them to stop it. Embarrassment lest someone should find him here like this impelled him up the stone steps and down the corridor past Peewit's room.

Then he remembered that Alphonse waited for him in his own quarters. He most definitely did not want any questions about it from the boy wonder. By the time he pushed open the door, Kursh had his countenance under control.

The wizard turned from the window with a half-eaten blueberry muffin in his hand. He brushed the crumbs from his light beard and said, 'You must have connections in the bakery. I had to settle for an oatmeal cake this morning.'

The dwarf's flinty eye went from the empty basket on the writing table to the red-haired man. If he admitted that the muffins were made especially for him, he would open himself to the youth's teasing – he could see merriment in the pup's eyes already. So he merely said offhandedly, 'Doesn't seem to have hurt you any. Didn't they teach you not to thieve on your precious Wizards' Isle?' He tossed his helm on the bed and began to unbuckle his broad belt to change his shirt.

The blue eyes sharpened, and Alphonse paused in mid-munch. 'What happened to your arm?' he asked.

'I was running through a training exercise with the squires' class.' The dwarf pulled the shirt off over his head and surveyed the cut. Satisfied that it was clean and not very deep, he went to the washstand and poured out some water into the basin.

'I thought training weapons were usually blunted.'

The dwarf slipped the leather patch off, facing carefully away from the wizard, and splashed the cool water onto his throbbing head. 'Some lessons can't be taught with dummy daggers.' He washed the sweat from his face. There was a knock at the door. 'Get that, would you?'

Jamison came in with a tray. He made the wizard as low a bow as possible with the two mugs brimming with beer threatening to slop over. 'I brought some linen, sir,' he reported to Kursh.

'Fine. Leave it.'

The young officer took his dismissal well. Wordlessly, he set the tray on the bed and bowed himself out of the room. 'I think he expected to wait upon you, Master Dwarf,' Alphonse said quietly, picking up one of the mugs.

'Doubtless. But I can't stand being treated like a simpleton.' Korimson scrubbed his face dry, replaced the eyepatch, and turned from the basin. Over the towel, his eye widened at the sight of Alphonse savoring the beer. He made no comment, but the youngling went up a notch or two in his opinion. He lifted his own mug and took a long pull. Dark and cool, the drink slid down in a most satisfactory way. Kursh lowered his mug and sighed gratefully.

He took up a strip of linen bandage and deftly tied it about the cut in his upper arm, using his left hand and his teeth. When he was done, he looked up to find the wizard's thoughtful gaze upon him. Alphonse said, 'Right. On a battlefield, you wouldn't have an orderly to do it for you.'

There was a gleam of surprised interest in the deep eye beneath its shag of gray brow. 'Exactly,' Korimson confirmed. He raised his mug once more and drained it before going to the trunk to get out another shirt. Unlocking it, he paused, regarding the note he had left for Peewit this morning, and wondered if the wizard had opened it by magic and gone prowling through his things. With controlled haste, he got out a shirt and closed the lid on the vellum. The sleeve caught on the new bandage for a moment, and he winced and pulled it roughly on. 'I hope you made yourself comfortable while you were waiting.'

'Oh, quite. I like the view you've got from here. Except that I stood on the bed to get a better look and went through your mattress to the floor. You really ought to get a new one from the quartermaster. Surely senior officers deserve better.'

Korimson controlled his expression. 'I like it,' he lied. 'You get soft, living in a castle.'

'I see.' Alphonse drained his mug. 'Think we could get more of this?' he asked, holding up the empty.

Kursh stroked the foam from his mustache, regarding him. 'I should think so. The cellar's barrel-to-barrel with it, they tell me, and Jamison's legs and wind are pretty good.' The wizard laughed, and the First Watchman stuck his head into the corridor and bellowed for the orderly. 'Bring us a half-keg and a tap,' he ordered.

Jamison betrayed his surprise at the amount, but quickly recovered. 'Yes, sir.'

'After that, we'll want supper in one turn of the glass, and after that, I won't require your service again till morning.'

'Very good, sir.'

Korimson closed the door. When he turned, Alphonse was holding his ax. Indicating the ruined face, he asked, 'How did this happen?'

The dwarf reached across the low bed to take it from him. 'It slipped out of my belt on the stairs and broke on the stones. Iron gets brittle when it's old.'

'May I fix it for you? It will take less time than if the armorer did it.'

Thinking of the letter – 'Please have my ax mended and give it to Jak Cooper' – Kursh replied shortly, 'No.' Then he added gruffly, 'Thanks. The smith's a friend for years and has worked on it before.'

Quiet blue eyes regarded him. 'Of course.' Kursh's head pounded and he looked away and leaned the ax against the wall with the feeling that the wizard knew everything.

Alphonse had settled with his elbows on the wide window ledge, and he was staring out across Willowsrill to the black-berry-colored mountains. 'I wonder how Peewit is doing.'

'Why don't you look and see?'

The wizard smiled. 'It isn't as easy as that. I could look for Peewit at need and find him, I think, but being a Littleman, he has a kind of mist about him that is difficult to penetrate.'

Kursh nodded. 'Like when he goes still.'

'Yes. I found him last night, and he was safe then. I saw a cottage and the face of an old woman. There was tea, I think, and fireflies.' The young wizard rested his bearded chin on folded hands.

'Well, that sounds good. If it was a true vision.'

The wizard heard the doubt in his voice and was amused.

Unexpectedly, Jamison returned at that moment, tapping at the door with his booted toe and raising a strained voice to ask, 'Sirs, the door?'

Kursh went to get it, and the orderly carried the smallish but heavy barrel in. He was panting, but he had been quick. 'Well done, Jamison,' Kursh acknowledged.

'Thank you, sir,' the yeoman managed. 'I filched it from the Second Watch's mess. I'd better get back down there and get a replacement for them before someone discovers.'

The dwarf hid a grin behind one broad hand. 'You'd better. Second Watchman Miller will have a thirst at dinner tonight. It was hot on the practice field.'

'Yes, sir.' Quickly the boy tapped the barrel and drew off pints to serve them. 'There you are, sirs.' He bowed and withdrew.

'A remarkable fellow,' Alphonse said.

'He's a good enough lad. Bit stiff.'

'He's scared to death of you.'

'Aye. Jamison was always the smart one.'

The wizard laughed. He raised his mug.

Kursh answered the toast and put words to it: 'To the queen.'

They drained their beer. Alphonse wandered over to sit in the room's one chair. 'So, what did you want to see me about?'

Kursh leaned on the fireplace mantel. 'That was no shooting star last night. It's a piece of firmament.'

The Wizard of the Three was still for a moment, then set down his mug on the writing table. 'You're certain?'

Kursh snorted. 'If there's one thing a dwarf knows, it's crystal. Trust me – what's embedded in the battlement is black crystal, the stuff from which Lord Aashis blew the firmament.'

Alphonse swallowed, thinking of the crack Patience had heard. 'He is breaking through, then.'

'Looks that way. Have you any idea how the Unnamed could crack the Sky Roof?'

Silently the wizard shook his head. When he looked up, the dwarf's face was creased with pain. 'Kursh, what is it?'

'It's nothing. I have a headache from being out in the sun.'

The blue eyes narrowed under the red bar of his brows, but he did not presume to pursue it further. Plucking the writing quill from the niche on the top of the table, he toyed with it as he asked, 'Do you know anything about a piper?'

'Which one?'

Smiling a little, the wizard clarified 'Patience . . .' He drew up; Kursh was not the sort one told about talking cats. 'That is, a friend told me something about piping last night that hurt the ears.'

The dwarf reached for the bottle of flotjin on the mantel. 'Sounds like your friend was in his cups. Festil's instruments are harp and lute, and most of the apprentices are training from him if ye can believe it, so I don't know where your friend would have heard a piper. Especially last night.' He held up the bottle questioningly.

A little surprised that Kursh was apparently intent on some serious drinking, Alphonse shook his head. 'She wasn't drunk, and she wasn't making it up, either. Are you really going to drink that?'

Kursh looked up from the thin stream of black liquor he poured into the beer. 'I am.' Though the wizard said nothing further, he added, 'It's been a long day, Freckles, and I am off-duty.' He took a swallow and measured the young man. After a moment the dwarf took a leather dice cup from the mantel and shook it hopefully. 'Are you any better at playing dice than you used to be?'

Alphonse parried, 'No, but I'm much better at cheating than I was.'

A rare grin swept across the bearded face and Kursh lumbered toward him. 'Set the table between us, then.' When he seated himself on the ruin of his bed, he held up a finger. 'And no sorcery.'

'You wound me, sir.'

'I will if I find you've put a spell on the dice.'

The wizard laughed. 'I'll bet you don't threaten Prince Ka-Salin when you play against him.'

Korimson gave him a look. 'I don't have to. His lordship never wins. Said once it was a game for taverns and brothels. He was right, of course. Your throw.'

Alphonse tossed off the rest of his beer, shook the dice cup, and rolled a double-six to beat Kursh's nine. He met the dwarf's baleful glare and smiled slyly. 'Sorry.'

Kursh grunted back, 'You will be.'

Chapter Twelve

There was a stain of old mold through the middle of the page, and Fidelis frowned and moved the lamp closer. The script was strong, but hastily written, and he was having trouble deciphering it. He bent close to the musty vellum again and read under his breath, '... yesterday being the third siege, and bye far the strongest yette. We fight on, tho it is all we can do to master oure fear and hold this ground. Alle about in the dark there comes the Wolfes snarlyng, so that none may sleep nor rest for fear of its next attack. Oft we see the winking of its eyes, blue as cold gems, blue as icy waters in some cave of earth, and –' A hand came down on his shoulder, and Fidelis jumped.

The wizard apologized, 'I'm sorry. I didn't mean to startle you – I thought you heard me come in.'

Fidelis rearranged himself on the high stool at the reading table, hooking his long legs back under the rungs. 'It's nothing. I was concentrating is all.'

The wizard regarded him critically. 'No offense, doctor, but you look like you've put in a hard day's work.' He explained, 'Your assistant told me.'

Fidelis pulled something from his pocket and tossed it on the table before Alphonse. 'What do you make of that?'

The redhead picked up the shiny sliver. 'A scrap of tin?' He shrugged, one eyebrow climbing.

'I just took it out of a dead man's foot.'

The wizard's eyes sharpened. 'He couldn't have run far with this in his foot.'

'My thought exactly.'

'Where were the hunters found?'

Fidelis shook his head and pocketed the tin. 'No help there. A clearing. No settlement, no house even.'

Alphonse took a turn to the window and back, halting before the doctor with a suddenly arrested look. 'What about wagon tracks?'

'What?' It took Fidelis a moment to get it, and then his eyes widened. 'I do not know,' he said. He went to the door, and beckoned the first guard that he saw. 'Give Sergeant Thatcher my respects and bid him come here, please. I want to ask him something about the hunters his patrol found this morning.'

The Watchman saluted – Fidelis was a senior officer of the elite group – and went briskly out. The doctor shut the door and went back to the table, where the wizard was running his eyes professionally over the first few lines of the manuscript. He saw Alphonse's breath stop, and the wizard bent to the book. 'Yes,' Fidelis confirmed. 'It is unmistakably the same wolf. That is why I wanted you to see this.' He waved a hand at two other volumes which lay on the table. 'There are three books – at least that's as many as I can find. I haven't been able to discover who the writer is. He represents himself only as the Painter. He was close to Beod, however, and very knowledgeable about the Powers, and, as you can see for yourself, they were under the same sort of attack as we are, and very near this actual place.' He nodded towards the window. 'The bog out there is the ancient battlefield.'

'You've sent us artifacts from there.'

The physician looked pleased that the young wizard would remember. 'Less than two miles from here is where Beod Greenbriar fought the Unnamed. The villagers at the foot of the Sweep have always claimed that the hill here is the barrow for all the slain who fought for the Powers, and these books,' he tapped a curling leather cover, 'seem to prove it.'

Alphonse heard Patience's voice clearly: 'He did this once before, you know.' 'By Nilarion Earthpillar!' he breathed. 'Then we've much study to do!' He strode to the door, asking, 'Have you eaten?'

'I have no appetite.'

'Right. Sorry.' He pulled open the door and called a page. 'Tea, boy, and keep it coming. Also, run with a message to the hospital – the chief physician is not to be summoned except in direst emergency. And no one is to be admitted here except the First Watchman or Her Majesty, of course. Oh, and we'll want another lamp, too.' Without waiting to see that the liveried boy followed his orders, the wizard shut the door.

The two scholars began to translate the Books of the Painter.

Sergeant Thatcher appeared some time later. There had been wagon tracks, he reported. 'How did you know, sir?' he asked, but Fidelis dismissed him without answering his question. When the doctor turned, the wizard was looking toward the window.

'Somewhere out there is a tinker who must have made a very narrow escape from the wolf. If we can find him, he may be able to tell us how.'

'We'll ask Kursh to alert the patrols first thing in the morning,' Fidelis agreed, settling himself again on his stool.

The doctor pressed the heels of his hands into his eyes, and

Alphonse looked over the top of a page. 'Anything?'

Fidelis shook his head tiredly and straightened, stifling a yawn. 'Not about the wolf. But they were apparently plagued with a rash of madnesses some time after the wolf's first attack, and the only relief they could find for the victims was an herb called dawn creeper.'

The young wizard closed his own eyes a moment to rest them. 'We may face a similar curse if the pattern remains the same.'

'I hope not, but I was thinking that this herb might be useful in treating the falling sickness. We have a few people in town who are afflicted with it.'

Alphonse reached for his tea, found it cold, and grimaced. 'Sounds reasonable.'

Fidelis' smile was weary. 'I just wish I knew what the stuff was: I know nothing called dawn creeper.'

'The ancients had much lore that we can no longer understand. If you like, I will ask some of my brethren at Covencroft. Many there have greater knowledge than I do.'

The doctor nodded, rubbed the back of his neck, and settled with a sigh once more. 'I am not finding much about the Painter's wolf.' He turned several pages. 'Maybe if I go a little ahead . . .'

Alphonse took a sip of cold tea and went back to his own book.

The midnight watch had changed some time ago; Alphonse had heard the shift of arms and exchange of password. He turned a fresh page, and halfway down the sheet, the Painter had begun a new entry. The wizard thumped his hand off the table, and his ring flashed.

Fidelis jerked upright from leaning on his elbows. 'What?'

Alphonse turned the book so that the doctor could read, and after a moment the healer's eyes flew to the snapping gaze of the wizard. 'Pipes? The Pipes he speaks of control the wolf?'

'That's what the Painter says. By the way, it is no natural creature. A few pages back, the Painter names him: Beldis.'

'By the Powers! The Wolf God?'

'Now you see why the Barreners have for so long confused their Wolf with the Wild Fire: Beldis was Tydranth's hound!'

The doctor had paled with more than exhaustion. 'And now he has risen to harry us.'

Alphonse grasped his arm. 'Yes, but don't you see? If the Unnamed was using the Pipes at the final battle and Beod cut them from him, then the damned things are still out there!'

Fidelis's weary face was washed with a grin.

They sat with the book between them for a moment, and the doctor's smile faded. 'The bog is a big place.'

The young wizard remained cheerful. 'If you were a beleaguered commander in a pitched battle, Fidelis, where would you position your troops?'

'On the highest ground, of course.'

'And the bog would have been a flat plain in those days, cupped between the hills all around, except for one spot.'

'The Wild Feller's Footstool!'

Alphonse stood up. 'Where can we get lanterns?'

Fidelis held up a restraining hand. 'It will be light in a few hours. Let's not take the chance of missing something in the darkness. The Pipes are made of black crystal, after all.'

The wizard blew an impatient sigh. 'You are right. And then there is the matter of the playing: we have no clue yet how they control Beldis.' He ran a hand through his ginger hair. 'We've still much to read, I'm afraid.'

The older doctor rose painfully, cramped from their long session. 'I for one must sleep a little, or I'll be no good to anyone. Come, Alphonse: tomorrow is time enough; thanks to you, there will be respite now from our woes.' He clapped the wizard's shoulder.

Alphonse allowed himself to be persuaded, and they turned out the lamps and left. Fidelis bade him an exhausted good night and headed for his quarters, but the wizard was too restless to sleep, so he decided to contact Chiswic. Perhaps someone on Covencroft would know what to do with the Pipes once they were recovered. And dawn creeper, he reminded himself. I must remember to ask about it.

Ariadne slept soundly until the moonlight stood bright in her window. She woke from a hovering dream of dark wind and pounding surf and was momentarily stunned at the silence that surrounded her. Meara's quiet breathing came from the pallet across the door, and Ka-Salin's even snores were muffled by the pillow. The queen had a fuzzy memory of candlelight and his voice asking her something hours ago, but she could not remember whether he had held her. Probably not. As usual, there was ale on his breath.

The moonlight bathed the room with a silver shower, dappling the curtained bed, and the oblong of night sky through the balcony door drew the queen's eyes. She had a sudden terror that another star was streaking for her window. So strong was the feeling that she swung lightly off the high bed and ran to the open shutters to look out. No flaming disc. No star. Ariadne suddenly felt stupid and weak. She leaned against the stonework and wished that the Powers would leave off making her their plaything. Her eyes filled with an attack of the nighttime-alones.

Alphonse had gone out on the small terrace in the queen's garden. From here he could keep watch on her window. From here, too, he could listen to the anxious yowling of cat voices all over

Greenbriar Castle. Patience had roused her folk to readiness. No wolf would go unmarked if it came near the walls.

The night around him breathed juniper and peppery nasturtium. Alphonse inhaled deeply, centering himself for his communication with Chiswic at Covencroft. Suddenly there was a flash of white at the queen's window. The wizard jumped to his feet, instantly alert, his ring hand already lifting against danger. Then he perceived that Ariadne herself leaned on the casement, looking up at the stars. She was too far away for him to see the expression on her face, but he thought perhaps she had wakened afraid. It would be like her to confront her fear, instead of shaking under the covers. I'm here, he thought at her. Look down, Ariadne.

The queen moved, leaning now on her elbows. Her head tilted down.

Neither Meara nor Ka-Salin had stirred. Ariadne combed her fingers through her hair and leaned her elbows on the stone sill. She was still uneasy, somehow afraid to leave the window. It was like being a little child again; she just knew that the moment she turned her back, something would come out of the sky to get her. She sighed, and her head dropped wearily.

Suddenly in the garden below there was a miniature fire rocket. It shot up only twenty feet or so, staying well below her high vantage point, and burst before she could fling away from the window in terror. In the next pounding heart-beat she realized this fire rocket was garnet-colored and that it hung in the air silently, with no explosion, as if to reassure her. Slow-motion, dreamily, the rocket opened to a rose, a beautiful bloom to decorate her garden. The queen smiled.

The rose faded. A second rocket streaked up, this one green. It formed itself into a tree shape and turned red, with white sparkles sprinkled through the boughs. Nilarion Earth Pillar overspread her garden.

Ariadne nearly clapped, but caught herself and glanced over her shoulder at the sleepers. Somehow she knew the wizard wanted this to be a private show, something between just the two of them.

She darted to the foot of the bed and snatched up her light wrap. Then she stood at the window and looked out into a night from which her wizard had purged the fear.

And the rockets went up and up.

Finally he sent up a last magic. Against the deep night shadow of boxwood and asters, he built a small cottage, whitewashed and thatched. There was a suggestion of a byre behind one corner and a half-door which stood open invitingly. Thyme spilled over the river stones that lined the dooryard path, and a rambling rose climbed for the eaves. With a final burst of inventiveness, he added a tendril of gray smoke from the chimney hole and conjured the smells of burning peat and new bread. These he sent wafting toward the window where watched the queen who would like nothing more than to have such a cottage and bake such bread. In this, the wizard guessed shrewdly.

He saw a white hand lift and wave and imagined that he heard her low laugh of pleasure. Then she was gone back into her room. Alphonse bowed to the window and stood for a moment watching that patch of dark against the stone castle wall. When he turned again to the small terrace, there was a smile on his lips.

He settled himself comfortably on the flagstones and began again to center within himself before attempting contact with Chiswic. First he Warded the area so that he would not be disturbed. Then he cast his thoughts toward the island where the wizards had their settlement. In a moment he smelled the sea and then the evergreen incense on the heights above the scattered small houses of the wizards and their apprentice adepts. Probing further with his thought, he narrowed his focus to Chiswic's cabin. No sense in troubling the dreams of everyone in the place. When he smelled a particularly acrid pipe smoke, he knew he had found his old master.

The ancient enchanter was dreaming of some long-ago encounter with a creature Alphonse did not recognize, but he got the impression that it had been real, no phantasm. Respectfully, the younger wizard let Chiswic know he was there. The old man, regarding the bronze scales of the creature, said, 'Quite a specimen, wasn't he?'

Alphonse replied, 'Indeed. What is it?'

'The authorities named it Pyrolus magnus, but the folk called it a t'ing. It was supposed to be fabulously wealthy.'

'Was it?'

The old man laughed in his dream. 'No, but he offered me tea very nicely and allowed me to keep my foolish head, which was rather more than I deserved. I was fond of him from that moment. Also, he taught me to smoke, and that was a rich gift, indeed.'

Alphonse smiled. 'I had always wondered where we got the inspiration.'

'Well, now you know.' The t'ing faded into a blurred background, and Chiswic gathered his robe around him, regarding his young friend with twinkling black eyes. 'Incidentally, you are really calling me, aren't you? You're not just part of my dream?'

'I am really here.'

'Ah, good. I can never tell the difference anymore. I seem to dream much more than I used to. Age, I suppose. I don't imagine you'll let me carry part of the Warding, will you?' Smiling, Alphonse shook his head, and the old man shrugged and

motioned him to a rock which had just appeared. Before the
younger wizard could begin, Chiswic asked, 'So, the Unnamed
has been throwing stars at your queen, eh?'

Alphonse registered surprise. 'You saw it all the way from
Covencroft?'

'Oh, I should say so! Besides, Realnor was only halfway home
with the barque from leaving you off at Greenbriar. To hear him
tell it over dinner last night, he was coming along at a spanking
clip – which, knowing how Realnor drives his boat, I can well
believe. Suddenly, there was a major flux in the Song which
drained power from his Warding and sent him flying on his face
on the foredeck. You really should apologize to him: his nose will
never be quite right again.'

Despite the gravity of the tidings he had yet to tell, the younger
wizard was momentarily amused. 'I'll see what I can do when I
get home.'

'I am sure he will be gracious. He's been quite the center of
attention all day. He guessed it was you immediately, of course,
and threw what power he had left your way. Did it help?'

Tactfully Alphonse did not tell him he had needed no power
other than his own. 'It must have. I brought down a piece of
firmament.' Even Chiswic, unruffled as he normally was, could
not hide the flash of fear that crossed his face. Alphonse said
quietly, 'The Unnamed is trying to break through Aashis's
Realm.'

'He is doing more than trying, if he can already shatter
firmament and use it to his foul purposes.'

That was something Alphonse had not considered, and it
stopped him cold. 'You think the Unnamed is already here?'

Striving for calm, Chiswic shook his head and reached to pick
an apple from the tree that thrust an obliging branch within
arm's length. In his hand the apple became a pear, but the old
man merely regarded it for a moment, thinking, before beginning to eat it. In real life, the crisp pleasure of that bite would
have hurt his teeth. Wiping juice from his chin, he waved away a
curious bee and said, 'Firmament. Now how do you suppose he
did that? I can hardly believe he has power in himself to break
the bonds of the Sky Roof.'

Alphonse hesitated. 'There is something else, Chiswic.' An
apple branch quested toward him, too, and he chose a winy red
one. 'What do you know of a painter of some sort who was close
to Beod Greenbriar?'

The old wizard set his half-eaten fruit down and dried his
fingers on his emerald-green robe. His black eyes fixed on his
student. 'Where did you find out about Aengus?'

'You sound as though it were forbidden.'

Chiswic stretched out his legs in the sun, and in the dream
they were not arthritic. 'Not forbidden, quite. Just a little . . .

tainted, I suppose might put it nearest. Aengus is not discussed.
Do be sure not to mention him when you get back.'

'Why? Was he one of us?'

There was a flicker of amusement across the lineless face.
'No. In fact, he was the only one ever to refuse to join us.'

Alphonse stopped chewing. To be sought out by the Meld as a
potential wizard was rare. Most would-be apprentices jour-
neyed to Covencroft and petitioned the masters to be allowed to
take the training. Very few actually were accepted, and fewer
achieved the rank of wizard. Refusing the privilege was
unthinkable. 'Was he mad?'

Chiswic shook his head. 'The sanest of men.'

'In league with the Unnamed, then?'

'Aengus had no more evil in him than you do.'

That was a lot sometimes, Alphonse thought. Because he was
controlling this Warding, Chiswic could not read his mind. His
master knew the youth well enough to guess what his sudden
silence meant, however.

The old wizard said, 'He was a good man and very gifted. We
lost one of the best when we lost him to the Meld.'

Something had been niggling at the corner of the redhead's
mind, and he scarcely heard this last comment. 'Wait.' He gave
his master a faintly accusing look. 'We have been talking all this
time about the Meld and Aengus, but there was no Meld in
Beod's time!'

'Not as such, no. Our formation as a group came somewhat
later. But there have always been wizards, whether they called
themselves such or not. We could recognize one another by our
power, though of course we had not yet figured out the Song or
how to use it in unity with one another.'

Alphonse glanced at him sidelong. 'When you say "we," do
you mean that you were one of them?'

The old man gave his dry-leaf rustle of a laugh. 'No. Even I am
not that ancient. I learned about Aengus from my master,
Merrithew. Even then, it was something of a scandal to mention
the whole affair. I think there was a good bit of jealousy mixed
in. As I said, Aengus was quite gifted and he helped the first
Greenbriar King immeasurably at a time when the Meld
couldn't.'

'What did he do for Beod?'

Chiswic tossed away the core of the pear. 'Not Beod, though
he was Beod's friend. You must remember that even though we
call Beod the first king of the Greenbriar line, it is a misnomer,
for of course the Crystal of Healing that makes the Greenbriar
was given only after Beod's death to his heir. Technically,
Berren, Beod's eldest son, was the first Greenbriar King, and it
was he to whom I referred. Aengus built Greenbriar Castle for
him, among other things.'

'He also used the Sweep as the barrow for the men who fell fighting the Unnamed in that first war, did you know that?'

'I know that is the legend. But I don't believe it. The hill is solid; I've sounded it myself. I could sense no crypts or passages. I think it more likely that the barrow stood in the middle of the plain where the bog is now. It has been swallowed up by the peat.'

'Maybe. Fidelis would not agree with you. He has found books about those days. The writer calls himself "the Painter." From what you tell me, it must have been penned by Aengus himself.'

'Extraordinary! Master Fidelis has quite scored one on us, hasn't he? We must have it copied at once. Will you speak to Her Majesty about it?'

Alphonse could not share the old man's enthusiasm for a scholar's pursuit. 'It is grim reading,' he said. 'Much of it concerns the Wolf, Beldis. It is the same wolf, master. I have read the description myself, and it fits.'

Chiswic's eyes narrowed. 'Why, how can you tell that? Has there been a survivor?'

'Imris.'

Chiswic leaped to his feet, staring, and Alphonse knew that his heart was pounding. Hastily he damped the shock to the old man and tried to undo any damage. He eased Chiswic back for a few moments into dreamless sleep, and when it seemed safe, extended the Warding again. The ancient wizard was calmer now and tried to help Alphonse regulate his pulse. 'Evil tidings, pupil mine. How is the Eldest?'

Alphonse, knowing the old man feared for Nilarion, answered firmly, 'The Elixir healed him, but he had a rotten time of it first.'

Chiswic released a held breath. 'Thank the Powers.' His black eyes sharpened. 'He was able to describe it?'

'Right down to the sapphire eyes.'

The old man stared, then refolded his hands and murmured, 'So the Hound of the Unnamed has risen, has he?'

'Yes, but we – Fidelis and I – have found a way to contain the danger he presents.'

'Extraordinary! What does Aengus's book tell you?'

'There is a set of Pipes. The Unnamed played them to set the Wolf on Beod's army.'

Chiswic's lips parted a little, and then warm satisfaction was in the look he gave his pupil. 'Well done, my lad!'

'But we don't know how to play them, even if we can somehow find them.'

The elder wizard thought a little. 'Caution is advised. We want to make no mistake. Let me ask Nicholas what he thinks.' Nicholas was the music master among the community and had studied much song from every corner of the world. 'Very well, now. Get out of my dream. You are tiring yourself unnecessarily,

and there is still much work to be done. You'll dig tomorrow for
the Pipes?'

Alphonse nodded.

'Good fortune, then. Call us immediately if you find them. And
don't wait till I am sleeping!'

The young wizard smiled and let the communication Warding
slacken. 'Oh!' He resumed the connection with a snap. 'For
Master Fidelis, will you ask if anyone knows of an herb called
dawn creeper?'

'Certainly. It's a small enough favor for the good doctor after
all he has done for us.' Chiswic flapped a hand. 'Go on now!' he
repeated.

Alphonse smiled. 'I have plenty of power left, master.'

At the faintly prideful tone, the black eyes firmed. 'Bear it in
mind then that the greatest danger to us all is not the Wolf: it is
you, Wizard of the Three. Should you fail in your control, we
would be undone.' At the disengaging of their minds as a chas-
tened Alphonse drew away, the old face softened to its customary calm. 'But we will help you bear it all that we can. Do not
hesitate to call.'

The young wizard whispered assent and was aware of his
master's fond good night. He came back to find himself cramped
from sitting so long on the slate terrace, and chilled with more
than the night's dew.

Chapter Thirteen

This was exactly the way Peewit had not wanted it to happen. To be alone at night, locked on the wrong side of the stout timbers that protected the village of High Heath, had not been his plan. But a wasp's sting, a wild ride, a snapped saddle girth, and a lame pony had conspired against him. He spread his bedroll under an old apple tree not far from the gate and told Snort in a low voice, 'You might at least have waited until we were on the way home!' But he wasn't really angry, and the pony knew it. Standing hip-shotten, favoring its bad foot, it whickered softly and pushed its nose into the Littleman's hand. Peewit relented and patted the shaggy neck.

He had tried to gain admittance to the village, of course, but as he had expected, the watchman had been immovable: rules were rules, and the rule was the gate did not open at night. Peewit had gestured toward the tree and told the gate man that he would camp there. Would the fellow keep an eye on him? The fellow would be glad to, and was in fact doing so. Brickleburr could see a red glow now and again from a pipe up in the watchtower. That was some comfort; at least nothing could sneak up on him ... if the sentry didn't sleep. Peewit put that thought from his mind and dug out his traveling rations. He settled with his back to the tree trunk and munched currants and a hard biscuit while he went over Tim Fuller's experience again.

There was nothing to suggest it was the Barreners, he realized, nothing at all, yet he couldn't shake the feeling that the Wolf Cult was linked to the star in some way. And if, as Tim had thought, there was a piper, then Peewit knew who would know. He and Muir Dach had crossed paths once in the old days, and the Littleman did not relish the thought of having to do it again. But the tinker was also the Nan Dir Nog – the King of Pipers – and if anyone was playing for Tydranth these days, Muir would know. If the tinker had not owed the Littleman such a huge debt, Peewit would not now dare to come anywhere within reach of his quick dagger.

But the last time they had met, nearly eight years ago, the Nan

Dir Nog had been mighty close to swinging at the end of a farmer's rope. There had apparently been a misunderstanding about the ownership of a fine fat lamb, and the farmer had taken Muir off-guard while the chops grilled over his campfire. Peewit had not recognized the tinker, knowing him only by reputation, but it seemed to him that the farmer's justice was extreme. He had rescued Muir and then had to fight him when the tinker would have turned on the hapless farmer. The owner of the lamb had meanwhile taken prudently to his heels, and by the time the tinker and the Littleman had bruised each other substantially, the chops were burned to a cinder and the two had developed a grudging respect. By the tinker code of honor, if such it could be called, Muir Dach owed Peewit any boon he asked for, up to and including Dach's life.

Brickleburr half smiled in the dark under the apple tree and hoped the tinker would recognize him when he caught up with his slow wagon tomorrow. He had been disguised as a dwarf then, too.

He finished his cold supper, drank a little water from his waterskin, and rolled in his blanket. Sticking Kursh's dagger into the soft earth near his head, he went to sleep.

Sometime during the night he came half awake and realized that Snort was not there. Looking around and sitting up quickly, he whistled once, low. The pony knew that whistle and would obey. But Snort must have wandered too far to hear, because the Littleman could not spot him coming back through the long grass. Resignedly, Brickleburr shrugged himself out of his blanket and followed the pony's hoofprints a little way down the road that bent around the town walls. Then the dark blotches of Snort's hoofprints in the dew struck off across a clearing. Must be looking for water, Peewit thought. He trotted after.

He was upon the camp before he knew it, so cleverly had it been hidden from the road. Snort was cropping the grass, and there was something by his forefoot – a pail. As Peewit made out the glint of moonshine off the tin, a strong hand caught him around the throat. Above him a voice said, 'That's my pony. You weren't thinkin' to steal him now, were you, Master Dwarf?'

Peewit managed to choke, 'No.' He meant, 'No, it isn't your pony,' but he hoped the answer would suffice.

The hand loosened its grip slightly, and he was quick-marched toward a hidden ravine where the field dropped off to the creek bed. Here, the camp's owner reached around the Littleman to stir up the small fire. 'Let's have a look at you, then. Just in case you don't try to steal him again, eh?' he suggested with heavy sarcasm.

By the growing light Peewit could see the heavy covered wagon, with its garish paint and tin-plated roof and wheels. He had thought he recognized the whispering voice. Prudently the

Littleman kept still, even when Dach relieved him of his dagger.
Finally the tinker pulled him roughly around to face the firelight.

Like most in his trade, Muir Dach had a good memory for faces.
There was barely a flicker of surprise across the sharp features.
The Nan Dir Nog sheathed his dagger and spat across the dancing
flames into the creek. 'Guess it isn't my pony.' He freed the
Littleman.

Peewit laughed. 'You're looking well, Nan Dir Nog. The lambs
have been fat this year.' Despite the real amusement he felt, he
got ready to go still if necessary. Muir still had his dagger thrust
through his wide belt.

In some long-ago fight, one of Dach's front teeth had been
knocked out and another chipped. He grinned raggedly, and the
black hollows showed. 'Aye, dwarf. You'd be amazed how careless the shepherd boys are getting.' He motioned to Peewit to
make himself comfortable by the fire and stepped to the wagon
to fetch an earthenware jug and two tin cups. Splashing some
liquor into one mug, he handed it to Peewit.

The Littleman knew this was part of the tinker hospitality code.
The liquor was potcheen, clear, nearly tasteless, rivaled only by
dwarvish flotjin for effect. It was one of the tinkers' best
weapons: by the time the fellow traveler woke up next morning,
the tinker was gone with purse, horse, or anything else of value.
Peewit sighed and took a sip. He did not cough, but it was only out
of sternest control. He did, however, wipe his eyes.

The tinker had watched over the rim of his own cup. Now he
smiled slyly and squatted down across the fire. He had no way of
knowing the only effect of any liquor on a Littleman was to make
him a bit silly, with an alarming proclivity to laughing until he fell
off his bench backward and went still. Muir Dach nodded com-
panionably up at the dappled pony that stood now on the rim of the
ravine looking down at them. He said, 'Your pony's foot should be
feeling much better in the morning. I've bound it with salve.'

'Thanks. I should have guessed that if there was a tinker round-
about, Snort would look him up.' It never hurt to pay respect
where due, and everyone recognized that tinkers were superb
with horses. Even the wild hill ponies would seek out a tinker to
have their hurts tended. There was some kind of power there, but
neither wizard nor Retreat Master had ever been able to figure it
out.

At the implied compliment, Muir Dach nodded complacently.
'I'd not ride him hard for a day or two, though,' he directed. The
tinker drained his cup and poured himself more potcheen. He
motioned for Peewit's cup, but the Littleman was not quite ready
for more.

Brickleburr cleared his throat. 'Actually, you've saved us quite
a step, Nan Dir Nog. I'd come up here to High Heath looking for
you.'

At this, the tinker's deep eyes sparked with interest. 'Did you now? And why would that be, Master Dwarf?' There was something in his voice that prickled down the back of Peewit's neck.

'I need a bit of news. Who better to ask than a tinker?'

'Any tinker would do.' Muir Dach put down his cup, and his hand moved to his belt.

Peewit sipped more potcheen, pretending he hadn't noticed. 'Not for this. I need to know about a piper.'

The Nan Dir Nog picked up his cup. 'Which one?'

The Littleman breathed a sigh of relief behind his cup, but if Muir Dach was the piper he was looking for, he wouldn't like the next bit. Peewit tensed, ready to go still. 'The one who is working with the Wolf Cult.'

Shaggy black brows drew down, and he dug one sharp-nailed finger into his ear in thought. 'The Barreners don't have any pipers,' he told the Littleman in a puzzled voice. That much was common knowledge.

'I have reason to believe there's one now. You've heard nothing of it?'

'No,' the tinker said shortly and swigged some liquor.

Watching him closely, Peewit could detect nothing beyond ruffled pride. Muir Dach, as Nan Dir Nog, was always told of a new piper. The King of Pipers had to test the new musician.

The tinker suddenly shot Peewit a look. 'What do you want him for? If it's a son you'd like apprenticed, I'd take him myself, dwarf. Claim your boon.' He had gone edgy again, and there was real anger in his eyes.

Peewit put his mug down and met Dach's look straightly. 'Nan Dir Nog, such a boon would be a king's gift. If I had such a son, I would not dare ask for this: it would be too much. But that is not the reason I am looking for the Barrener piper.'

The tinker said nothing for a long moment. He stared at Peewit, took a drink, and decided the dwarf was being honest. That was unnerving, and he responded quietly, 'Tell it. You've ridden a long way, I can tell that from your pony. And if you would dare ride looking for a tinker, then you must have a fear that's bigger than any I could put on you. Drink your potcheen, and tell me what this piper has done.'

He seemed to have struck some chord in the tinker, so Peewit went carefully on. He matched the other's grave tone. 'At first, Muir Dach, I thought I was looking for the only piper I knew who would be mighty enough to work a spell with his piping. I thought that you were in league with the Wolf Cult.'

The Nan Dir Nog snorted. 'What would I want with those blackguards? They'd sooner cut your heart out than look at you. They work their horses to death, too, and break the mountain ponies with whips and fire.' He spat again. 'We tinkers have never even traded with them, much less been in league with them.' Thoroughly disgusted, he poured himself another drink and irritably signed Peewit to finish his. 'By the Powers,' he swore under his breath, 'we have some honor, you know!'

Maybe it was the potcheen, or maybe it was relief, but Peewit believed him and grinned. 'I'm glad it isn't you!'

Grudgingly, Muir Dach showed his teeth in a matching smile. 'Aye. I'd not like to fight you again, Master Dwarf. I've a feeling neither of us is as young as he used to be.' They toasted each other, and the tinker gave Peewit back his dagger. Then Dach's smile faded. 'You still haven't told me why you're so keen to find this Barrener piper.'

In for a penny, in for a pound, Peewit thought. 'You know, of course, of the wolf that's been attacking folk everywhere?' At the tinker's terse nod, the Littleman said, 'The piper I'm looking for has that wolf following at his heels like a kennel hound, and whatever music he's playing is so powerful that it can deafen a shepherd boy.'

Dach stared. 'A mighty piper. Or mighty pipes he's playing.' There was silence while both of them sipped. Speculatively, Muir said, 'You're no hunter, Master Dwarf, so it isn't the bounty you're after.'

'No.'

The tinker asked, 'Have you lost kin?'

Peewit replied carefully, 'I have lost folk I was responsible for.'

The silence this time was longer, and the Littleman was fairly certain that Muir had figured out that only one of the queen's soldiers would have answered that way. But the tinker did not ask, so Peewit did not tell him.

Finally the Nan Dir Nog stirred. 'Last year at the Crowning Feast, the queen healed a tinker, young lad by the name of Ferric.'

'I remember.'

Muir shot him a look. Peewit understood what the other was saying: for tinker honor, Muir Dach would make the search for the Barrener piper his own.

They drank another cup of potcheen, and both understood that it was the giving of a pledge. Then Muir Dach slapped his hands on his knees briskly, so that Snort's ears shot up where he dozed above the ravine. 'You've come to the right place for your news, Master Dwarf,' he said. 'I think there's something afoot tonight you'll be interested in.' He began kicking dirt over the fire. The Littleman stood up. The tinker explained, 'We'll have to walk a bit. Your pony will be all right here. You might tie him with my two over there.' He gestured beyond his wagon. By the time Peewit had done this, the fire was banked, the cups rinsed, and the potcheen jug safely stowed. Muir Dach beckoned from the lip of the ravine. 'Come.'

They slipped around behind the village of High Heath and
followed the worn track that led up over the ridge. The rocky
bones of the hill were covered by thin patches of heather and
some sparse gorse. There was not much cover in the moonlight,
but Muir Dach had an uncanny way of taking advantage of the
lay of the land to hide himself from any possible watcher. He
was nearly as good as the Littleman, and for a human that was
very good, indeed. What a scout he would make! Peewit thought,
wondering if anyone had ever tried to enlist the tinkers. Probably not. He didn't think the independent rovers would take well
to army discipline.

Near the crest, Muir dropped to his belly. 'We'll have to take it
carefully over the top. Move like a dozing sheep, if you can.' He
rose to all fours and ambled his way across the sharp rocks.

Hoping that no wolves, real or human, spotted them, Peewit
followed.

The other side of the ridge was darker, and they made it down
to a verge of trees not far from the top. Under the covering
branches they paused to catch their breath. Muir Dach was
listening intently, but it was the Littleman's keen ears that heard
it first. The thump of a drum. Their eyes met. Peewit whispered,
'A ritual?'

'Sounds like it. I heard mention of it in a tavern a week ago.
This is the right night and the right place. If the Wolf Cult is
meeting, your piper is probably down there .'

Peewit straightened from leaning on a tree. 'All right, Nan Dir
Nog. Your service has been most valuable, and I thank you. But
I'll go on alone from here. Keep Snort till I come for him, will
you?'

Muir Dach frowned and took hold of the Littleman's shoulder.
'Wait just a minute, dwarf! You've drunk my potcheen and I've
said I'll help. If you're going down there, I'm going, too.'

'One alone is safer.' The Captain of the Queen's Watch did not
want to say that he could disappear at need, while the human
would be left visible amidst enemies.

'True enough.' The tinker pulled down the brim of his hat. 'So
I'll go. Who better to go sneaking about in the dark than a
tinker?'

'I'm a pretty good sneaker myself,' Peewit said mildly.

'Well, if you must go,' Muir Dach said impatiently, apparently
forgetting that the Littleman was the searcher, 'remember: if
we're seen, it's every man take to his legs and fend for himself.
We'll meet back at my wagon.'

That suited Peewit. He nodded and led off through the woods.
Guided by the sound of the drum, they wound down the slope
until finally the Littleman motioned the tinker to a crouch. 'Just
through the trees there. Do you see?'

The King of Pipers squinted. With the barest movement of his lips he answered, 'That will be their horse picket line. There will be a lookout with the animals, I think.' In the dark, Peewit could see the glint in his eye. 'It might be useful if all their horses got loose somehow, except for two.'

The Littleman grinned back. 'I'll get the lookout.'

As soon as he had moved far enough away from the the tinker he went still. Nearly soundlessly, he walked unseen toward the Barrener sentry. The man was leaning up against a tree near the horses, idly digging at the birch bark with his dagger. Every once in a while, he would glance off into the woods toward the drum. The horses were quiet, most dozing. Suddenly one caught wind of Peewit and swung its head to look right at him. Its ears pricked, its nostrils flared. Don't whinny, the Littleman prayed. The horse shifted its weight, but did not otherwise move again. Had the man been more alert, he would have noticed.

Peewit's fingers closed about a palm-sized rock. He probably could have brought the man down with a flying kick, but he had to do it silently, and this was the easiest and surest way. All Littlemen were expert marksmen, and Peewit loved to test his aim. Usually he practiced with apples, though. He hefted the rock, drew back his arm, and let fly. There was a solid thud, and the man sprawled. He groaned once and tried to rise, but then lay still. Powers, don't let me have killed him, the Littleman thought belatedly as he ran forward. Quickly making certain that the fellow was out cold but still alive, Peewit straightened. He barely had time to flicker back into view before Muir Dach was at his elbow, grinning fiercely, dagger in hand. The Littleman put out a hand. 'No. There's no need to kill him. He never saw me, so he won't be able to tell them anything when he wakes up.' He cut a piece of the picket rope and lashed the fellow hand and foot, finishing off by stuffing a piece of horse blanket from the ones dumped on the ground into his mouth for a gag.

'Not bad,' Muir Dach said, 'but you want to be sure to tie his thumbs as well.' He dropped to one knee and did this expertly.

Peewit filed away that useful bit of knowledge, and said, 'I'll leave you to take care of the horses. If you hear a sudden commotion, go.'

'Right,' the tinker agreed, already moving down the line of horses to gentle them by hand and voice.

The Littleman went toward the sound of drumming. Almost immediately he went still as a precaution.

It seemed quite a long way from the horses to the drum, and when he was close enough to hear more than the rhythmic thumping, Peewit realized why. He heard snarling. Should have thought of that, he told himself. Of course they wouldn't want the horses to smell wolf. Or vice versa. He stopped for a moment and craned to see through the trees. There seemed to be an opening ahead. Creeping silently, he went forward.

The members of the Wolf Cult were assembled in a small pocket of meadow in the middle of the forest. Peewit saw robed figures ringing the edge of trees. There was the sound of a voice, but he was not near enough to hear what it said. The robed figures were silently listening. The Littleman went nearer.

There must be a fire, but he could see no light from it. The clearing was thick with smoke, though, and this was probably because they had laid some wet branches on to make the fire smolder. The smoke had a thick tang that he identified as hazel. Seer's Smoke, it was called. Even some of the Retreat Masters used it to produce visions. Taking a closer look at the nearer faces, he weighed the risk of going closer. The smoke could produce in him the same intoxication it had in all those silently watching cultists. He was nearer to the ground, though, and the smoke hung wavering nearly shoulder-high on the humans. Wishing he had a wet cloth to tie over his mouth and nose, the Littleman slipped behind the few people farthest back and made his way through to the front rank. A fierce snarling and the rattle of wooden bars came just to his right, and Peewit jumped back so hastily that he brushed the robe of a Barrener. The man looked around vaguely, then relaxed again into the ritual.

The Littleman clapped a hand over his mouth to stifle the sound of his jerky breathing. He stared at the caged wolf, and the savage eyes glared back at him. Peewit realized after his first start had passed that this was not the Wolf: though big enough, this was no monster, and its eyes were dark in the night. Its nose had him targeted. The wolf hurled itself against the cage once more, gnashing at the stout wooden ribs that held it, for now, captive. Peewit took a slow step sideways, and the beast's yellow eyes followed him.

The Littleman caught his breath and moved into the clearing. If there was a wolf here, there would also be a sacrificial victim waiting to meet his doom. Peering through the smoke, Peewit scanned the crowd. To his left, in front of the man who beat a slow drum, stood a lone robed figure. At first the Littleman thought that this might be the victim – his robe was dark where the others' were white – but the man raised his hands to the night sky and Peewit realized that this was the priest-seer, and the quiet yet penetrating voice was coming from him. There was no piper that Peewit could see.

Set into the forest floor near the seer was a thick post, and bound to this was the intended victim. The man raised his face at that moment, and only Peewit's training kept him from gasping aloud. Through the bloody mask, he recognized Lyle Brewer, one of the spies he had sent out to gather information on the Barreners. The young Watchman must have made straight for the border country and had the ill luck to be captured. His right shoulder was twisted unnaturally, and Peewit guessed it was broken.

Standing alone in a ring of enemies, the Littleman wondered
how he could get both of them, plus Muir Dach, safely away. His
heart sank, and he wished that Kursh and Imris were with him.
He fingered Kursh's dagger and eyed the rope that bound young
Lyle. Taking a deep breath, he edged nearer to the post. While
he did, he tried to translate what was being said. His Barrener
was rusty, but the seer seemed to be begging Tydranth's mercy
and asking the Wild Fire to avert the calamity that had befallen
his people.

The drummer was the problem. Peewit could circle behind
young Brewer and cut his ropes, but the drummer would see
them parting and surely would say something to alert the others.
Besides, even if he got Brewer free, they would still have to
break through the ring of cultists and elude capture in the
woods. At least they hadn't broken Lyle's legs yet; that was part
of the ritual, Peewit knew.

The seer was saying, 'Protect us, Lord Beldis, from the foul
magic of the unbelieving wizards, who have turned your creatures against us. From attack by mad wolves protect us.' Peewit
was shocked. The Barreners also had lost people to the wolf!
Why would a Barrener priest-seer be inflicting that on his own
folk?

The wolf gave a shuddering howl and the Littleman jerked
back to action. He returned back across the clearing toward the
cage to do the only thing he could think of. If Lyle Brewer was
held still by his ropes and all the others were fleeing meat,
maybe the wolf would give chase. In the confusion Brickleburr
might be able to get them both away from the clearing. The cage
was pointed away from the horses, so the beast would probably
leap out in a straight line and go after the first thing that moved.
Judging by the ribs that stuck through the creature's rough fur, it
had been starved in preparation for tonight. The Littleman had
begun to sweat, and he knew the smell of that fear was his
greatest danger. He tried to will himself to become calm.

Around the clearing, the smoke-stupored Barreners were
joining in the priest's chant. Peewit used the covering sound to
dart past the cage and fling himself up the trunk of the tree
which hung over it. If anyone heard the scuffling against the
bark, or saw tiny bits of twig fall, no one remarked on it. The wolf
knew, though. Straddling the thick branch, Peewit drew his dagger and looked down at the rope that was stretched taut to open
the cage upon the seer's gesture. The beast, snarling, looked
back up at him.

Would it leap the cage and come for him? Peewit wondered.
He had no more time to consider it, because a change in the
tempo of the drum made him look across the clearing. A huge
man with what looked like a smith's heavy hammer stepped from
the crowd and strode purposefully toward the bound victim. This

would be the leg-breaker. Sucking in his breath, the Littleman hung by his feet from the branch and cut the rope.

So quickly that Peewit barely realized it, the wolf was out the door and leaping for the top of the cage, where it could smell fear and danger. The Littleman strained every muscle and threw himself upright on the branch. The teeth missed him by the thickness of his leather vest. He watched the thing land, whirl, and fix on the leg-breaker, who shouted and pointed. For a moment, there was dead silence in the clearing except for the growling of the wolf, and then people began crashing through the trees. The wolf went in a flattened run across the clearing toward the man with the hammer.

As though sleepwalking, the seer moved into its path and opened his arms wide in a gesture of homage and acceptance. Appalled, Peewit watched the wolf spring. By the time he had jumped from the tree to the top of the cage, retrieved Kursh's dagger where he had dropped it, and leaped to the ground, the seer was a red blur under the slashing fangs. Still bound to his post barely five paces away, Brewer stared wild-eyed and strained at his ropes. Except for them, the place was deserted. Even the man with the hammer had escaped. Peewit halted in the middle of the clearing and let himself flicker back into view. 'Hold still,' he ordered the young officer.

Brewer's frantic stare caught his commander, and then the sense of what Peewit had said must have gotten through to him. Abruptly he stopped struggling, though Peewit could hear his ragged breathing. The Littleman gave him a hand sign: At ease. Courage.

Lyle clamped his lips and stood stock still while his captain circled behind the feeding wolf. Peewit went still again, though this was little protection. Very quietly, Brickleburr said, 'If we make no sudden move or noise, I think he'll leave us alone.'

'Very good, sir,' Brewer whispered. The wolf snarled and lifted its stained muzzle to stare at him a moment. Then it resumed its grisly meal.

Brickleburr breathed again. He had halted in his tracks, and now resumed his cautious circuit closer to the post. 'How are you?'

'Well enough, sir. My shoulder's out of its socket, though.'

Peewit spoke from Brewer's elbow. 'All right, young fellow. Let's see if we can get you out of this. I'll cut the rope. It will hurt, but you must not cry out. When you feel yourself free, don't move. Remain as you are until I say so, then move slowly to your left.'

The wolf ignored them. Brewer gave the tiniest of nods.

'One more thing,' Peewit murmured as he cut the ropes. 'Have you ever been invisible before?'

While Brewer was still wondering whether he had heard

correctly, the ropes fell away, the Littleman took him by the uninjured arm, and they both went still.

They were scarcely halfway back to where Peewit hoped Muir Dach would be waiting with the horses when they ran right into the drummer. The Barrener was obviously circling back to get to the horses. Brickleburr and Lyle were visible, for the Littleman could not hold the stillness for them both very long. They jerked to a stop, and young Brewer grunted with pain.

The drummer's knife was poised for throwing, aimed at Peewit, and the Littleman's dagger hand was tangled in Lyle's arm. To throw the Barrener's aim off, Brickleburr went still.

Behind the drummer, a horseman suddenly plunged through the trees and leaned to thrust his own sharp blade into the drummer's back. Muir Dach pulled up the horse and was looking straight at Peewit when he flickered back into view. 'Ah,' was all he said. Then he turned his head and clucked to the second horse and it came up, trailing the rein he had used to lead it. 'Hurry,' the tinker said. 'There are more of them about.' With his help, young Brewer scrambled into the saddle. The tinker squinted over at the Littleman mounted in front of the injured man. 'Friend of yours, I suppose?'

'And their victim,' the captain panted. He pulled the horse around and followed the Nan Dir Nog back through the trees.

Because they could not climb the ridge and had to go as carefully as possible for the sake of Brewer's dislocated shoulder, it was a few hours before they walked their horses through the clearing to the edge of the ravine. In the gray light before dawn, the bright paint of the tinker's wagon looked a little darker, but inviting still. Snort's piercing whinny lifted from the trees where he was tethered with the tinker's horses. Peewit grinned.

After getting Brewer down from the stolen horse, Muir Dach went directly for the potcheen jug. He tipped some down his own throat and poured for the injured man. 'Drink it,' he ordered. When Lyle hesitated, looking to Peewit, the tinker added, 'You don't want a clear head when we set that shoulder, do you?'

Shortly, with very little talk between them because they both realized what had to be done, Peewit and the King of the Pipers had settled the young officer in the bed of the wagon and made him as comfortable as possible. Then they set the shoulder and bound it while Brewer was still in the faint. The Littleman clapped the tinker on the shoulder. 'How much of that potcheen is left?' Silently Dach passed him the liquor.

When Peewit lowered the jug, Muir Dach was motionlessly watching him. 'Quite a night's work, Master Teazle.'

Peewit licked the strong spirits from his lips and began to peel away the fake beard that had scratched the skin off his jaw in places. 'Yes, it was,' he agreed. He knew what would come next.

'Your queen has gritty folk dealing for her, Captain Brickleburr.'

Peewit returned the compliment deftly. 'And some of them she doesn't even know.'

The tinker grinned his jagged grin and drank.

Between them, Lyle Brewer stirred and woke. He stared muzzily up at the two faces over him.

The Littleman said, 'You got yourself into a tight spot, Brewer. I'll hear all about it when you get back to Greenbriar. For now, there's one thing you can tell me. Did you hear anything of a piper? Or of the star that fell out of the sky the other night?'

Brewer stared. 'How did you know?' At his commander's gesture, he continued, 'That's how they caught me. I stayed too long to listen in a tavern a couple of villages over. All of a sudden I found myself attracting a great deal of interest.'

Peewit sat forward. 'What about the piper?' he asked urgently.

'Oh, yes. Well.' Brewer paused to lick his lips and focus his eyes. 'The Barreners seem to know a lot about some pipes: black crystal they are – belonged to the Wild Fellow himself an age of the world ago. Play the Music of the Spheres, or some such. I didn't get that part very well. At any rate, these things summon . . .' He licked his lips again. 'Beldis, the Wolf himself.' His eyes sought the captain's. 'They're saying it's the end of our queen, sir.'

'I doubt that,' Brickleburr said briskly. 'Her Majesty has fought him before and won. Now, this piper: did they say where he was? Is there anything that would help us find him?'

Brewer actually grinned despite his pain. 'I should say so, sir. I got the whoreson's name.' Peewit's jaw dropped and the young Watchman started to laugh, but caught his breath instead and bit his lip. He darted a look at the tinker, and Peewit thought that odd until Lyle reported in a strained voice, 'It's Tomasheen, sir, Tomasheen the tinker, and he's at Greenbriar, or headed there.'

Muir Dach growled a curse.

'By the Powers!' the captain breathed. 'Well done, Brewer, well done! We'll see you knighted for this!' Lyle flushed with embarrassment. The Littleman looked to Muir Dach. 'I ask for my boon now, Nan Dir Nog.'

'What is it?'

'One of your horses. I need to ride faster than poor Snort can take me. Also, I need a place for Brewer to stay until he can follow along on his own. Will you give him your protection?'

'Pah!' the tinker snorted. 'That isn't a boon at all. You'll have to do better than that. My honor wants satisfying.' He edged past the injured man on the floor.

On a sudden inspiration, Peewit said, 'All right, then. Someday when this is all over, come to Greenbriar and pipe for the queen. That will be my boon.'

Muir Dach dug his finger in his ear and spat out into the woods. 'Done. Next time I'm down the river road, I'll play your queen such a song as she's never heard before. They should know down there what a real piper sounds like, not some pisser like Tomasheen.'

He left Peewit smiling and went to saddle the horse.

Chapter Fourteen

His headache split him right through the ears, but Kursh went grimly about his business. He had known that the flotjin would not work eventually, and that seemed to be what was happening now. Also, he had not had a good night's sleep; the howling of cats all over the castle had been nerve-racking.

Over breakfast there had been a hasty meeting with Fidelis while Alphonse similarly took the news to the queen: they had found a record of Pipes to control the Wolf and would dig for them today. The doctor added a special warning from the wizard. 'He says to be certain Her Majesty and Gerrit are guarded well, for the Unnamed will likely become aware that we seek his Pipes and therefore throw an attack at us as a feint.'

Kursh's head pounded as he gave Fidelis a look over his breakfast cup of thin ale. 'Tell the stripling to mind his own skin – and yours. I'll hold up my end.'

The doctor frowned at his tone and said mildly, 'I am sure he meant no slight to you, Kursh.'

The dwarf grunted, 'Good luck,' and Fidelis nodded, washed down the rest of a scone with his tea, and hurried to meet the wizard at Armorers' Gate.

Kursh watched him thread through the bustle of Watchmen entering and leaving the mess. A sudden image of the Wolf flashed before his inner eye, and he called in a strained voice, 'Don't fall down any bog holes!' But in the noise, Fidelis did not hear.

The news whipped along the gossip vine. In the tense atmosphere the only light spot had been the consort's decision to take the litter of new hunting pups out on the Sweep between Gerrit's Wood and the castle. There he could run the dogs after some rabbits and yet still be under the watchful eye of the guards on the battlements. That was all the heed he would pay to Kursh's insistence that he not go hunting until the Pipes had been safely recovered. Gerrit had wailed to go, and after some hesitation, Ariadne had allowed it on the condition that they were not to go

out of bowshot of the walls and were to be accompanied by a
mounted escort. Ka-Salin rolled his eyes, and Gerrit copied his
father.

Kursh had caught the queen's eye. 'I'll accompany them per-
sonally, Your Majesty,' he told her. Ariadne's look lightened a
little. She would be closeted with Imris out on the north terrace
and would remain there, she promised. The First Watchman
approved; the terrace was at the top of the north wall of the keep,
a place obviously inaccessible to a wolf, and the wizard had her
Warded from another bit of falling firmament.

So now Kursh was hurrying to his room to discard his cloak and
arm himself with a second dagger. There was no sense taking
any chances. He was already wearing his mail tunic under the
uniform surcoat. If the Unnamed sent his Wolf, Powers forbid, the
dwarf would be as ready as he could. Before he left, he swallowed
what was left of his flotjin, hoping it would do something. Then he
put his ax over his shoulder and took the stairs down, headed for
Rose Hall, where he would meet the rest of the escort. He swung
around the landing and came face to face with Thyla, who was
carrying a covered tray, probably to the queen's apartment. The
dwarf stepped aside. 'Good day, Mistress Njordson.'

The dwarven bakeress nodded. ' 'Day, First Watchman.'

They both stood poised, one to go up, the other to go down.

After a moment, Kursh said, 'I'm attending on the consort and
the Lordling. We're going to try out the beagles.'

'Are you? Well, I'm for the rabbits.' She smiled. There was a
spot of flour along the side of her generous dwarf nose, but she
was unconscious of it, and to Kursh it seemed homey somehow.

'Well, I'd best be going,' he said.

There was a flicker of disappointment in the bakeress's eyes,
but she agreed lightly, 'You'd best.' She turned to go.

'Thyla.'

When she looked back from a few steps up, the First Watchman
did not know why he had called her back, because he could not say
what he wanted to: that he had put aside his suicide dagger for
her muffins and been somehow glad of the choice. She was waiting expectantly. He had to give her something to remember him
by. He cleared his throat. 'Thank ye for the muffins. They were
. . . very fine. And the tea, too.'

Something that may have been amusement showed in her face
for a moment, and then she nodded gracefully. 'You are very
welcome, First Watchman. Kursh.' The barest tinge of blush
crept over her cheek, and she made a business of straightening
the napkin that covered the tray she carried. She made herself
look at him. 'Starflower's good for a troubled mind, they say. With
all your responsibilities, I thought you could use it.'

'I could use a gallon of it,' he muttered before he caught himself.

'Aye. It's been a hard few days. It's good that you're taking the little master out to play. He needs to get away from the fear for a while.'

'That's what I thought myself,' Kursh said, though he had not thought anything of the kind until she put it in that light.

Thyla smiled. 'Shall I leave you a teapot with some starflower? For later?'

'That would be very nice,' he told her, and he meant it.

'Right, then.' She gave a push to her cap and nodded to him once more before hurrying up the stairs. 'Don't catch any rabbits!'

Then she was gone around the corner and the dwarf was staring after her ample figure. It was a moment before he realized that he was smiling just a little. He tugged at his mustache, put on his customary scowl, and went down to whip the escort into shape. His head was pounding abominably, but he almost didn't care.

The sun came warmly to the north terrace, but there was a fine breeze up from the river that made sitting out quite comfortable. The queen lifted her face to the racing clouds and, with her eyes still closed, sighed. 'Why does it have to be such a beautiful day? It makes it too hard to believe that the Unnamed is moving against us.'

'That may be part of his plan,' the Eldest warned, sweeping his fingers lightly along the strings as he tuned his harp. Festil had been delighted to give him replacements, and Imris had not had the heart to tell the man that the originals had been spun silver.

'Oh, do hush,' she murmured, though she knew that he was probably right. She looked at him. 'Are you certain your throat is well enough to sing, Master Harper?'

The Yoriandir smiled. 'I think Fidelis is overcautious. Certainly after Elixir and rest, there can be no harm in testing.'

Ariadne returned the smile. Despite the tension, she really was looking forward to this. Then her thought returned to the wizard and the doctor and what they sought, and she glanced at the sky fearfully. He had assured her that she was Warded, and that ought to have made her feel better. He was the one in danger – and Fidelis, of course. Determinedly, she brought out her embroidery from its basket. It was no good worrying about it. She was on the north terrace and they were squelching around in the bog to the south, so she could see nothing anyway. Ariadne threaded her needle, listening to the snap and flutter of the Greenbriar standard that flew from the highest turret.

The Eldest marked the conflicting emotions racing across her countenance – clouds across the sunny landscape – and decided his song would be something soothing and light.

He glanced over the parapet to the scene out on the Sweep,

and a smile came to his face. 'Those pups will run them all ragged before an hour is out. I think the rabbits are amused at the whole spectacle.' One of the kennelboys had brought out a hunting horn and blew it badly, trying to call the pack to some semblance of order. In the kennels it had worked, and he had thought the pups were ready for Prince Ka-Salin to take to the field. Now he was frantic at having so wretchedly messed up his first chance at becoming a packmaster. Wildly, he threw down the horn and grabbed a multithonged whip from a grinning younger boy.

On the terrace the Yoriandir murmured chidingly. 'Oh, no,' but he need not have worried. The thongs all tangled as the kennelboy whistled the lash about his head. He was reduced to throwing himself bodily at the racing knot of pups as they frolicked past. When he missed grabbing even one of the brown-and-white blurs and landed heavily on the springy sod, the Eldest could almost hear his oath.

Gerrit's squeal of delight came from below as one of the dancing pups licked his face. Instantly there was a rustle of silk and the queen was at the singer's elbow, fear etched in her features as she leaned past him for a look. He put a hand on her arm. 'My lady, 'tis well. He plays, that is all.'

She had seen that it was so, and the color came back into her face in a wave.

Imris asked, 'Would you rather have him up here with us?'

The queen brushed a tendril of hair back behind one ear. 'No. I'm being silly.' Her chin came up. 'If I keep him by me like a hen with her only chick, my people will think their queen is afraid, and we can't have that.'

The Yoriandir looked down at the slight tremble to that firm chin, and wondered what it had cost her to learn such royalty. 'Maybe, this once, it matters not what people think,' he said gently.

Ariadne put on a smile and patted his arm. She went back to her carved chair at the edge of the mosaic floor and deliberated over a choice of colors from the knotted skeins. When Meara called from the open terrace door, the queen nodded that she might bring tea.

In the seat built into the parapet, the Eldest set his bow by his foot and strummed his harp once more, raising his voice to sing away her fear.

Tomasheen leaned against the tin-plated wheel of his wagon, idly picking his teeth and gazing up the Sweep toward the knot of activity near the north wall of the castle. Through the trailing branches of the willows by the river's edge, he could see the bowmen that lined the battlements and the mounted escort that ringed the hunting party. A lot of soldiers about this morning, the tinker thought. Wonder what the flap is? And then it came to him and he smiled. They were all afraid of Badulf!

He turned to look up at the lean dark man on the high seat. 'I believe you've got their wind up proper.'

The red lips drew back in a smile. 'You are quite right, Tomasheen. Even now they are expecting fresh corpses.'

A cold bead trickled down the tinker's spine. 'What are ye starin' away to the bog for? What are those men doin' out there?'

The incredibly blue eyes rested on him for a moment. 'They are looking for your Pipes.'

The tinker gave a start. 'How'd they know about my Pipes?'

'They have found an old book, and they think, they hope, that by finding the Pipes, they may control me.' He began to laugh, and for a moment there was the rising sound of a howl, but Beldis quickly stifled it.

Tomasheen swallowed. 'What did we come here for?' he asked suddenly. 'I never said I had somebody around here that I'd like to pay back.'

The lean man sprang lightly from the seat to the river-bank, and in spite of himself the tinker flinched. But Beldis merely regarded him for a moment. 'I told you when we began that I had some enemies of my own to tend to. Now is the time to do it, that is all.' He reached under the seat of the wagon and brought out a small well-wrapped bundle. 'Play, Tomasheen.'

The tinker's breath came short, but he demanded, 'Are you goin' to hurt somebody up yonder?'

Sapphire eyes fixed on him, and he heard the snarl, though there was a half-smile on Beldis's face. 'And what could you do to stop me, tinker? It is in your mind to try, isn't it?'

Tomasheen swallowed. 'I got no quarrel with them,' he stubbornly insisted, but he knew already that he would do it.

Beldis nodded. 'It is them or you,' he suggested lightly. 'Master says.'

By now, the tinker guessed well enough who master was. He bit his lip and began unwrapping the Pipes. Beldis laid one long-nailed hand on his arm. 'Good man. Play us a song of triumph now.'

As always when Tomasheen's hand touched the dark and gold-bound instrument, music came into his mind. Even wrapped as he was in the spell, he knew very well that he himself had no such song in him, but the compulsion was irresistible. He slid down to sit with his back against the wheel and began to play.

Hearing those first few notes, Beldis shivered with anticipation. 'Soon, my Wolf,' came the master's whisper. 'Soon we shall be free. Make you ready.'

Keeping to the screening growth along the riverbank, he walked quickly away north toward the town.

He looked back once. *It is them and you, Tomasheen, you fool.*

Alphonse had probed with his Warding, of course, first thing. He had expected the Unnamed would have screened the Pipes from his finding them that way, and he was right: he could sense no dark crystal shapes anywhere near the Wild Feller's Footstool. Then Fidelis, with his more extensive experience at such work, took over, assembling several teams of diggers and starting them at different probable locations.

After three hours' digging, ditches radiated out from the high rock. Though there had been no grumbling among the soldiers yet, there were some glances at the wizard. 'They are tiring,' he observed to Fidelis, who stood with him on the scrub that crowned the Footstool.

'Nonsense,' the doctor replied absently. 'These are seasoned men – they can dig the whole day yet.'

Alphonse made no reply.

' "Long they strove, Lord Beod and the Cursed One, and the shadows of earth wheeled a full turn ere my lord drew back and cast a look at me. 'I weaken, my friend,' he whispered. 'Seek your own safety!' I looked at the storm clouds gath'ring above his helm and measured the distance to our camp in my heart. 'My lord,' I sayde to him, 'I will stay with ye till the ende. But ye must strike for the Pypes full soone, for my heart misgives a foul wind breweth.' " ' Fidelis must be a quick study, the wizard thought, to have memorized critical passages after only a couple of readings. The doctor was frowning. 'That's an odd phrasing, don't you think? "Measured the distance to our camp in my heart"?'

Alphonse was alerted. 'Perhaps it was dark at the time?'

'The storm hadn't struck yet, and it was not night because he'd not have been able to see the clouds.' Fidelis swung to face the south. 'But you know, if Beod's camp was on the Sweep – the logical place, since Berren later built his castle there – and the Unnamed had stood here' – the doctor stepped a few paces away and faced Alphonse – 'then Beod would have been just about where you are now, with Aengus next to him.'

'And the Painter would not have dared to turn his back on the Unnamed to look back toward their camp!'

'Yes. Now Aengus says that when Beod cut the Pipes from the Unnamed's hand, they were flung off the high place.' He made a casting gesture with his right hand, and though he actually threw nothing, both of them followed an arc through the air with their eyes. 'Just about where that pool is,' the physician murmured. He was already shouting for a team of diggers while the wizard scrambled down the steep rock.

Alphonse beckoned urgently, and when the soldiers came running he pointed. 'Here. The Pool.'

Fidelis landed beside him. 'No, wait.' He waved the men back and described an intersecting line to the dark brown water. 'Earl, we need to drain this water,' he told the corporal. 'If you dig here, the ditch will lead the water away. Some others of you dig as deep a well as you are able where the ditch will end. Quickly!'

'As you will, sir,' the soldier said. His men had heard and caught the urgency. Turves began to fly. Other teams, attracted by the flurry of activity, left their own work and gathered at the spot. There was silence on the bog except for the thud of spades and the whir of insects. Very soon, the deep well that would hold the water was done.

Earl took a few more chunks of peat out of the ditch that he and three others had made, smoothing a channel. The last thing was to dig out the thin dam they had left at the pool's edge. He glanced to Fidelis, and the doctor nodded. The corporal sank his spade in the marshy ground and broke the plug. The bog water began to drain. The soldier leaned on his spade and hawked and spat. They waited.

The men edged closer, peering into the opaque water. Alphonse extended his Warding, probing for crystal, but still he could not sense the Pipes. Fidelis crouched beside the pool.

The water rushed down the channel to the well, and the level of the pool dropped moment by moment. Something about the shape of the banks made the doctor frown. He turned his head to remark to Alphonse that the edges looked as if they'd been cut.

One of the men cried hoarsely, 'What's that?'

Dyed to the color of the peat in which it had been submersed, a human hand rose from the water.

A few of the nearest men jumped away, but then, unwilling to be shamed in front of their comrades, they stiffened and held their ground, staring. A wrist was exposed, and the wizard saw that it had no iron guard. This was not a warrior. For a moment, he wondered if it might be Aengus himself who lay beneath the water. He found that he was holding his breath.

Inch by inch the water drained, and the tip of a massive stone broke the surface, then another. That is why the body did not float to the surface, Alphonse thought: the rocks were filled in on top of the grave. Didn't Fidelis say all those who fought in that battle were entombed in the Sweep? Maybe Master Chiswic was right and the slain lie here on the battlefield.

But then an iron slane showed above the water, and a piece of something that might have been a rough cloak, and he knew. Sick foreboding swept over him. The young wizard suddenly jumped down into the last few feet of dark water. His stomach turned at the grisly task, but he heaved the restraining stones out of the pool, and in a moment the corpse floated to the top. Cries of dismay and fear went up.

The acid of the peat had preserved the body as though embalmed. Cobb's ripped throat gaped to the sky.

The wizard raised his devastated eyes to the doctor. 'We are too late. The Pipes are already found!'

The huge Wolf trotting through the dappled sun and shade of Gerrit's Wood sensed the wizard coming back empty-handed up the south slope of the Sweep and laughed at the echo of Alphonse's despair.

Finally, finally, the boys had gotten the beagles formed up into a pack. Kursh thumbed his aching temple and squinted against the fierce sun. The consort came striding across the turf, shouting over his shoulder, 'All right, Harry. Let go the ferret.' His huntsman nodded and put the muzzled ferret down the hole into the rabbit warren. When the hares were flushed from their underground protection, the pups would chase and catch them. That was the theory, but Ka-Salin was shaking his head as he joined the First Watchman at the top of the slope.

Behind them, Jamison's voice said diplomatically, 'I'm sure the dogs will do well, my lord.'

The consort laughed and swung Gerrit up to see. 'It should be good for a jest anyway, eh, First Watchman?'

'Aye, my lord,' the dwarf answered shortly. Ka-Salin did not notice, pointing out to his excited son where the rabbit would spring from, and Kursh was glad no further words were necessary. It had become unbearably warm, and he was sweating freely under the mail shirt. His ears roared with a pulse like piping, and the pain in his head brought a sickness into his throat. He had never fainted, even when he had lost his eye, but now he knew that he was going to. 'Not here,' he said and stumbled a step toward the gate.

Ka-Salin turned and looked down. 'What?'

The dwarf opened his mouth to say that he must go, but his vision narrowed and there was darkness all around. The Sweep tilted crazily, and suddenly the blood-streaked muzzle was opening and the blue, blue eyes gleamed. The ax flew from his shoulder.

Too quickly for stopping, it happened. No horseman was close enough, no bowman even had an arrow out of the quiver, when the First Watchman hewed at the prince consort as though he were a tree made for cutting. The heavy blade, wielded by the best axman Ilyria had ever known, severed half Gerrit's small right foot and bit deep through silk and linen, bone and tissue to find Ka-Salin's life. Jamison flung himself on the dwarf. On the nearest turret the bowmen swung their weapons up as one, but hesitated, not wanting to hit the young yeoman.

High above on the north terrace, the Eldest cried out in horror and leaped up on the parapet. So quickly that the terrified queen never saw his hands move, the only archer in the kingdom who could have hit the mark let fly his arrow.

It struck true, taking the dwarf through the chest. He went down with the yeoman still grappling fiercely. On the battlement Imris stared. In a sudden paroxysm of shock, he flung his bow off the castle wall and sent a mind-shout thundering over the Willowsrill Valley: 'Kursh!'

Hearing that sent cry of anguish, Alphonse knew the Enemy had struck. 'Damn! The Sweep – run!' he shouted to Fidelis and sprinted past Armorers' Gate, quickly outdistancing the doctor.

Imris turned to catch the queen, but Ariadne had seen, and she broke away from his uncertain restraint and flew for the door and the stairway down.

The wizard pounded around the southeastern turret and raced beneath the firmament embedded in the wall. There was a flash from the trees by the river, and his eye was drawn to it. The sun glinted off unmistakable pipe shapes in the hands of some-one leaning against a tinker's wagon. At the time, raging that he had been blind to Tydranth's spell, the wizard did not stop to consider how it was that he could perceive the piper so clearly. He shot out his ring hand. Claws gripped his ankle, and Patience, who had hurtled out of Queen's Gate, warned, 'Control! He wants you to fail!'

That admonition hit him like icy spring water. Grimly, he threw a stream of garnet Fire that knocked the tinker from his feet and sent the Pipes skidding to the edge of the river.

'I will guard them,' the cat said. 'Go!'

It was the young yeoman who had the presence of mind to clamp his hands around the stump and hang grimly on while the dazed child told the first horseman who slid to one knee beside him that his leg hurt 'because Daddy fell on me.' Jamison and the horse corporal exchanged a glance over the boy's head and prayed that reality might be blotted out for a few moments more. 'Put your coat over him,' the yeoman told the other, nodding toward the consort's corpse. The man stripped off the surcoat that he wore over his mail and dropped it over the dreadful wound. Quickly others did the same until Ka-Salin lay draped with Greenbriar emerald. Most of the blood was hidden.

Then the wizard came running up, from where no one really knew, and went first to the dwarf. Swiftly his glance took in the bright point of iron just protruding from the back, and he bent to hear whether breath came from between the bearded lips. He looked up a moment later along the blade of a sword. 'No,' he told the soldier who held the weapon. 'It is the queen's judgment now, not yours.' For an instant, Alphonse thought the man would

strike regardless, but then the soldier rammed his sword home in
its scabbard and turned away. The wizard hastily turned the
dwarf on his side, and a trickle ran from Kursh's mouth into
the grass.

Alphonse got to his feet and told the horse corporal, 'There's a
tinker down there by the river. Near him are the Pipes we sought.
Take men with you and bring them both here at once. Handle the
Pipes carefully!' The horseman signaled his men, and they raced
to their mounts.

They galloped past the queen, who was running up from the
gate. The wizard dropped down next to Jamison. 'Let go his foot.'
The young man's eyes flew wide, and he began to shake his head.
Alphonse said roughly, 'I've got to cauterize it or he'll bleed to
death. Hurry, before she sees, you fool!' He put a hand to the
child's head, and Gerrit lapsed into unconsciousness. Jamison
drew his hands away just as garnet light gathered on the wizard's
ring and arced to sear the small mangled stump.

The alarm bells were ringing, and people spilled out of the castle like ants out of a pile that has been stepped on. Through the
screams and shouted orders Alphonse heard a Binoyr's mournful
cry back in Gerrit's Wood. The wizard felt the pulse in the boy's
throat. To one of the Watchmen who stooped over he said quietly,
'Send a horse for Master Fidelis quickly.'

'It's been done, sir.'

'Good.' In the same tone, Alphonse warned, 'Be ready to catch
the queen, if need be.'

'I will, sir.'

The wizard wrapped his light cloak around Gerrit, being careful not to let it touch the wound, and stood up. As the queen burst
through the group of kennelboys and Watchmen, Alphonse
stepped forward with the boy in his arms. 'Madam, your son
wants tending,' he said as evenly as possible.

She threw herself on him, gasping, 'What – where –?'

'His foot. No, don't look!' He pulled away, or tried to, but not in
time. Ariadne had pulled back the covering cloak. One hand went
to her mouth, then she feverishly brushed back the tousled hair.

'Is he –?'

The wizard cut across her breathless question. 'I put him to
sleep.'

But even as he was saying it, she saw what was behind him.
'No,' she cried, darting the few steps. Alphonse hurriedly turned
to Jamison and thrust Gerrit into his arms. Then he stooped to the
queen, staying her from pulling back the concealing pile of
surcoats.

'Steady, my lady,' he murmured.

Her fingers were clutching, but she did not touch her husband's
body. 'What happened?' she whispered in a suppressed scream.

The circle of men and boys exchanged glances and shuffled

uneasily. Plainly she had not seen the killing itself, only the aftermath. Alphonse swallowed hard. 'It was Kursh, lady queen.'

'Kursh?' she asked, uncomprehending. She reached to touch Ka-Salin's face.

One of the Watchmen went to one knee and gestured. 'He's there, Your Majesty, awaiting your judgment.'

In the same vague tone, she repeated, 'Judgment?' Her gray eyes followed where the man pointed. Of a sudden, she seemed to understand. Her face writhed with anger. 'Kursh did this?'

'Aye, my lady!' the Watchman answered strongly, while at the same time, Alphonse tried to say over it, 'It was the Unnamed's plan.'

The queen thrust away the wizard's supporting arm and sprang to her feet. 'Is the traitor dead?'

The wizard flushed and stood in her way. 'I tell you, it was the Unnamed!'

She glared, teetering on the verge of hysteria. 'You told me you had Warded us, too, wizard! Yet look at this!' One fist swept out over her consort's corpse. 'I'll hear no more of your sayings!' She pushed him out of the way with unexpected strength and angrily strode to the crumpled figure of the dwarf.

Alphonse made to follow, but a Watchman with drawn sword leaped between him and the queen. Garnet sparks gathered at the wizard's fingertips, and he could feel the hot tide rising in him.

Young Jamison, with the wrapped child in his arms and his hands stained to the elbows with Gerrit's blood, walked around them all and stood across the dwarf. With no trace of defiance, he said, 'We must look to the Lordling, Your Majesty.' He nodded down the Sweep. 'Master Fidelis comes.' Ariadne was still staring at Kursh, and now the yeoman added. 'There will be time to deal with . . . this . . . later. If the Fir – if the dwarf lives that long.'

Fidelis ran up the lane the crowd of bystanders made for him, and Alphonse angrily swung to meet him. 'The boy,' he told the doctor when Fidelis stooped to the consort. The physician gently pushed past the queen and hastily examined the child. 'Hurry. Get him down to the castle. We need Elixir.'

Ariadne was crumbling into shock. 'What's this?'

The queen's physician kept his finger on the pulse in the boy's wrist. 'He's weakened by loss of blood, my lady. If he doesn't get Elixir quickly –'

She cut across his words. 'Make more! Right now!'

He gestured to a soldier for his dagger, and Ariadne ripped at the Crystal of Healing on its fine golden chain about her neck. The chain let go and the Crystal fell into her hand. 'Damn the knife!' she told Fidelis and darted to an outcropping of rock.

With the Crystal in her palm, she slammed her hand down on the rock. In the next instant Alphonse had reached her. He grasped her wrist and pulled her hand up. Crystal fragments glittered in the sun amid smears of the queen's blood. The Greenbriar seeds rolled from the surface of the stone into the grass and a benumbed Ariadne crouched over them, her hand streaming, bits of jagged crystal embedded in her palm. The wizard knelt beside her and nudged the seeds into the growing shower of blood. The crowd craned to see.

After a moment Ariadne reached with her other hand to rearrange the seeds. Tensely she and the wizard stared down, but nothing happened. The queen began to cry and mindlessly pressed the seeds into the turf as if by willing it, she could make the healing miracle happen.

Leaping up, Alphonse shouted at one of the horsemen, 'Take the Lordling to the castle!' And to another, 'Give the doctor your horse!' He pulled Ariadne to her feet. 'Come, my queen. We can do no good here.'

She allowed herself to be led away, but then shook off his arm and cast herself beside her husband's body. The wizard signaled a man to stay with her and watched a burly horseman gallop for the gate with the small boy tucked in his arms, followed by the wiry figure of the doctor bending low over his mount's neck. Alphonse spoke low to Jamison. 'Take the First Watchman to the dungeon – a dry one. Cut the arrowhead off and draw the shaft out. Then pack the wound and keep him as warm as you can. Wait with him until I come.'

'Right, sir.' Jamison's voice was firm and his eyes were steady.

The wizard gave him an approving nod. 'Good man.' He turned to a Watchman with the brass badge of a commander of fifty clipped to his sword belt. 'Sir, we need a detail set around the place where the queen broke the Crystal. No one should be allowed near. Inform us at once if there is a change in the seeds, of if the fragments come together.'

The commander eyed him. 'Are you in charge here, sir?' There was wary challenge in his tone.

'Only until the queen is more herself.'

The commander nodded, and turned to his men.

Alphonse left him to walk to where the horse guards had brought up their prisoner and the Pipes. The wizard narrowed his blue eyes. Tomasheen's eyes were glazed, and the young wizard knew that his Warding had not done it. The Pipes themselves must have bewitched him. 'Where is the Wolf?' he demanded. The tinker did not answer. Alphonse's ring sparked, but he damped his urge. 'You will await the queen's justice,' he told the vacant eyes. To the horse corporal, he added, 'Chain him in the deepest hole you've got, and under no account let anyone near him.'

Something flickered across the man's face. 'Badulf,' he murmured.

The cavalry escort sat their horses woodenly. The corporal's eyes went to the queen. 'We'll just wait for the queen's word, if you don't mind, sir. I don't dare take responsibility for not presenting this whoreson to her immediately.'

'Very well,' he said shortly.

All the while, he had been conscious of the queen's despairing sobs, the dwarf's harsh gasping, and the insidious lure of the Pipes. He did not trust himself to touch them. One of the cavalrymen held them gingerly at arm's length and leaned from the saddle to give them to the wizard, but Alphonse drew away. 'No. Take them . . .' He was about to instruct that they be taken to his own room when he thought of Patience. 'Take them to the First Watchman's chamber, and lock them there. You, yourself, stand guard at the door. Admit no one.' The man nodded, but indicated by gesture that he, too, would wait for the queen's approval of this course of action.

Alphonse looked around to the queen. All around her, kennel-boys and Watchmen, courtiers and servingmaids, and now people who had come from the town, stared in stunned sympathy and horror. Not a few of them had sunk down where they were and wept bitterly for the queen's grief. The wizard found a patched azure cloak suddenly at his side, and he grasped the Yoriandir's shoulder thankfully. 'Help me with her.'

Imris gazed at him with green eyes gone dead. 'I shot Kursh.'

'You cannot dwell on that now. Help me.' They went up to the queen together. Awkwardly Alphonse touched her shoulder. 'My lady, will you not come away from here now? Please?'

He did not think she had heard him, for she rocked on her knees and stroked the thick black hair. She was no longer making any sound, though her eyes were wet and she blinked rapidly. 'I couldn't bring him back,' she said in a small lost voice. 'I couldn't make the Crystal work.'

The wizard had the eerie feeling for a moment that she was reliving Captain Tristan Faring's death, and he saw by the look Imris gave him that the Yoriandir had thought of it, too.

The Eldest took the queen in his arms to comfort her. Gently but firmly he told her, 'You would not have been able to bring him back anyway, my lady, even if . . .' He stopped, not wanting her to think too much about the Crystal. Her son might be dying even now because her Greenbriar power had deserted her.

The queen ignored him. 'I told him hunting would be the death of him, the way he rode.' Her face twisted. 'I told him that. And it was.' Her head went down and tears fell on Imris's tunic.

Meara, who had been standing at the edge of the crowd, her own tears streaming, stepped forward, thinking to help. But Alphonse, sweeping the gathered faces, knew that the pity of

her people would not carry Ariadne through the next days.
He stilled Meara with an understanding gesture, while the
Yoriandir said, 'Come, my queen. Your little son needs you now.
You must go to him.'

The redheaded wizard leaned close to whisper urgently, 'Come
on, Ariadne, get up! Do you think the Unnamed is done with us?'

She looked up at him then, dashing her good hand across her
eyes, and her face became a mask. 'He's done with me,' she said
coldly. 'Because I am done with him. Let some other take up the
fight. I have given all I intend to.' She got to her feet. People drew
back for her to walk down to her castle and bowed low as she
passed on the Eldest's arm.

They found the cavalry escort in their path. The corporal
bowed in his saddle and saluted. 'Your prisoner, Majesty. The
piper.'

Ariadne looked up at the tinker. 'Why have you done this?'

Tomasheen did not answer. 'He's mad as a hare, my lady,' one
of the escort said.

Another of the horsemen saluted. 'And here are the Pipes themselves, Your Majesty.' He held them out for her inspection.

Cradling her injured hand against her gown, Ariadne took the
Pipes.

'Badulf,' Tomasheen said again.

The wizard frowned and reminded her, 'Gerrit, my lady.'

Her voice was flat. 'I know. I am well aware of what this demon
has cost me.' With eyes gone the color of dense smoke, she
regarded the prisoner. 'I think it only fair that he should suffer
as much.'

At that moment, Kursh gave a loud groan. Alphonse swung
around to look at him and thus did not see the queen put the Pipes
to her lips and blow them in the tinker's face.

There was an instant frozen out of time in which the Greenbriar
Queen and the instrument of Tydranth stared at each other, and
then Tomasheen began to writhe at the newer, stronger music in
his mind. He raised his bound hands and clapped them to his head.

The wizard jumped for the queen with a cry, wresting the Pipes
from her and flinging them away. Watchmen spurred to her
defense, unsheathing their swords, but pulled their horses to a
plunging stop at the sound that came from the sky.

From everywhere and nowhere came the rushing sound, and
people's caps were blown away in a suddenly rising wind. The
beagle pups cowered fearfully under their kennelboys, and the
boys themselves were shaking. Clearly on the air came the
staccato burst of Pipes.

Someone at the edge of the crowd near the wood cried out in
terror as a dark shape streaked from the trees. People flung
themselves aside.

Beldis sprang for the tinker, and the terrified horse bolted.

Tomasheen came off in a heap, and the Wolf killed him with one snap of his powerful jaws. Then he turned, sapphire eyes glowing.

Alphonse threw his Fire, but the beast only laughed as the Warding rebounded back upon the wizard and drove him to his knees. Beldis loped easily back toward Gerrit's Wood.

Whipping his dagger from its sheath, the Eldest of the Yoriandirkin followed.

'Imris, don't!' the wizard gasped painfully.

A kennelboy shouted and flung up a hand, pointing.

Northward over Yoriand a bright fire hung in the sky, a dinnerplate, a horseman's shield, a mill wheel.

Alphonse hauled himself to his feet, gathered his Warding, and threw it at the chunk of firmament streaking toward earth. People began to stumble instinctively toward the stone safety of the castle.

The meteor grew to the size of a turret platform.

Cold sweat dripped from the wizard's brow, and his ring hand began to shake. A web of garnet and seafoam pearl quickly grew about him as he combined Wardings of Earth and Wind and hurled them desperately at the falling firmament. A stream of molten debris flared from the huge meteor where his power cut at it, but still it came on, and now there was sardonic laughter all around. Patience, streaking up from the river where she had been left when the horsemen brought the Pipes to the Sweep, passed the northeast turret and heard the two elements of Earth and Fire commingled, and she believed Alphonse teetered on the brink of disaster. 'Do not,' she shouted, 'do not reach for the third!'

The meteor grew to the size of the Rose window, and the wizard could hear Nilarion's leaves crisping in the heat.

He brought up his other hand, clasped his fists, and tearing through the mental defenses that had been set upon him, the Wizard of the Three reached for his third Warding. A pure golden light shone through his web of garnet and pearl, and he could feel himself begin to dissolve. He attacked the shooting star.

High above Yoriand he drove the flaming disc, but he could not destroy the Warding of Tydranth that was upon it, and in the end he had to let it go. The meteor slid sideways out of the sky, ducked behind the Rimwall west of the enchanted forest, and completely obliterated the little country of Westphalia between one heartbeat and the next.

Alphonse came back to himself screaming mindlessly with the pain of the ring that had burned into his flesh. Knowing what was coming, he threw himself on a stunned Ariadne to shield her.

A shrieking blast ripped through the air, and the blast wave tore into the wood where some of Nilarion's Children had found such a welcoming home.

Because of the flying debris, it was hard to see what was going on near the ground, but Alphonse knew that whole trees were tossed like straws in the leaden sky. He dug his fingers into the turf and clung like a rooted plant while all around them horses bolted from their thrown riders and people crawled downhill in the flash fire.

There may have been words in the shrieking wind, but Alphonse refused to hear the Unnamed's triumphant bellow. One moment there was a cacophony of splintering wood and screaming horses, and the next it was nearly quiet. The wizard raised his head.

Away across Willowsrill the blast wave raced, pushing a waterspout before it. He saw a boat upside down near the top of the surge. Then the fiery wind spread across the lowlands on the other side of the river, pressing the fertile cropland flat, every stalk of hay facing in the same direction. As it went, it drew up from the earth, thickening near the top, and just before it disappeared over the foothills, resolved itself into the shape of a giant dark hand in the rolling sky. The fingers reached out for Alphonse and the queen. Then it was gone.

The wizard sank his blistered face in the grass and tried to get his breath back. Sounds gradually penetrated his overloaded ears: the tinkle of broken glass falling, the terrified bawling of a calf, the crash of a roof down in the town. Beside him the queen stirred from under his protecting arm. He swung his head to look, but she was already running across the scorched grass, headed for the gate, for her son. Wearily the wizard who had made himself the Abomination to save them all pulled himself to his feet and made for what was left of Gerrit's Wood.

In mockery of his best efforts, Tydranth the Wild Fire had broken through the fragile Sky Roof. The Realm of Aashis of the Winds was shattered.

PART 3

The Keep

Chapter Fifteen

Across Willowsrill, in the meadows between High Heath and Waysmeet, the Littleman heard the Yoriandir's sent cry. Reflexively Peewit reined in his trotting horse. The big black champed the bit and blew, glad to rest, for they had ridden hard.

Brickleburr stared in the direction that he knew Greenbriar lay, but the intervening hills screened his view. He knew it had been Imris's voice; he knew there had been anger and fear in that one-word cry. The Littleman found that he was twisting the reins in his hands and standing in the stirrups that Muir had shortened to the saddle for him. Though he searched the sky, he could see no falling firmament, no streaking wizard's Fire. But there was no doubt in his mind that the Unnamed had attacked once more. Peewit sank into the saddle and urged the strong black horse into a flying race down the road that led to the lowlands.

He had just gained the overarching branches of a hedgerow when a blast of warm air whoofed against his ears and clashed the tree limbs above his head. For a second while he tried to control the shying horse, his mind flashed back to the charges they had set off to entrap the Bastard so many years ago. By the time he had mastered the black to a standstill, though, Peewit's mind had jumped to the falling star of a few nights previous, and he spurred for a vantage point. When he topped the next height, a fearsome sight met his staring eyes: a dark, rolling cloud hung in the Willowsrill Valley, and above it from the line of hills that marched away north and south, east and west of Greenbriar, the signal beacons blazed. The leaping fires called the Captain of the Watch home.

His heart turned to ashes and a stinging came to his eyes, for he knew the queen was dead. Cursing, he spurred recklessly down the folded slope, half hoping the black would die under him and take him with it.

Across the strait that separated Covencroft from Yoriand and Westphalia, the wizards of the Meld heard the sent cry. They were meeting in council when Hrontin of the copper robes

suddenly lifted his hand to halt the discussion, and they all
listened intently for more. But from Ilyria there was silence.

Chiswic's parchment skin had paled, and he said quietly, 'We
are too late.'

Across the table from him, Nels made a fist around his Meld
Mariner's pearl ring. 'By the Wind!' he gasped and shook his
head wildly as though some hornet were in his hair. Next to
him, Galen, who was also representing the Wind Wizards, was
holding his ears.

Chiswic leaned to them. 'What is it?'

Nels seemed to be running through a quick control meditation,
but he replied, 'The Wind's Song – it's been laid over with something else.' He winced. 'It hurts to listen to it!'

Galen gripped his shoulder, and reinforced by the mind link,
the two Mariners cleared their minds of the destructive melody.
'There,' said Galen, as a bright pearlescent glow came from his
ring. 'That's better. At least I can bear it now.' His face, tanned
mahogany by the sun on the ocean, relaxed a little, but Chiswic
noted that he gathered his aquamarine robe about him as though
he were cold. The lean Mariner's blue eyes, surprising in such a
dark face, lifted to the old wizard across the table. 'The Realm
will not take much of this before it begins to blow away, master.'

At that very moment Nels threw himself bodily across the table
and knocked Chiswic to the floor. Then, even through the stone
of the chamber, they all saw the flash, and a moment later were
lying stunned or writhing on the floor as the concussion
hammered their eardrums and ripped off the vaulted roof.

Moments later Galen crawled over a fallen beam and found
Nels and the old man emerging from under the stout table. 'Thank
the Powers you're well, master!' He reached to help Chiswic to
his feet.

Nels brushed his blond hair out of his eyes. 'What was it?'

'The Unnamed has broken the Sky Roof,' the elderly wizard
answered. The young Mariner began scrambling for the door
while Chiswic raised his voice to call, 'Hrontin? Where are
you?'

'Here, master.' The copper wizard had his hands pressed to his
bleeding ears, but his chin beneath its immaculately groomed
beard was firm.

'Can you send a Warding across to Nahomish and Ka-Lil? We
must check on Nilarion!'

'I have done it already.' Hrontin, second in rank on the council,
climbed dizzily over a fallen chair. 'Earth Pillar took the blast
well, they say. Ka-Lil tells me that a few branches are broken, but
he can bind and graft them. Apparently the blast came from
Westphalia, and the Rimwall protected Yoriand from the worst
of it.' He sat down quickly, drawing a breath. 'It must have come
right across the water at us.'

By now the adepts and wizards outside the Meld hall had managed to force open the bronze doors, which had been warped. Nels threw his weight against the portal, and it grated the last few inches open. At the sight outside, the Mariner stopped on the threshold. 'Powers!'

Galen was quickly beside him. Chiswic, clambering slowly after with the aid of his staff, saw the mahogany face go pale. He cleared the last twisted wreckage – closing his eyes to the hand that in death gripped the crushing timber – and stepped through the door.

Covencroft was a mess of rubble. Small cottages lay tumbled like children's blocks that some willful imp had kicked. The pines that fringed the volcanic cone's crown had been struck down all in one direction, regular as if a woodsman had laid logs side by side before hauling. The neat rectangles of the herb and kitchen gardens were pressed flat and scorched.

The old wizard surveyed the damage, his black eyes unwinking. Already the stretcher bearers were trotting to and fro, and he could hear the grating of stone being shifted. Some of the Earth Wizards were Warding to move the heavy blocks. He was momentarily proud that there was no panic. Chiswic said to the young Mariners, 'Let us see how many we have lost. Galen, will you send the Summons?'

But before the aquamarine wizard could bend his mind to the task, Nels grasped the master's arm and pointed. A moment the three of them stared, then together they sent a blast of Warding to warn all the others.

From ruined Westphalia's shore, a tidal wave was racing.

Down on the stone-built pier, a small gray-robed figure crouched, trying without much success to haul in some of the dinghies which had slipped their moorings. 'Zachary!' Nels gasped. His apprentice obviously had no idea of the danger he was in.

The two Meld Mariners flung up their pearl rings and aimed to throw a Warding about the end of the pier to hold the wave at bay. But their rings did not light. The Wind Warding was broken, and they could not use it.

The surging water smote the shore, drove the boats splintered on the strand, and took the struggling boy out with it while those who watched tried vainly to save him.

Nels turned and threw his fist into the bronze door, cursing, and Galen walked silently away around the corner. Old Chiswic had closed his eyes, leaning heavily on his staff. 'I am so very sorry,' he murmured to Nels.

The Mariner looked down at the blood streaming from his split knuckles and nodded, but he could not speak past the lump in his throat.

'Have the healers see to Master Hrontin, would you? Then I'd like you and Galen to join me. I will wait for you in the pocket garden.'

He left the Wind Wizard bowing and tapped his way along the path to the secluded garden spot. He needed a little time and quiet to be certain before he told them, but he was nearly sure, listening to the clear Song that rose in his mind: Alphonse had broken his vow and used all three of his Wardings. As master of the Meld, Chiswic must now order the garnet wizard stripped of his powers – even if it took all of them together to do it – and then killed.

His black eyes filled with pain, and he angrily dashed away his old man's tears.

In the artificial dusk that had fallen with the ash cloud, Alphonse thrust aside the broken limb that blocked his way and forced his way through the splintered trees. 'Imris?' he shouted, but there was no reply except for the leaves rustling in the breeze which still eddied through the wood. The wizard halted and extended his Warding around him, looking for the Yoriandir. He got a sense of the tree-tender, coming from deeper in Gerrit's Wood, and there was no echo of the Wolf. Ducking under a branch, Alphonse went on.

Gone was the ordered, parklike forest. In its place was a twisted, tangled ruin where the wind had run riot. Great swaths of fallen trees blocked his way, and he had to search for a way around the log fells. As quickly as he could, he went toward Imris. After a time, he found him.

The Eldest was about twenty feet off the ground, tangled in the broken branches of one of Nilarion's Children, and the tree, half its roots wrenched from the earth, was leaning dangerously over the small clearing where the wizard stood peering up. Tentatively he called, 'Imris?'

The Yoriandir did not stir, and the wizard felt cold dread sweep over him. He snapped a Warding on the tree, eased it to the forest floor, and ran to see if the Eldest lived. When he bent, reaching for the neck pulse, Imris opened his eyes. 'Don't move,' Alphonse cautioned immediately. 'Where are you hurt?'

The Yoriandir stared blankly up through the ragged canopy of Gerrit's Wood. The young wizard bent to look into the fir-green eyes, but still Imris gave no sign of being conscious, except that his eyes were open. Alphonse hastily searched him for broken bones, finding none. He must be in deep shock, he said to himself. Very carefully, he shifted the tree-tender to carry him. Imris drew a breath. 'Do not, please.' His eyes were clearing.

'Where are you hurt?' the wizard asked again.

The singer pulled himself upright until he sat. 'I was knocked out by the blast, but I think I am not hurt.' He put a hand to his head.

'Did you climb the tree to escape the Wolf?' Fear flashed across Imris's face, and Alphonse assured him quickly. 'The beast is nowhere around.'

The Yoriandir swallowed, and after a moment answered, 'The thing was waiting for me, Alphonse, and I nearly walked right into it.' He gestured at the tree where the wizard had found him. 'Nilarion's Child bent and plucked me from the earth, else I should have been killed. Nilarion knows the Wolf now,' he said grimly.

Alphonse nodded. It was well known that at need the trees would protect their tenders.

The Eldest suddenly searched the wizard's face. 'Is the queen well?'

'She wasn't harmed by the blast. She was running for the castle when I came up here to find you.'

Imris had been gingerly fingering his head, but what he heard in the wizard's voice stopped him. 'It was not your fault, Alphonse. None of the whole wretched mess was your fault.'

The red brows drew down in a straight bar across the wizard's eyes, but he made no reply, only pulling the Yoriandir to his feet. They set off back through the woods.

The wizard helped the Yoriandir over the fallen logs, and when they were nearly to the wood's verge, he asked, 'Will you help Jamison see to Kursh until Fidelis or I can get there?'

Imris stopped. 'I do not think I can do that, Alphonse.' One hand came up in a helpless gesture. 'It was my arrow!'

'And had your eye not been good, Kursh would have been dead.' A ghost of a smile touched his face. 'If you had meant to kill the old sod, you would have shot for his head.'

'That's so,' the Yoriandir said in a puzzled voice, as though he had just realized it, and then his eyes clouded once more. 'Perchance he will die anyway. It is hard to think of such a valiant companion ending so. Alphonse, why did he do it?'

The wizard murmured, 'I should have guessed that of all of us, a dwarf would have been most susceptible to an instrument designed to interrupt the Wind's Song. He heard the Pipes, Imris, and went mad from the evil song. He cannot have known what he did.'

They were silent. Standing still at the edge of the tangled trees, they began to feel the grief which shock had held at bay until then. After some moments, the Eldest spoke. There was unaccustomed flint in his voice as he said, 'The Unnamed has much to answer for.'

Alphonse regarded the tattered Greenbriar standard flapping from its broken pole and the jagged hole where the stained-glass Rose had been blown out of its window frame in the great hall. His gaze fell to the honor guard forming beside the improvised bier on which they would carry the consort to the hall of mourning.

'Doesn't he, though?' the wizard grated. He coughed in the ash-filled gloom.

Fidelis straightened from taking the boy's pulse. His look had lightened, and he nodded to the queen. 'Much better. He'll gain his strength back now, and in a few days, he'll be well enough.'

Ariadne said bitterly, 'Except that Ilyria's future king will be a cripple.'

The physician said carefully, 'It is not unknown for a king to be wounded in war. And make no mistake, young as he is, Gerrit has been in one. We must think of it that way.'

The queen turned away and gestured that Meara should bring up a chair to the bedside. They were in the Lordling's chamber. 'If the wizard had not burned my son, the Elixir might have restored his foot completely. He would not now be left with a stump.'

Fidelis recognized her brittle composure for the only defense she had against the overwhelming events of the past hour. Quietly, he told her, 'If Alphonse had not done as he did, the little master would not now be alive, my lady. It was the only course of action.'

Her fingers cut him off with an abrupt gesture, and he knew reason told her he was right, but she still could not forgive the man who had burned her son. The doctor began packing away his herbs and instruments, except for a twist of parchment containing soothing mallow, which he left on the table. 'This will ease you. You'll take it for me?'

'No.' After a moment, she amended, 'Later, maybe. Not now. I want to be here when he wakes.'

'That will not be for some hours yet.'

'Quit fussing, Fidelis.'

There was no gainsaying that tone, so the physician bowed and picked up his bag. 'By your leave, my lady, I must see to the others.' He reached for the blue bottle of Elixir.

'Where are you going with that?'

Surprised, he answered, 'There were folk severely injured. I will need it if I am to heal them.'

'Leave it. Don't look at me that way. You have more put by. We made plenty of the stuff the day before yesterday. I want a bottle of Elixir near my son at all times from now on. There was no excuse for that business out on the Sweep.'

Fidelis reddened at the rebuke. 'I little thought this morning that I would need Elixir in the bog, so I did not bring my bag with me.'

The queen took Gerrit's hand and regarded him as he slept. 'That's another thing: from now on, you must not use the Elixir on every Tom, Dick, and Harry who complains of a splinter.'

Despite the pity he felt for her, the doctor was angry, and this

was so rare for him that he could not speak for a moment. Then he
said, 'My queen, I have never misused the Lady of Earth's gift,
and I will not do it now.' He added dangerously, 'But other people
have hurt sons, too.'

The gray eyes she turned on him did not waver. 'My son comes
first, Fidelis.' He bit his tongue, and she waved him off. 'You may
go now.'

His steel-colored hair bristling, he stalked to the door, where
Meara waited silently by the rocking horse.

'Fidelis.' He stopped with his hand on the latch, and the queen
told him, 'If you had any thought of giving Elixir to the dwarf,
forget it at once. That murderer does not deserve it.'

His jaw corded. 'You cannot –'

'I made the Elixir. I will decide what is to be done with it!'

There was tense silence. Meara did not dare breathe. The physician shifted his kit to the other hand. 'As you will, madam. But I
was healing folk before ever you had the Crystal, and you will not
tell me that I cannot use the skill I have, and you will not say who
my patient may be.'

Not since she had ascended the Greenbriar throne had anyone
spoken so directly to Ariadne, and her waitingwoman was
appalled. The queen merely flicked her fingers to dismiss Fidelis,
and the doctor jerked open the door of the Lordling's chamber
and left.

Outside, Theodric fell into step as the healer stalked past the
Watchmen who crowded the corridor to guard the queen and her
son. The assistant doctor's square face was worried. 'How does
the Lordling?'

'Well enough. The Elixir brought him most of the way back.
With rest, he'll recover fully, except for the damage to the foot,
and that is already as healed as it will get.'

'Ah, that's good,' Theodric sighed with relief. When the chief
physician who had trained him said nothing, Theodric gave him a
look. They were going down the stairs. 'It is, isn't it?'

'Of course.' Fidelis suddenly stopped on the landing. 'She's
forbidden me to use the Elixir on Kursh, Theo.'

The stout man looked like a bad excuse for a bull, but he
had deft hands and a manner that made patients trust him.
As a fellow healer, he knew what his mentor was suffering.
He jammed his hands through his wide belt and said, 'She
didn't say someone else couldn't give it to him – me, for
instance.'

But Fidelis was shaking his head. 'She was adamant.'

Theodric regarded him. 'Well,' he said, and in the one syllable
put aside that worry for the moment. 'I was coming up to let you
know we've set up hospital in the barracks of the First Watch. I
had a word with Will Quint, and he saw the need. It's the only
place that would serve: it has enough hearths to keep the injured

warm, and the well is right outside, so the orderlies won't have to spend a lot of time hauling water.'

Fidelis straightened. 'Are there many people waiting for treatment?'

'More from the town than from the castle here. The stone protected most who were inside. One of the serving-maids got it when the window in Rose Hall blew out. She's pretty badly cut, but Ruel is working on her, and he says if we can keep him in catgut, she'll make it.'

The chief physician nodded. 'Tell everyone to be sparing with the Elixir. Save it only for the critical cases, and even then administer it diluted. There's likely not to be more.'

Theodric caught his breath. 'So it's true! Someone who was out on the Sweep said that she tried to use the Crystal and couldn't.'

'It's true,' Fidelis confirmed grimly. He hefted his bag once more. 'Can the rest of you keep things under control without me for a time?'

'Going to the First Watchman?'

'Yes.'

The square peasant face was kind. 'You'll only be saving him for the executioner, master.'

'Maybe.' He looked off up the stairs. 'But maybe she'll be merciful in view of his long service to the Crown. She cannot have forgotten that.'

'With her husband dead and her son left maimed, she may not be able to remember it.' Theodric grasped Fidelis's arm and walked with him down the stairs. The chief physician had no reply, for he feared it was true.

After he left Theodric, Fidelis headed outside for the stair that opened off the courtyard and went down to the dungeon. He met Alphonse just coming down from the Sweep, where he had cast a Warding for the Wolf and been unable to find Beldis anywhere. The wizard asked, 'How fares the Lordling?' The doctor told him what he had just finished saying to Theodric, and the wizard nodded. 'Are you going to Kursh?'

'Yes. I wish I could have gotten to him sooner, though.'

The redhead swung toward the stairs. 'I'll stay with Ariadne.'

Fidelis stopped him. 'I wouldn't. Just now there's no one there but Meara. Let the queen have some time alone.' When Alphonse still seemed inclined to go to her, the doctor told him, 'She isn't herself right now, you know. She . . . she holds it against you that you burned Gerrit, even though without it, the lad would have died.' Alphonse's face fell, and he looked all at once like the very young man he was, wizard's training or no. Fidelis guessed that his former apprentice needed at least as much tending as any of them in this aftermath. 'Come,' he said. 'Let us see what we can do for our friend.'

They were met by the iron lances of the Watchmen who guarded the dungeon door. One of them swung it open and allowed Fidelis to pass, but when Alphonse made to follow the other said, 'You'll not try removing the prisoner from here, sir? Nor any wizardry? I'd not like to have to report it to the queen if you did.' His tone was respectful but firm.

The wizard bristled, but reminded himself that the man was only doing his duty. 'I won't move him, sergeant.'

The Watchman motioned him through. As Alphonse followed Fidelis down the rough stone steps, the door was shut and fastened behind them.

The damp stone walls were lighted at intervals by torches, and they could see well enough to avoid stumbling on the uneven floor. A puddle ran down the center of the narrow corridor, where the condensation ran off the sweating walls. Lime from the mortar had made crumbling stalagmites overhead. Both men drew back as a large rat scurried past. 'What a place!' Alphonse commented.

'It is not much used,' the doctor explained. 'Only the occasional soldier who has drunk too much and started a fight, or some ruffian from the town awaiting the queen's justice.'

They came to another iron gate, another sentry. This one unlocked for them immediately. 'The Yoriandir king and that young yeoman are already with him, doctor, but I suppose it will do no harm to let in two more.'

'Is it necessary to have him so heavily guarded? Surely you cannot think he could escape, in his condition,' Fidelis said.

The guard eyed them. 'It isn't to keep him in, sir. It's to keep others out. There's many a man who saw what he did out on the hill, and a few of them might think they'd have the queen's thanks for taking care of the dwarf for her.'

'But you are not one of them,' Alphonse said quickly.

The Watchman looked down a moment, then up again. 'No, I can't say that I am. The First Watchman always was fair-handed with me.' His hand went to his sword hilt. 'Besides, till the queen says what she wants done with him, he's in my charge, and there'll be no foul thing done during my watch.'

'Let us hope your fellows are as clear-headed as you,' the wizard told him.

Under his helm, the man's face was worried. 'Aye, sir, I've thought of that myself.' They stepped through into the large open dungeon, and he locked the door after them. Leaning to peer in through the grille in the solid wooden portal, he told them, 'Give a call if you need help,' and then turned away.

Across the low-vaulted room there was a torch stuck in a bracket, and under it a stone bench with rusted iron manacles bolted into the wall. Imris and Jamison were bending over the bench, and Fidelis hurried toward them. 'Is he still alive?'

The young Watchman straightened. 'Just barely.' His voice was tight.

Imris made way for them, and Fidelis stooped. Alphonse stood off to the side and hoped it was just the bad light that made the dwarf's skin so gray.

'Bring the light closer,' Fidelis ordered, and Imris reached to take it down for him. The doctor's lips tightened and he put an ear to the barrel chest. After a moment he straightened. 'We must prop him up, almost sitting.' Together they swung Kursh upright, and Jamison held him. Fidelis put his fingers to the entry wound on the dwarf's breast. 'You did a good job getting the arrow out,' he told the young officer. 'I see where the mail was driven into his flesh by the force of the arrow. When you drew out the shaft, do you think there were any pieces of metal left in him?'

'I don't think so, sir, but I wouldn't want to say positively. I . . .' He swallowed. 'I opened the wound as much as I could without a knife, and it looked clean to me.'

Fidelis nodded, probing with his fingers. He nodded again after a moment. 'All right. We'll hope that you're right.' He began digging through his medical kit. 'I need hot water. Imris, would you?' The Eldest left to get it without a word. 'And, Alphonse, we need a fire. The damp alone could kill him.'

'I can't make Fire indefinitely,' Alphonse warned. 'We'll need wood eventually.'

The doctor glanced at Jamison. 'Would you get us some?'

'Right, sir.' He slipped his bracing arm carefully from about the dwarf's shoulders and propped Kursh against the wall with the Yoriandir's cloak for protection from the wet. Standing to go, he looked down at the gray face. 'Do you think he'll live?'

'I've treated a few arrow wounds in my time, son,' Fidelis replied. 'At least we know that Imris doesn't venom his arrowheads.' The last such wound he had worked on had been the old wizard Llodin's. That had been a grim hurt, too.

Jamison watched the glow come up on Alphonse's garnet ring, and he moved toward the door. 'I'll just get that wood, sir.' He left.

Only when they were both gone did the doctor look up at the wizard. A warmth was beginning to permeate the air. 'He'll never make it without the Elixir, and the queen has forbidden me to use it on him.'

Alphonse looked as though he could not believe what he had heard. 'She cannot forbid the use of a Power's gift! It is not for her to say!'

'Nevertheless, she has done it and it is certain she will not relent – not in time to do Kursh any good.' Fidelis had his hand above the dwarf's heart.

The wizard moved to stand beside the bench, casting warmth on the dwarf, and met the doctor's eyes. 'Then you'll have to pull him through on your own. Or disobey, and use the Elixir anyway.'

'There is a third alternative,' Fidelis said, chewing his lip. 'But it will depend on you.'

'What is it?'

The doctor beckoned and pointed to Kursh's chest above the wound. 'Put your ear there and listen.' Alphonse cast him a doubtful look, but did as requested. 'You remember how to listen for a patient's breath, I hope; it was one of the first things I taught you.'

The wizard straightened, frowning. 'It sounds fairly clear to me.'

'Right. Now listen there.' He indicated the lower part of the dwarf's chest, below the wound.

'I can't hear a thing.'

'Right again. And that indicates that the lung is filling.' He nodded at the look on the wizard's face. 'He is drowning in his own blood.'

Alphonse cleared his suddenly thick throat. 'And what do you want me to do?'

'I want you to do for him what you did for Gerrit.'

'No! I can't, Fidelis! By Earth Pillar, do you know what you're asking? I'd have to guide my Fire through him! That's a far different thing from touching it to a limb.' He ran a hand through his hair nervously, and it grew noticeably warmer in the dungeon.

Fidelis got stiffly to his feet. 'He has no other chance, Alphonse. Even if you did him harm, it would be nothing more than the fate that awaits him an hour or two from now.'

The young wizard stared down at the dwarf and thought suddenly of the evening before, and of how Kursh had tried to teach him the finer points of betting on dice. 'All right,' he said suddenly. 'I'll try it.'

Fidelis smiled. 'Good lad,' he said, just as he used to when a young redheaded bondsman had tried hard to please around the infirmary.

By the time Imris and Jamison returned together with their supplies, it was done. Alphonse now sat on the stone bench next to the dwarf, and he was visibly trembling. Fidelis had his hand to the First Watchman's brow. The Yoriandir darted forward, alarmed that the wizard's face reflected that the worst had happened. 'How is he?'

'Kursh is holding his own,' said the doctor, 'but I'm afraid our young friend here is a bit worse for wear. He's just performed his first surgery.' There was something like a smile in his tone.

'What?' the yeoman asked.

The doctor answered, 'Alphonse used his Fire to –'

'I'd really rather not discuss it,' the wizard broke in, and they could not tell if this was modesty or a queasy stomach.

Fidelis poured some of the hot water from the kettle Imris had fetched over a piece of linen cloth and set about to wash the dried blood from his patient. 'Well, at any rate, we've done all that can be done for now, except to administer a draught to keep the fever down and ease his breathing. When I get him bandaged, we'll wrap him in those blankets you brought, Jamison – good thinking – and then time will tell.'

Alphonse sat forward with his head in his hands. 'Jamison, would you mind setting up a fire? I feel as though I'd like to rest a little from Warding.' The temperature of the dungeon had climbed to a comfortable level by now.

The yeoman made a fire below the one small window grate not far from the bench and set up the small tripod he had lugged down from the kitchens. He swung the kettle over the fire. 'There,' he said. 'It will serve us to have a pot going, I should think. It will probably be a long day.'

Imris smiled. 'You are a wonder, Master Jamison.'

'Oh, no, sir,' the young man said easily. 'My job is to look after the senior officers. That's all I'm doing.' But the slight flush that reddened the back of his neck belied his words. 'I'll fetch more water,' he said hastily and went out.

Fidelis mixed some water with dried herbs from his bag. While the mixture steeped in an earthenware cup Jamison had brought, the doctor cast a professional eye over the wizard. 'Do you want a draught, too?'

'No, thanks.' Alphonse stood up. 'I should go to the queen. Don't worry,' he said in answer to Fidelis's look. 'I'll not take anything she says seriously.'

The doctor shook his head as the wizard left. He sighed and said to Imris, 'I'm due in hospital. Will you stay with Kursh?'

'I have no intention of leaving.'

The physician picked up the cup to feed the medicinal draught to Kursh. 'A little of this every few minutes. Take care not to give him too much at once, or you risk his choking on it.' The Yoriandir's eyes were cast down, and the doctor added quietly, 'Be easy in your mind, Imris. You did what you had to. If it is any consolation, he would have done the same if you had suddenly gone crazed.'

'That is small cheer,' the Eldest muttered, nauseated as much by guilt as by the crackling of the fire. The doctor clapped him on the shoulder, picked up his bag, and left.

Imris sat still for some time, thinking of quick-tempered arguments, and battles lost, and a kingdom regained. Kursh's breath rattled and the wood in the fire hissed. Looking over the low flames, the Yoriandir saw the fire reflected in two pinpoints of light near the farther wall. He groped for a piece of loose mortar in the floor and heaved it suddenly. 'Hai, you – get out of here, rat. You'll not take him yet!'

But he felt in his bones that it would not be long.

Chapter Sixteen

Night was falling. The black horse's flanks were streaked with sweat, and it held its head low, stumbling. Never in his life had the Littleman treated a beast so, and he promised himself that he never would again, but he had to keep going.

Peewit had skirted Waysmeet in the early afternoon, avoiding the town for fear that one of last night's Wolf Cultists might have ridden that way. Though no one had seen him, the horse might be recognized. Now he had gone back to the road, thinking that it would be safer riding at night. At least if there was a huge wolf with sapphire eyes stalking him, he might see it coming. He tightened his reins, helping the black hold its head up, and watched carefully in the fading light for ruts or stones. This night of all nights he did not want to be thrown.

Urging the horse on, he made the best speed he could, and wondered why Kursh had not thought to send Riders posting with fresh horses for him. The dwarf had known he would likely be on the Waysmeet road. But, he told himself, Kursh no doubt had other more important matters to tend to at the moment. How had it happened? How had the queen been killed? And why, oh why, had he thought she would be safe until his return!

Tears formed in his eyes as he angrily slapped the horse to a jog.

The heavy violet evening blanketed the valley by the time he had to stop to let the horse blow at the top of the slope leading down past Ned Weaver's ruined cottage. Though the Littleman could not see much – there was a pall of ash – he could still smell the burning. He straightened painfully in the saddle that was too big for him, sighed, and kicked the black to a shambling walk once more.

Dusk had deepened to night by the time he made the next rise, the one where Liam and Kip Potter had halted their wagons to stare down into the ruined valley. This time, the horse balked at the upward climb and Peewit had to let it plod like a plowhorse. Clearly the black could go no farther. 'Just to the other side,' he told it. 'There is good grass there for you.'

When they stood finally at the crest and the Willowsrill Valley lay spread downward to the river, Peewit guided the horse to deep grass under the verge of the wood that had been cleared back from the road by the queen's troops. The black dropped its head, too exhausted even to nibble. The Littleman slid down from the saddle and had to hold on for a moment to keep from falling. His stiff legs did not want to hold him. When he could, he unbuckled the girth and pushed the saddle off. Then he unbridled the horse and turned it free to graze and roam at will when it had rested. 'There, stout heart. I hate to leave you unprotected this way, but there's no help for it. Wait here for the tinker – he should be along in a few days. If you've taken any hurt from your work this day, he'll care for you. All right?' The black could not raise its head, even if it had understood him, but one of its large ears turned in the Littleman's direction. He patted it and slowly made his way back to the road. It took some minutes of walking to get his legs loosened, but once he did Peewit broke into a trot. If he had to run all the way to Greenbriar, he thought grimly, he would, and wolf be damned.

The miles rolled slowly by. Coming down a gentle slope, he took a cramp in the calf of one leg. With a stifled curse, the Littleman tried to rub it out and took a step to see if he could. Now that he wasn't hearing the sound of his own panting and his running foot-steps, Peewit picked up another noise on the night wind: hooves approaching, and it was more than one horse. He flicked Kursh's dagger into his hand and hoped he would not have to use it, but one way or another, he would have a new mount.

The night hid the approaching horses until they were only a few feet from the unmoving small figure in the middle of the road. The lead animal was a big dark one, maybe a chestnut, with a white forefoot, and the single rider was leading another, a packhorse, probably. Peewit ordered, 'Halt for the queen's business!'

The chestnut shied and plunged and the rider cursed and pulled it around when it would have headed for the woods. 'Captain! Am I glad I've found you!' He dismounted in a flurry and led both horses forward.

Peewit had put his dagger away as he recognized Jak Cooper's voice. The queen's foster brother was saluting. The Littleman returned it and said, 'I saw the beacons. What –?'

Simultaneously Jak was saying, 'The Riders have been looking for you all day, sir, to let you know the news.'

Peewit braced himself. 'What has happened to the queen?'

The Littleman sensed rather than saw the other's shake of head. 'She's left a widow, sir. The consort is dead. The Lordling is sore hurt, but they were saying he would live when I left.'

Peewit could not at first take this in. 'The queen is not dead?'

'No, sir.'

Relief flooded through him, but was immediately overtaken by shock. 'Tell me what happened!'

Cooper pulled the ends of the reins through his hands. 'They had gone out on the Sweep to try out some beagle pups – the consort and the Lordling. We all thought it would be safe enough with them right under the bows of our archers on the walls, and there was even an armed escort with them. The consort had just taken Gerrit in his arms to show him the rabbits, and that was when he attacked them. The wizard says –'

'Who attacked them?' Peewit broke in.

In the dark, he could hear the young officer swallow. 'Well, sir – it was the First Watchman.'

For a stunned instant, Peewit was sure that he must have fallen asleep in the grass at the side of the road and must now be dreaming. But then he remembered Imris's sent cry: the Yoriandir had shouted Kursh's name. Suddenly Peewit was unbearably tired, and he felt sick. He sat down heavily in the middle of the grass track and put his head in his hands.

Alphonse climbed the Sweep wearily, taking the road up from the city of Castlenigh. Ariadne had refused to see him, so he had spent much of the day lending a hand to shift heavy timbers or to pass buckets with the others who tried to fight the fires started by the blast wave.

He stopped to rest a moment. Smoke drifted from the town up the hill, but the slight breeze thinned some of the ash sifting down and made the fumes bearable. Alphonse looked back down the road, and now that he was high enough, he could see the lantern-lit area around the market hall. The teams of fire-fighters had managed to save the inn next door, but the market itself was mostly gone, only the stone pillars and a few blackened beams still standing. The embers had not fanned up into blaze again, he noted. The guilds were taking it in turns to watch through the night.

The wizard sighed. All at once he was very tired, and the black mood that he had held at bay by force of will and hard work finally seized him. Grateful for the covering dark that would hide him from the sentries' eyes, he sank down upon a rock and rested his head on his knees.

Kursh dead or dying, Gerrit's Wood a scrambled log fell, the Wolf still loose to murder, half of Castlenigh burned or blown down, folk still crying from the rubble. Ariadne so angry at him for burning Gerrit that she would not even send a page to answer his message of condolence. And himself with the Rule broken, the three-stranded Song that he had made still straining to escape his control. He knew that if he let himself slip just a little, he could well become exactly the Abomination that the ancient wizard seers had prophesied, the one wizard who would wreck the Great Song so badly that it would never be right again.

He knew, too, that the Meld must realize by now what he had done and that Master Chiswic would have no recourse. The ancient injunction was adamant: for a wizard who broke the Rule, there was only one penalty – death. Even now the master must have sent his Unmakers, the fellow wizards who would be charged with the task of stripping him of his power. Though it would be quite impossible for them, since his power far outstripped their own, someone would have to try. Likely Chiswic would come himself, alone. Powers, be it not so, the garnet wizard prayed. *I could not use force against him even to protect myself.*

Alphonse felt the gritty ash sprinkling the back of his neck. Already the ground was thick with the stuff, looking as if an unseasonable snowstorm had whitened Ilyria. He suspected there would be several more inches yet. At one stroke, the Unnamed had both destroyed this season's crops and made it difficult for next year. *If there was a next year,* the wizard thought.

Suddenly there was a brush of fur around his feet, and he started, reaching for a Warding against the Wolf, but even in the dark he could see the pied black and white. He regarded the cat, feeling immensely glad that she had sought him out. 'I didn't think you'd want to see me again, after what I've done.'

Patience tucked her tail around her feet. 'It was bad,' she agreed. 'We have both failed the charges laid on us. I was not there to stop you.'

'You could not guard me from myself every minute of my life, little one. This was bound to happen sooner or later.' He brushed the ash from her head.

'Don't be a twit. Of course I could have stopped you,' she snapped and irritably ducked away from his touch. 'You don't think Master Chiswic would have sent me for your guardian if I could not, do you?'

The accustomed asperity in her tone made him smile a little. Something was still the same.

'You needn't twitch your whiskers at me, either, wizard,' she told him. 'Just promise you won't do it again and then let's get inside before this nose-dust buries us.' She sneezed.

His expression hardened. 'I promised once, Patience, and it did no good. I'll not swear again. You know the pressure on me,' he added. 'I shall need all my Wardings to fight the Unnamed. I will try to hold back from using at least one of them, but I cannot disarm myself again.'

They stared at each other, the green eye and the blue ones meeting. Alphonse was prepared for her to spring, to rake him with her claws, to become a hissing, spitting ball of fury.

She sneezed again. 'I have failed once,' she said. 'I will fail again. No other Song I know can blot out the Evil One's, and it would be ridiculous for all us four-legged and feathered to perish on account of some musty bit of human lore. Abomination you may be, but that is of no account to me. Master Chiswic warned me against some great evil if ever you failed.' She sniffed at the hem of his robe. 'But I can smell no evil on you, wizard.' She stood up and stretched. 'Could we get something to eat now?'

Alphonse began to laugh, but coughed instead. He tucked her under his arm and slogged up toward the main gate. He did not really feel as though he could eat, however, so he left her off at the marble steps into the keep and made his way to the dungeon door. There a new pair of guards was on duty, and they eyed him distrustfully, but finally allowed him through. There was no sentry at the inner door. The wizard frowned, not liking the feel of things. As a precaution, he set a Warding on the door to admit only friends of the dwarf. Anyone else who tried to enter would get a nasty jolt.

Inside he found the fire carefully tended and Jamison watchful by it, while Imris and Fidelis murmured by the bench. As Alphonse came through the door, they looked up. 'Where have you been?' the doctor called in a low voice. 'You look like a charcoal burner!'

Alphonse absently brushed at some of the soot on his clothing. 'How is he?'

'If he weren't a dwarf, he'd be dead already,' Fidelis said. 'Then again, if he were a younger dwarf, I would be more hopeful.'

The wizard leaned beside him. One look told him more than he wanted to know. He said nothing as he straightened.

'We cannot allow this to take its course,' Imris said, obviously continuing the conversation he and Fidelis had been having. Apparently, they were debating about the Elixir. 'I will do it,' the Yoriandir volunteered. 'What can the Queen of Ilyria do to the Eldest of Yoriand, except send me packing home? Let me do it, Fidelis. You have too much to lose. You must stay here at court.'

Before the physician could reply, Alphonse cut in. 'No, I should be the one; she is already angry at me. Why let someone else incur her wrath? He smiled. 'Besides, what could she do to me? Wage war on the Meld?'

Fidelis said quietly, 'You are both wrong. Kursh is my patient. That is reason enough for me to take the responsibility. I will go up to the hospital and get a bottle of Elixir, and I will give it to him.'

'And then you may find yourself down here in irons, waiting for the headsman,' young Jamison said unexpectedly. He got up from the fire. 'All of you will be needed to help the queen against the Unnamed. I am not so important. And after all, I am acting as the First Watchman's yeoman. If I stole the Elixir and brought it to him, it could even be taken as part of my duty.'

Fidelis looked at Alphonse speculatively. 'You know, if she has given orders that the Elixir be guarded by the Watch, they may well be looking for me to take it. The same goes for you,' he nodded to the wizard, 'and for Imris. But they may overlook Jamison. Much as I hate to let him risk it, he may be right.'

The idea made sense, and after some hesitation, Alphonse nodded. Imris said, 'Good luck.'

The yeoman grinned and headed for the door. 'I shall be right back.'

When they unlocked for him, the guards on the outer door gave him a surly look. 'Lot of runnin' back and forth for a traitor.'

'I am running errands for the First Watchman. If you have aught to say about it, see the sergeant major,' Jamison answered, having taken one remark too many about it.

One of the men, who had a crooked nose and a long scar down one cheek behind his helm, put his hand to his sword hilt. 'Keep a civil tongue, or you'll eat it.'

Jamison kept his hand carefully away from his dagger. 'And if he recovers, and somehow finds the queen's grace so that he is still First Watchman, will you boast in the mess that you kept watch over him and did not let some rogue in to do him harm while he lay helpless?' For a moment, the yeoman thought he had miscalculated, that the scarred one would draw on him.

Then the other guard made a gesture telling his watch mate to put up, and Jamison knew that this one, quicker-witted than the other, had taken his meaning. If Kursh lived to be second-in-command for years to come, and if Jamison should ever mention what these two had been thinking on this night, the dwarf would thrash them both.

Silently, they made way for the young officer, and he went by them, but he did not feel safe until he had turned the corner of the keep and put stone between himself and their blades. He went past the marble steps into the castle and followed along the wing which spread out to the north. Shortly he had reached the First Watch's barracks, which was lit by lanterns and full of activity. A line of people waited in the courtyard, some on rude crutches, some with rags bound about their brows, some lying on improvised litters attended by friends or family. He stepped carefully around them and went inside to the ordered bustle of the temporary hospital.

Long rows of pallets lined both walls, and there were fires burning on the hearths down the center of the room. Tripods burned sweet-smelling herbs to dispel fear and induce sleep. Here and there a doctor with his assistants knelt by a bed to tend a patient. Jamison looked about, wondering – now that it had come to it – how he was going to get hold of one of the blue Elixir bottles. The only ones he saw were in the hands of the healers. A voice came at his elbow. 'Pardon, sir, but could you tell me some news of the Squiremaster? How fares he?'

Jamison turned to find a worried Rory Fisher clasping soiled linen. He was obviously on his way to the laundry. The yeoman answered, 'He lives. I suppose that is all that can be said for his condition.'

The boy's face fell, and he looked away. 'I thought . . . I mean, I hoped . . .'

Jamison had not intended to say it, but it came out anyway: 'We had all hoped, but our hopes look bleak.' When the boy dropped a blood-spattered apron and bent to retrieve it, the yeoman understood it was to give him time to get his face under control. 'You have been working with the healers, I take it.'

Rory straightened. 'Yes, sir. I turned the senior squires out and we've been running errands here all day.'

The germ of an idea formed in Jamison's mind. Taking a quick look around to see if anyone had noticed their conversation, he murmured, 'Fisher, would you dare a very dicey mission for your Squiremaster?'

'Of course,' The reply was quick and certain.

'The queen has forbidden him Elixir. I am going to steal a bottle and take it to him. I need someone to distract one of the healers long enough –'

'There's a better way,' the squire interrupted. 'The apothecary has set up pharmacy in the weapons room.' He nodded at the door at the other end of the barracks and added, 'I've been in and out of there getting ointments and draughts for the doctors. There is Elixir, too.' The boy said calmly, 'I'll just go in and ask him for an infusion or something and while he makes it up, I'll decant some Elixir into a cup. Will that do?'

Jamison, looking at the set young face, warned, 'It is no game, lad. If you are caught, we will both face the headsman.'

The squire took another covering look around. 'I reckon I owe Master Korimson this much, at least.'

'All right. Off with you. I'll wait outside by the well.' He raised his voice for any listener. 'When you finish here, the sergeant major wants to see you.'

'Aye, sir. I'll be right along. Let me just get this draught made up.'

Jamison nodded and went out the door. Rory walked down the aisle past the hearths with his armful of soiled linen and went into the makeshift pharmacy. From where he tended a patient, Theodric watched the boy and had a fair idea what was shaping up. He was smiling as he took the splints from his orderly and began wrapping a broken leg.

Rory walked past the racks of burnished shields and halbards. 'Master Theodric needs a posset. The comfrey one for boneset, he says.'

The herbalist reached for a clay jar. 'They're keeping you running, aren't they, boy-o?' He took up a wooden spoon and a measure.

'I'm glad to do it,' the squire answered truthfully. The pharmacist had set up a couple of planks on up-ended barrels to serve for a worktable. On this was a wooden box, heavy enough not to be knocked off the table, and in this the Elixir bottle was nestled in straw. The herbalist was taking no chance that a careless move might send the precious fluid crashing to the floor. Several small bowls were set out, ready for mixing the medicines required by the doctors. Rory took all this in at a glance. To get the man talking, he pointed to the array of bottles on the table. 'Are any of these poisons?'

'What, do you think we kill our patients if they can't pay?' The herbalist laughed. 'No, they are all beneficial herbs. Of course, there are others. Try cooking rhubarb leaves in a pie, if there's someone you don't like.' He laughed again and turned, as Rory had known he must, to lift the kettle from its hook and pour steaming water into a bowl.

The boy dropped the laundry and his hand shot out to grasp the bottle. The clink against the bowl went unheard in the brisk stirring the herbalist was doing. The man was saying, 'And of course there are mistletoe, laburnum, and columbine. Black bryony, too. They'll all do the job.' Rory's hands flew, slipping the bottle back into its nest. He was bending to cover the small bowl with laundry by the time the man turned around and set a cup of hot liquid on the plank table. 'There you go, young fellow. Carry it carefully, now – it's hot.'

Straightening, the squire held the Elixir bowl under the laundry heaped over his arm, and took the comfrey tea with the other. 'Thanks. No, sir, you needn't take those sheets – I can manage.' He nodded to the herbalist and went out through the hospital, breathing a little easier when he made it to the dark courtyard. Rory veered through the crowd toward the well where the yeoman should be waiting.

Jamison saw him coming, but did not attract attention by hailing him. Rory went right by the yeoman, whispering, 'Got it. Follow me in a minute.' He crossed the courtyard, heading in the direction of the laundry.

That boy's got pluck, Jamison thought. He lounged a moment more on the wide ledge of the well, and then made his way toward the corner where the boy had disappeared. When he rounded the turn, Rory was waiting. The boy looked around and held out the bowl with the healing Elixir.

'What's the other?' Jamison asked.

'I had to ask him for a posset to distract him. I'll just dump it here and leave the bowl. If they find it in the morning, they'll just

think one of the patients didn't like the taste of the stuff and
threw it out. Or up.'

Jamison had to laugh a little at the youngster's cool. 'Thanks,
squire. You've done good service tonight.'

'I'd not like to try it again, and that's the truth,' Rory admitted,
shifting the laundry.

'Wouldn't want to try what again?' a voice said behind them.

Jamison did not jump, but it was only because he had heard
the sound of a booted footstep an instant before. He turned now
to find the crooked-nosed man staring with a most interested
look. The man's voice was edged. 'Why would you be throwing
out medicine?' he demanded of Rory.

The squire did not reply, and the man shouted, 'Answer when
you're spoke to!'

'It is none of your affair!' Jamison said, putting himself
between the soldier and the boy.

The surly man gave him a shove, and some of the Elixir
slopped over the edge of the bowl. 'Don't tell me what's my
business and what ain't!' He drew back his fist.

Jamison moved back quickly, taking Rory with him and holding
the bowl for dear life.

But a broad hand caught the cocked fist and Sergeant Major
William Quint demanded, 'What is going on here?'

Anxious to clear himself of blame, the man with the crooked
nose said, 'I seen this kid sneakin' medicine and bringing it out to
him. As you'll know, sir, the queen has forbid the Elixir to the
dwarf, but I'll bet that's what's in the bowl!'

They were done for. Jamison squared his shoulders and prepared to take the blame, but William Quint pursed his lips and
said quietly, 'Well, now –' His eyes flicked to the brass badge
clipped to the man's sword harness. 'Corporal – as it happens
the yeoman is on an errand for me. I asked him to fetch something for the headache I've got from dealing with people like you
all day.' His tone got icier word by word of the lie, and Jamison
realized with a shock that the burly man knew!

Rashly the man objected, 'He'd only just come from the
dungeon, sergeant major. I seen him.'

Quint moved up a step, towering over the man. Dangerously
quiet, he asked, 'You wouldn't be calling me a liar, would you,
corporal?'

A moment the man stood the glare of those eyes, and then
moved back a step. 'No.' He saluted pointedly and turned on his
heel. The three watched him out of sight.

Rory and Jamison waited for the sergeant major to speak.
After a moment, Quint looked down at them. 'Better cover that
bowl with a towel or something. That way if anyone asks, he
can't say that he actually saw you carry it into the dungeon.'

Silently the boy handed the yeoman the freshest one he had.

Jamison began to say, 'Thank you, sir . . .'

But Will Quint waved him to silence, 'Get on with you, yeoman. If Fidelis sent you for it, there's no time to waste.' He regarded Rory. 'I take it this young fellow helped you get it?'

'I ordered him to do it,' Jamison said quickly.

'You did not!' Fisher objected hotly. 'I did it myself! Sir,' he added, remembering the sergeant major.

Quint scratched his beard. 'I see. All right, Jamison, you can go. Mind yourself around that ugly fellow.' The yeoman saluted and left. The sergeant major said genially, 'Now, young Master Fisher, isn't it?' At Rory's nod, Quint continued, 'I am thinking that I will need a yeoman tonight, what with all there is to do. Drop that dirty stuff off at the laundry and on your way back, pop into the kitchen. They're holding a plate for me, I think. Fetch it to the antechamber of the queen's apartment, would you?'

'Yes, sir.' The boy touched his forelock and sped off, trailing a sheet.

Quint watched him go, and hoped that the Elixir they had stolen would be in time. He had no wish to be First Watchman.

The man with the crooked nose said nothing when Jamison approached the dungeon, merely staring at him angrily while he unlocked the door. The yeoman ducked under the low lintel and the door swung to. If he had not moved quickly, his fingers would have been smashed. All right, Jamison thought angrily, I'll deal with you later.

Alphonse's Warding admitted him at the lower door, and he carried the bowl of Elixir quickly across the wet floor. 'Here you are, sir,' he said to Fidelis, who had jumped to his feet.

'Well done!' the doctor approved, and a smile broke across the Eldest's face. Alphonse held out a hand to congratulate him.

Jamison handed the bowl over and told them, 'It is a young squire named Fisher that we must all thank. He's the one who filched the Elixir.'

'Well, however you came by it, I swear I would be glad to go to the gallows if this works.' The doctor measured out a sip into the earthenware cup. 'All right. Alphonse, hold his head, will you? And be ready: the first thing he will probably do is start coughing.'

Imris said, 'And the second will be to curse me for shooting him. Guard your ears, friends!'

Carefully, the physician reached to dribble a sip of the fluid between the dwarf's blue lips. A sudden cry echoed down the dungeon steps: '*Stop!*' Rory Fisher cried again, 'Don't!'

Fidelis had started, and the Elixir spilled, running down into Kursh's beard. The doctor muttered an exasperated oath. Imris was hurrying to the door to see what was the matter, and

Alphonse, Warding the guard that had the squire by the scruff of the neck, grasped the physician's arm. 'Wait,' he said.

The boy clattered down the steps and darted past the Yoriandir, slapping garnet sparks off his tunic. 'Don't give him the Elixir! It's poison!'

The wizard jumped up, and Fidelis whirled, demanding 'What are you talking about?'

Rory panted, 'It's got to be the Elixir, sir. Everyone who has been given it is dying – I heard it in the kitchen and came straight here!'

Alphonse extended his Warding as the doctor stared. 'It is true,' the wizard reported grimly. 'I perceive death everywhere.' He ran past the squire with Fidelis a step behind. Both of them had thought instantly of Gerrit.

Fisher had eyes only for his Squiremaster. He advanced to stand by Jamison near the bench, and though he was but a boy and had never seen a dead man, he knew enough to guess that the dwarf was in very bad straits. Mumbling that the sergeant major would be looking for him, he fled up the steps.

Imris met Jamison's despairing eyes. 'Do not give up hope. Being a dwarf, Kursh is much stronger than any of us.'

The yeoman nodded for courtesy's sake, though he did not believe it, and threw another stick on the fire. 'Will you have some of this tea, sir? The bakeress sent it down. 'Tis soothing, she says.'

Imris sighed. 'We are low on the draught for Kursh, and Fidelis will have no time now to send more for a while. Let us mix what is left with this tea and give it to Kursh. It will be liquid for him, anyway. It may help with the fever.'

The officer nodded once more and bent to lift the dwarf's head.

The heir to the throne of Ilyria moaned and thrashed on his bed, while Ariadne tried to hold him and Cele stood white-faced in the corner. The queen threw a desperate look over her shoulder. 'Fidelis, what took –' Her eyes narrowed when she saw the wizard behind him. 'Get out, you!'

'He is my assistant,' the doctor said curtly, slinging his bag on the bed. Alphonse stepped in and shut the door on the curious and fearful crowd outside. Quickly Fidelis examined the gasping little boy, probing the abdomen and noting the pale, clammy face. 'Does he seem to hear you?' he asked the queen. At her shake of the head, his brows drew together. As gently as possible, he pried Gerrit's mouth open, checking to see whether the tongue might be discolored. It was: dark purple, as though the Lordling had eaten a quantity of blackberries. Fidelis caught the writhing boy's head and thumbed up an eyelid. The whites of his eyes were bright red, as bright as if something had gashed his eyeballs. Ariadne made a strangled sound, and the doctor pushed her away. 'Please stand over there with Cele.' He threw a look to Alphonse at the door, and the wizard came forward to tug her back from the bed. Angrily she flung away from him, glaring, but did not stoop to touch Gerrit again.

The physician motioned to the wizard to hold the boy while he quickly mixed packets of powder from his bag and dumped the lot into a cup of water. 'He has had no food or drink since the Elixir?'

Ariadne shook her head. 'He did not wake, and I did not try to force drink on him.' She had let Alphonse gently hold the boy down, but hovered at his elbow lest he should try any wizardry.

Fidelis was nodding. 'It is the same with all the others, I am told.'

'What others?'

Plainly no one had told the queen. The doctor looked up at her as he knelt with the cup. 'It is the Elixir, my lady. Somehow it has become poisonous.'

Her hands went to her mouth to stifle a gasp, but Alphonse and Fidelis had no time to comfort her. They fed sips of the medicine to Gerrit. Since Fidelis had no idea what kind of poison this was, he could guess at no antidote, so he had only mixed a heavy sedative to ease pain and spasms. Though Gerrit swallowed, the medicine soon came back up. Clearly, this was not going to work.

Worriedly Fidelis put the cup aside, reached in his kit for a knife and a straw, and bared the child's thin arm.

'What are you doing?' the queen demanded.

'When Master Llodin was poisoned by the Fallen, this worked,' he told her. 'I think perhaps the Unnamed may have turned your Elixir to something like that poison.'

Trembling, she nodded and signed him to continue.

The doctor nicked open the vein in Gerrit's arm, drew a sip of medicine into the straw, and blew it into the incision. They waited tensely for some result.

Alphonse was holding the boy's head, and he counted thirty racing beats in the pulse at the delicate temple. Then, suddenly, there was nothing under his finger. Gerrit groaned and went rigid. The wizard hit the physician on the arm to alert him, but Fidelis had already marked it. He swallowed and raised his eyes to the queen.

'No!' she cried, and was moving to catch the child up when Alphonse thrust her back, summoned all his Wardings for the second time that day, and plunged down the black tide of death after Ariadne's son.

Ice stung him and wind howled through his mind, but what drove him mad was the laughter. All the time he wove a Song to drag Gerrit back, he heard it. Resolutely the Wizard of the Three

refused to listen to the gloating words, but he marked well the
Unnamed's disdain and the burning hate, and the desire for
mastery. 'All right, lad,' he told the boy now clutched in his
arms. 'Let us go back.' Gerrit stared at him, and his countenance
twisted and aged until Alphonse was looking into the burning
eyes of a resentful youth. What he saw in those eyes gave him
pause, but the wizard shut the gates of Sight, turned, and began
fighting his way back with a sleepy little boy nestled on his
shoulder. The laughter followed him.

He came to himself crouched over the bed, his hand on Gerrit's
brow. The last vestiges of a garnet, pearl, and gold web were
flickering out. His vision narrowed and his ears roared, then the
queen was beside him, weeping and kissing the sleeping child.
Alphonse straightened and, waving away Fidelis's concern,
walked out the door.

Jamison tapped at his chamber door some time later. When the
haggard wizard pulled it open, the yeoman bade him come
quickly. The doctor was with the First Watchman again, he said,
and there had been a significant improvement. In fact, Fidelis
thought Kursh would wake within the hour.

They clattered down the dungeon stairs together. The dwarf
was gasping, and as Fidelis predicted, had begun to cough. He
pushed Alphonse's arm away and swung his feet to the stone
floor, sitting on the edge of the stone bench and coughing as
though he had a winter croup. The wizard put an arm around his
shoulders. 'You had us worried, old fellow!'

Kursh looked at him, and his face drew into a rictus of fear. He
shrugged away from Alphonse and clubbed wildly at the young
wizard with his fist. A solid blow knocked the wizard from the
bench, and the dwarf dove for the doctor. Fidelis tried to catch
him, and Kursh hammered him two-fisted. The doctor fell,
dazed.

'Kursh!' Imris sent. 'Stop this!'

The dwarf seemed to have turned to stone, and the Eldest
rejoiced. But Kursh suddenly pointed an accusing finger and
said coldly, 'You keep your bloody music out of my head.'

'But I –' the Eldest began to protest.

Alphonse had risen to a crouch and now brought up his ring
hand. A flicking arc of garnet knocked the dwarf from his feet
and held him pinioned on the floor.

'Don't hurt him!' Fidelis cried, staggering to his feet.

'I won't,' the wizard assured him. 'I just want to hold him until
we get some irons on him.'

The Eldest had backed slowly until he came up against a wall.
His fir eyes were wide and afraid. 'By Nilarion, he is still mad!'

Jamison and Alphonse between them carried the dwarf back
to the bench, and the wizard closed the manacles around the

brawny wrists. 'How will you get them off, sir? We've no key,' Jamison pointed out.

They stood back. 'I'll burn them off, if necessary,' Alphonse answered absently, regarding Kursh. He shook his head. 'I should have expected it,' he murmured.

Fidelis sighed and ran a hand through his hair. Alphonse motioned Imris and the yeoman back and released his Warding upon the dwarf. Kursh glared at them, writhing and pulling at the chains that held him. 'Damn you, Rasullis!'he roared, looking right at Alphonse. 'Let me go!'

Pity filled their hearts. 'He may be calmer if we move closer to the fire, gentlemen,' Imris murmured, but in spite of themselves, they stayed, staring.

Chapter Seventeen

The early cocks were crowing when the guards at Queen's Gate opened up and the Captain of the Queen's Watch rode through with Jak Cooper. The sergeant on duty saluted from the platform above the ironclad oak doors. 'Glad to have you back, captain,' he called in a low voice. 'It's been a right awful few days.'

The Littleman turned on him, eyes like knotholes in a hollow tree. 'I know,' he replied. His voice was husky with exhaustion, and he did not return the salute, but kept the rawboned red gelding moving. 'Find Tomasheen the tinker and bring him to me at once.'

'But, sir –' the sergeant began to protest, but the Littleman did not turn back.

In the unnatural darkness – it should have been lightening toward dawn – some of the castle folk went about their early-morning chores, but there was none of the usual banter. Peat smoke rose and new loaves were baking, but the ash drifting down scoured the clean aromas from the morning.

Peewit drew up before the broad steps into the keep. One of the Watchmen on duty came down to take his horse. 'Thank the Powers you're back, sir!'

The Littleman slid wearily from the saddle, and his knees buckled. He caught himself on the stirrup and waved Jak away when the young officer would have taken his arm. Looking up at the guard, Peewit asked, 'Where is the First Watchman being held?'

The man made a business of gathering the gelding's reins, though the horse was too tired to move. 'Well, sir, he's . . . in the dungeon.' He could not meet the Littleman's eye.

Without a word, Peewit pushed himself away from the horse and began to walk in that direction.

The man watched him go, then beckoned his watch mate urgently. 'Best go fetch the wizard right away. The captain isn't going to like what he finds down there.' The other man left, running.

Jak Cooper asked, 'Why? Is the First Watchman dead?'

The man reached for the chestnut's reins, and Jak let him take the horse. 'No, not dead. I'll say no more, as I haven't seen it myself, but all you want to know is that the captain will need someone attending him when he walks through that door.'

The queen's foster brother was mystified, but he took the fellow's hint and quickly followed the captain. He caught up with Peewit as the man with the crooked nose, scrupulously correct in manner now, unlocked the dungeon door. 'You'll find all is in order, captain,' the man was saying with a sidelong glance. The Littleman said nothing, merely gesturing to swing the door open.

When Jak took the torch from its bracket and would have accompanied him down the steep steps, Peewit stayed him. 'I'll go alone, Mister Cooper, if you don't mind.'

Mindful of the guards, Cooper inclined his head. 'Of course, sir. I'll await you.' He took up a position on the top step, making it impossible for the guards to lock the door again unless he moved, which Jak had no intention of doing. This whole situation was appalling, keeping the First Watchman dungeoned like a common thug. He guessed that it had hit the captain hard to find his old comrade so roughly treated.

The guards were in a quandary, but they wisely decided against making an issue of it. They withdrew, one to either side of the door, and maintained rigid attention.

Peewit said quietly, 'Thank you, Jak.'

'Aye, sir. Try not to take it hard.'

The Littleman shook his head slightly and turned down the stairs alone. The green-slimed steps were slippery under his exhausted, shaky legs, and he put out a hand to the rough stone wall to steady himself until he stood before the studded wooden door. The grille was set too high for him to see through it, and he stopped for a moment to gather himself. He had to keep his expression under control: Kursh must not see any sign of horrified disgust. Doubtless, he would be feeling enough of that himself. The Littleman drew a breath, set his face, and put a hand to the door, which yielded before his slight push.

The dungeon was very dim, for the gray light outside the small window did not do much against the darkness, and the fire had burned down to embers. It was just enough to show the Yoriandir nodding over the tripod, the dwarf – in chains, Peewit saw to his shock – on the bench, and a scurry of rats rummaging through the remains of a loaf of bread that Imris had set in the opposite corner to bait them away from the prisoner.

Peewit had not meant for the gasp to escape him, but it did. Imris did not move, but Kursh heard it and raised his head from his drawn-up knees. He stared for a moment, and then a smile broke across his face. 'Orin!' he breathed. 'Ah, lad, I knew you'd come for me!' The Yoriandir stirred and woke, squinting at the brighter light.

The Littleman moved toward the dwarf. 'Not Orin, Kursh – you must have been dreaming. It's me.' He tried to smile.

'Don't go near him, Peewit!' The Eldest sprang from the fire and crossed quickly to the Littleman. When Peewit glanced at him, frowning, the Yoriandir repeated. 'Don't go near him. He'll attack you.'

Kursh put his feet to the floor and sat forward, tugging at his chain. Hoarsely he whispered. 'They've got me, see, they've got me. But you can get me out, Orin – you were always a clever lad. Come on, get the key – quick or they'll get you too. There's no time to waste, because they're very sly and they sneak up on you and throw a net over you when you aren't looking and then – fsst! It's out with your eye and the deuce they care that you can't see a sodding thing and the darkness all around.' He nodded, as though imparting wisdom. His voice dropped even more. Peewit stared, open-mouthed. 'But we have two eyes, boy, two eyes, and that's where we'll get them. Two eyes to see, see? And they don't know it. We can see the stars falling, even if they can't!'

Only the fact that he had not eaten for nearly a day kept Peewit's stomach from revolting, but it tumbled and turned over. He whirled blindly and, having no other outlet for his grieving anger, hurled himself at the squeaking rats. The dagger was in his hand, and he hurled it into the pack of them and then flailed with his hat and kicked and cut until the bread crumbs were scattered across the floor and the rats had fled. He swallowed and threw the dagger off the stone wall. It clattered away in the gloom.

A hand came down on his shoulder. He could see the garnet stone catching what light there was and refracting it in a wine-colored star. Past the lump in his throat, he said to the wizard, 'Nobody told me.'

'We did not know until late last night. The Elixir has become poison, so we could not give it to him. The gravediggers will have a busy day.'

Peewit gasped. 'Gerrit!'

'Is well.' The wizard did not explain how. 'Though Kursh's tough constitution is healing his body, the madness left by hearing the Pipes remains.'

Brickleburr was staring. 'Pipes? That's what I was coming to tell you – Tomasheen has them.'

Alphonse nodded. 'He was here. Dead now, of course. The queen played the Pipes.'

Peewit's exhausted eyes grew bleaker, if that was possible. 'That was the Unnamed's plan all along, wasn't it? She's corrupted her own Power.'

And I have corrupted mine, the wizard thought, but aloud he answered, 'Yes. We'll have to figure out what to do with the damned things themselves. For the moment, they're locked in Kursh's room.'

A sudden bellow filled the low chamber. 'You keep your hands off him, Rasullis, you whoreson!' Angry oaths echoed off the stone and the chains rattled as Kursh strained at his manacles.

'He thinks I am Rasullis,' Alphonse explained over the noise. 'Come, let us get out of here before he wakes the entire place.' He guided Peewit toward the stairs. 'Come, Imris,' he called. 'You can do no good here now. Keep watch beyond the door, if you must, but the Warding will be guard enough.'

'I will stay,' the Eldest said shortly. 'The grille in the door is no proof against an archer, as who should know better?' The three of them went out together.

From the dungeon came a despairing cry. 'Orin! Orin, don't leave me!'

Peewit pulled away from the young wizard and ran up the stairs, stumbling.

The Yoriandir murmured, 'Speak to him about changing the guards on the door.'

The wizard nodded and climbed slowly after the Littleman.

When he stepped through the upper door the relative light made him squint. It was a moment before he realized the guards were saluting. He looked about for Peewit and saw what had snapped the men to such rigid attention. Ariadne was staring at him. Flustered, he bowed.

'Orin?' the queen repeated, questioning.

Peewit straightened from the deep obeisance he had made her. 'His nephew, Your Majesty. Apparently, he confuses me with the boy.' The Littleman hesitated and added, 'He is quite mad, my lady.'

'Still, a strong madman for one who just yesterday supposedly lay so close to death that the chief physician spent most of the day and evening here, I am told.' The cool gray eyes swept Alphonse.

'A dwarf's native constitution is much stronger than ours, lady queen,' he replied noncommittally.

'Alas for that,' she said bitterly and drew her cloak about her shoulders. Peewit shot her a look and drew breath to protest, but the wizard gripped his shoulder and the Littleman bit his tongue. If Ariadne noticed, she did not pay any attention. Her lips tightened at the howls and cries from below. 'Shut him up. Gag him, if you must, but keep him quiet. My son is still sleeping.' Alphonse bowed, and she swung away from them in the direction of the garden gate. Over her shoulder she ordered, 'Attend me, captain. There is business we must discuss.'

The Littleman's exhaustion was apparent to all but the queen, who ordinarily would have been the first to notice. Her foster brother, Jak Cooper, frowned. 'The captain is weary, lady queen. Can't –'

But Peewit cut him off. 'Her Majesty is weary, too, and should not have to wait upon my rest.' To Ariadne he added, 'I am home now, my lady, and ready to help all that I can.'

Meara, who was attending on the queen, suggested delicately, 'I could fetch tea and a bite to the garden, my lady, if it would suit?'

The queen nodded, and the waitingwoman bowed herself away. Alphonse asked, 'May I also be part of your conference with the captain, lady queen?'

She avoided his eyes. 'No. We have no need of wizardry to plan my husband's funeral, I think.' Her voice was chill as dew. The wizard bowed his head. When the queen and the captain had gone, he went to the dungeon to gag the dwarf.

In the deep shadow of the garden where they walked, Peewit limped at a respectful pace behind. They had said nothing since leaving the dungeon door. The queen followed the buried tile walk to the birch in the middle of her garden, where the dim light was enough to show the curled leaves. She gestured to the bench. 'Sit, if you wish.'

Peewit glanced at the ash. 'I'd rather be on my feet, my lady. At least I'll know I am awake.' His attempt at a light tone failed.

The queen swept past him. 'Suit yourself,' she said and leaned a little to regard the powdered border plants, a marigold here and there sticking above the layer of ash. 'It can be washed off,' she muttered. Peewit was alarmed at the flatness of her voice and her brusque manner. Though he had expected to find the queen grieving, he had not thought her shock would take this form. A bright orange butterfly, its wings barred with iridescent emerald, fluttered around her head. She batted at it impatiently, and the Littleman caught his breath for a moment, fearing that she had hit it, but the bright wind-rider lifted to skim over the drifted yew and was gone. Peewit wanted to tell her that she should not treat Lord Aashis's messenger so, but he did not think she would appreciate the reminder at the moment.

The Littleman hesitantly cleared his throat. 'The Lordling is strengthening well, they tell me.' In fact, no one had told him anything of the sort. He was guessing from what Alphonse had said.

She shot him a withering look. 'Oh, aye. He woke before cockcrow. And do you know the first thing he said to me? "Mumma, I saw Master Kursh's ax." That was all, just that. And then he started to cry.' The queen kicked at the ash blanket over the rosemary.

Cold dread filled Peewit. 'Your Majesty . . .' He stopped, not knowing how to continue. 'Please.' The Littleman tore out the words: 'He has served so long!'

Pale stone eyes were colder than the breeze that was beginning to swirl. 'One day too long.'

Exhaustion made him heedless of ceremony. 'It was the Pipes!' Desperately he added, 'It could have happened to any of us! To me, Imris, Alphonse – even to you yourself! You know Kursh loves Gerrit!' In his anguish he had taken a step toward her.

'I know that when a plant is blighted, you tear it out and destroy it before it spreads!' she said angrily, glaring down at him.

'That's a plant! We're talking about a loyal soldier of the Crown who has fallen ill!' he fought back.

'You forget yourself, captain!'

'No, you forget yourself, my queen. What kind of healing is this, for the Greenbriar to choke out its own?'

'Enough!'

When he mentioned the healing she could no longer give her people, Peewit knew instantly that he had hit at the heart of the rage she barely controlled. He went to one knee. 'Forgive me,' he said simply. 'I am tired beyond thought.'

'That is the only reason you will not be flogged for your insolence!' she snapped, and Peewit knew that he had done just what he had fought to prevent. He had sealed the dwarf's doom.

He risked one more try. 'Please don't take my stupidity out on Kursh.'

But she cut him off. 'My lord's brother, Prince Ka-Treer, will represent his father at the funeral. He will arrive by boat from Shimarron this evening. Tomorrow morning will be the funeral. Before that, at dawn, we will witness the traitor's execution, so that my lord's killer will precede him to Ritnym's Realm.'

Peewit felt the garden swing dizzily around him. 'No,' he begged. 'Can't you see the Unnamed's hand behind this?'

'I see all my hopes blighted by one whom I trusted with my son's life. That is what I see, Master Littleman. And I will have blood for blood.'

When she turned back to the garden, Peewit choked, 'If you will kill him, at least don't make a public spectacle of it. Grant him the boon of a noble death, a private one, without the world to see.'

She would not look at him. 'His crime was public; the penalty should be the same.' After a moment, she added, 'But because he is First Watchman, I will grant the mercy you have asked. It will be done in the practice yard with only the necessary witnesses.' When he remained silent at last, the queen looked at his bent head. 'You may refuse to head the detail of the First Watch, if you wish. I am sure everyone will understand.'

She had never seen such an expression on his face. Indeed, no one in Ilyria had ever seen the wrath of a Littleman kindled. He said woodenly, 'I am the Pledged. It is my duty, and I will be there. Kursh merits one friend's company.'

There was noise at the gate into the garden, and one of the guards opened it for Meara, who carried a covered tray. Peewit rose to his feet. 'I cannot share breakfast with you. Later, when I am bathed and properly dressed, I will be back to see to arrangements.' Without waiting for her leave, he turned on his heel and stalked away past the puffing waitingwoman.

Meara set the tray down on the stone bench. She cast a look after the Littleman, then asked uncertainly, 'Shall I pour, my lady?'

'Feed it to the dogs, for all I care,' Ariadne muttered and abruptly walked away up the path that led to the terrace. Plainly Meara was not to follow.

Tears came to the woman's eyes, and she wrung her hands, looking back to the gate now closing behind the captain. Her mistress walked between the bordering rosemary and slumped down in a cloud of ash upon the bench on the terrace, facing away. Meara regarded her for a moment, then shook her head and sat down next to the tea tray to wait. After a moment, she took a pastry from the covered basket and nibbled it, just to make herself feel better. 'Seems like people have all gone daft,' she complained to the choked asters. She took another bite of nut-filled honeybread.

The idea first came to him in his coldly formal attendance on the queen while they planned the ceremony that would send the consort on his way. Through the council meeting in which, despite the captain's report that the Barreners were also prey to the Wolf, Ariadne gave the orders for the extermination of the Wolf Cult, he pondered how he might do it. By the time the hasty noontide meeting with the senior officers of the Watch was over, Peewit had made his plans.

In the quiet early afternoon, he took himself off duty and slept, while Jamison stood outside his door and would not let him be disturbed. I'll have to give the boy some protection, Peewit thought as he lay abed upon wakening. Otherwise, they'll never believe Jami didn't know.

He swung his feet over the edge of the bed and stood up, buttoning his tunic. When he pulled the door open, the orderly came to attention. 'Come in for a moment, Jami. I've some orders for you.' The young Watchman entered and Peewit motioned him to the table. 'I'll need you to do two things for me. First, there's the matter of the First Watchman's execution.' It was remarkable how steady he managed to keep his voice. 'There must be no shoddiness. I should supervise the building of the platform myself, but I must find time to meet with Alphonse and Fidelis. So I'd like you to do it for me.' Jamison nodded, reluctantly. 'If it's going to be done at all, yeoman, I want it done right.'

'But he shouldn't be killed at all, sir!' the young man burst out.

'Our queen has decided otherwise. Let us tend to our business.' When Jamison nodded once, the Littleman went on. 'Now, the second duty I have for you: when you are done supervising things in the practice yard, report to the queen's antechamber and represent me. If she needs to see me, fetch me at once. I'll be either in Fidelis's room or in Alphonse's.' That should keep the yeoman in plain view of all the courtiers and nobles who would crowd the antechamber that night.

'Very well, sir. You will be sure to have something to eat, won't you?'

The Littleman gave the ghost of a smile. 'You have taken good care of me, Master Jamison.'

The yeoman was not quite sure what the captain meant by this, but he saluted and went briskly out the door.

Peewit took a sip of the cold tea left in the cup on his table, gave the boy time to get outside, and, tucking a stump of candle inside his tunic, went to the dungeon once more.

'Orin!' the dwarf shouted. 'Come here, you little whoreson, and give me a hand with this block and tackle. I've got the damned thing all wrapped around me.' He tugged at the chains.

Imris had accompanied the Littleman into the chamber. 'I took the gag off some time ago to let him eat, though he nearly knocked my head off.' The Yoriandir laughed a little.

Peewit smiled up at him. 'You've had a long watch. Why don't you go to the kitchen and get something to eat and a sniff of fresh air? I'll stay with him awhile.'

The Yoriandir said gratefully, 'That will be welcome. I shall return shortly. Remember: don't go near him!'

Peewit waved him off and closed the door. He saw the snap of garnet and guessed that the wizard had it Warded. Better and better, he thought. Leaving the door unguarded for any length of time had bothered him, but he had had to get rid of Imris for a while. He turned to Kursh. 'Hello, old friend. Listen, do me a favor, won't you, and stay quiet for a bit while I just take a look about?'

'Orin, you are the slowest, dumbest bloody ox ever made. Get me out of here!'

Peewit walked up to him. 'Kursh, if there's anything of you left behind those eyes, I beg you to shut up!' He glared.

The dwarf shook the long gray hair out of his eye. 'Cheeky little bastard,' he muttered, and drawing up his feet, he turned his face to the wall and went silent.

By the Powers! Peewit thought and caught his breath. Maybe he knows what's going on after all! Cautiously he patted the dwarf's arm. 'Good fellow. Don't give us away now.' The dwarf remained unmoving.

The Littleman looked over his shoulder to check that no one watched through the grille, and then dug the candle from his tunic. Lighting it from the flint and iron Imris had left beside the fire, he held it out in front of him, drew his dagger as protection against the rats, and walked into the corridor that ran back under the keep. It had been long since he had been this way, but like most of his people, Peewit had a good head for direction, and he went quickly along the dank corridor. At regular intervals dungeons opened off the corridor to either side, but he passed these by. Once a torch bracket was low enough and he took down the torch, but it was old and damp and he could not light it from the candle. He made a note to himself to bring a fresh one, or better yet, a candle lantern.

He could see eyes in the darkness just outside the pale circle of light that his little candle made, and from the space between the eyes, he knew that some of the rats would make short work of almost any cat going. Maybe even of a Littleman. He shuddered and kept his knife ready.

Then, just where he remembered it, another corridor intersected at a right angle. He turned and followed it. The air was clammy, but the timbers were stout and some of them were new. The floor had been smoothed and there was sand underfoot, meant to muffle footfalls. The queen would know about this passageway, of course, but he hoped she would not think of it right away. Besides himself, the only other person who knew was Kursh. Not even Alphonse, Imris, or Fidelis guessed that the ancient escapeway for the Greenbriar monarch had been rebuilt.

In the first year of her reign, Peewit and Kursh had pressed the queen to reopen the blocked tunnel through which her mother and brother had once escaped death at the hands of her uncle, the Bastard. At the time the Barrener killed her father in battle, explosives had been set to seal the tunnel with debris, preventing the royal family's capture. With Ariadne's permission, Kursh and Peewit had supervised the removal of the rubble and the shoring up of the old passageway. However, where once it had led to the solid bulk of the hill behind Greenbriar and thence by a rocky conduit up into the forested heights, now the tunnel was blocked. It appeared to end in a stone wall, a dead end.

But that was an illusion. The mason had been a master, and the Littleman's love of puzzles had supplied the design. There was a door in the ceiling of the tunnel, and if one knew which blocks of the end wall to press, and in what order, that door would open and a stair would swing down. Ariadne had tried it once when they had spirited her down here to look at the finished job. 'Oh, Peewit, I might have known!' she had laughed when he had showed her. At the time, he had been miffed that she would

not take it seriously enough to practice it more than once. Now
he was glad of it, for she might not remember the code.

Quickly he went to the wall and unerringly pressed the coded
pattern. There was the click of a spring, the creak of a cable,
and the wooden stair swung down. For the first time since he
had left Muir Dach's camp, the Littleman smiled. He left the
stairway down and retraced his steps to the dungeon.

He got rid of the candle with not a moment to spare before the
Eldest descended the steps. 'Thank you for the relief,' the
Yoriandir said. 'Did he give you any trouble?'

'Oh, no,' the Littleman replied. 'None at all.' He bent to the
dwarf and the one eye turned to him. 'In fact we had a nice bit of
chat, didn't we?'

Kursh regarded him. 'Go take a long walk off a short pier,' he
said distinctly in his old venomous way. Then he coughed and
brought up blood. He closed his eye wearily.

Peewit straightened. 'I'll be back to see you again later,' he
told the dwarf quietly. Kursh did not reply. Peewit nodded to
Imris and ran up the steps into the courtyard.

Peewit went to his own chamber and threw a change of clothes
into a stout sack. At least he would not have to get one for Kursh,
too. The dwarf's uniform had been cut away, and then someone –
Jamison probably – had gotten him into a fresh shirt. Except for
the color of his breeches, there was nothing to identify him as an
officer of the Watch.

Into the sack went an extra cloak, a bit of rope, and the small
sack of silver that was some of the winnings he had made over
the years at dice. He had rarely needed coin before, but he
thought he might now. The tin lantern with its good candle he set
ready on the table, and also his sword in its scabbard. He would
pack his pipe and tobacco later, with a cheese, a loaf, and a
flask. These he would get from the kitchen when he took his
supper. He dug in a box under his bed. As captain, he had a key
to every lock in the castle. Finally he found the ones tagged
'dungeon.' The key that fit the door had been made to fit the
manacles as well. He put both the key and its duplicate into the
pouch at his belt so he wouldn't forget them later.

Now for Kursh's effects.

He took a look out his door. The hall was empty. He went
quickly down the corridor and around the corner to the dwarf's
room. He had no way of knowing there was supposed to be a
guard on the door, that the wizard had commanded the security.
In the wake of the queen's public sharpness with Alphonse, the
guard had done the diplomatic thing and ignored the wizard's
order. He had left the door locked, though.

This was no particular problem, except for the noise. Peewit
broke the lock with his dagger and went in. The first thing he
saw was the Pipes lying on the bed. The second was the gory ax,

thrown in the corner by the fireplace. He shut his eyes quickly and tried not to think of Ka-Salin and Gerrit. While he crossed to the trunk, he thought it was probably a good thing he had been sobered this way. Whatever rapport he thought he had established with Kursh that afternoon, his old friend was still mad enough to kill. Peewit decided maybe the manacles were a good idea, after all. But there was time to decide that later.

The trunk lock also gave to his dagger. Peewit knew this was where Kursh kept his Weatherglass. Such a precious thing should not be left behind, and it might prove useful where they were going. He lifted the heavy lid. On top of the clothing was a sealed parchment, addressed to him. Peewit picked it up curiously and walked to the window to better light. Breaking the seal, he opened the letter. A moment later his eyes began to sting and he realized what Kursh's headache, the headache he had had off and on since last spring, meant: for months, his friend had been fighting the power of the Pipes. Long ago, the Unnamed had set this trap for them all.

He drew his sleeve across his eyes. It occurred to him that if the letter had clarified things for him, it might do the same for others. One certain other, at least. She could not ignore the line about the brooch and the pommel stone. Peewit turned back to the trunk and dug through it quickly, taking the Weatherglass Kursh had given him and an extra cloak for the dwarf. He also took the dwarf's other boots, but the ruby brooch remained at the bottom, still wrapped in its soft leather protection. The letter he left right on top, open.

Next he went to the bed and stood regarding the darkly shining crystal Pipes. Even in the broad light of day, they looked menacing. He swallowed, debating. Clearly they were a threat to the queen as long as they existed. If Alphonse had been able to do anything about their power, Kursh's madness could never have harmed the Lordling, so whatever Warding the wizard had was little protection against the Pipes. On the other hand, if the Pipes were at the bottom of the sea, no one could blow them. The Littleman picked up the dark crystal Pipes and wrapped them in a shirt.

He was done. Probably no possession of Kursh's meant more to the dwarf than his ax, but Peewit would not look at it again, much less try to clean it and bring it with them. The Littleman stuffed the wrapped Pipes into his tunic, put the Weather-glass in his belt pouch, and slipped into the corridor. A moment later he was in his own room. The Weatherglass went into the sack with the Pipes. It was time to get some supper.

The sun was going down when he returned. He stuffed the cheese, bread, and bottle into the sack, added the candle lantern, then went out with Kursh's boots to perform the last task.

Taking no chances at this stage, he went still and thus was

able to go outside and make it to the postern in the north circling wall that was used for the convenience of the shepherds.

The wind had come up strongly, and he was thankful that it would cover his tracks now, but it presented certain problems. The wooden door was locked, but left unguarded in peacetime. The captain took the appropriate key and tugged it open against the ash. In the lee of the door, the ground should stay fairly clear. Quickly he swept a clean patch and made sure one of his small footprints was clearly visible in the soft earth beneath. Then he slipped both his feet into Kursh's roomy boot and jumped as hard as he could. He landed awkwardly and pitched forward to his hands and knees, but that was all right because the wind would cover over it. When he looked behind him, there was a satisfactory track. It would never pass a skilled inspection, but it might do for a hasty one. He smiled and pulled off the boot. Leaving the postern ajar and the key in the lock, he returned to his room to wait for the midwatch of the night.

The castle settled for the evening, though it had been nearly as dark as night all day. The Littleman sat smoking his pipe. He had never thought it would come to this, that the Pledged would break his kin's oath to the Greenbriar, but Ariadne had put him in a cruel position. If he remained in her service, his best friend would be killed at dawn. That would annihilate whatever Littleman glow Peewit still had within him. Break his Oath, or break himself: that was his choice. He had found it was no choice at all.

Peewit knocked out his pipe and put it in his pocket. With the sack over his shoulder, he went still and crept down the stairs. Out of the keep he went. There were two guards on duty at the dungeon door, but he had expected this. Stowing his sack in the ash drift near the wall, he flickered back into view and slogged toward the two men. 'Good evening,' he bid them.

In the whistling wind they had not heard him coming, and to them he seemed to have materialized right in front of them. They stiffened, and one tried to hide the flask. Peewit pretended not to have seen it. 'I'll take your watch,' he said.

They exchanged a glance. 'Begging your pardon, sir, but do you think that's proper?' one had the courage to ask.

'I am his friend. It's an accepted tradition.' That much they could not argue with. The condemned's next of kin or closest friend was by age-old custom allowed to watch outside the dungeon on the night before an execution. Peewit said to allay their suspicion, 'Sergeant Major Quint is coming, too, and the Eldest of Yoriand.' He let some of what he was feeling into his voice. 'Come, let us do him this honor at least, if we can give him no other.'

They saluted and handed him the iron key on its ring. 'As you will, captain.'

'Thank you.' They nodded and left. He smiled a little in the dark. Now for Imris.

He unlocked the door with the key from his pouch and clattered down the steps. Imris looked up. 'I'm your relief again,' Peewit told him.

The Eldest looked back into the fire. 'I would rather stay.'

The Littleman read his morose mood. 'Well, I'm afraid that isn't possible. The queen has sent for you,' he lied.

'For me? Why?'

Peewit could barely restrain his exasperation. 'I don't know – I didn't question her orders,' he said pointedly.

The Yoriandir rose slowly to his feet. 'You should never lie, Peewit,' he said quietly. 'You do it badly. You will try to escape with him?'

Brickleburr grinned ruefully, but added, 'It would be a great help if you would go up and sing in the antechamber. Hold them as long as you can.'

The fir eyes were relieved but somber still. 'Fare you well, my friend.' They shook hands, and suddenly Peewit could not think of even one good jest. Imris seemed to understand, for he patted him on the back and left.

The Littleman sniffed and turned to the dwarf. They had gagged Kursh again with nightfall, and Peewit was thankful for it. 'I'll be right back down. I just have to get our provisions.' He darted to the stone steps and raced up them. The sack was where he had left it. He slung it over his shoulder and was about to swing the door shut when someone he recognized as the dwarven bakeress came hurrying across the courtyard. The Littleman's heart sank, but he gave her a friendly nod. 'What brings you out so late, mistress?' he asked lightly, but as she got closer he was startled to see tears in her eyes. My word! he thought. What's this?

'I couldn't sleep,' she was explaining in a low voice. She swallowed. 'May I see him?'

'Well, it isn't allowed,' Peewit began, flustered.

She nodded as though she had expected to be rebuffed. There was a tankard in her hands, and she held it out. 'I just wanted to bring him some starflower tea. It's . . . it's good for easing the mind, and I thought . . . tonight . . .' Thyla stopped, unable to finish.

Belatedly, the Littleman realized there was something between the crusty First Watchman and this woman. He set down the sack and took the tea. 'I will give it to him.'

Her eyes went to the sack, then flew to Peewit's face. Hope came alight in her eyes, and he knew she had guessed.

After a moment, the Littleman asked, 'Would you help him?' At her eager nod, he said, 'Then take this key and lock the door after me. When you have done it, drop the key down the nearest cistern.'

Her eyes had widened, and she was shaking her head, thinking that she would be sealing them into the dungeon. He held up one hand. 'Ask me no questions – what you don't know cannot be held against you. But trust me: I have no intention of seeing Kursh die.'

Thyla shut her mouth and straightened her cap. 'Just you two be careful of yourselves.'

Peewit handed her the key. 'Think well of him. He did not mean to do what he did.'

'I never doubted that,' she said sturdily and waved him through the door. 'Go on. Time's a-wasting.'

The Littleman picked up the sack and the tea, and turned down the steps. The door was quietly shut behind him, and he heard the snick of the lock.

Quickly he picked up an empty bottle that stood by the bright fire and poured the tea carefully in. Corking it, he threw it into the sack and lit the lantern. Finally he ran to Kursh with the duplicate key. He opened the huge padlock that secured the chains to the wall ring, and the dwarf stood up. 'Now, let's get out of here!' Taking Kursh by the arm to guide him and the sack in the other hand he made for the rough passageway. As they went, he clapped the dwarf on the back. 'You never told me you had a lady, you old rogue!'

Even through the gag, the First Watchman's curses were impressive.

Chapter Eighteen

Fidelis was checking the swelling of the acrobat's broken limb when Theodric came puffing up the aisle. 'Master!' he called, and it was so unusual for him to ignore medical decorum this way that Fidelis raised his head and frowned.

'What is the problem, Theo?'

'In the yard. Quickly, please. I'll take your patient here.' The portly man was waving him out.

The chief physician straightened from leaning over the cot. 'Another case?' At the other's breathless nod, Fidelis headed for the door at a run.

When he emerged into the blowing cold of the small courtyard that fronted the two-story wing of the hospital, he recognized young Miles Spinner, who twitched uncontrollably while his wife tried to lead him to the door. Fidelis had delivered the couple's first child not long ago. Suddenly the victim let out an unearthly screech and collapsed, writhing as though he was having a seizure. The physician covered the last few steps at a run and pulled the woman away, fearing that in his flailing her young husband might hurt her. 'Don't touch him, Maire!' He knelt quickly and cradled the patient's head, getting his own hands beaten against the cobblestones in the process. To the first assistant who came running, Fidelis snapped, 'Get the posset and some bindings, quickly!'

The assistant doctor scrambled up and ran for the apothecary's workroom at the end of the wing, and two others raced for the strong canvas strips that were the only thing the physicians had found that would hold the madness victims. In the last few hours, there had already been a dozen. Fidelis bit his lip as his knuckles caught the full force of Miles's pounding head. 'How long has he been like this?'

Maire was nearly beside herself, but she tried to calm down and answer. 'It come on sudden, sir. He was fine at supper, but when I gave him the baby to dandle for a while, he fell asleep. I managed to rouse him, and he said he felt awful tired and thought he wanted to go to bed early. Climbing the ladder, he

started to twitch, and I knew we had to come up here to you.' Her
eyes were swimming. 'It's the madness, ain't it, sir?'

'I'm afraid so,' the doctor answered. She had seen enough
cases in the town to know.

Maire reached to touch her husband's hair. 'I figured it when
I seen this,' she whispered. As with all the victims, whatever
other symptoms of madness they had, the hair on Miles's head
had gone completely white in a matter of hours.

And I have no idea what dawn creeper is, Fidelis thought
tiredly. Damn!'

'Right here, my queen. You can see where the dwarf's print is
here, and this small one would be the captain's.' William Quint
rose from pointing out the tracks. Only proper chagrin was
showing on his face, but his heart was smiling.

Ariadne looked out through the open postern across the
crown of the Sweep to Gerrit's Wood. 'So. They are headed for
Yoriand, and thence, no doubt, to Covencroft. Both of them have
found refuge there before.' Quint said nothing, and she took it
for assent. But William had been forced to live the life of an
outlaw in the forest during much of the Bastard's reign, and if
there was one thing he knew, it was woodcraft. He was sure
from the tracks that they had not left this way. She turned to the
wizard. 'Your Meld will welcome them, no doubt.'

The deep wine of his cloak made a splash of color amid the
crowd of nobles attired in the black and white of mourning.
Alphonse answered quietly, 'Perhaps. I imagine Peewit is
thinking my brethren there may be able to help Kursh's
madness.'

There was a hush as people strained to hear. She rearranged
the fold of the black wimple that framed her face. 'And I suppose
you want me to believe you had nothing to do with this.'

'Madam, I did not. I spent most of the night in the library.
There is a book that Fidelis and I thought might help us learn
how to help the victims of the madness.'

'That had better be the truth, Master Wizard.'

Or what? he retorted silently.

Prince Ka-Treer was as tall as his brother had been, but
where Ka-Salin had been slim, Ka-Treer was broader in the
shoulders and thicker through the forearms. Alphonse could
guess even without his reputation that the man would be a
swordmaster. His hair was as black as Ka-Salin's, however, and
the eyes the blued metal of stirrup iron. The black velvet doublet
and heavy wool cloak he wore were threaded with gold, for he
was next King of Shimarron. He said brusquely, 'So they are
afoot. Send your Riders after them, lady.'

The queen looked off to Gerrit's Wood again. Mindful of the
curious crowd, she murmured, 'And how would Riders, or any-

one else for that matter, find a Littleman, my lord, if he chose not to be seen?'

Ka-Treer flushed.

Alphonse held his breath. Now she would command him to find Peewit and Kursh through his Warding. He had his excuse prepared. Ariadne's woodsmoke eyes met his, and the wizard knew that he was lost.

The queen said, 'No, there is no way to find them now. Let Covencroft receive them if it will. But hear my judgment: Riders will indeed be dispatched this forenoon to all our borders and coastal patrols, and if either of our former Watchmen is ever seen again in Ilyria, his life shall be forfeit.'

Ka-Treer stared at Alphonse. 'Then you will have no objection, my lady, if the Shimarrat Crown takes vengeance for my beloved brother.'

'You will do as you must, my lord.' She gathered her skirts. 'For now, let us think no more on it. Other, more important concerns must occupy us.' She signed to her pages, who led the way to the hall of mourning.

Ka-Treer held the wizard's eyes a moment more. Then he took the queen's hand on his arm and escorted her away. Alphonse had not been invited to join the royal train. He waited for Fidelis and Imris and attended the ceremony with them.

All the while, the memory of that woodsmoke glance thrummed in his mind.

It was as well that the weather had been dry, Peewit thought, because with any more water the bog would have been treacherous indeed. As it was, only his Littleman sense of the land had kept them out of trouble so far. He looked back to Kursh. 'Watch it! Step only on that ferny-looking thing there – the rest of it's muck.'

The dwarf whispered hoarsely, 'Don't be telling me what to do. I was hunting Barreners before you were born.' He muttered something further that Peewit didn't catch, and the Littleman sighed, though he was glad that at least Kursh seemed to grasp that he must not shout.

They had made their way to the secret stair with no trouble, and Peewit had drawn it up after them to seal the passageway once more. The upper escape tunnel had still been in sound repair, and they had come to the exit on the south side of the Sweep below a line of trees while Alphonse was still poring over the books of the Painter and Ariadne rocked her son to sleep.

The bog had been much nearer to that escape hatch than Peewit had remembered, but he put this down to faulty recollection and led the dwarf through the tussocks and pools unerringly, turning back only once to look at the far lights of Greenbriar.

Now they were not far from the Hurdles, if the Littleman
guessed correctly. The swift-flowing section of the Willowsrill
was about ten miles south of the castle, and there was a bridge
across to the east bank. Peewit reasoned that if everyone was
searching for you to the north, there was some sense in heading
in another direction. Besides, tomorrow or the next day, he had
to have the dwarf on the east side of the river, on the road
coming down from Waysmeet. The bridge was the sticking point.
No doubt it would be guarded, and no doubt they would be looking for him and the dwarf. They would not see them, of course,
but they might hear them. Kursh's manacles clanked.

His feet knew the ground was rising before his head did.
Shortly they were standing on the low bluffs overlooking the
bend in the river where Willowsrill entered a narrower channel
and went hurtling through the gorge. The dwarf and the Littleman stood under the low trees and looked down on the guardhouse and the bridge. One of the keepers was staring from
the wooden span into the water, and the other whittled at the
bonfire on the bank. If they were supposed to be on alert for
escaping prisoners, they did not look it. For once, Peewit was
glad to find a dereliction of duty. He clapped Kursh on the shoulder. 'We'll rest here and have something to eat. Powers, it's
cold! How would you feel about some starflower tea?'

Fidelis straightened on his stool and flexed his neck. He was
cramped with hunching over the antique manuscript. 'Here's a
little more.'

Alphonse looked up. He had been deep in an account of the
slaughter of innocents by the power of the Wild Fire. 'What?'

The doctor turned the book toward him, pointing to a passage.
The wizard translated aloud, ' "This siege hath sore stretched
oure supplyes. Meat hath run out, and there be little enough
meal to make bread. Of fresh water, tho, we have plentie
thankes to the One We Nameth Not and his cursed rayn. Quite
by accident we discovered that the flower of dawn creeper
maketh a right good tea, calming to the mindes even of those He
hath driven madde. This was the first remedye we found to have
any effect at alle. Oure healers feed it to the afflicted as often as
the madmen will take it, and those of us who have stille the use of
oure wits drinke it allso. It is beneficial, seemingly preventying
any more of us from falling under the Pypes spelle." ' He looked
up from the page. 'This comes earlier in the book than the part
you were reading before we went out to dig up the Pipes?' Fidelis
nodded, and the wizard frowned. 'It still tells us next to nothing.'

'True, but let us consider the clues we have. First, it is a
flowering vine, hence the name creeper. Second, it is quite likely
that it only blooms in the early morning, else why call it dawn
creeper?'

Alphonse added, 'And it is a plant one would not ordinarily consider for making tea.'

'I would hazard a guess that it is a bog plant. Even in Beod's day, the land to the south of the Sweep must have been fairly marshy, cupped all around by the hills as it is. We know that is where Aengus and Beod and the rest were besieged, so the plant must have been near at hand.'

Hope stirred for an instant in the blue eyes, but then he glanced toward the shuttered window. 'Even if it is still out there, Fidelis, we'll never find it now. It will be covered with ash, and there is no sun to make it bloom at dawn or any other time.'

The doctor stood and caught himself on the edge of the table, for he was exhausted. 'Still, we must look for it. Hourly we have more patients. More and more people are hearing the Pipes, Alphonse. So far, none have been murderous, but it is only a matter of time. And . . .' He looked down at the book. 'There is a lung flux breaking out. I fear it is connected with the fumes.' His weary face made the wizard lean to grasp his arm. 'Gerrit has it.'

'Powers!'

'I was hoping this dawn creeper may have some effect on the malady. Otherwise . . .'

Alphonse was already on his feet. 'I'll get my boots.'

When they came in late in the afternoon, Fidelis and his assistants made straight for the hospital to try out the drooping flowers of a vine that had been buried in the ash. The wizard went to his room to strip off his muddy boots, and decided to establish a Warding to contact Chiswic. Surely one of the herb masters on Covencroft must know what dawn creeper is, he thought, and though I am abhorrent to them now, they could not refuse to help the needy.

Patience tried to calm his trepidation. 'Say hello for me,' she thought. She liked to watch him work, especially the times when he lost himself in the Warding and floated off the floor a little. It was funny to see him hit with a thud when the Ward was released. There would be little fun today, she thought to herself. By the look of him, the wizard was dreading this.

In the dark room, the wizard sat himself on the floor, palms on knees, spine straight but relaxed. This posture was the most useful for him, though others of the Meld could attain the necessary detachment standing in the middle of a crowd. He had wondered sometimes if it was harder for him to enter the Warding state because he was attuned to all three modes of the Song at once. He always had to choose which entryway into the Song he was going to use, and that made his process somewhat longer than anyone else's.

For the present moment, however, his resolution was firm; he would use only one Warding, the simplest: the Earth. He let himself down quickly into trance and reached for his power. His first image, probably because he had been thinking of them so much, was of Peewit and Kursh. Alphonse got an impression of rushing water and a bridge. The Littleman and the dwarf were dozing under a tree. The bridge looked like the one at the Hurdles. The wizard smiled a little: so they had headed south! His Warding glanced off them and he redirected it north toward Covencroft.

There was a rumble of thunder. Patience cocked an ear at it and her whiskers twitched.

Alphonse went deeper into the Song, casting his Warding now over the Rimwall above Yoriand, now over Aspenglade where Nilarion reached for the rolling sky with hands of red leaves. Then, casting over the strait to the home island of the wizards, he perceived too late the net that Tydranth had spread for him: the island was encircled with a Warding web dark as the darkest night and burning like pitch.

Reflexively Alphonse tried to withdraw, but his Warding had already touched the Unnamed's. There was an explosion in his mind of jet-and-wine-colored energy and he was blown somewhere where there was no Song and there were no stars and only the ether streamed by his benumbed mind.

Patience sprang for the floor when the lightning bolt shot its blue finger through the shutters. When the awful bright light had gone, she rolled on the stone floor, trying to quench the burning fur along her side, but her overriding concern was for the wizard. He had fallen backward, and she jumped on his chest to peer intently into his still face. He was smoldering – she could feel it beneath her paws. Panicky, the Queen of Cats knew this was beyond her power to help. She yowled with fear and pain and leaped for the door, which stood slightly ajar. She needed the one who smelled of peat and nice herbs.

The black-and-white cat streaked down the hall, past the guards, who were still holding their ears and expecting another blast. Her nose led her toward the herbs she had smelled on Fidelis. Straight to the hospital door she went. When she found the doctor, she jumped up into his arms and put a claw into the front of his tunic urgently.

This human was much quicker than the others. He stroked around the burn on her side softly, then whirled and caught up his bag from the table. He snapped something to the orderlies as he went by them, then they were all pounding across the courtyard and up the stairways toward the room she shared with the wizard.

In this extremity, she did not hold it against the peat-and-herb man that he dumped her to the floor when he barged through the door. A sound came out of him, and he knelt, touching her wizard carefully. One of his hands came out, pointing to the water bucket. An assistant handed it to him, and he dashed it over the wizard. Patience sank down and treated her own burn to the cooling puddle. Possibly she fell asleep then.

There was a tapping somewhere. No, it was water dripping. Very nice, very soothing. Drip. Drip. Plink. Must have hit something. No, idiot, that was a bottle being set down. Shake yourself, wizard. Something important has happened. Wake up.

He opened one eye; it was much more difficult than he had expected. There was welcoming firelight. A shadow moved somewhere above.

'How do you feel?'

Alphonse considered and finally said, 'I feel fine,' It took him a moment to recognize the croak as his own.

'Good,' Fidelis approved. 'Give it a little while to work better. Do you remember what happened?'

The wizard licked his lips; there was a bitter taste of herbs on them. He sighed, his head feeling as if it were full of wool. What happened? he thought. I was . . . in my room. I sat down to . . . yes, and there were Peewit and Kursh by the river. Yoriand and Earth Pillar. I wanted to talk to Chis . . . Oh! He recoiled when he touched the raw place in his mind.

Fidelis's hand came down on his arm. 'It's all right. It's all over. Relax now.'

'I ran into his Warding, Fidelis.'

The doctor corrected gently, 'You were hit by lightning.'

Alphonse shook his head and discovered that sensation was returning. He caught his breath at the pain.

'I know,' Fidelis told him. 'There will be some after-shock for a few hours. Try not to move.'

The wizard swallowed and tried again to grasp the tail of the thought that skittered around the corner of his mind. 'It feels as if my head were empty or something.'

That grunt must have been a laugh. 'I don't wonder! That happens to some victims of such an experience. Usually the shock to the mind heals with time. Don't push too quickly for complete memory.'

A spark of irritation flared in him. 'No, you are not understanding me. I do remember: I ran into the Unnamed's Warding. I was trying to contact Chiswic, and the Wild Fire had the island blocked from me. Before I knew it, his Warding . . .' He winced.

'Ah. Well, you may be gratified to learn that the Unnamed made a special point not to leave out your body when he blasted your mind. I don't know as we've ever had a lightning strike inside the castle before.'

'Was . . . anyone else hurt?'

'No. The Unnamed has good aim, give him that.'

Alphonse gave him a look.

Fidelis grinned and leaned to say, 'She's fine. Gerrit, too.'

Alphonse nodded and closed his eyes. 'I am not fine – thank you for asking.'

Startled, he turned his head on the pillow, which rustled with herbs. One green eye in a black-and white face was at his shoulder. 'I forgot you were there!'

The doctor reached across him to rub Patience's ears. 'If she hadn't come to fetch me instantly, I don't know that we could have helped you.'

'If he had been as dull as most humans you would have been gone,' she returned the compliment.

A faint smile crossed the wizard's face, and he fell asleep without remembering that he had to warn his brethren on Covencroft about the Unnamed's net of Wild Fire.

Peewit finished wrapping strips of shirt around the chain linking Kursh's manacles. He gave it an experimental shake. There was a little noise, but it would be lost in the sound of the rushing water. 'All right. Now, one more time: remember that we have to stay together. If you pull away from me, they'll be able to see you. Got it?'

Kursh made no reply, and the Littleman bit his lip. There was no way of telling what, if anything, the dwarf understood. If he said anything when they were nearer the guards – anything – the game would be up. Peewit would have liked to hitch up the gag again, but Kursh had pulled sharply away when he had tried it, and the glare he had given the Littleman made Peewit decide he would lose whatever rapport he had managed to establish. He got to his feet and beckoned. 'Let's go.' With the dwarf beside him, he picked a way down the steepish bluffs.

They crept through the scrub, and just before they stepped onto the cart road that ran beside the river, Peewit took Kursh's arm and they went still. 'Quiet, now,' Peewit reminded him in a whisper. He led the dwarf down the middle of the road. When a sudden flare showed near the door of the guardhouse, the Littleman halted, his heart jumping, but it proved to be just the draw of the fellow's pipe. With Kursh in tow, the Littleman walked quietly past him onto the span.

The rushing water showed as white streaks between the timbers of the railings, and Peewit was careful not to let Kursh get too close to the sides for fear he might suddenly take a notion to jump. He peered ahead to the other landing, but there was no sign of the second guard. He must be asleep in the guardhouse.

They were nearly to the other side when the dwarf tripped on a loose plank and pulled up sharply. Peewit managed to keep his hold of Kursh's arm, but the manacles scraped along the bridge loudly enough to be heard above the roaring torrent.

The guard clapped a hand to his sword. 'Halt! Who goes there?' He was staring right at them, but the Littleman knew he could not see them. In the next split second he was reaching to clap a hand over the dwarf's mouth, but it was already too late.

Kursh bristled. 'The Queen's Watch goes here! Guard yourself, Barrener!' He flung Peewit aside like a terrier shaking off a rat and charged for the guard. The stillness spell was broken.

With the two apparitions appearing suddenly before him, the guard was momentarily dumbfounded. Before he even had his sword out, Kursh was on him. The dwarf swung his joined fists and the bridge sentry dropped to the planks. The Littleman had scrambled up and now seized the dwarf's arm. 'Come on, will you?' He tugged the First Watchman away. But before he could make them both still again, the other guard came running from the woods on the east side of the river and dropped the load of firewood to whip out his sword. The Waysmeet end of the bridge was held against them.

Peewit drew his own sword and jumped in front of Kursh. Surprise dawned in the guard's face. 'It's you!' His mouth firmed into a line. Plainly there had been a Rider this way while they were sleeping this afternoon, the Littleman realized.

'Just let us by and we'll cause you no trouble,' the captain said, though he knew it was useless.

The guard did not even bother to reply. He attacked, sword at the ready.

Peewit parried, and there was a flurry of sparks as metal met metal. Because of his size the Littleman could not close with the human to grapple, so he sprang sideways. The guard met his counterblow with his own parry. Peewit deliberately let the blade skitter down along his own until it nearly touched him, and at the last second went still and disengaged.

Caught off-balance by an enemy he could no longer see, the sentry faltered, and the Littleman whipped the flat of his blade across the fellow's knuckles. With an oath the guard dropped his sword and clutched his hand to his stomach. But some sixth sense or perhaps pure chance made him suddenly lash out with one foot, and he caught Peewit right on the knee.

The Littleman collapsed and rolled in a ball, grasping the wounded leg. The pain drove everything else from his mind, and he flickered back into view. The guard saw him, grabbed up his sword, and lunged.

Kursh dropped the chain of his manacles over the man's head from behind and pulled. Grasping for his throat, the kicking guard fought madly, but, even still convalescent, the dwarf was much too strong for him. Kursh dragged him to the side of the bridge and put his shoulder into the guard's back to pinion him against the railing. 'No, Kursh, don't!' Peewit yelled. When the man slumped, the dwarf unlooped the chain, lifted him easily over the rail, and threw him into the rapids.

Peewit had risen on an elbow, one hand stretched out to Kursh as though to prevent him from doing it. When the dwarf turned around, he clenched and unclenched his hands, and the Littleman had a bad moment wondering whether the dwarf would now come for him. But Kursh ignored him, gave a clap of his hands, and began to dance a sailor's jig. The bridge timbers thumped and shook while the Littleman stared. Kursh looked over his shoulder for a moment. 'Makes a good dancing floor, this,' he remarked. He threw back his head and laughed.

Listening to that bullroarer voice shout above the rapids, Peewit lay back and put his hand to his eyes, wishing desperately that he could go home, and not just to Greenbriar.

Old Chiswic was tired, and because of it he was not sure that he had read the passage correctly until he read it a second time. The ancient vellum flaked under his fingers as he smoothed the page and pulled the lamp closer. His was the only light in the scriptorium except for the distant flickers of lightning. The only sound to break the utter quiet was the even breathing of Bremen, who slept in a chair by the door, waiting for his master to be done. The stout building was the best on Covencroft and had withstood the meteor's shock wave well, except for the windows. Planks now covered the holes.

The book Chiswic had pulled from the shelves was a miscellany of odd pages of manuscripts now lost. These had been bound together to protect them, but it had been long since anyone had opened the collection. He had discovered the book some years ago and took it down to look at every once in a while when he was sleepless. The short fragments were a good length for the elderly wizard: short enough to finish in a sitting, and intriguing because they were pieces of puzzles he could only guess at.

Tonight, however, he had come to the book deliberately looking for something that had jogged his memory. He had seen Aengus's name once while he was leafing through the pages for something else, he was sure. Now, in the small hours of the morning, he had found it.

By the Three! he thought. How could all our lore over the ages have missed this? Can the early members of the Meld have been so jealous of the Painter that they deliberately suppressed it? And where is the rest of the manuscript this fragment came from? There would be a book worth reading!

In his excitement he said aloud, 'Alphonse, I have the most astonishing news for you, my lad.' From Bremen in his chair there came a murmur and a sigh, but the boy did not awaken.

Chiswic pulled up short. How could he be thinking to aid

Alphonse, fallen as he was? The master debated for a few
moments with himself, then made the decision his heart had
been urging all day: he could not give up on Alphonse. There was
no evil in the boy.

The elderly wizard debated sending his adept to fetch Hrontin
to help him with the energy drain, but then decided that he could
manage it on his own, since the news had put such heart into
him. Besides, he smiled to himself, he'd like to pay Freckles back
by entering one of his dreams. He set the lamp before him and
stared into the steady flame, centering his mind. Then with the
practiced ease of long years, he listened for his own Earth notes
of the Song and began to weave a Warding that would carry his
thought to his protégé. Because Chiswic's power came from
Ritnym, the Lady of Earth, his bit of the great Song was
unaffected by the Unnamed's interference in Aashis's Realm,
and he was soon smelling the damp breeze off Willowsrill and
the sharp tang of ash. He followed the river southward. There
was a smell of burning, and he glimpsed a darkened city with a
ring of lanterns posted about a charred building. He knew by the
size of the place that it must be Castlenigh. Chiswic cast a little,
and his thought carried him up the Sweep until he knew from the
sharp smoke of a smithy and the rich gravy smell of a kitchen
that he had found the castle. He centered on the pungent aroma
of Lipopo cheese and found Alphonse.

This was not a pleasant dream at all – all gore and flashing
axes and voices in the dark screaming for help – and Chiswic
knew if he did not get into the redhead's mind quickly, Alphonse
would wake himself up from the nightmare. Very quietly he said,
'I should think you might like to think about something else for a
while.'

Alphonse groaned, both in his dream and in his physical self,
and murmured, 'I would if I could.' His mental voice got
stronger. 'Master! You shouldn't be here!'

The old man let an amused and affectionate thought float back
so that the younger wizard could read it. 'Then you wouldn't
hear what I've found out about your friend Aengus. Still ready to
send me back to my bed?' he asked, for he guessed that Alphonse
would be readying a counter Ward. 'I'm not there, by the way, so
please don't try it. It would completely undo little Bremen if he
found me here in the morning staring blankly off into space and
he couldn't find my mind anywhere about.'

The young wizard chuckled his relief. 'As you wish. But don't
tire yourself. What's the news?'

But Chiswic had discovered Fidelis's presence in the room
and the sharp smell of unguent. 'What's this? Have you hurt
yourself?'

Fear shot through Alphonse's mind, and Chiswic winced at
the strength of it. The redhead was suddenly scrabbling about

for something he could not seem to remember. 'Yes, there was something I was supposed to tell you.'

'Calm yourself,' the old wizard said in alarm. 'It will come back, surely.'

'No, but it's important!'

'If you're going to wake yourself up, at least have the sense to listen to me first!' Chiswic relaxed a little as Alphonse's frightened thoughts settled. 'There. Now. I have been reading in a very old book tonight, and here's a bit of information for you: Aengus apparently made your Ariadne's Crystal of Healing.'

'What? But the Roll of Kings says a Yoriandir smith fashioned it after Ritnym had given her seeds to be the heart of it!'

'Yes, well, I think you can blame jealousy for the Yoriandir-smith part of that story. At any rate, the lore that we have believed and taught all these years is regrettably in error. Aengus made the Crystal. Also, Ritnym was not the only one of the Powers who gave a gift to be part of the Greenbriar legacy – oh, my, that was a close one!'

'Chiswic, what's happening? I lost you for a moment.'

'Oh, sorry. It is just a storm. I was distracted by the lightning.'

The elderly wizard cried aloud at the surge of terror that swept over his protégé. Alphonse was screaming. 'Break the Warding! Break –!'

In the next instant, the roof of the scriptorium was shattered by a bolt of lightning and Chiswic snapped his connection just in time to keep the Wild Fire from reaching Alphonse.

The young wizard shot upright in his bed at Greenbriar, screaming his master's name, and certain he had seen one white hand lift in farewell, though of course that was impossible.

Fidelis's strong hands caught his shoulders. 'Alphonse, wake up! It was just a dream! Easy now!'

The door flew open and the queen was there, a stuffed toy horse in her hand. Plainly she had been checking on Gerrit.

The wizard resisted the doctor's attempts to ease him back to the pillows. 'No! The Unnamed struck him with lightning, just like me!' He was panting, and his voice was caught between a sob and a shout. 'He killed him!' He seemed suddenly to focus on the queen in the doorway. 'If you hadn't let the Unnamed loose by blowing the damned Pipes, Chiswic would be alive!' Rage quickened in him, and the effort of fighting the three Wardings back snapped his control. 'Damn you, Ariadne, you've killed us all!'

There was stunned silence. Fidelis pushed Alphonse back into the pillows and grasped his shoulder warningly, but he did not try to draw the sting by apologizing for his patient. In his heart, he agreed with the wizard.

The queen's thought went to the gentle old man who had

helped her to her throne, and this gall spilled over, mixing with all the griefs of the past days. For a moment, her frozen mask crumpled and terror and unbearable sorrow showed through, but then her chin came up. 'Give him a strong posset, Fidelis. He obviously needs to sleep.'

The chamber door closed behind her. Later, after the wizard had let the drugged potion take him, the doctor stirred up the fire and discovered the toy horse on the floor where she had dropped it. Fidelis slowly bent to pick it up and set it carefully on the mantel.

Chapter Nineteen

There was a rapping at the door. Fidelis roused with an oath and jumped to open it before the wizard was wakened. When he swung it open, William Quint stood there, breathing heavily. 'She's gone!' the big man blurted.

Alphonse struggled up in the pillows. 'What?'

Quint found himself pulled inside by the doctor, and the door shut. 'Never mind that, doctor – the whole castle knows by now. The queen is missing!' Alphonse was already fumbling with his robe. 'Meara thought she was in the Lordling's room attended by Cele, and Cele thought she was in the royal apartment. She was last seen by the Watch outside your door, sir.'

The doctor and the wizard exchanged a glance. Fidelis said, 'She left hours ago, Will.'

The wizard's eyes were closed as he clutched his boots. He broke the Warding. 'Call off your men, sergeant major. The queen is not in the castle.'

Quint's mustache bristled. 'She couldn't have been abducted. There have been guards –'

Alphonse grasped his arm as he went past. 'No. Not abducted. I will bring her back. If you would do something useful, send search parties down the river. Folk must be given something to talk about.'

'Are you sure you know what you're doing?' Quint demanded.

'I know she has come to no harm.' He pulled open the door and strode down the corridor through the buzzing people.

Fidelis said quietly, 'I am sure we may trust him, Will. Search the river.'

The Fire effectively kept the rats at bay, but the damp of the dungeon passageways still beaded the shoulders of his cloak. Ariadne had passed this way, he knew, and he could also tell from his Warding that there was an opening above him, but he could not open the trap door by his power, because it was not a thing of magic, only a mechanism.

Alphonse peered at the wall, wondering whether he was

supposed to twist something, or if there was a hidden trigger. Engraved on the squared stones were nine different designs. He could make out what seemed to be a wavy line with a tree; a spire of rock that may have indicated the Guardian; a Rose; two circles, one larger, one smaller; a sword; a bottle or urn; the sun; a horse. It would have to be something so obvious that she could remember it even in a panic, because obviously this tunnel was built as an escape. Quickly he pressed the symbols exactly in the order that they were engraved on the wall. Nothing. He reversed the order, working from the bottom row up. Nothing. Down the rows. Nothing.

'All right,' he grumbled. He stepped back to see the symbols better, pulling at his beard, and went silent for some moments.

An idea suddenly occurred to him. Stepping to the wall, he pressed the larger circle, the smaller circle, the Rose, and the bottle.

The stairway swung down on its cable.

In the crystal is the seed, which makes the Rose, which makes the Elixir, he thought. A sequence no Greenbriar monarch could ever forget. This has Peewit's mark all over it. She must have known all along that Kursh had been taken this way.

At length he emerged behind the trees that screened the escape hatch from the battlements, though in the blowing dimness, it was doubtful that any sentry could have seen him. An upward path was just visible in the scruff, and the wizard ran after the queen.

A little over an hour later, after leaving First Falls behind, Alphonse caught up with her. Before them was a stretch of open ground with huge boulders strewn like a wall. The dark finger of the Guardian, a massive outcropping which stood like a sentinel above the Willowsrill Valley, loomed in the ashy mist to their right. If there had been daylight, they could have seen down to the sea.

The queen turned at the sound of his scrambling footsteps, fear flashing across her face. She had obviously been listening all the while for the Wolf. When she saw it was only Alphonse, the fear vanished and was replaced by anger. 'I did not ask for your company.'

'No, you just threw the whole bloody place down there into a panic and expected us not to look for you. You haven't even a cloak!' He swung off his own and threw it around her shoulders.

In spite of herself, Ariadne drew it close with her frozen hands.

'My lady queen, what are you doing here?'

She regarded him for a moment, weighing whether to tell him. 'I am going to Ritnym's Realm.'

His lips parted. 'Surely you can't ...' He swallowed and flushed. 'Look, I am sorry for what I said last night. I didn't mean it.'

The gray eyes were steady. 'Yes, you did. And you were right. I did exactly what the Unnamed wanted me to do.'

Words tore free. 'I did, too. Oh, Ariadne, I've become something horrid. I am Abomination,' he said miserably.

'I know. I saw, when you healed Gerrit. His fate was to die, like all the others, but you brought him back.' She looked down. 'I think that is not so horrid as you believe. Surely the Powers cannot begrudge that you used your power for such a purpose.'

He shivered in the wind. 'I don't know, and I am afraid to find out.'

The queen looked up then. 'You need not come with me into the Guardian. In fact, I don't want you to.'

Regarding the ash powdering her hair, Alphonse reached to brush it off and said, 'Well, in fact, I intend to. It's too bloody cold to stay out here.'

She did not quite smile, but she put her hand on his arm and they went across the broken ground together.

Unhesitatingly, the queen stepped under the curved arch into the tunnel, which was a pitch and living dark. Alphonse felt ancient wardings brush his mind. 'Do you want a light?' he whispered.

'No. There are torches, remember?' On her words, the first of the Warded lights flared silver in the darkness, apparently triggered by her presence. As she walked ahead of the wizard, the torches lit one by one to show the way. He saw her tug at the cloak, and guessed she might be as nervous as he was. One rarely toyed with a Power.

Shortly they came to a corner in the tunnel. Alphonse remembered it: he could still see Peewit wriggling around it on his stomach, uncertain of what they would find and half expecting to die on the spot. Now the wizard followed the queen around the turn. There before them were the doors of the chamber where they had found her brother Gerrit's shade waiting to conduct them to Ritnym's Realm. The door was heavy wood, with columns on either side carved with the Greenbriar motif. Ariadne set her hand to the large iron ring to pull it open, but Alphonse touched her shoulder. 'Are you certain you want to do this?'

Her chin came up. 'Very certain,' she said grimly. 'I want Ritnym to tell me why she has allowed him to break my Crystal and turn it to evil poison.' Alphonse knew she was angry. Not the best frame of mind in which to approach a Power.

'Be careful what you say, Ariadne. You are not dealing with another mortal queen here.' She gave him a look that convinced him further cautions would be useless. 'At least let me open the door, then. Stand back, just in case.'

Ariadne pushed by him. 'It was made for my forefathers, Alphonse. The Warding cannot hurt the Greenbriar.' Before he had time to do more than hope she was right, the queen swung the door open and stepped through.

She paused. Alphonse stood stock-still. Here was no royal bed-chamber where they had found a little boy asleep in the great bed. The Guardian that had been prepared for this Greenbriar monarch was far different, subtly suited to her. The walls were whitewashed stone, the floor of beaten earth. A small window was shuttered on the far wall, with a spinning wheel set ready under it, fluffy wool already on the spindle. The hearth was open, and a peat fire there made a kettle sing. Looking about, Alphonse shivered to think that his cottage in the firerockets the other night had been a vision; this was the same place. 'Ritnym knows you surpassing well,' he whispered.

The queen advanced a little into the snug room, pausing to touch the dyed yarns in the basket by the spinning wheel.

Her eyes traveled to the kettle, and she saw two cups set ready and a new loaf for the slicing. Comfort was offered here, and rest from a heavy burden of fate. Her shoulders squared. 'She may think she does,' Ariadne said. 'But I have come for an explanation, not to play at being goodwife.' There was bitter resolve in her voice, and the atmosphere of the room was jarred visibly.

At first Alphonse thought that the weakness from the lightning must have crept up on him, but then he perceived that the gentle peat light was indeed flickering. In another heartbeat the walls of the cottage disappeared and they stood on the same bank of a river in a cavern where a barge had come to take them across the echoing water to the kingdom of the dead. The wizard found himself afraid, and he was not ashamed of it. This wasn't my idea, Lady, he silently told the Power of Earth.

Rippling water lapped at the wooden landing on which they stood. Alphonse cleared his throat but said nothing, waiting as Ariadne did for the barge to come for them. He listened out over the water but heard nothing, and try as he might he could extend his light no farther than halfway across.

The queen's voice broke the silence. 'Sal?'

Alphonse looked around quickly, but saw no one. 'Where?'

Ariadne shook her head helplessly. 'I thought she might send him as our guide.' She was fighting tears, and he realized belatedly that this journey had been as much to say goodbye as to seek Ritnym. He put an arm about her shoulders, searching for something to say, and then wisely decided there really was nothing except to hold her.

But the queen veered again into anger. She pushed herself away from his supporting arm and stood on the edge of the landing. 'Lady of Earth!' she shouted. The wizard wondered if the shock of it was in his ears alone. Ariadne groped in the purse at her waist and extracted a small cloth-of-gold sack. The fragments of the Crystal of Healing had been collected from the Sweep and from her hand. Meara had dumped out one of her rings and put them all carefully in the pouch, together with the Greenbriar seeds. Now she held it up. 'My Crystal is broken, Lady, and you must help us!'

From across the water there was no answer.

'Come on, help me if you want me to fight the Unnamed! I cannot do it alone!

This was dangerous. Alphonse found that he was holding his breath. He moved up beside her to touch her elbow. 'She might take it better if you asked politely,' he murmured.

She turned desperate eyes on him. 'I cannot beg for something we are entitled to! How shall we survive, if the Immortals will not help us?'

To that, he had no answer at all, because it was true.

Alphonse held out his hand. 'Give me the Crystal, then,' he said. When she frowned, he nodded at the still water. 'I'll try to swim it.'

She backed a step, clutching the cloth-of-gold bag. They both knew if he reached Ritnym's Realm he would not do so alive. As the implications of what he was offering to do sank in, Ariadne shook her head. 'Oh, no. I will not lose you, too, ' she whispered so that he barely heard.

'Look, we'll never know if I don't try, will we? I don't think the Lady will blast me – that's her brother's tactic.' The wizard tried to smile, but it was no success. He sat to pull off his boots. 'She wouldn't have let us get this far if she didn't want us here, after all.'

'But she would have sent a barge if she had wanted us to reach the other side,' the queen pointed out.

Alphonse pitched his boots behind him onto the landing. 'Maybe she just wants proof of how serious we are about needing help.' His face was grave but set, and he cast aside his belt.

The queen was saying, 'I know Gerrit has the lung flux. I would dare it to save my son, but I cannot swim.'

The apologetic fear in her voice made him swing around and catch her in his arms. Prompted by the dark water, he bent his lips to touch hers. She was startled and pulled away, but only slightly. After a moment, the wizard straightened. There was much he wanted to say, but between embarrassment and fear of what she must think of him, he suddenly snatched the Crystal and dove into the water.

As the dark river closed over his head and the cold struck at him, he knew that he had been wrong – so wrong – about the Lady's not blasting him. His heart fluttered and went still.

On the landing, Ariadne was still reaching out to where he had been. She opened her mouth, ready to call him back when he surfaced.

But the wizard did not come up. 'Alphonse?' she searched the water frantically. 'Alphonse!' There was no sign of his ginger hair. She screamed a wild and wordless protest and made to cast herself headlong into the lapping water. Then she saw him bobbing at the farther end of the landing. Crossing the boards in two steps, she threw herself down on the edge and reached down to grasp his hair and pull his face out of the water. He was deadly cold to the touch, and his skin was blue.

Ariadne got her hands under his frozen arms and hurled herself backward, trying to pull him from the water, but he was too heavy and slipped from her grasp. 'Damn you,' she hissed at the Lady. 'Give him back to me, at least!' At the moment she began to pull again, there came a slightly higher wave which lifted Alphonse nearly to the level of the landing. The queen hauled back as though heaving a net to land, and this time she was able to pull him to safety.

Desperately she searched for some sign of life, but her trembling fingers found no pulse in his throat, and under her palm there was no lifebeat. With a moan, she flung herself on his clenched right hand, prying it open to get at the Crystal in its pouch, but when she got his stiff fingers open, the pouch was gone. The wizard must have dropped it. Ariadne shrieked, 'Don't you do this to me!' She did not know whether she hurled this at the still man under her hands or at the Lady who had given, and now taken back, her Greenbriar power. 'Live!' she shrieked.

From somewhere, there came a sardonic laugh, and she knew that it was not the Lady who had done this, but Her brother: the Unnamed must control the river now. Anger flared. 'You!' she breathed. 'You.' The cavern narrowed in her vision until all she could see was the wizard's still face, no forget-me-not blue eyes sparkling with fun, no fiery red hair catching the sunlight, no lips . . .

'No,' she told the Unnamed. 'You will not have him!' Ariadne reached in her mind for the feeling of the Crystal in her hand and closed her fist about it. There was a smell of springtime flowers. The Greenbriar Queen saw her hand – the one holding the Crystal that was only a dream – come alive with a light that shone like an alabaster lamp. 'Live,' she told Alphonse again, but this time it was a quiet command.

His heart gave a bound, and he drew a ragged gasp. The light of her hand faded to a glow that steadied his lifebeat and sent the warm blood coursing through his veins. Just before she lost the light completely, a woman's voice whispered in the queen's ear. ''The Crystal Keep, my daughter. It is not for me to do.'

'I'm sorry,' Ariadne murmured. 'I was frightened.'

The only thing she could hear was the wizard's hoarse coughing. When the queen lifted her eyes to look over to Ritnym's Realm there was a light like sunlight through a canopy of living leaves, and by that greenish glow she saw the cloth-of-gold bag floating in the water.

Ariadne took up the bag. A tinkle of fragments came from inside, and she set it aside to dry. The wizard opened his eyes. 'I guess she really doesn't want us over there,' he sighed feebly.

Ariadne touched his wet hair. 'I guess not.'

Chapter Twenty

Peewit rested against a tree trunk and kneaded the muscle above his bruised knee. It ached from all the walking, so he was glad to sit and wait. It was two days since he had escaped with Kursh, and with any luck, Muir Dach would be coming down the road sometime in the next few hours. He hoped he could stand the dwarf's mutterings that long.

Peewit had thought the passage of time after Kursh's attack on the consort might serve to heal the dwarf's mind somewhat, but in this he had been wrong. If anything, the First Watchman was worse. He talked to himself almost incessantly, and had taken to chewing the end of his beard. Then he would go suddenly silent. At such times Peewit would look back and find the dwarf's eyes on him with an unreadable expression. The Littleman could well believe the dwarf might kill him and never even know it.

Watching him now as he nodded and muttered, Peewit wondered if Kursh's brother would even recognize him in the stringy-haired idiot that he had become. The Littleman had to swallow hard and look away.

From the road there came a creak of wagon wheels and the clanging of tin pots. Peewit jumped up and walked stiffly to the roadside. He went still just as a precaution, in case Dach had the young Watchman, Lyle Brewer, riding up on the seat with him. But the tinker was alone, so Peewit limped to the middle of the road and suddenly appeared. Muir Dach reined in, the surprise on his face changing to his jagged grin. 'You could make a fortune as a highwayman,' he called.

Peewit peered past him anxiously and put his finger to his lips.

'If it's your young soldier you're looking for, he up and left me yesterday. There was a group of Riders went past us and he hitched a ride with them. Seems my wagon was too slow for him.' The tinker spat through the gap in his front teeth and looked the Littleman up and down as Peewit grasped the bridle of the horse nearest him. 'You're looking worse for wear, captain.'

'Nan Dir Nog, I'm in trouble.'

'I guess to hell you are! The story of how you helped the dwarf

escape is on everyone's lips from here to Waysmeet.' He
sobered. 'Is he with you?'

Peewit nodded.

The tinker spat again. 'Well, get him loaded in the back and
let's get out of here. Are you heading for Yoriand or what?'

The Littleman put up a hand. 'I want you to understand that
this is my boon, and if anyone should catch us at it, I'll say you
did it at swordpoint.'

The tinker laughed. 'Is that so? Well, I want you to
understand something, captain.' The smile stayed on his
lips, but his expression had darkened and Peewit guessed that
he had hit too close to the man's pride. 'There ain't nobody,
with a sword or without one, who rides in my wagon unless I
want him to. Now, I happen to like you, don't know why. If
you want to claim this as your boon, go ahead, but I aim to
give you and your mad friend a lift to wherever it'll suit you
to go.'

Peewit nodded. 'He's in the woods over there. I'll go fetch
him. And, Muir, don't be offended by anything he says. He
doesn't even know me. I warn you that he's dangerous.'

'I gathered that. But mad folk are the innocents of Aashis,
it's said. I won't take offense.'

The Littleman had started for the woods when a soft whicker
brought him up. Snort was pulling on his lead rope at the rear
of the wagon. 'Hello, old friend! How's your foot?'

'He's fit as a fiddle,' the tinker said. 'My liniment works
pretty well.' Peewit gave the pony a pat, then limped for the
woods once more. Dach called after him, 'Looks like you could
use some yourself!'

'Kursh, our ride is here,' the Littleman was saying as he
passed under the trees. The dwarf was gone.

Peewit swore and ran back out to the road. When he heard,
the tinker guided his horses under the trees and joined the
Littleman in the search. Dach went east toward distant
Waysmeet, and Brickleburr went west toward the river, the
way they had come. The ash fall had been thinner on this side
of the river, and after a few moments Peewit bent to look
closely at a track and then gave a hail. Shortly the tinker came
through the trees. 'He went this way,' the Littleman pointed.
They set off, trotting to catch up.

Here and there were freshly turned leaves, where the end of
the manacle chain had caught under the dwarf's feet for a
moment. They broke into a lightly forested patch, and suddenly
the land became trampled. Muir Dach pulled at the Littleman's
arm. 'Horses,' he panted. 'A lot of them.'

'Why would anyone be riding here when the road is faster?'

The tinker did not answer but drew his dagger. 'Your daft
friend has gone right after them.'

Peewit's heart froze at a sudden thought. 'Or they are following him.' His eyes lifted to the man beside him, and as one they raced after the dwarf. A thread of smoke came to them, but not wood or peat. This had a foul reek to it, like a burned barn. He made a sign to Muir Dach, and they slowed and carefully crept forward.

The hoofprints went trampling through a small field of flattened oats, and the Littleman knew then that they were on the track of marauders. There were not many outlaws left in Ilyria, but obviously some brutes had ridden this way. There must be a secluded farmhouse about, and he could guess now what the burning smell was. He glanced at Muir Dach; the tinker's face was grim. Peewit drew his sword and ran low across the field with the tinker following. The field of oats had a small path cut through to it from the house, which stood back in the trees. They could see flames through the woods. Above the roaring of the thatch they could also hear coarse laughter and the neighing and stamping of horses. Whoever had done this was obviously still there.

When Peewit reached the verge of the woods he stopped until Dach was beside him once more, then picked a way through the trees, holding his sword at the ready and hoping the outlaws would be intent on their blood sport.

He pushed aside the last screening bush. The first thing he saw – all that he could see – was the green-and-gold surcoats of the First Watch, and then the terrified expression of the Barrener woman who knelt with her baby by the well. The intense heat of the blazing house made the air waver, and there was a loud pop as one of the beams gave way. The byre was engulfed, and between the structures lay what had been a man before the soldiers had hacked him to pieces, and the twitching form of a stripling youth transfixed by a thrown spear.

So enraged by the sight was the Captain of the Watch that he sprang out of the bushes without thought as the leader of the group – a corporal by his badge – swung down from his horse to grasp the woman by the hair and pull her up. 'No!' Peewit roared. 'You will not!'

From the Littleman's left another figure leaped for the nearest horseman, wresting the sword from his hand. Kursh, who had never been a swordsman, waded into the thick of the troop, hewing about him as though he were wielding his ax. The soldiers were taken by surprise and tried to wheel out of his way, but their already skittish horses trampled against bit and spur. Faced with the figure of the enraged Littleman, who flickered into and out of view so fast that they were not quite sure what they were looking at, and the shouting dwarf who laid about him with the sharp blade, the troopers were slow to regroup. Muir Dach leaped to the man who had seized the

Barrener wife and knocked him from his feet with one well-placed punch. He sprang for the next nearest.

By now the troopers were beginning to answer the attack. Their swords flashed up. A bull voice rose above the tumult, singing one of Imris's old songs – the lay of Marian the Fair – and Peewit knew that in the dwarf's mind, this was the Bastard's attack on Greenbriar castle. The battle heat rose in the captain, and he flickered back into view to drag a soldier from his horse. Catching the reins, he vaulted to the saddle. Now his sword could be put to good use.

Meanwhile, the tinker flung himself to the side as a horseman leaned to hew at him. Muir slashed his knife across the man's wrist. The ugly cut spurted, and the fellow dropped his weapon with a hissed curse and pulled himself upright in the saddle to send his plunging horse pelting off through the trees.

Kursh had dispatched two of the troopers, but now three others circled him, and he was desperately parrying the thrusts of their spears. One of the soldiers began to systematically work to the dwarf's blind side. When Dach sized up the situation, it was apparent they would kill the dwarf within seconds. The tinker put his fingers to his lips and whistled shrilly. Every horse but Peewit's stopped short and swung its head to look at the tinker. Try as they might, the riders could not make them budge. Shouting oaths, they jumped to the ground.

Peewit spurred his horse to rear, towering above them all. 'Stop!' he shouted in his parade-ground voice. Even in their bloodlust, the Watchmen heard that order and hesitated, glancing up at him. The Littleman's eyes flashed. 'Put up your weapons and look at what you have done!'

One or two did. But then from the back of the pack rose a shout at Kursh: 'Hai, you old murderer!' No power of Peewit's could reach the dwarf and make him break off his attack, and he had thrust his sword through a man's midsection while the fellow's mate jumped to his defense with a cry. The dead man folded over the blade, trapping it. Kursh was left defenseless against the other soldier's charge. Hampered by his manacles, he could not even throw up his hands to ward off the blow.

But the man had reckoned without Kursh's mad strength. The dwarf grabbed the soldier's wrist and snapped it like a twig. Peewit spurred to his side and deflected the blow that would have taken the dwarf in the back. Muir Dach grappled another before he could hurl his dagger at the captain.

The dwarf swung the end of his manacle chain and caught the trooper that fought Peewit across the back of the head. The soldier dropped like a stone, and Kursh whirled to Muir Dach and the soldier he fought. But at that moment, the next to the

last soldier left alive caught at the Littleman's foot and pulled
him from the borrowed horse. The animal shied. A hoof grazed
the Littleman, and Peewit was knocked out. Muir Dach tackled
the soldier and Kursh cracked the trooper across the head. The
tinker jumped to his feet and then stooped to the Littleman.
He looked up an instant later along the sword the dwarf had
grabbed. They stared at each other. Dach's dagger was in his
hand and he said quietly, 'If you go for me with that, old pot, I
swear I'll drop you where you stand.'

A moment longer they held each other's eyes, while the
Littleman stirred between them and brought a hand up to
finger the rising bump on his temple.

A broad grin split Kursh's bearded face. 'A good bit of work,
eh, Tristan? You were slow with that last whoreson, though – I
could have taken him in half the time if you hadn't got in the
way.'

The tinker's eyes narrowed, but then he nodded. 'I reckon
you probably could have.' He gestured to Peewit. 'Help me get
him to the wagon, will you?'

'Aye.' Kursh bent and easily lifted the Littleman, throwing
him over his broad shoulder like a sack of meal. Peewit
protested dizzily, but the dwarf overrode him and struck off
through the trees.

Muir Dach looked after them, then walked slowly to the
woman, who wept on her son's body. He wanted to say
something, but she raised a wild face to curse him in Barrener.
He bowed his head and left her.

The massacre they had witnessed left both the tinker and
Peewit silent. The Littleman nursed his aching head while the
horses clopped along, and Muir Dach sucked his teeth and
cursed the stinging flies near the river. Kursh was in the back
of the wagon, happily singing nonsense to himself. Finally the
tinker twitched the reins over the horses' rumps and cleared
his throat. 'I reckon to have to take a little trip to Greenbriar
when I've left you and the dwarf off.'

'The queen must be told,' Peewit agreed, 'though I don't
suppose she'll thank the messenger.'

'Especially if he's a tinker.' Muir Dach's lip curled. 'Thanks
to Tomasheen, curse him.'

'I would give you a letter and a token to get you past the
guards, but that would put you in greater danger, as one who
had helped Kursh and me escape.' An idea came to him. 'Will
Quint is the man you should see. He could bring it to the
queen's attention. After all' – there was the barest hesitation
before he continued – 'Will must be captain by now.'

The tinker heard the loss in his voice and skirted around it.
'This Quint is someone to trust?'

Peewit smiled. 'No fear there.'

'All right, if you say so.' They left it that way and talked then of other things until they made camp that night. By the flickering fire, the Littleman wrote his report to Quint of how the queen's order to eradicate the Wolf Cult had led to cold-blooded murder and the massacre of innocents. He did not know the Watchmen involved in the incident, but he gave as accurate a description as possible of the man who had gotten away and informed Quint of where the bodies could be found. After he was done, he held up the shirt and regarded the charcoal letters on it. He hoped it would serve.

Two days later they reached the fishing port at the mouth of Willowsrill where the great river met the sea. Peewit and Kursh stayed hidden in the woods with the wagon while the tinker hiked in and made inquiries for a boat to take them to Jarlshof, a long day's sail away. With Peewit's small stash of silver coin, he had no problem hiring a boat and crew. He came back to the camp at sunset.

'Got it,' he reported. 'Fellow named Pers Half Hand will take you.'

Peewit looked unconvinced. 'Half Hand?'

'Relax. He's no brigand. The hand got caught in a winch as he was pulling in a net, and he lost a couple of fingers. He's a fisherman.' The Littleman's brow cleared, and Dach added, 'Says the tide'll be on the turn about three hours from now, and that's when you'll sail.'

'You told him there would be two passengers?'

'Of course,' the tinker answered, pulling a strip of rabbit from the stick where Peewit had set it to roast. 'I couldn't very well pass Old Wind-in-the-Thatch off as baggage now, could I?'

The Littleman smiled at this epithet for Kursh, who was tearing into his portion of the hare meat greedily. Then he sobered. 'Does Master Half Hand have any idea what will be done to him if we're caught?'

Muir Dach threw a bone into the fire and wiped his greasy chin on his sleeve. 'No, But he's being paid enough to take the chance. Didn't blink an eye either when I offered that much money, so he must have a glimmer that it's not a couple of honest traders he's carrying.'

'He may be thinking to take our coin and then turn us in for the reward,' the Littleman worried.

'No,' said the tinker, 'I don't think so,' He patted his dagger in its sheath. 'I made clear how ill it can make a fellow feel to run afoul of a tinker's curse.'

That made Peewit feel a little better, but not much.

Later, in the fog streaming off the ocean, the tinker's wagon rumbled down the cobbled main street of the town to the waterfront. If any of the sailors who crowded the seaport tavern thought it odd that a tinker should have commerce with a fisherman, they did not follow the wagon to satisfy their curiosity about it.

Dach drew up at the landward end of the pier. 'Good fortune, captain,' he said, and they shook hands on it.

The Littleman returned the traditional tinker farewell: 'Free roads and plenty of mutton to you.'

Muir grinned, and Peewit jumped down from the seat to walk around the wagon. Snort ducked his head to be patted. 'Well, old fellow, it's come to this, I guess,' the Littleman murmured. 'Behave yourself and stay with the Nan Dir Nog. He'll treat you well, I know.' The pony's ears pitched and he whickered softly. Peewit stroked the length of his nose and stepped quickly to the small door of the wagon. 'All right, Kursh, let's get aboard this boat.'

The dwarf had been dozing. 'Eh? What?' He settled the eyepatch. 'Boat?'

'Yes. Boat. I'm taking you home to Jarlshof.'

The shaggy gray head leaned from the door, and Kursh glanced around, his eye fixing on the dark shape that swung at the bollards. 'All right,' he said and, climbing down, strode out onto the pier.

Peewit took their sack and darted forward to have a last word with Muir, but the tinker waved him off. 'I know, I know. Go get him now before he tells Half Hand all about how his lines are strung wrong!'

The Littleman grinned, gave him a hasty salute, and ran after the dwarf.

Pers Half Hand was smoking his pipe on the foredeck, and what Peewit hadn't reckoned on was that he should be a dwarf, too. Peewit saw Half Hand's gaze on the chains and he put out an arm to catch Kursh. 'He's mad,' he explained to the watching fisherman.

Half Hand blew a thin stream of smoke reflectively. 'That's what I hear,' he said.

The Littleman met his eyes steadily. 'Will you still take us?'

'You've paid your money. Come aboard.'

Peewit stayed where he was. 'There may be trouble for you.'

'Don't think so: the wind looks fair for Jarlshof.' He had squinted out to the mist-shrived sea, and now he looked at the Littleman. 'I'm just taking a kinsman home. What trouble could come of that?' He beckoned, and the Littleman, reassured, led Kursh aboard.

When Peewit came on deck the next morning rather late, he was cheered to find it sunny ahead. He glanced around and discovered the black line of the ash cloud behind them. Half

Hand saw him frowning. 'We've crossed over into the Weather-glass Zone.' He gestured off the bow. 'It's an inconvenient time for it to be rotten weather on the home island, you see, so everyone has used his Weatherglass to hold the cloud off.' He grinned at Peewit's surprise, offering him a hard biscuit and a shot of flotjin. He pointed off the starboard bow. The Littleman had his first look at the home island of Jarlshof.

Seventy feet the cliffs dropped to the sea. The island was stacked behind them like a beehive-shaped pile of drying turves that someone had knocked sprawling. Topping this vaguely conical mass was the sheer towering peak of Barak-Gambrel, wreathed in cloud. Deep bays ran back from the rocky headlands, and Half Hand was tacking expertly to make port in one of these. He waved a pipestem. 'Our main city, Skejfalen. It is my harbor and Korimson's home.'

Peewit climbed on a coil of rope, bracing himself with one hand on the mainmast to see better. 'What is that shining? A mirror for signaling out to sea?'

'No, but that is a clever idea. What you see is the roof of the guildhall of crystal blowers.'

The Littleman gave him a startled glance. 'That's all crystal?' Pers nodded, and Peewit began to realize just how important a family of Glassmakers like the Korimsons might be. Guiltily he regarded the dwarf, who stood braced in the bow with his manacled hands gripping the rail. He shouldn't be going home like this, the Littleman thought, and resolved that when they landed he would unlock the chains.

Half Hand knocked out his pipe on the steering oar. 'There is a thing you should know. Early this morning a fast ship was off our port bow. We could barely see her in the fog, but my best lookout says she was flying the Lion of Shimarron.' The Littleman paled, and the dwarven fisherman added, 'She was on a course from the Isle of the Wizards to Jarlshof. We may find her lurking about offshore of the harbor mouth, behind one of the headlands. Our coastal patrol will not let her hold the harbor against us, of course.' When he finished, Peewit was silent. 'Don't worry. I won't stop for them, but it would be well if you and Korimson were not on deck. Also, you might let him free; the Shimarrats may try to drive us on the rocks or hole us. That would be the simplest way for them to resolve their problems, if they have any idea that you two are aboard.'

The biscuit lay heavy in Peewit's stomach. 'All right. But even if they come aboard, Master Half Hand, they will not see Kursh and me, I promise you that. So perhaps it might be best to heave to and let them satisfy their curiosity.'

The dwarf's beard bristled. 'Not while I am master of the *Puffin*, unless it damn well suits me.'

The Littleman smiled and went forward to coax the pro-

testing Kursh to go below. The cabin was small, only enough
room to let the fishermen not on watch get in out of the
weather. The smell of fish from the hold was overpowering to a
landlubber, and after sitting Kursh down on a pile of oiled
leather hoods, Peewit stood at the foot of the companionway
and called up to Pers on deck, 'See anything?'

'Not yet. Would you like to place a small wager on this?' He
cocked an eye over the shaft of the steering oar.

'No. I'm sure you're right, unfortunately.'

The fisherman smiled and refilled his pipe. He called
something in dwarvish to his crew, and when Peewit climbed
the few steps and peered just over the hatch, the dwarves were
ranged about the small boat, busily mending nets, coiling lines,
or trimming sails. What would not be seen by an approaching
boat was that each of them had a gaff or boathook close to
hand. Peewit felt better at that.

Until he saw the Shimarrat vessel.

She glided out from a hiding place beyond the headland
west of the harbor and tacked to intercept them a good mile
from the entrance to the bay of Skejfalen. Half Hand's lips
tightened, and he jammed his cap down until it sat just above
his eyes.

The double-forked pennant snapped from the mainmast, and
the Lion of Shimarron seemed to be running on the wind. The
Shimarrat vessel was sleek, painted black, with a raked stern
and a bowsprit that looked as though it could easily run right
through Half Hand's much smaller boat. Two painted eyes
glared balefully from her prow. It was well that Peewit and
Kursh had gotten out of view when they did, for a lookout was
swinging in the highest crosstree and would surely have been
able to see them at that distance.

The fisherman said. 'Keep Kursh quiet, please.'

Going below, the Littleman apologized, 'Sorry about this, old
fellow.' Before Kursh could react, Peewit drew back his fist
and hit the point of the shaggy chin with all his might. The
dwarf's head thudded off the bulkhead, and he slumped into
the corner. Quickly the Littleman replaced the gag. He had a
bad moment wondering what he would do if the Shimarrat
vessel tried to sink them and he could not rouse Kursh, but a
shout from the mad dwarf would spell disaster.

Half Hand had not changed course; he was still bearing for
the harbor mouth. At another order in dwarvish, some of his
men jumped atop the cabin and into the rigging to shout in
dwarvish and wave the bigger ship off. 'So we will look like a
normal small fishing boat about to be run down by a
high-handed sloop,' he explained to Peewit, who was peering
up at him from the cabin.

Presently there was a hail from the Shimarrats. 'Ahoy!' one

of them called in accented Ilyrian, the common language of trade. 'Small fishing boat *Puffin*, you will heave to immediately!'

Half Hand took the pipe from his mouth and yelled back something in dwarvish.

'What does that mean?' Peewit asked anxiously.

'It is not flattering to his mother.'

'Oh.'

'They are signaling us to stop,' the dwarf reported, and he gestured emphatically that the Shimarrats should give way, reaching to seize the mallet and ring his ship's bell in warning.

Peewit went still and looked over the hatch. What he saw froze him. The Shimarrat racing ship was barely one hundred and fifty yards off and closing like a greyhound. 'S-stop!' he begged Half Hand..

'I've been wet before,' the dwarven skipper answered tranquilly. 'Can you swim, by the way?'

The terrified Littleman did not have time to answer before the racing ship's red eyes passed just off their bow and the length of the Shimarrat slid past so close that they could see the caulking in her planks. Her wash rocked the small fishing boat, and Peewit grabbed the rail to keep from being thrown down the steps.

Half Hand grinned. 'Now I'll stop.'

He raised a fist and bellowed a stream of dwarvish at the stern of the Shimarrat. Calling to his crew, 'Pile on the sheets, boys!' he held the tiller straight for the harbor mouth. To Peewit he said, 'They will come about now and cut across our bow again just outside the harbor. This time, of course, I will stop, as any normal fisherman would do.'

About twenty minutes later while Peewit was double-checking Kursh's gag, Half Hand called down the hatch, 'Here they come!' The Littleman went still and hurried to the deck. This time as the Shimarrat vessel closed, the dwarves furled their sail and floated.

'Ahoy, *Puffin*!' the same voice called from the deck which loomed alongside. 'That was very foolish race. Now you listen, eh?'

Pers spat over the gunwales and shook his fist. The Shimarrat captain grinned. 'Yes, all right, you hate me. That is of no importance. Stand by to be boarded.' He gestured, and a dinghy swung from the davits. A tall man with broad shoulders and a familiar look sat in the boat, and the oarsmen jumped in to row him to the fishing boat.

'I think that's Prince Ka-Treer,' Peewit warned. 'Be careful none of your men gives him a reason to make trouble.'

Half Hand glanced toward his voice, but the Littleman could not be seen. For an instant the dwarf's eyes widened, then he carefully nodded. With his hands on his hips, he strode to the gunwale and shouted what was obviously an angry question in dwarvish. One of his crew tugged at his arm and pointed up to the deck of the Shimarrat vessel. Crossbowmen were sighting in over their weapons at him. Half Hand went rigid with fury, but made no further resistance.

Three of the oarsmen leaped into the fishing boat, and then Ka-Treer sprang lightly to the deck. He swept the crew, his eyes resting on Half Hand. 'We are searching for a murderer. We will examine your boat. If we find nothing, you will go on your way a silver sovereign richer for your pains.' He held the coin up before the dwarf, who frowned in pretended incomprehension. Ka-Treer gestured, and one of his men moved to the open hatch.

Peewit, grasping Kursh's arm, crouched in the corner and kept them both invisible.

When he saw the smoking censer swinging on its chain, his heart sank, for he knew how Ka-Treer planned to find an invisible Littleman and the dwarf he protected under his stillness. The smoke began to eddy in the confines of the fish-reeking cabin. When it filled the small space, he and the dwarf would be clearly outlined.

He waved his free hand gently to keep the smoke swirling and hoped that neither Ka-Treer or the censer-swinger would notice.

The Shimarrat prince and his man-at-arms were silently listening and watching intently. The prince's hand was on his dagger. From the sounds on deck, some of the dwarven fisherman were giving the rest of the Shimarrat boarding party all they could handle.

Ka-Treer coughed and waved irritably at the smoke that stung his eyes, and the Littleman was hopeful. The man with the censer murmured a question in Shimarrat, and the prince grunted a reply. Drawing his jeweled dagger, he stepped around the man and slashed the air. Peewit's heart stopped, for he had missed Kursh's face by a scant finger's length. Enough of that, the Littleman thought and got his feet under him to spring for the dagger. The hatch slammed back. Both humans swung around.

Half Hand's head was framed against the azure sky, looking down at them angrily. He pointed at the censer – at fire on his ship – and jerked a thumb. Out! he said unmistakably.

Ka-Treer took a final look around, then brushed past his man, and they went up on deck. Through the open hatch the Littleman watched as the prince chopped a gesture at his men and they climbed back in the skiff. From his belt pouch Ka-Treer took a silver sovereign and gave it to Half Hand.

The dwarven fisherman regarded the coin for a moment. Then he bent to the hold cover in the deck at his feet. Pulling open the door, he straightened and laid a cold and gaping fish across the Shimarrat's hands. Ka-Treer stared, and Half Hand made him a very passable bow, smiling and holding up the coin.

The Shimarrat's face contorted with disgust and anger, and he whipped the fish into the sea and glared down at the dwarf, whose face showed only hurt puzzlement. With a curse, the prince vaulted the gunwales into his own boat, and the oarsmen pulled away. The dwarves began to cheer and wave goodbye. Their laughter rolled across the water. Half Hand did not take his eyes off the crossbowmen. 'All right, lads, let's not beat the wasps' nest, shall we? Up the mains'l. Let's shake these dogs.'

They slipped away past the stern of the Shimarrat sloop, and the sail billowed, driving them straight for the harbor. 'Are you still with us, Master Littleman?' Half Hand called, glancing into the open hatch.

Peewit flickered back into view and sank down on the steps. 'Could I trouble you for a drop of flotjin?' he asked, and the fishermen broke out the liquor locker very happily.

On the way in, they passed a patrol boat of the Jarlshof navy on its way out to investigate the Shimarrat sloop. Half Hand stepped to the rail and cupped his hands about his mouth. 'It's the Shimarrat prince, Karl, so you'd better not sink him, but if you get close enough, kick him in the nuts for me, will you?'

The officer gave him a laughing salute, and the solid defense vessel sped by.

They passed the headland that protected the harbor. The city of Skejfalen, with its magnificent domed guildhall of the crystal blowers glittering in the noonday sun, swung by to starboard. Half Hand ordered the sails down and the oars out, and they rowed through the crowded slips until they reached the main pier, well built of stone.

Peewit swept the bustle of warehouses and docks, the teeming fishmarket, and the dark green pine heights that lifted to the knees of the mountain above the city. Then he looked again, squinting at the specks of bright color that danced in the sky far overhead. 'Are those kites?' he asked incredulously.

'They are,' Pers answered as he cupped a flaring splinter to light his pipe. He looked for a moment while his crew tied the boat up fore and aft. 'Aye, they've got some fine fliers this year, it looks like. I'd put a silver on that red one, for sure.'

The Littleman turned from the rail. 'You bet on them?'

Half Hand laughed. 'We bet on anything! But yes, we do bet on the kites. It's a mock war, you see. One flier will try to knock another out of the sky, like two big eagles having it out over a salmon.' When Peewit gave him a doubtful glance, the dwarf waved his pipestem. 'This is just the preliminary stage of the competition. They're establishing which flier will get the most points for his kite's grace in riding the wind. Tomorrow the real fun starts.' He looked over the glowing bowl of his pipe, and there was a hint of speculation in that look. 'By chance or by design, you've arrived just in time for Aashnasse, the Festival of the Wind. That's why the place is so crowded with currachs: Aashnasse Eve is the time for the gathering of the clans, and most ancestral homes are here in Skejfalen. By twilight, every window in every house will be lit with new candles made just for the occasion and it will look like the stars themselves have come down and made their homes here on Jarlshof.' He reddened and cleared his throat. 'Anyway, it's a grand sight, and the rest of the week will be the same. Of all the times of the year, it's the best for a dwarf to be coming home.' He puffed. 'It's funny, you know.'

Peewit picked up the sack of his own and Kursh's belongings that a crew member had brought up from the cabin for him. 'What is?'

'Well, one of our traditions is that on Aashnasse Eve all quarrels are set aside and a new start is made. We're a rather hasty folk, as you might have noticed, and I suppose if we didn't have something like this, there'd soon be no family on the island that wasn't split right down the middle by a fight. But this way, there's time for both sides to cool off and then the younger ones come home at Aashnasse and nothing more is said about it.' He turned to look where Kursh was being helped over the side by two fishermen. 'And now here's Korim's son home, and Korim not here to see it.' Half Hand gave Peewit a quietly sad look. 'Kursh could have come home any Aashnasse: why did it have to be this one?'

Peewit watched his friend stand on the pier with his hands in their manacles clasped before him, like a man surveying his garden in the cool evening.

When the Littleman said nothing, Half Hand cleared his throat once more. 'Well, Lord Aashis baits his own hooks, 'tis said.' He took his own duffel bag on his shoulder. 'Come now, I'll show you to Kursh's home, and then my wife will be waiting for me.'

'I want to take his chains off first,' Peewit said, and the fisherman nodded with approval in his eyes. 'What did that proverb mean, just now?'

A sharp glance from beneath the bushy brows. 'Hah? Well, only that ... that is ...' He frowned. 'Well, look, you didn't think you got all this way through the Queen's patrols and past the damn Shimarrat without some help, did you?'

Peewit knew the dwarf did not mean himself as the help. 'No,' the Littleman murmured. 'No, I suppose not.'

The fisherman nodded. 'Right. Now let's get a move on: I'm starved and Aashnasse Eve cake is waiting!'

Chapter Twenty-one

The dream came again, and even in the midst of it, Ariadne was resentful because she had only just gotten back to sleep. There was a tower of glass, chiming in the wind like a thousand wind chimes, while the waves smashed against the cliffs and spray rose up to patter the turrets high above. Fog and gray clouds lowered, and the sea-touch was cold upon her. A butterfly winged in over the crests of the waves, exhausted and ragged, and she put a hand out to give it a place to light, but it was blown past in the rising gale. She fought her way across the rocky strand, the water surging about her feet, wanting to drag her out with the tide, but she gained the crystal steps that wound upward. She knew she had to go up, but she didn't know why. The glass stairs were slick with wet, and she was afraid. She paused on the first step, feeling the whole structure shaking. Impelled, she began to climb into the dark and swirling mist. It was cold, so cold – then something came down the stairs at her, all fangs and evil eye. Its breath was poison, and she got a whiff of it though she tried to hold her breath and cried out in fright and –

Meara's face was concerned in the growing candlelight. ' – just a dream, my lady.' As Ariadne came fully awake, the waitingwoman straightened and reached for the small bag of herbs Fidelis had left the night before. 'There's more of the posset,' she said hopefully, 'if you would like it?'

The queen drew the covers up to her chin. 'No, thank you. I'll not sleep again anyway.' She did not say she didn't want to, but Meara understood. 'You may go back to bed.'

'I'll leave the lamp lit, my lady.'

Ariadne lay awake a long time, waiting for Meara to sleep again, but in the end she had to feign slumber herself, with slow and even breathing, before the waitingwoman relaxed enough to drop off. The queen gave it a good half hour, then quietly rose, pulled her nightrobe about her, slipped into soft shoes, and made her way through the dressing room with its rack of gowns to the secret door behind the arras. She made sure to oil it now

and again with lamp oil, so it swung soundlessly to her touch.
She followed the stairway down a flight by touch, until her hand
found the torch that waited. With its light, she went more
quickly, and soon the door that opened into the kitchen corridor
was before her. Dousing the torch in the bucket of sand that
stood there for the purpose, Ariadne put the flint and iron where
she could find them again and eased the door open. There was a
torch lit along the corridor somewhere: its light swelled and
ebbed with the wind through the open window arches. By this,
she saw that she was alone.

The night guards would be stationed at the foot of the grand
staircase at the entrance to the keep itself, so there should be no
danger of being caught in her shift, unless one of the servingmen
came out of the sleeping barracks that was Rose Hall. She had to
chance it.

When she stood before the painted fresco, the queen stared at
the mural with her eyes half closed, trying to see again what she
had seen in the vision she had had the night before Crowning
Day. The Crystal Keep had glowed over there, near the left
border. She moved a few steps to come before the section. Peering intently, she willed the diamond tower to sparkle to life and
the fire of the rising sun to show through it once more.

But there was no tower and there was no rising sun. The
vine-and-flower border ran up the wall as it always had, the
blue sky stayed blue. Unconsciously she took a step closer. A
torch flared, but it showed her only a long crack in the plaster
that she had not noticed before. Probably from the falling star,
she thought, or the lightning that almost got Alphonse. *I shall
have to have the plasterers to mend it most delicately.*

The torch flared again, and now she saw a network of cracks,
a web that checkered the painted surface, thrusting out fingers
across the painted fields and into the vine border. The queen
squinted in the uncertain light and put out a hand to be sure. At
her touch some of the plaster flaked off, and to her surprise, the
wall was warm.

What's this? she thought. Then, even as she shrugged deeper
into her wrap, her eyes widened. There it was, unmistakably,
just inside the frame made by the border: a tower was rising in
the clouds. As she stared, the torches flared a third time. In the
gleam of hundreds of starry crystals seen from afar, the Crystal
Keep winked in the fresco. A network of dark crystal fingers
groped across the fresco toward it. The queen tried to blink
herself awake, but the Crystal Keep and the dark crystal net
remained. She reached to touch the black stuff and snatched
back her hand. It was hot, just like the star that had – 'By the
Powers!'

The queen whirled to the kitchen corridor and ran for the
secret passageway. When she reached her own solar, she

stooped to shake Meara's arm. 'Send a page to fetch the wizard. Hurry!'

The waitingwoman was only half awake and glanced at the dark window befuddled. 'Now, my lady?'

'Now.' Ariadne darted into her tiring room and grabbed a dress at random.

'I'm sorry, sir, but she said now.' The young boy in the livery of the queen stood at the door, shifting from one foot to the other. He had the good training not to knuckle the sleep from his eyes, but he could not quite stifle the yawn.

Alphonse jumped for his robe. 'What's happened? Is it the Lordling? What's the matter?'

'Nothing I know of, sir. She just desired speech with you immediately.'

That would be Meara's phrasing, Alphonse thought: Ariadne's command would not have been such a nicety. His heart was thumping and he could not get his cloak pin closed. 'All right. Let's go.' He was still pulling on his boots as the page sketched a bow and led him down the sleeping halls.

By the time they received the salute of the guards on duty at the antechamber doors, the wizard had readied a Warding to try to meet whatever danger had suddenly presented itself. The ladies eyed him over their blankets, pink with shame. No other man save Fidelis would have been admitted in the middle of the night. He averted his eyes and marched after the boy, who gave a light tap at the door and went to one knee as the queen herself opened it. She nodded Alphonse in and left the gossip to fall where it might.

'What's the matter?' he was demanding as the door shut.

'Nothing. I've something to show you, that's all.'

'Now?'

Meara thrust a teacup into her mistress's hands. 'Tea?' she asked the wizard. He did not realize for a moment that she had put herself firmly between them. When he did, he hid a flicker of amusement and stooped to the small fire on the hearth, warming his hands. 'What couldn't wait till morning, my queen?'

Ariadne took a swallow of tea that would have done a hay-raker proud, then beckoned him to follow. They went out through the antechamber, and the Watchmen followed as a bodyguard.

'There.' Her finger described the area of the Keep. 'Do you see it?'

'By Nilarion, you're right!' He beckoned a torchbearer closer, and now the Crystal Keep glittered in the streaming light. With the stronger illumination, the dark web glowed. Their eyes met. The wizard steeled himself and reached experimentally to touch it. Before his finger made contact, a faint crystal spark leaped

from the tower to his hand and drove his touch aside, as if to
protect him. His eyes flew open. 'It is Warded! By the Three, the
whole wall is Warded!' He seemed struck by a thought and
moved his hand close to the surface again, studying the reaction
of the spark. 'Aengus,' he murmured. 'Aengus must have painted
this.'

Ariadne frowned. 'His work is about to come to grief from the
black stuff. See how it works its way through the wall even as we
speak.'

Alphonse probed with his Warding and was thrown back a
step by the hint of the Unnamed Warding still on the black crystal. 'It is all the way through the wall and spreading like a
canker.'

'Can you stop it?'

He was already making a Warding to try to seal a perimeter
around the black crystal web. The wizard set it in place, and
they watched tensely as the fingers grew toward his garnet line.

When the black met the garnet, Alphonse gasped and grabbed
for his ears. The garnet perimeter lapsed and the black crystal
crept nearer the Crystal Keep. 'I couldn't hold it!' He did not
know why protecting Aengus's painting seemed so desperately
important, but he immediately bent his mind again to the task. A
bright crystal spark flashed from the Keep to his eyes, and he did
not throw up a hand in time to stop it.

Ariadne cried out, but he was smiling. 'So that's how you did
it,' he murmured, listening to the new fragment of Wind
Warding that Aengus had left for him to discover. Clearly,
sweetly, the Painter's notes showed him a way around the
Unnamed's Warding.

The wizard quickly set the perimeter again, this time using
Aengus's warding. He stepped back.

'What – ?' the queen began to ask.

'Watch, lady queen.'

The black advanced, a malignant threat. Crystal glowed, a
stable line. The two Wardings met.

The black crystal shattered.

'Oh, well done, sir!' one of the Watchmen guards approved.
'Send the Wild Feller to the rightabouts!'

'I cannot do that,' Alphonse cautioned. 'This is only a tiny bit
of Wind Warding,' he told the queen's hopeful glance. 'Not
enough to fight the Unnamed, but still – it is something, and we
may find a use for it yet.'

'Any weapon for us is a weapon against him,' she agreed.
Mindful of the guards, she motioned him to withdraw with her to
one of the windows. The queen leaned her chin on her hand and
gazed out into the cold and powdered dawn. There was silence
for a time. Finally she stirred. 'Have you any idea where the
Crystal Keep is? How does one find the stronghold of the Wind?'

'I know only the legends, my lady,' he answered, leaning on the casement. 'They have never been proven.'

'The legend of the Guardian had never been proven until we went there,' she pointed out. 'And of course the legend about the Crystal of Healing hadn't, either. You and I are surrounded by legend, Alphonse.' A slight mischief touched her mouth and eyes. 'I suspect that we are probably legendary ourselves, or shall become so.'

His breath came suddenly short at the echo of Sight that couched her words. 'Don't say that!' At her startled expression, he tried to smile. 'One is not usually a legend within one's lifetime.'

The queen looked down at the cloth-of-gold bag she had been toying with and remembered the voice in her ear. The Crystal might be broken, but she was sure now of her direction. She would seek the Keep even if the wizard would not dare it. 'The signs can be no clearer. The Powers want me to find Aashis's Realm.'

'Yes. All the Powers do.' When her eyes came up, he reminded her, 'The Unnamed controls the sea now. Do you think he will suffer us to voyage across it?'

'Ah, so it is an island? You still haven't told me.'

He sighed and ran a hand through his ginger hair. 'The Crystal Keep is reported to lie far to the northwest of Jarlshof. How many days' journey, no one can tell. Some say the island floats in the waves, drifting here and there as Aashis wills. Mariners catch a glimpse of it and then it is gone and they can never find it again.'

She did not seem nonplussed. 'Then a reasonable course would be to Covencroft first, thence northward.'

'There is no reasonable course, Ariadne. That is what I have been trying to tell you! And why do you think Aashis will help if Ritnym wouldn't, anyway?'

For answer, the queen opened the sack and spilled the fragments into her palm. 'Look. It isn't the seeds that are harmed, is it? Ritnym's Gift, the Greenbriar seeds, is still just as it was. It is the glass that is broken, and what Power knows more about crystal than Aashis? If the seeds will not grow, though everything else remains the same, then obviously the breaking of the Crystal in the Ritual of the Rose is a trigger to the whole magic, and we must restore it. Do you see? That is why I have to find the Keep. Aashis himself must blow me a new Crystal, or mend this one.'

Something she had said stirred a fragment of memory. He frowned, worrying at it until he dragged it out of the darkness. The color drained from his face, and he groped for the edge of the sill.

Ariadne said sharply, 'Alphonse, what is it?'

The wizard drew a steadying breath. 'That's what he told me right before . . . right before . . .'

'Chiswic?'

'I had forgotten! Chiswic was saying something about Aengus making your Crystal and . . . yes, he said, "Apparently Ritnym was not the only one of the Powers who gave a gift to be part of the Greenbriar legacy." '

The queen gripped his arm. 'So Lord Aashis did have something to do with my Crystal!'

He nodded, the blaze of excitement in his eyes matching her own. 'The Power must have given Aengus the Painter a piece of his own Crystal to work with.' He grasped her hand as the thought struck him. 'Maybe it is a chip of the Crystal Keep itself!'

'I'll warrant you're right!' She looked around for Meara. 'Would you get us some breakfast? We've much to do today and time's a-wasting.'

The woman was bowing herself away as a Watchman hurried up the marble stairs and saluted. 'A message from the gate, Your Majesty: there is a craft docking at Castlenigh.' His eyes slid to the wizard. 'It is a barque from Covencroft.' Alphonse's face drained. 'Shall I take my lord wizard someplace safe, Majesty?' the soldier was asking. It was known that somehow the wizard had broken his Rule, but he had saved the Lordling's life and that was all that mattered to the castle folk. They would protect him for Gerrit's sake, whether the queen was still angry with him or not, and it didn't look as though she was.

Before she could speak, Alphonse said quietly, 'It would do no good, corporal.' To the queen he explained, 'They could find me by Warding. I will meet them on the Sweep. Please keep your people away, lady queen. I would not have anyone hurt on my account.' His eyes were bleak.

By the Powers, she thought, they've sent Unmakers for him, as he was sent for Rasullis! 'Nonsense, Master Wizard. We ourselves shall go with you.' She took his arm, and he was forced to walk down to the gate with the Queen of Ilyria and a complement of armed men as escort.

Outside it was cold and the air was acrid. Quietly they crunched down the Sweep. 'This is not a good idea,' he told her.

'Hush,' was all she answered.

He sent a Warding. 'Nels and Galen. By the Powers, did they have to send my two best friends?' At his anguish, she tightened her grip on his arm. After a moment, he disengaged his arm, made her a half-bow, and walked to meet them.

Out of the dark dawn came a hail: 'Ahoy! Alphonse!'

'Hoi, Galen,' he answered steadily. 'Hello, Nels.' He Warded only a minimal protection about himself, but shielded the queen and escort.

The two Meld Mariners reined in the horses they had been

given at the landing. Around them more Watchmen sat their horses. Nels frowned as he looked around at the armed men, but Galen suddenly grinned.

Alphonse shrugged helplessly, though he kept his Warding up. 'I couldn't keep them home.'

The mahogany face stayed creased in a smile, and Galen swung down. 'Powers, I am tired! After piloting a barque by Warding, it's bloody hard work to sail the thing the conventional way.'

Nels was regarding the garnet wizard from his saddle. 'What's all this, Alph?'

The Wizard of the Three answered simply. 'I am afraid, and they know it.'

The blond Mariner stared. 'What, of us?'

Galen had sobered. 'He thinks we are Unmakers.' He kept his aquamarine pearl ring carefully in Alphonse's sight.

Nels slid from his horse and flung the reins to a soldier. 'Alphonse, you idiot! Did you think that anyone could order us to do that?'

'I had hoped not.' But he did not relax his Warding, and they knew it. His blue eyes went to Nels. 'You of all people – I thought . . . because you are Westphalian . . . I'm sorry.'

The blond Mariner looked away up to the turrets until he could master his voice. 'There is no blame to you. We all knew it was the Unnamed.'

'Besides – and here's the proof – you are not thinking.' Galen twisted off his ring and handed it to Alphonse. 'We are Wind Wizards, and the Wind Warding is gone. We can't throw a spell at you!' His white teeth showed in a smile. 'Neither of us could drive a rowboat on a duckpond right now!'

Nels similarly gave over his ring. 'Relax. Master Chiswic sent us.'

Alphonse's face darkened as he thought he was betrayed. He flung the rings into the drifted powder. 'Chiswic is dead!'

Galen nodded. 'We had met with him that afternoon and agreed to bring a barque. He seemed to think you would need it, though he would not say why. That night after . . . he was killed, we slipped away.' He added reluctantly, 'Hrontin may have sent Unmakers for you after we left. Guard yourself, my friend.'

Nels said, 'In the meantime, we have brought my ship. The *Gannet* is yours, if she will help. Why did Chiswic want us to bring her to you?'

Alphonse bowed his head. How had his master guessed the doom that was laid on him? 'Because I must take Ariadne to the Crystal Keep,' he told his friends, and at their gasps turned away back up the Sweep.

There was, as she had said, much to do. Over a disappointing breakfast of underdone scones and more tea, the queen laid her plans. The biggest problem was Gerrit. Reason told her he would be much safer in the castle with Imris, Fidelis, and William Quint to guard him than he would be in a boat sailing for an island that disappeared at will. But her mother's heart was horrified at the thought of leaving him alone and ill. Where were Peewit and Kursh when you needed them? she asked herself angrily, and it did not seem odd in that moment that she should think of the dwarf as he had been of old.

Her councillors came as near to open rebellion as they could come and still remain loyal. It was absurd, they told her, couched in more politic terms, of course. The queen could not go off on some wild goose chase with the improbable object of gaining back her Crystal. Let the Crystal remain broken, they said; she was still Queen of Ilyria.

When she remained adamant, they tried a different tack. Send a champion on the quest, they advised. The Captain of the Watch, for instance, or the wizard, for they plainly thought Alphonse had talked her into this madness.

Ariadne had heard enough. She leaned back in her gilded throne, laid her hands along the carved rests, and said, 'In the first place, gentlemen, the Captain of the First Watch is unavailable at the moment.' She paused to let them think it over and saw the glances that went to William Quint. The burly man lifted his head, and a broad grin spread over his features. It was answered by a glance from the queen. At least they understood each other.

'In the second place,' she continued, 'Master Alphonse has his own tasks. This is not one of them, though he will accompany me on the journey as my safeguard. No offense to our brave Watchmen, of course, but I think this situation has more to do with magic and less with swords.' Quint frowned, and Kelvin Miller's mouth opened to argue. 'I will require no protection, gentlemen. I will risk no other lives, though they be freely given.' Quint pulled at his mustache, and Miller folded his large hands on the table. An order was an order.

'Now, for other things. As of this time, I want our southern border sealed, very quietly and without any fuss. The Shimarrat ambassador is to be treated with all respect, but his correspondence is to be held. Without his knowledge, of course.' She saw the glances they gave each other and the approval. 'The longer before the Shimarrats know that I am not here, the better for us. Other trade and treaties will continue as usual.

'While I am gone, and in the event I do not return' – she said this steadily, and that helped to take some of the shock out of it for them – 'I will name a council of regents. First Watchman William Quint will have full authority over all our troops. His will be all military decisions and his the responsibility for protecting the realm in our absence.' Quint stood at the table and saluted, then resumed his seat.

The queen nodded. 'Next, we name our beloved foster brother, Jak Cooper, to be our chancellor.' Jak's head jerked up from the stool where he sat behind Quint, acting as his adjutant. Ariadne smiled at his confusion. 'We are sure you will approve our choice, gentlemen, and approve also the elevation of Master Cooper to the peerage.' There was surprise, then someone thought of the queen's pleasure and began to clap. Amid the applause, Jak, red to the ears, stood and bowed. 'I name you Lord of Nevelston, and yours will be the supervision of our material possessions, this to include both Greenbriar Castle and also taxes and treasury. We will, of course, expect a strict accounting.' He summoned an embarrassed smile and sat at her nod.

'Last but certainly not least in our heart, we name the Eldest of Yoriand to the council of regents.' Across the table she met his fir-green eyes. 'His shall be the governance of my son.' She dropped the formality and said simply, person to person, 'Take care of him for me, Imris.'

The silver torque about his neck gleamed as he bowed his head. 'I shall, my queen. Rest you easy.'

She looked around the council table. 'I expect that you will support these regents as you would support me. That goes without saying, I know.' She had said it anyway, just to be sure they got it. The council broke up a few minutes later, and she went to walk in the garden, sending Meara to collect some tea and a bite from the kitchen.

When the waitingwoman returned with the tray, her manner was distracted. 'What's wrong?' the queen asked.

Meara looked up. 'I found out why the scones were so bad this morning, my lady. Thyla's up and left!'

'The bakeress? Whatever for?'

'I don't know. She didn't let on to anyone that she was going. Just left the bread rising and the tins greased and slipped off at first light, seemingly.'

'Perhaps she had word from home, and had to rush to Jarlshof.'

The waitingwoman's worried expression cleared as suddenly as steam wisping off a mirror. Though she said no more, Ariadne had the impression that Meara was immensely satisfied about something.

At candlelighting, the queen went to her son's room. Taking a deep breath, she pushed open the door. Gerrit stood on the bed while Cele dropped his little nightshirt over his head. His eyelids were already drooping, but he looked up as Ariadne came in and held out his arms. 'Mumma!'

'Hello, my poppet. Almost ready for Blanket Fair, I see.' She nodded to the girl. 'All right, Cele. I'll put the Lordling to bed.' The news must already have gone the rounds, for Cele curtsied and let herself out with not more than a sympathetic glance. Ariadne set Gerrit in her lap. 'Well, now, what shall we talk about? Have you been a good boy today?'

He nodded. 'But do you know what, Mumma? My horse flew away!' His lower lip came out. Alphonse had given him the magical toy this morning.

With her eyes on the window where he had pointed, Ariadne said, 'Sometimes we can't hold on to the things we treasure, little one. They have lives of their own, and sometimes they go away from us.' She looked down and hugged him.

'Like Daddy,' he murmured against her shoulder.

It was a moment before she could say, 'Yes, dear. Like Daddy.' She rocked him, and when his thumb found his mouth, she said, 'I have to take a boat ride, Gerrit, and I think I shall be from home awhile.'

He was sleepy and comfortable and did not raise his head. Around his thumb he asked, 'Are you going to see Master Kursh?'

I hope not, she thought. 'Whatever gave you that idea?'

'Cele said he probably went to his house. I said I wanted to go find him, but she said I'd have to take a boat.'

To Jarlshof? Ariadne thought and then realized that she had known that was what Peewit would do. 'If I find him, I'll tell him you miss him.'

He frowned, but his head was on her shoulder and she did not see it.

Ariadne went on. 'I've given Uncle Jaki a big castle of his own near the ocean, Gerrit, and I must go and see that it is in good order before he moves in. That's why I have to take the boat ride.' And I'll skin Cele if she tells him differently.

'Oh,' he mumbled around his thumb.

'I've asked Master Imris to look after you while I'm gone. You like him, don't you?'

A vigorous nod. 'He's going to make me a bow!' Indeed? the queen thought. We'll see about that! Gerrit raced on. 'He wanted to make me a harp like his, but I said I liked the bow better and he said he would make me one. But he won't give me any real arrows, though.' No, he will not, his mother assured herself.

'Well, it's getting late. Let's get you into bed.' When the covers were drawn to his chin, she gave him a good-night kiss and held his hand. 'Mumma loves you, Gerrit. Remember that.' He coughed and turned his head on the pillow.

She watched him sleeping, and it was a long time before she could force herself to leave.

Alphonse stood on the aft deck, arms akimbo, staring steadily at the full-bellied sail. 'How am I doing?'

Nels lounged on the main deck, or pretended to, though actually he was keenly aware of the two blended Wardings. 'Not bad, for a landlubber.' He would travel with them to the mouth of Willowsrill and teach Alphonse what he could about piloting the *Gannet*, which the redheaded wizard had temporarily renamed the *Minnow*.

The queen sat under the canopy and had not said much since they had pulled away from the landing at Castlenigh. Her hands gripped her woolen wrap, though, and Nels guessed that between fear of the unknown and homesickness, the Queen of Ilyria was feeling pretty miserable. He presented a silver flask with a bow. 'Sileaught, madam. It helps the stomach.' His smile was meant to be engaging.

'Oh, I am not feeling sick,' she said, but she took the flask and helped herself to a good swallow.

She would have given it back, but he pressed it into her hand. 'Keep it, please. It helps other things besides the stomach, I have found.'

Ariadne's hand dropped to Patience, who was curled on her lap. 'Thank you.'

Nels swarmed up the short ladder to the piloting deck. Alphonse stretched. 'The fatiguing part is casting ahead to make sure there's a clear channel.'

'Yes,' the Meld Mariner agreed. 'That usually takes a while to get used to. You've picked it up quickly.'

'Good teacher.'

The Wind Wizard suddenly began to chuckle as he looked over the clean lines of his vessel. 'By the Powers, did you have to name her after the smallest fish in the sea?'

'Ever tried to catch a minnow with your bare hands? Small and quick – that's what I want us to be.'

Nels laughed obligingly, but did not voice his thought that there were many fish in the sea that ate minnows.

A heavy swell was running when they slipped past the lighted beacon that marked Willowsrill Mouth, the place where the great river met the sea. They had set Nels ashore at Waterford. Ariadne sipped steadily at the Sileaught, but did not otherwise betray the fact that she was scared silly. Alphonse drove the *Gannet* in the face of the freshening wind, checking the boat's trim with his mind. 'Would the Greenbriar Queen still remember how to make tea, do you think? There is a paraffin stove in the cabin and, if I know Nels, a goodly supply of tea.'

Summoning a smile, Ariadne answered in the same tone, 'Just drive the boat, Master Wizard, and keep a civil tongue if you expect to eat anything on this trip. Do I remember, indeed!'

Chapter Twenty-two

The first thing that Kursh did when he saw his brother Trondur was to smash him in the mouth. He stepped over the prone body and strode into the house.

Peewit was more shocked than Trondur was. He leaped to help the dwarf to his feet, stammering, 'I – I'm sorry! He's mad, you s-see!'

Trondur Korimson got up slowly, wiping away the trickle of blood from his split lip. 'Sane or crazy, he'd have done the same thing.' He spat ruefully. 'Kursh has owed me that one for a long time.'

Peewit hadn't a clue what to say or do, so he just stood there with the sack at his feet.

After a moment, the dwarf seemed to recollect himself. Wiping his hand on his vest, he extended the other awkwardly. 'He's driven my manners clean out of my head! Trondur Korimson, at your service, captain. Be welcome – our home is yours.'

The Littleman made him a bow. There was much to take in in that moment. Trondur looked much as Kursh had in his younger years, with the same hawk nose and square jaw, but he was lean, for a dwarf, and beardless, having recently shaved it in mourning for his father's death, and his eyes were less piercing than Kursh's, not as proud or stern. He was obviously of quieter temperament, too: Kursh would have beaten the daylights out of anyone who had hit him that way, brother or no.

Peewit eyed the lump rising in the corner of Trondur's mouth. 'Maybe I shouldn't have brought him here, but –'

That brought a quick glance. 'And where else would you have taken him?' Trondur bent to pick up the sack. 'No, whether he likes it or not, Kursh was due to come home sometime. Now is as good a time as any.'

To try to make the situation lighter, the captain admired the house. 'This is magnificent! I knew you Korimsons had your ancestral home on Jarlshof, but I must say, I wasn't expecting anything like this!'

Trondur beamed and turned with him to regard the intricate carved fretwork that rose above their heads. 'The family has lived here, father to son, for sixteen generations. We are one of the oldest clans on Jarlshof.'

If you wanted to capture the full warmth of the winter sun, you could not have done better than to pick this hill overlooking Skejfalen, Peewit realized. He had found on the hike up from the city that nearly all dwarvish homes were built into the hills, like the Korimsons', earth-cooled in summer and protected from winter snow and gale. Only the south-facing wall was of timber, and this was intricately carved and painted, with an overhanging peak like the prow of a ship. The Korimsons', however, was far bigger than any other he had seen, and had more windows. Peewit took a closer look and realized with a start that the panes were all of crystal, thick and perfectly clear. A low whistle went through his mind, and he wondered that the dwarves were so casual with their wealth.

On studying the carving more closely, though, he realized that there was a difference here. Most of the houses he had seen were bright with color and window boxes bloomed under each window. This old house was faded, the paint lightened by sun and rain, and there were no window boxes at all. There were brackets for them, but no planters. There was an indefinable sense of things gone downhill. Kursh's father had been elderly, Peewit remembered, and then he wondered why Trondur had not kept up the house for him.

But he had no business asking, so he gestured to the smaller house off to the left. 'Who lives there?'

'That's mine.'

'Oh,' Peewit said, flustered. 'Forgive me, I thought –'

'That I was Korim's heir?' Trondur shook his head, and the same rueful smile came to his twisted mouth. 'No, Kursh is the elder of us. He is the Korimson, now, and master of Ledgelawn.' He gestured Peewit through the great oak door. 'I welcome you in his name.'

The place was a regular warren, but Peewit liked the low ceilings and neat bedrooms on the second floor. For the first time in his life, all of the knobs were within easy reach and all the furniture comfortable, and if it was a little dusty and a little musty, what of it? Trondur had given him the best guest chamber, the third room on the right at the top of the stairs, with a wonderful view out over the front garden and the city and the harbor bobbing with boats. A fire roared on the hearth, drawing out the damp, and the bed was thick with feathers and a good wool coverlet. He looked longingly at it, but thought it best to go looking for Kursh.

He descended the stairs and found himself in the large room

that formed the heart of the house. Massive tree trunks supported the roof, and the room was flooded with light from the multipaned windows to either side of the entrance. A hearth easily large enough to roast an ox was on the right wall, with a carved, high-backed settle drawn near. The floor was covered largely with woven rugs that must have been at one time very fine, but had worn threadbare in places. There was a crystal chandelier, too, but its candles were mere stubs, and even from where he stood, Peewit could see the cobwebs.

He glanced twice to be sure Kursh wasn't sunken in one of the armchairs, then followed the sound of water being drawn. There was a short hallway to the left under the stairs and then the kitchen. This was cheery, well lighted, and there was a built-in planter for kitchen herbs along the width of the windowsill. The hearth looked in fairly good shape, and wonder of wonders, there was a pump in the sink. Peewit had heard of them, but never seen one, not even at Greenbriar. Trondur had been cranking on the handle and looked up over the bucket. At the Littleman's expression, he smiled. 'It's a convenience in the dead of winter, I can tell you! And the spring it's drawn from never goes dry.' He dipped some water into the kettle and set this on the hook over the fire. 'There. Now while that's boiling, let me just step over to my own place to fetch us some tea. I am afraid the mice have been into what was left of my father's.'

'A cup would certainly be welcome, thank you. Say, Trondur, have you seen Kursh?'

'He wasn't upstairs?'

'I don't think so. I heard him come down here.'

The dwarf nodded. 'I know where he is, then.' He beckoned, and Peewit followed him out across the main room to a door set in the fireplace wall. 'The workroom,' Trondur explained and quietly lifted the latch.

Inside was a long narrow room stretching to take in as much of the south light as possible. The walls had been given a lime wash to brighten it further, and when Peewit saw the hearth, with its conical hood of beaten copper, he understood why: it needed good light to blow and then cut the crystal.

Kursh stood at the long workbench. His hands roved restlessly over the calipers and blowtubes, the etching tools and heavy leather mitts, but his eyes were not following his hands. He was staring out the window at the sky and sea.

Trondur watched him for a moment, then murmured to Peewit, 'Some of the instruments are sharp.'

The Littleman nodded and went quietly to Kursh's side. 'Time to take a break, Kursh. Come have some tea.' The unfocused eyes swung to his face. 'Come have some tea,' he repeated.

All of a sudden, tears were spilling down the dwarf's face, and he let Peewit lead him out of the workroom and to the settle before the fire. 'There, old fellow, there.' He tucked a rug about Kursh's legs and murmured to Trondur, 'I think he knows he's home.'

'Aye,' the younger brother sighed, and, going to the workroom door, he turned the lock. Then he went quietly out to fetch the tea from his house, and Peewit was left to pat the broad back and say sympathetic things he was positive Kursh could not understand.

Later, Trondur and Peewit shared a salt-fish stew at the huge wooden table in the kitchen. Fourteen people could have been seated, easily. Trondur saw Peewit's eyes tallying the seats. 'Dwarves have big families,' he explained. 'I remember when I was young, this house would be full to bursting at Aashnasse, with relations and the hired folk. My mother always complained about feeding that many people, but she always made the best Aashnasse cake in Skejfalen.' He caught himself with an embarrassed grin and noisily slurped his stew.

They had not been able to get Kursh out of the settle, so they had left a bowl for him on a stool drawn close by. Peewit wiped his lips on a finger towel and swallowed some tea to take the salt out of his mouth. Trondur wasn't among the best cooks, but the meal had been hot. 'You were four brothers, I believe? Were there any sisters?'

'No, just the four of us.' He went silent.

Peewit had never known just what had happened, but he knew that Kursh had been disowned and that young Orin had been the son of a brother who had settled in Swiftwater Shallows along with Kursh. With his Littleman sensitivity to matters of family, he knew also here was a broken one, even before the old dwarf had died. He looked over the rim of his teacup to find Trondur's eyes on him.

'My brother has never told you, then?'

Peewit set down his cup. 'It's none of my business.'

Trondur looked down at his stew, then left his spoon in it and pushed it away with a grimace. 'You're as much brother to him now as any of us ever were, except maybe Finnivar. Finn and Kursh were closest in age, the middle two. I guess that accounts for it.' Trondur got up and fetched a bottle from one of the shelves. 'Will you have a taste of flotjin? It isn't the properest Aashnasse Eve feast, but it will have to do.'

'Your hospitality has been warm,' the Littleman said stoutly and took the short glass of black liquor the dwarf offered.

Trondur let that pass unremarked and sat down again, leaning back in his chair. 'Has Kursh ever mentioned kjeggles to you?'

'No. It sounds like a delightful pastry.'

Trondur laughed. 'It's a game.' His smile faded. 'It's supposed to be a game. We play it only at rather important occasions, like wedding feasts, birth celebrations, that sort of thing. Outlanders have sometimes called it a form of bowling.' Peewit's brow cleared. Bowling he understood.

'But there is an important difference,' Trondur said. 'I think in other places the pins are wooden and the ball is hard leather sewn around stone.'

Peewit nodded. 'Sometimes it is clay, but more often a river rock.'

The dwarf continued, 'Well, here we use pins of wood, right enough, but the balls are Weatherglass.'

The Littleman gasped.

'Yes, it is a little expensive, you see, and that is why it is only played on the merriest occasions.' Again he gave a lopsided grin around the swelled lip. 'At the end of the game, the winner gets to break the Glass over his opponent's head and call down a little weather on him. Usually it's a dash of the iciest water he can summon!' His smile flickered and went out, and he poked his glass of flotjin about the table for a moment.

Peewit did not move as Trondur's voice became lower. 'The day of Kursh's wedding –' He broke off and looked up. 'You knew that he had been married?' Peewit nodded tightly, and Trondur resumed, 'Yes, I thought he might have told you that. She died in childbirth, and the boy, too. Finn sent to tell us from Swiftwater Shallows. But that was later. The day of Kursh's wedding they could hear the party clear down to the harbor, they tell me, and my mother and aunts fed nearly everyone in Skejfalen.' He waved. 'A wedding is an important occasion for the city as well as the clan, you know. It means the traditions will be unbroken, the skills passed down for another generation.' He sipped. 'There was quite a lot of drinking, as you may imagine.

'By late afternoon my older brothers were ready to play kjeggles. A lawn was cleared for them, and the pins set up. I wasn't allowed to play yet, for it is an adult's game and I was only twelve. So it was Finnevar, Kursh, and my eldest brother, Llew.'

Trondur stirred in his chair. 'To understand what happened, you must know that Llew had a fierce temper. He was a fine kjeggler, and my father was prouder of him than of the rest of us. He was the heir, and that made a difference. Anyway,' he sighed, 'the three of them began to play. Hours later, they were still at it, and torches were brought out to light the field. None of them would yield, and the scores went up and up. Small fortunes were won or lost that night by the spectators, for, of course, no one went home. At length, Kursh lost and he dropped out of the game, going to stand with the crowd and shout encouragement to Finn. Llew always won, you see, and so he wanted to see Finn take it for once.'

Trondur went silent for so long that Peewit thought he had changed his mind about telling the rest, though the Littleman figured he could guess it. 'Why didn't your father stop it?'

'He had some bets of his own,' Trondur said briefly. 'And besides, it was fun. Nothing like it had ever been seen before!' He drew a breath. 'Finally, around midnight, it was over: Finn won. The shout that went up from the crowd woke those who had fallen asleep out of the torchlight, and they carried Finn about the field on their shoulders. I was near enough that I could see Llew's face, though, and I remember thinking that he was going to be a sore loser.' He tossed off the rest of his flotjin. 'They set Finn down before Llew. He hefted his Weatherglass and teased Llew for a minute about what he was going to do to him – freeze his nuts right off, things like that. All good fun. Finn was much younger than Llew and still at the age when boys don't know when to shut up. Then he raised his Glass, broke it, and brought the iciest, coldest dump of snow down on Llew that you ever did see. Midsummer it was, and there stood Llew, covered with snow like a snowman. People laughed until their sides ached. Llew just stood there brushing himself off, his face red with cold – we thought. Then he swung and lifted Finn right off his feet.

'Kursh came between them, and Llew knocked him down, too. It all happened so fast no one had time to stop Finn when he picked himself off the ground. He put everything he had into the blow, and it caught Llew square. He went over backward and hit his head on a rock. He was dead before anyone could even get my father from the house.'

Peewit was silent. When some minutes passed, he said, 'I take it that your father blamed Finn, though Llew had started it.'

Trondur nodded. 'Kursh tried to speak for Finn, but it was no good. Father cursed them both, and Kursh cursed him back. Then I got into the act and said some things I shouldn't have, and it wound up with Kursh and his new bride and Finn all leaving on the morning tide. None of them ever came back.' He raised his eyes to the Littleman. 'Until now.'

It was, as Half Hand had promised it would be, as if all the stars in the night sky had come down to make their homes on Jarlshof. Peewit leaned on the wide sill at his open window and smoked a quiet pipe. Down the dark expanse of the hill of Ledgelawn, the lights of other houses in the city came faintly, a twinkling carpet rather like fireflies, he thought. The old house stood dark and silent around him. On an impulse, he set his night candle on the sill next to him and watched it reflect off the crystal panes. 'Go in peace, Korim. Your son's come home.'

Next morning, as Peewit shaved with Trondur's razor, he heard a clop of hooves outside. When he glanced out the window, a grin broke across his face, and he toweled the soap off, flying down the stairs.

Trondur already had the door open, and the expression on his face was something to behold. She was saying, 'How d'ye, sir. My name's Thyla Njordson, bakeress to the queen, and I'd like to see Master Kursh if he's to home.' Behind her, the milkman pulled his beard, eyebrows reaching for his hairline. Peewit brushed past Trondur and for no reason he could have put into words, gave her a hug. She beamed. 'Well met, captain. He is here, then.' The fellow with the milk wagon was positively gaping.

Peewit took her arm. 'Master Trondur Korimson, allow me to present the noble lady who bakes the finest blueberry muffins and the most delectable honeycakes in all of Ilyria!'

'Tut, I ain't noble,' she was saying, plucking at his sleeve in embarrassment.

Trondur shut his mouth with a snap. 'Welcome, mistress. May I take your bag?' He looked over her shoulder. 'Thank you, Ollie.' The milkman came to with a start and touched his cap. The cart rolled back down the hill.

Trondur bowed and waved her in. She caught sight of Kursh, still in the settle where he had spent the night, and went toward him. Trondur caught Peewit's arm. 'Is she . . . that is, are she and my brother . . .?' he whispered.

The Littleman watched her stoop and search Kursh's face for any sign of recognition. There was a glint of merriment in him, but for Trondur's benefit, he whispered back gravely, 'I think it is all very proper.'

'I see.' Plainly he didn't, but as Kursh was in no condition to play master of the clan, he would have to. If the woman had come all the way from Greenbriar, she had to be welcomed, especially during Aashnasse. He cleared his throat. 'I am sorry we can give you no great reception, mistress, but tea we have, and toast. Would that do?'

She had straightened. 'Lovely. Thank you. But I reckon I know my way around a kitchen. There's no missus, I take it?' At his shake of the head, she threw her cloak on the settle. 'Then if you'll just point the way, I'll fetch some breakfast for all of us. I've even brought a pot of elderberry jam to have with our toast!' She dug in her satchel and emerged triumphant.

Peewit was grinning. Trondur, though flustered, handled it well. 'Right this way.'

While he led her toward the kitchen, Thyla putting him at ease by exclaiming at the views, Peewit crossed the room to Kursh. 'You're a lucky old dog and you don't deserve it,' he twinkled.

Kursh moved then, looking up. 'Piss off,' he growled, and the Littleman laughed.

In remarkably short order, she was calling from the kitchen, 'Breakfast is ready. Any hungry folk out there?'

'Coming!' Peewit sang out. He reached to get Kursh up, but the dwarf pulled his arm away and refused to budge. The Littleman sighed and went along to the kitchen. Thyla was pouring tea, and Trondur was already happily wolfing thick toast and jelly. When Peewit took his place at the table, she looked beyond him and frowned. 'He won't come,' the Littleman explained quietly.

She pursed her lips and finished pouring for him. 'Yes he will,' she said shortly.

From where they sat, Trondur and Peewit both watched over their breakfast as the stout dwarven woman marched to the end of the hallway. She put her hands on her hips. 'You're no invalid,' she told Kursh sternly. 'Now, there's good tea and toast waiting. If you want some, get off your hind end and come out here.' She gave a push at where her cap would have been if she had still been in the queen's service and waited for him.

Trondur's brows shot up and he choked a little on his tea. Peewit crammed a half slice of bread into his mouth.

There was a movement in the living room, and then Kursh lumbered past her. 'I thought you might be hungry,' she said with satisfaction. 'And I've made you some starflower special, too, so just sit you down and drink it.' He grumbled something as he pulled out a chair. 'You can save your mumbling, too,' she told him crisply, but she patted his back as she went by him to the hearth and he did not shake her off.

Trondur and Peewit exchanged a look.

Kursh picked up a thick slice of toast and began to eat. The starflower tea must have been good, because he drained the mug and held it out for more. As she poured it for him, she winked over the shaggy gray head at Peewit.

'He just needs time to come to himself,' she told Trondur as he pumped water for her to wash the breakfast things. 'In a few days, when I've put some good food into him, he'll get built up a little, and then we'll see if the starflower does him any good. Who knows? Maybe the Wild Feller will leave him alone, now that Kursh has . . . done what he's done. Pump me another bucket, would you? And is there a mop?'

He set the washing bucket on the hook to heat. 'I think you should see the house.'

She dried her hands on her apron. 'I'd like that.'

They went through to the living room. Peewit had fetched out his own pipe and Kursh's from the sack, and they both sat with their feet stretched out to the hearth, smoking. Contentment was thick in the air. Trondur picked up Thyla's bag and cloak and led her upstairs.

At the top of the stairs, he turned into the right-hand wing. At the end of the hall he swung a door open, and Thyla stepped past him. The room was large and bathed in light. Not only did it share the large south windows that every other room had, but a smaller window had been cut in the end wall, so that it would catch the afternoon light from the west, as well. A small patch of posies bloomed just outside it. Lace trimmed the bed canopy, and there was a lace runner on the table that held the china washbasin and pitcher. The walls were lime-washed and the coverlet on the bed rich rose velvet.

'It was my mother's room,' Trondur said from the door. He shrugged a little. 'It is the only one suited to a lady, I'm afraid. We were all males in the family.' He looked around. 'Everything is just as she left it. My father could not bear to come through the door after she passed on.'

Thyla touched a silver handmirror and the ivory comb that lay beside it. She blinked. After a moment she faced him. 'You're a dear lad.' She drew her shoulders back and straightened her apron. 'I am staying, you know. At least until he's well again.'

He smiled briefly. 'I know. You are welcome.' He dug a finger in his ear. 'It will be good to hear pans clanging in the kitchen again.' They understood each other very well, it seemed.

She saw the upstairs bedrooms and the downstairs pantry, laundry, bathroom, and weaving room. They finished up back at the kitchen. Her eyes sparkled. 'It's a good big house!'

He pulled at where his beard was growing back in. 'It is,' he admitted.

'Would you mind very much if I did a bit of cleaning?'

He laughed. 'Not hardly!'

Thyla smiled and poured herself some wash water. 'Why don't you leave Kursh with me and take the captain up to the kite competition? It's his first Aashnasse, and he shouldn't miss that!'

Trondur looked doubtful. 'Will you be all right?'

'Right as rain. Go on, now. Put a copper or two on the green one for me: I thought it looked good when Ollie was driving me up this morning.'

'The green one! The blue will win!'

'In your eye!' she replied, and they bet on it on the spot.

She kept Kursh busy all morning, drying dishes, pumping water for laundry, moving furniture to be swept beneath, beating rugs. Every time he faltered she was at his elbow with more starflower tea, and he drank it all. Finally near noon, she found him asleep in one of the armchairs. Thyla regarded him for a moment. 'Face it,' she whispered to herself. 'He may get better, but he's never going to be well again.' She climbed the stairs and went to her own room to unpack at last.

When she had everything put away to her satisfaction, she

repinned her hair and headed back briskly for the stairs. She
heard a noise across the landing and three doors down. When
she stepped quietly to the open door, Kursh had the Pipes out of
the sack and was turning them over and over in his hands.

'Kursh?'

He swung his head to look at her.

'Put them down and help me with this rug, would you?' She
pointed to the hall runner.

He looked down at the Pipes once more. 'Thyla,' he said,
'someone has to destroy these.'

He knew her! She kept the jubilation out of her voice.
'Yes, dear,' she agreed calmly. 'But not today. Help me with
the rug.'

When they had it rolled and Kursh was carrying it outside for
cleaning, Thyla took the Pipes and put them in another room,
under the mattress.

There was new-baked bread for supper, and thick slices of ham
with roasted new potatoes. The menfolk pushed themselves
away from the table, groaning, and she promised, 'Tomorrow,
I'll make Aashnasse cake.' Trondur took Kursh out to the living
room to make up the fire and set the checkerboard between
them, but Thyla caught Peewit's eye and he stayed to wipe the
dishes.

When he heard about the Pipes, his brows drew together.
'And two minutes later, he didn't know me again,' she finished,
wringing out the dishrag.

'Which room have you put them in?'

'I forgot to count. It's the little one with the cradle and the
trundle bed.'

'Good enough. I'll tell Trondur. We should keep an eye on
Kursh.' He pulled the towel through his hands. 'I meant to throw
the damned things overboard on the trip here, but the Shimarrats
drove it right out of my mind.'

'Well, there're any number of ships down at the port. You can
do that anytime.'

He nodded. 'Say, I brought you a present today!' Dropping the
towel, he dashed out to the front door and returned in a few
moments with a big box. Thyla leaned to see. Candles, dozens of
them. Their eyes met. 'Let's put them in the windows, shall we?'
the Littleman asked.

In an hour's steady going, they had lit every window of
Ledgelawn, and all four of them went out to the yard to look back
and admire their handiwork. 'Doesn't it look fine?' Trondur
glowed.

Thyla's hands were on her hips, and her eyes were shining.
'Just you wait till tomorrow night, when I've washed those
windows!'

Kursh looked at her. 'I suppose you'll want me to help with that, too,' he groaned.

'Ho, Trondur!' one of the fliers called next morning when Peewit and Korimson came up to the competition field. 'I saw your place all lit up last night.' He grinned. 'Who is that woman?'

Trondur never batted an eyelash. 'She's my brother's betrothed,' he answered, and Peewit nearly swallowed his tongue.

They kept at the windows, he on the inside, she on the outside, and after each one they finished, she fed him more starflower tea. 'My kidneys are floating, woman,' he growled.

'It's good for you,' she answered serenely as he came back from the outhouse.

They did another window.

She fed him more tea and went back outside to start another expanse of crystal. But he was not inside looking out at her. Thyla gave it a minute, shook her head, and went back inside. She had set her foot to the stairs when she realized the door to the workroom was open. She found him at the bench with a blowtube in his hands. His eyes were thoughtful. 'He didn't leave any crystal,' he said. He put the tube down and held out a hand to her. 'Would you like to take a walk?'

A pink blush came up in her cheek, and she went with him toward the shed that stood higher on the hill. 'This is where we keep the raw crystal,' he explained. 'If the old man had any left, it must be up here.'

They stopped to pick some flowers, and by the time they got to the shed, he had gone blank again. 'What was I looking for?' he asked her.

She kept the disappointment out of her face. 'Raw crystal, dear.'

He frowned. 'What for?'

'I don't know,' she told him gently.

Kursh stood looking into the empty shed, and then allowed her to take him back down the hill to the house and the windows.

She duly reported it to Peewit, and that night he and Kursh played checkers. The dwarf studied his moves and finally jumped four of Peewit's men to end up with a crown. 'Well done!' the captain exclaimed.

Kursh said gruffly, 'I'm not stupid, Peewit, I just have trouble remembering things.'

The Littleman mentally held his breath. 'How do you feel?'

'Well enough, only I have to use the chamber pot every two minutes,' he grunted.

Peewit laughed, and Kursh held out his broad palms for

inspection. There were blisters, big blisters, Peewit agreed. The dwarf leaned across the board confidentially, glancing to include Trondur where he sat in the settle smoking. 'Do you know that woman made me wash every sodding window in this house?!'

'Cheer up!' his brother advised. 'There can't be much she hasn't cleaned yet! Tomorrow should be an easier day.'

Peewit ventured, 'Do you have any headache?'

'Headache? No. Why do you ask?'

'Oh . . .' The Littleman shrugged. 'You had quite a lot of them before . . . we left Greenbriar, that's all.'

Kursh nodded and sipped his tea. 'I remember, a little.' He fell silent.

Peewit glanced at Trondur, and he nodded slightly. 'Kursh, do you remember anything about . . . about the consort?'

'Nice fellow. Likes his wine a bit too much.'

The Littleman had to bite his lip. Obviously Kursh did not even realize that Ka-Salin was dead by his hand. 'Yes,' he mumbled and then he got hastily up and went to his own room.

Kursh stared after him. 'What's the mackerel stuck in his gullet?'

'Haven't a clue,' Trondur lied, and handed Kursh his pipe. 'Outlanders are funny sometimes.'

Next morning, Kursh knew them all and even teased Thyla about her muffins. Was there some problem with the blueberries this year? he wanted to know. She slapped him with a dishtowel and then they all took the day off and went up to the kite competition.

On this day of the kite battles, there were five fliers left. The blue one that Trondur liked had been knocked out on the day before. He paid his wager and Thyla doubled her money on the green.

On their flaxen tethers, the silk kites rode the wind, lofting so high they were nearly out of sight, and then – at a flick of the flier's wrist – screaming down the thermals to attack one of the other kites. If the flier under attack was skillful enough, he could make his kite swoop in time to avoid the strike and then launch a darting attack of his own. It looked uncannily like two birds buffeting each other with their wings to knock each other out of the air. Fouling the lines was not allowed, and when it happened by accident points were deducted from the score. So far the red one that Half Hand had picked was at the top of the standings.

The gold one swooped and there was a crack and the sound of silk ripping, and the black kite fluttered to the ground. There were some good-natured curses and some scattered applause from the crowd. Kursh said to Thyla, 'Did you bring anything to drink?'

She had brought a flask of starflower. 'It's not hot,' she warned.

'That's all right. It's wet.'

Vendors wandered among the people sitting on their quilts to watch, and Trondur bought some soft pretzels and light amber beer. Kursh unexpectedly stuck to his flask of tea, and it seemed he realized it kept his mind clear. He was able to answer some of the dwarves who stopped to welcome him home, calling them by name.

The summer day wore on, and Thyla's nose grew sunburned beneath her bonnet. The gold kite went down, and the contest was ended for the day. Tomorrow the red and the green would fight it out for the championship.

Peewit and Trondur, who had had several beers apiece in celebration of Kursh's recovery, sang all the way home, and Thyla and Kursh followed a little behind in the twilight. 'Think I'll get some paint for the house,' he told her.

She turned her head to regard him under a tilted bonnet. 'And how about flower boxes?'

'Of course. Got to have flower boxes. I don't know what you'll put in them, though. It's nearly fall.'

Thyla smiled. 'I'll find something.'

He had seemed so much better that it took them all completely by surprise when they found him gone the next morning. Peewit pounded down the hall to the nursery and plunged his hand under the mattress on the trundle. The Pipes were gone.

'He's been into the workroom, too,' Trondur reported grimly. 'Some of the tools and Father's mitts are missing.'

Thyla sank down at the kitchen table. 'I thought he was getting better,' she whispered.

Chapter Twenty-three

The wind blew coldly, but at least the air had begun to clear a little. No longer did ash swirl and flurry with every breeze. Near noon it could almost be said to be as light as a winter's dusk. The Eldest had decided to allow the Lordling out in the garden for an hour to give him some fresh air. Gerrit, well wrapped, stumped along clinging to Imris's hand. To give the boy credit, he had not complained at all about his foot, and with the increased exercise he had been allowed for the past few days, seemed to be gaining back some strength. If it were not for his persistent deep cough, one might have thought him well on the way to recovery.

The Yoriandir shifted his bow and motioned to the stone bench beneath the deadened birch. 'Would you rest, my lord?'

Gerrit headed for the bench without answering and clambered up. 'I wish my horse would come back.'

'Likely Master Alphonse will make you another when he returns. Here, sit on my lap. You will be warmer.' He pulled the child onto his lap and enfolded him in his azure cloak. 'You are getting to be quite a big fellow! Soon we shall have to find you a real horse.'

Gerrit twisted his head to look up. 'When?'

'Soon. When you are big enough.'

'How big is that?'

The Eldest was trying to remember how to talk to a child. 'When you are belt-high to Master Quint.'

'But I want a horse now!'

This looked like the beginning of a royal tantrum, unless Imris missed his guess. 'I have been working on your bow, my lord. Would you like to try it out?'

Eyes shining, the Lordling nodded vigorously.

Imris shifted him off his lap and went behind the tree, where he had earlier secreted the gifts: a small bow and a quiver of scaled-down shafts, unpointed of course. Gerrit crowed as the dim light caught the silver lacing of the quiver. He held out his hands. 'Give it here, old sod!'

The Yoriandir blinked. Then he realized that Kursh had been the boy's bodyguard. Though the dwarf would never have used such language to Gerrit, the prince had obviously overheard him talking, perhaps to Peewit. Imris had an impulse to laugh, but stifled it. 'That is not appropriate language, my lord,' he said mildly, but handed over the bow.

Gerrit slid from the bench and fumbled a shaft from the quiver. He tried to fit it to the string, as he had seen the castle archers do. Imris knelt to guide his hands. 'Turn your body so. Yes, good. Now, draw back the string to your ear . . . and . . . release!' The blunt shaft made a solid thwack against the tree trunk. 'Well shot, my lord!'

The prince began to laugh, but coughed instead.

'That is enough for today. We shall practice again on the morrow,' Imris decided quickly.

Gerrit's little face set. 'I want to shoot my bow again.'

'Very well. Once more.'

The Yoriandir had expected to have to help him again, but Ariadne's son repeated exactly the steps he had just been taught. As he was about to release, a butterfly fluttered across the frostbitten tansy. Immediately, Gerrit swung the bow and shot. 'I hit it, I hit it!' the boy chortled.

The green face had gone still. 'You have done an ill thing, Lordling. It is not right to kill Lord Aashis's creatures.' The ice in his voice brought the boy's lower lip jutting. It was not the child's fault, Imris thought. It was mine. 'Why don't you aim at that clump of foxglove down there if you want a mark. Come, we'll try a few more times.'

Three arrows remained in the small quiver, and Gerrit sent all of them down the slate walk a fair distance, but none so far as the dried stalks. 'Very good, my lord. In no time at all you'll be able to hit whatever you wish. Walk down now and collect your shafts and then let us go.'

The Lordling gave him a bright smile and ran heavily down to retrieve his small arrows. In the dusk and against the boxwood, even Imris's sharp eyes very nearly missed the streaking blackness. Out of the gloom came Beldis.

The Yoriandir whipped an arrow from his quiver and fitted it to the string, sending an enraged mind-shout: 'Me! You want me!'

The sapphire eyes gleamed, and for an answer Beldis blasted Imris's mind with a wild shriek of Song, even as it cleared the yews with a bound. Only a low bed of chrysanthemums and the clump of foxgloves stood between the Wolf and the child, and now Gerrit raised his head where he stooped over his toy arrows. He froze.

Imris had fallen to one knee, his spirit riven by that dark Song, his own gentle music dying under its cacophony. He knew his hands clutched his bow, but he could not feel them. He knew his mouth was open to yell to Gerrit, but he could not speak. In the narrow dark of fading consciousness, he saw the little Green-briar prince and the savage enemy. He wrested his mind to his control and sent a desperate plea: 'Ritnym! Lady!'

The Wolf laughed and gathered itself to spring.

A hurtling flash of white-and-emerald swooped between Beldis and the boy. For an instant the Hound of Tydranth paused, its head lifting to follow the Binoyr.

Imris heard a soft woman's voice command quietly, 'Now, my Eldest.' He loosed his silver arrow.

The shaft took Beldis through the sapphire eye.

The Wolf fell dead for that age of the world.

Imris, dagger in hand, had already reached young Gerrit. The boy stared down at the long length of the beast, then raised wide and solemn eyes to the Yoriandir. 'Well shot, my lord.'

Imris drew a breath, and not to make too much of the narrow escape, answered offhandedly, ' 'Twas an easy mark, my prince – there was so much of him to hit. Shall we go in to lunch?'

Gerrit slung his bow and quiver in an exact copy of his teacher, reached for the Yoriandir's hand, and they went from the dark garden under the wondering eyes of the sentries on the walls. 'Clean that up, would you?' Imris ordered quietly as they passed the Watchman at the postern into the keep. The soldier bowed wordlessly.

But the magnificent shot was the talk of the castle within the hour.

Aboard the *Minnow*, the Queen of Ilyria clutched the rail. They sailed north in an overturned bread bowl of fog, only the water curling back from the prow showing that they were moving at all. Though the position of the sun could not even be glimpsed, Alphonse cast his Warding ahead and found the way. There were still scars in his mind from the lightning clash with Tydranth's Warding, so he went warily and less quickly than he could have. He spoke to her as often as he could, but watching him she knew that the work was exhausting, so she tried not to bother him.

It was a good thing she had Patience for company. The one-eyed cat played like a kitten with a ball of embroidery silk from the queen's small bag, and since Ariadne knew she could do no embroidery anyway, she laughed at the cat's antics. Alphonse, of course, knew how much Patience detested the whole charade.

Their days became defined by mealtimes. While Ariadne fixed their third lunch, she became aware that they were not moving. She went out and looked around fearfully, but there was nothing to be seen, only fog. Alphonse stood rigid on the pilot deck. 'What's wrong?'

He raised a hand to slick back his hair, then sighed and came down the ladder. 'It's rough ahead, that's all. I think I had better rest before I try it.'

'Come in out of the wet, then. There's something hot to eat.'

He wolfed the stew hungrily with a piece of the hard biscuit that had been wrapped in oiled leather in Nels's stores. Chiswic must have directed that the boat be provisioned. Patience hopped up on the table and demanded cheese. The queen trimmed some off the wheel for her, and the cat was soon washing her face contentedly. Ariadne said hesitantly, 'There's a big storm ahead?'

Alphonse nodded. 'There's no way around it, either. I can't find the edges. We'll have to go through. Don't worry – the *Minnow* will ride well enough. Barques can't sink, you know.'

Then why won't you look at me? she thought. 'That's comforting.'

He looked at her then. 'Truthfully. They can't.'

'Then why are you afraid?'

Alphonse hesitated. 'We're lost,' he said. 'I think we've been going in circles, though I thought I was steering due north all the time.' He looked down at his empty bowl. 'And now I can't see anything at all in my mind except that damned storm.'

On the word, before she had time to say anything, the *Minnow* canted sharply and there was the crack of her linen sail filling with wind. Ariadne frowned. 'I thought you said you wanted to rest. You might at least have given me time to get the supplies stowed away!'

His blue eyes met hers. 'I am not piloting,' he said.

The storm had sucked them in, and the *Minnow* refused to answer to her pilot. She sailed cleanly enough through the mounting seas, but when he tried to let down the sail, he could not, and when he tried to turn her with his Warding, there was a vivid blue snap in his mind and he was thrown backward down the ladder to the main deck. Tydranth had his boat.

Alphonse clung to the mast and wrapped the other arm about his aching head. When he saw the first ice floating by, he knew. Ariadne fought her way to him, and he grabbed her arm to steady her, shouting above the wind, 'He's going to send us over the Falls at World's Edge!'

'This is what it looks like,' Thyla had told him. 'I've made up a flask, but the fresh is better anyway.' He nodded and took the leather bottle. A coil of rope was already over his shoulder. From tracks leading to the shed and then off across the hillside, they knew Kursh was climbing. 'You'll have to pick it as you see it, though; starflower only blooms in the early morning, with the morning star. It's a vine – mind you don't trip yourself in it.'

Trondur waited at the door. 'Don't worry,' he told her. 'He's just gone up to our quarry, I'll bet.'

Thyla nodded, but her hands were making a rag of her apron. Peewit patted her shoulder and followed the dwarf out.

Now, two hours later, Peewit had a small sack full of white starflowers, and they stood on the edge of the deep workings where the Korimsons had mined crystal for time out of mind. But there was no sign of Kursh, and they could hear no tapping of a hammer in the stillness. The ground was mostly thin turf over rock and left little imprint, but from what they could tell, Kursh had veered past the Korimson quarry and set his feet to the lower slopes of Barak-Gambrel, the forbidden mountain of Aashis. Trondur rubbed his brow and sighed.

Peewit's head was tilted to the summit, lost in cloud. 'I'll go,' he told the dwarf quietly. 'That way, no law will be broken. And I am a little lighter than you: I can go more quickly alone.'

'I don't give a hang about the law,' Trondur said, but Peewit knew by the pallor of his face that he was afraid to venture where the Power had spoken with Olin long ages ago.

The Littleman grasped his shoulder and shifted the coil of rope. Tying a knot in the end of the sack, he tucked it quickly under his belt in back. He was as ready as he could be. 'Have the candles lit in the windows.'

'Captain? There's one thing more I found missing down at the house. The bloody fool's got a kite up there with him!'

The sack kept swinging around to the front, and the rope was far too heavy to be lugging. At least he wasn't too warm, Peewit thought with an attempt to convince his aching legs and shoulders that it was all very normal to be climbing at such an uncomfortable angle. The sun had vanished into thin mist at this elevation. Normally Peewit had a good head for heights, but he had looked back over his shoulder once and that had been enough. He toiled steadily up, trying to follow where loose rock and fresh grazes showed Kursh's trail. To pass the time he tried to devise what he would do to the dwarf when he caught up with him. Might as well put the rope to good use, he decided; there ought to be enough kick room for a good hanging.

He climbed up onto a wide shelf, and there was Kursh, smoking his pipe. 'Hello,' the dwarf said.

Peewit did not know whether he should go closer. Was Kursh himself? 'Hello,' he puffed, studying the bearded face.

The dwarf regarded him through the fragrant smoke. Suddenly his brows drew down. 'Did my wife send you?' he asked suspiciously.

Wife? I don't think you could call her that, Kursh, he thought. 'No. I came looking for you myself.'

The dwarf nodded. 'That's good.'

Peewit carefully sat down nearer the edge of the shelf than he'd like, but he dared go no closer right now. 'Where are you going?'

A jerk of the pipestem. 'Up there.'

The Littleman did not take his eyes off him to peer upward. 'Why?'

'I've a thing or two to say to the Wind.'

Peewit nodded. This might be Kursh talking. 'Do you know who I am?'

The one eye narrowed, and the dwarf looked him over carefully. 'Can't say as I do,' he said cheerfully. 'You're a little fellow, though, aren't you?'

Not Kursh: this was the madman. Peewit carefully unslung the leather bottle. 'I've some tea. Would you join me?'

'All right.'

Quickly Peewit handed him the flask, and the dwarf took a long pull. 'Go ahead,' Peewit invited. 'There's more.' Kursh nodded and toasted him as he downed the rest.

'Ah, that's better,' he sighed. 'I was getting parched.'

The Littleman gave it a few minutes, while the dwarf puffed away, unconcerned. Finally he said, 'Kursh?'

'Hmm?'

'Don't you think you'd better come down? Trondur and Thyla will be worried.'

The dwarf rubbed his eyepatch. 'Well, the thing of it is, Peewit, if I come down now, they'll make sure there's no way I get back up here again.'

Holding his breath, the Littleman scrooched further over on the rock shelf until he sat beside the dwarf. 'And why is it so important that you go up Barak-Gambrel?'

Kursh looked at him clear-eyed. 'Because that's where the best crystal is. Doubtless Olin's old workroom will be there, too. That will be useful.'

'You're going to try to make crystal?'

The shaggy hair blew in the wind coming down the mountain. 'I've got to melt down the Pipes first,' he said.

The Littleman masked his shock. He had been sure he was talking to the sane Kursh.

'I know you think it's a daft idea,' the dwarf continued, 'but look – it's for certain that no other furnace than the one that Lord Aashis showed Olin how to build is ever going to be hot enough to melt down the ugly things. And somebody's got to do something about them. Why, right now the queen's in the thick of a terrible storm that's coming this way, and no Weatherglass that's been made is going to be able to help her. Alphonse thinks he sees ahead, but he doesn't, not really, and they're already closer than I like to World's Edge, and –'

Peewit had grasped his shoulders. 'Steady, old fellow, steady!'

Kursh drew a breath and wiped the sudden sweat off his forehead. The effort of hanging on to his mind was exhausting. 'If I lose my memory again, just keep me aimed up this damned mountain, all right?'

The Littleman did not answer immediately. He was weighing the bit about the furnace. Finally he clasped the other's arm. 'All right. I've more starflower. If we can get to the top, maybe we can find someplace where the water has collected, and then I'll make you some more tea.'

Kursh nodded. 'There must be a stream to quench the crystal, of course. And the first piece I'll make will be a teapot.' He pulled at his mustache. 'If you've got your wind back, we really should push on before I go bonkers again.'

'Let's use the rope.' While he was helping the dwarf rig a harness, Peewit asked, 'By the way, what's the kite for?'

Kursh stilled. 'Kite?'

'The one sticking out of your pack.'

The good eye swung to regard the leather pack against the face of the mountain. Then he stared at the Littleman, confusion and fear mingled in his expression. 'I really am crazy as a March hare, aren't I?' He grunted a laugh. 'Well, at least there's no more the Wild Feller can do to me. Guard yourself, Brickleburr!' He caught hold of the pack, buckled it on, and began to climb.

By late in the afternoon, the dwarf had begun to mutter about his shrew of a wife and his weak son, and Peewit knew that Kursh had slipped again out of himself. If the Littleman read him correctly, he was Olin now, climbing to challenge Aashis on Barak-Gambrel. The Littleman wondered who Kursh thought the small stranger on the other end of the rope was. They toiled upward, the rock cold and slippery under fingers worn to bleeding by sharp edges. Once Peewit lost his foothold and started to fall, but the rope brought him up short, swinging out over the clouds below, and Kursh silently hauled him back onto a narrow ledge. The Littleman tried to call his thanks, but his heart was hammering in his throat, and the most he could do was rest his face against the mountain until Kursh began to climb again.

By the time he hauled himself over the last edge, Peewit was too exhausted even to realize in the streaming darkness that they were at the top. He took a step and walked into Kursh. 'Ease up,' the dwarf growled, and Peewit froze. He was standing very near the edge.

Then Kursh walked forward surefooted, seeing in some way that the Littleman could not. They passed under a low dark arch, and the wind was no longer in their faces. A cave, Peewit thought. He felt his way a little along the wall and heard Kursh ahead of him by a step or two.

'All right, Lord Aashis, I'm here!' the dwarf suddenly yelled. It was not a belligerent yell, just a matter-of-fact one, to let a friend know you're borrowing something from his barn, for instance.

Peewit had jumped. There was a rustle in the darkness, and he realized Kursh had sat down. 'I'm going to sleep now,' the dwarf said, and judging by the snores that rose shortly from him, he had done just that.

Peewit arranged himself where he thought the dwarf would have to fall over him to get out the mouth of the cave, kept the rope tied about him, and let sleep take him. Just before he went under completely, he thought he heard a wild jangling, as of crystal bells tolling madly in a shrieking wind.

There was ice in the rigging, and finally the *Minnow*'s mainmast bent one way before a shivering blast and snapped when the wind suddenly veered. Alphonse cursed, made sure of his life-line, and slid across the canted cabin roof to try to clear the lines with his knife. But the flax ropes were frozen to iron, and he had to burn them off. The *Minnow* righted herself abruptly when the broken section of the mast and sail were freed, and the wizard fell hard. The next wave buried the rail and reached for him. He threw himself over the edge of the cabin, finding the door and careening through it. Ariadne sat rigidly braced on the floor, in the angle of his bunk and the partition. She was white, and her jaw was clenched to keep her teeth from chattering.

He was so cold that he had to draw the leather mitts off with his teeth. 'We've lost the sail,' he reported.

'So now we can't steer at all, not even to stay bows-on to the wind?' She had picked it up quickly.

'Well, we're being driven before the wind anyway, so we'll just have to hope that the *Minnow* doesn't swing around.'

Her eyes were huge. 'What will happen if we do?'

'The waves will break over the deck.'

'We'll go under?' There was a note of panic.

'For a moment. Then she'll breach again – come to the surface.' He made a diving and surfacing gesture. 'Like a porpoise. That's the way the Mariners design these boats.' The explanation was better than nothing, and he had kept his voice deliberately businesslike. She wanted to believe it, but the rolling cabin was far more convincing. She did not loose her grip on the bunk.

It was true that barques were engineered to be extremely seaworthy, but they were never meant for sailing off the rim of the world, nor were they intended to stand such a maelstrom as this forever. Searching the boat's struts and ribs with his Warding, he knew she was flexing with the stress of the wave action, and that it had been well enough that the mainmast let go when it did: it had buckled its stepping blocks and could easily have ripped through the deck given more time. He Warded the bilge and found only a few inches, nothing to worry about. So far, Minnow was doing well for a boat with no pilot, no rudder, and no sail.

He sat down and put his arm about the queen, and she clutched his hand. 'I just wanted to try to take the Crystal to Aashis,' she murmured apologetically.

'I know. It was the only choice.' He leaned his cheek on the top of her head, and after a time they slept.

And that was when Minnow was holed.

There was no sun in the morning, but at least there was enough light to see. Peewit got to his feet stiffly, looking about. 'Kursh?' There was no answer, and he realized the rope dangled at his waist. The other end had been untied. Hastily unknotting it and letting it fall, he went out of the cave.

The dwarf was standing on the little landing outside, beard flying back over his shoulder in the gale. His arms were folded on his chest, and he stared into the fog. Peewit hesitantly repeated, 'Kursh?' He did not answer, and gave no indication that he had heard. The Littleman tapped his arm, but there was still no response. Dread swept over Peewit, and he seized the dwarf and shook him. Still Kursh gave no sign of being conscious of his presence, only blinking and resuming his intent gaze.

Quickly Peewit ran back into the cave and emerged with the rope, which he retied about the dwarf's waist. Bringing the line back inside, he tethered it to a rock spur and dug for the sack of starflowers. On a thought he went to Kursh's leather pack and unstrapped it. There was a fat candle, with flint and iron. He did not light it yet, for they might need it if he couldn't persuade the mad dwarf to go down the mountain today. There were blow-tubes and other glassmaking implements, a few of Thyla's biscuits, and a tin cup. The kite was wrapped tightly about its light wooden crosspieces, and a huge ball of flaxen twine was at the bottom of the pack. There's water, Peewit reminded himself; Kursh said there was water to quench the crystal. He knelt, listening. He thought, but could not be sure because of the wind's roaring, that he heard running water from farther into the cave.

Damn! Now what's to do? he wondered. Kursh won't budge, but I must get some water to get tea into him.

He bit his lip, entrusted the dwarf to Aashis's protection for a few minutes, and lit the candle. Taking the tin cup, he made his way toward the water.

When the first of the silver torches lit, Peewit dropped the candle in shock, and it snuffed out on the rock floor. He stared at the silver, clean-burning cresset until he remembered where he had seen one like it. The Guardian. The Littleman bent stiffly to pick up his candle and went carefully along.

The underground springs welled up in the section of the cave that widened to form Olin's workroom. One spring steamed as it leaped up to fall back into its own pool, and Peewit realized he would not have to worry about trying to boil water to steep the leaves. 'I don't know if the water's for drinking, Lord of the Winds,' he murmured, 'but my friend really needs a cup of tea.' Hesitantly, sensing nothing evil about the place, he filled the tin cup and sipped. The water was hot enough to make him blow quickly to cool his tongue, and it tasted sweet. He had been afraid minerals might make it undrinkable.

He sighed with relief and dumped a liberal amount of starflower into the hot cup. Then he went to fetch Kursh.

The dwarf was flexing his arms above his head and rubbing his neck when Peewit came out of the cave. The Littleman did not know whether Kursh thought he was Olin, but it was a safe bet, because he'd been so long without the mind-calming tea. 'Master Olin,' he said, 'your workroom is ready, and I've a nice hot cup of tea for you.'

Kursh turned and stuck his thumbs in his belt. 'Have you got the furnace lighted?'

Furnace? 'No, sir, but I will just as soon as you've had your breakfast. We must keep your strength up.'

A lopsided grin that was not Kursh's came to his face. 'I don't know why Lord Aashis sent me an assistant. I didn't have one before and it worked out fine.'

'But your task now is much more difficult, sir.'

Kursh sighed and stroked his mustache. 'Aye, that's true.' He shuffled into the cave, muttering.

Peewit drew a breath and followed, stopping to collect their baggage. The silver torches burned steadily, and somehow they comforted him, though the Pipes banged against his knee through the leather pack at each step.

When he got down to the work chamber the dwarf was sipping his tea, sitting on the edge of a deep firepit that Peewit could have sworn was not there just moments ago. He blinked. Kursh drained his mug and stood up, dusting off his breeches. He regarded the firepit. Suddenly he put two fingers to his lips and whistled piercingly. He followed this with a bellowed word in dwarvish, and fire shot up to the roof and then subsided to a moderate fountain. The dwarf rubbed his hands together. 'There.'

Peewit crept to his side, and the dwarf looked at him. 'Get the roof window open, will you?'

The Littleman tilted his head to look up, and sure enough, the top of the cavern was roofed with crystal. A silver chain hung down,and he tugged at it gently. One section of the huge window swung down silently, and the smoke from Aashis's Furnace spiraled out to be grabbed by the vicious wind.

'Peewit? Could I have another cup of tea? And hand me those rotten Pipes.'

I should have expected it, Peewit told himself. Of course it could not be so easy.

Even the furnace of Aashis would not melt the Pipes. Kursh had held them gripped in the long-handled tongs until the iron glowed red-hot, but the dark firmament did not even change color. From the wind outside, from the cold spring, from somewhere, came a sardonic chuckle.

The sound had enraged Kursh, and he had hurled the Pipes to the floor, seized the heavy hammer, and brought down a blow that should have smashed the dark crystalline shapes, but the hammer bounced harmlessly off and the rebound threw the dwarf back against the rim of the firepit. Peewit tackled him to safety from the side, and they sat for a long time while Kursh spewed curses that gradually subsided into brooding silence. There was only the splashing of the hot spring, the roaring of the furnace, and the gnashing of the wind around the roof window.

'Let's go home, Kursh.'

'Aye,' the dwarf mumbled. 'There's no more to be done here.'

They picked themselves up, and Peewit began to gather up their gear. Then he hesitated. Why carry all of it back down the mountain? There would be little enough time to use any of it, even if Kursh still had his brief moments of sanity. Without saying anything to the dwarf, he filled the flask and took the sack of starflower – much depleted – and the rope. Forcing heartiness, he said, 'I can't wait for some of Thyla's muffins! I'll bet they've saved us some.'

The dwarf did not answer, merely taking an end of the rope and tying on his harness once more. Peewit put an arm around his shoulders, and they walked down the cave to the arched opening, leaving the Pipes as safe as they would be anywhere, in the workroom of Olin.

The wind must have slackened, for the fog hung almost still about the landing outside the cave, and Peewit was relieved. He had wondered whether they would even be able to attempt the descent of Barak-Gambrel. This looked manageable enough. The Unnamed must be content with his victory. The Littleman was suddenly angry that the Three – especially Aashis – had done so little to help them. He bit his lip and said nothing that might hurt Kursh more than he was already aching from the sure knowledge that his madness could not be healed.

Peewit finished tying his own end of the rope. 'Do you want me to go first?'

Kursh was staring over the edge. 'I think it best. Wouldn't want to pull you down.'

Sitting down on the edge of the shelf, Peewit swung his feet over, turned to face the rock, and let himself over the edge. He had gone nearly the length of the rope when a pummeling wind plastered him against the cliff face so suddenly the breath was knocked out of him. His hand slipped from its hold and he began to slide down the rock. Desperately scrabbling for a handhold, he was brought up short by the rope. The wind seemed determined to make him part of the cliff. He twisted to shout upward, 'This is no good! Pull me up!'

The rope jerked and he was pulled up a few inches, then a few inches more. There was a crack of lightning somewhere too near, and he squeezed his eyes shut and could not breathe for fear. The rope hauled him up some more, and he found a foothold to help. The wind pasted him to the rock, then something hit him on the shoulder. When he squinted up he was hit on the forehead. It had begun to hail. First it was the size of a sparrow's egg, but quickly grew to pigeon-egg proportions, and then one came down the size of a duck egg and smashed his index finger. He screamed for Kursh, and the rope lurched as he hung straining to grip the icy rock and protect his head at the same time. 'Kursh!' But the line only swung sickeningly against the edge of the shelf as the flax twisted and frayed. The bellowing wind was a giant hand in the middle of his back.

Up on the ledge, the dwarf hauled the rope in hand over hand as though hauling in a fishline with a little fish on the end of it. When the lightning cracked he ducked instinctively and saw the weird greenish light. He went stolidly about pulling up the rope. The hail began to bounce off his brawny arms and shoulders, piling up around his feet. A goose-egg-size chunk glanced off his shaggy head, and he winced. The part of him that was still the First Watchman had a passing thought: Interesting. These things make good missiles.

The rope slackened unexpectedly, and he found himself overbalancing. Instinctively stepping back to save himself a fall, he slipped on the hailstones, and the gusty wind blew him off the other side of the narrow shelf. He and Peewit were strung like saddlebags across the summit of Barak-Gambrel.

Had a rock spur not taken up some of the slack, his greater weight would have pulled the Littleman right over the top and they would have both fallen to their doom. He shook his head to clear it and, mad or not, had sense enough not to look down between his dangling feet. At least he was out of the wind for a moment. His broad hands found holds, and he began to haul himself up the cliff.

Peewit was having a bad time holding to the cliff face with only one good hand. There were specks of black swimming before his eyes. He clung desperately and expected at any time that the dwarf in his madness would untie the rope and send him to his death on the mountainside. He tried to climb, but could not.

All at once, the rope twitched a little, and he rose a foot, then two, and he fended himself off a spur and his lifeline pulled him steadily up to the shelf. A broad hand caught his belt and hauled him over the edge. There came a bright flash and the stink of ozone, and lightning lanced into the cliff face where he had hung only moments before. Heedless of the hailstones rolling under them, he and the dwarf flung themselves toward the arch of the cave. Kursh had barely cleared the entrance when the mountain shook under their hands and knees. There was a flash of too-bright light and a whoofing concussion. Peewit saw a net of blue fire reaching for them, and then there was falling stone and darkness.

They sat under a steady silver torch. Peewit leaned against the cave wall and cradled his hurt hand, drawing his twitching legs up to his chin. Kursh sat next to him, fingering the crown of his head where the hair was singed and thin. He looked toward the sealed entrance. 'I could do with a spot of tea. Actually I could do with a keg of flotjin, but tea will have to do.' He swung his head to Peewit and tried to smile.

'Me, too.'

They got to their feet slowly, and Peewit reached automatically for the small sack he had tied to his belt, but it was not there. The Littleman gulped.

Kursh had seen his motion. After a moment he smoothed his eyepatch. 'Well, let me get your hand bound up, anyway, before I forget how to do it.' When Peewit nodded and turned wearily up the cave corridor, the dwarf cleared his throat. 'Brickleburr? Arm yourself with one of the heavier blowtubes. I expect you to use it if you must.'

The memory of the murders he had committed must have come to him. Peewit wished the dwarf could have been spared that, at least. He summoned a smile. 'You won't hurt me,' he declared.

But later in the day when the dwarf began to mutter and pace and there was no starflower to stay the madness, the Littleman quietly laid one of the heavy iron tubes by his side and did not dare to let himself fall asleep. He sat against the wall and listened to the wind groan beyond the crystal roof vent.

Chapter Twenty-four

Alphonse exerted his Warding and forced the pouring water to a trickle, but he would not be able to hold it for very long. Working quickly, he fashioned a patch from the spare stores and nailed it over the fist-sized hole in the *Minnow*'s hull. But when he withdrew his Warding, the water gushed around the edges and the patch blew out like a child's dam in a spring brook. He threw his Warding on immediately and tried to ignore the ice water lapping at his knees. Every time the *Minnow* climbed a wave and then slid down its long trough, the ballast of water surged from one end of the hold to the other and the barque wallowed, slow to recover and get her head up again.

He held the Warding with his mind and passed buckets up to Ariadne. They bailed for what seemed an eternity, and still the water level had not gone down much. The ship took a sudden lurch, and the wizard lost his feet. The ice water soaked him. 'Are you all right?' she called from the hatch where she clung.

'Yes,' he growled disgustedly. He sloshed aft, leaving the heavy oak bucket floating in the bilge. 'Leave it,' he told her, and they climbed to the cabin. 'Stay here.'

The wizard went out on deck. The wind howled, and he nearly slipped on the ice that coated everything now. Anger for his ship's torment flared in him, and his Fire snapped over every line of the *Minnow*, melting the crust in an instant of wonderful warmth. He could not hold the Fire and the patch both, however, and before he had made it to the pilot deck, there was a coating on the ladder once more. It might have been only the sea breaking over the prow, but he could have sworn he heard laughter.

Bastard! he thought savagely. Whoreson bastard!

Ice loomed off the starboard bow. It was not much taller than the maindeck rail. Struck by a sudden idea, he reached for the floating miniature mountain with his Warding and drew it near. As delicately as he could under the circumstances, Alphonse guided the ice to the *Minnow*'s bow until the ship and the berg rose and fell in the waves together. When he thought he had the right place, he Warded the block, binding it to his ship. There was a bad moment as a crest reared up behind them, taller by twice than the ship was long, and he thought perhaps the *Minnow* would be crushed finally between the wave and the ice, but the floe moved with the *Minnow*, acting as a sea anchor. Their flying speed had been slowed a little. He brushed the ice from his eyebrows, climbed perilously down to the maindeck, and made his way through the cabin to the hold.

Sloshing through the bilgewater, he bent to look at the hole. Beyond the glistening garnet light of his Warding, there was solid white. He grinned a little and eased the Warding off. The iceberg plugged the leak.

His whoop brought Ariadne leaning down through the hatch. Her face relaxed at his laugh. He went up the ladder, and she made way for him. 'Have you found a way to steer?' she asked.

'No, but I think I've found a way to keep us from sinking!' he said cheerily and went back out on deck.

Ah, so we *can* sink, the queen thought. She set her bucket on the floor tiredly.

He had the full use of his Warding this time, and kept the deck clear of ice while he climbed to the pilot deck.

Scanning quickly around in the driving cold, he spied a small ice block that would do well. He bound this to the port stern. Then another and another, systematically around the *Minnow* until she rode the waves collared in ice. As the ice was lighter than seawater, she could not now sink. The ice ring had another salutary effect: the waves no longer broke directly over the boat, and her flying speed had been stalled. The wind summoned by the Unnamed still drove them, but far more slowly. There might be time now for him to think of some way to save them.

He took the ladder easily and in the cabin found Ariadne already lighting the paraffin stove for the first hot food they had been able to make in longer then either of them could tally.

He sopped a piece of hard biscuit in his tea and looked up to find her watching him. 'What is at World's Edge?' she asked.

He shrugged. 'There's the Falls and a lot of water. Beyond that? Stars, I guess,' he answered lightly.

The gray eyes were thoughtful. 'We rode a falls once before in a Warded boat.'

She was thinking of the time five years before when Ritnym had sent them from her underground realm. Alphonse said gently, 'But I have not the Lady of Earth's Power, my queen.'

She hesitated, then said, 'I think I do. At the Guardian when you –'

The *Minnow* suddenly bucked. Alphonse flew up the stairs to the deck and grabbed for the rail. Everywhere the sea was the same, the slanting ranks of waves, the ice churning and bobbing beyond their white collar. The *Minnow* bucked again, more strongly, a decisive up-and-down action that had nothing to do with the waves.

The hatch flew open, and the queen stood muffled in her mantle, signaling him urgently. 'There's something under us!' Then her hand went to her mouth to stifle a scream, and she flung up a pointing hand. Alphonse turned to look behind him.

For a moment, all motion seemed suspended. There was the blunted point of the head, an open mouth ringed with huge incurving teeth, mottled black-and-white hide. Then the wave carried them down into the trough and the creature slid with them, ducking under the barque so that its sleek flukes rose higher than the mainmast would have. A third buck and some of the ice collar along the port side fell away, leaving the boat nearly foundering in the mountainous waves.

The wizard perceived in an instant Tydranth's intention. 'No!' he shouted and leaped to the stern rail. When next the ring of teeth towered above him, he threw his Fire into the open maw.

There was a hiss of steam, a quick sideways sliding of the mottled creature, and it sank beneath the waves. Alphonse and the queen waited tensely for the buck, but it did not come.

After a moment, Ariadne turned for the hatch. But off the starboard rail arose another set of flukes, and this time the barque was shuddered by a strike from the side which cracked away all the ice that had held out the water. Alphonse was aware of seawater gushing into the hold even as he grimly hurled Fire and saw the next creature rise to port.

From raging sea, from frozen rigging, from somewhere, came a sardonic chuckle.

'Some hell of an assistant you are,' the gruff voice said above him. Peewit's head snapped up. Kursh was standing there with the Pipes in one hand and the kite in the other. 'Get the window open again.'

The Littleman ached in every bone. He discovered this when he tried to scramble to his feet. 'Window? What are you doing, sir?' Don't put the Pipes anywhere near your lips, old fellow, or I'll have to do it. He had the heaviest blowtube in his hand.

'Just open the window,' Kursh-Olin repeated patiently, 'and stand by to make some crystal.'

Peewit risked a look upward. The window vent must have been sucked shut by the force of the wind. He regarded Kursh. Why not? he thought. If it will keep him occupied to fly a kite, let him. Walking to the chain, the Littleman pulled the roof window open. The shriek of the wind was unnerving, but at least no hail fell in, and it did not seem as though the lightning was anywhere about.

Kursh-Olin squinted up. Then he nodded, and crouched to tie the Pipes to the kite's crosspiece.

Oh, wait now, Peewit thought. He took a step. 'Don't you think – ?'

He never got the chance to finish his question, because the dwarf sprang from the floor and the Littleman rode his fist halfway across the cavern and lay stunned. Quickly now, the mad First Watchman picked up the kite, unwrapped some flax cord from the ball, and looked toward the firepit. He whistled and shouted the word in dwarvish, and the fire fountain shot up. On the warm upcurrent of air, the kite rose to the roof, bounced a little along the crystal window until it found the opening, then was caught by the howling wind. It shot into the open air, and the cord burned through the dwarf's fingers as he spat on the twine to keep it from parting.

He battled the wind as though it had been another kite, pulling and paying out twine to take his kite higher. The lightning began to flash and fear shot through him, but he kept his silk flier attacking the heavy clouds. For so long that it seemed an entire age of the earth, he fought the wind, then he came to the end of the ball of twine. He could go no higher; he could not get above the clouds to come shrieking down the sky and attack.

Still he played the cord back and forth across his cut hands, keeping his flier moving at least so the Other could not easily attack. The assistant groaned and rose to his knees, but Olin paid him no attention.

It was coming now – he could feel it – and he took precaution, winding the flaxen cord a half hitch around a spur of the crystal cave wall.

There was the sound of an arrow passing much too close to his ear, a blast of hot air as though the firepit had flared beyond its hearth, and then his eye was full of darkly spangled light.

Peewit barely had time to throw himself flat before the work chamber shuddered and flared. When he could think to look for Kursh, the dwarf was still on his feet, though his hair and clothes were smoking, and he was hauling in the kite. Incredulously the Littleman tried to get up and help the dwarf to the cold spring to douse the burns he must have, but the blast had thrown him on his injured hand, and the chamber momentarily swam before his eyes.

When the Littleman came to himself again, Kursh was leaning over him with a charred kite in his hand. Swinging from the crosspiece was the clearest blob of crystal Peewit had ever seen.

'Are ye all right?' the dwarf was asking.

'Are you?'

'Come on, Peewit, don't muck about – are you all right, or aren't you?'

The captain laughed. 'I don't know when I've been better!'

Kursh regarded him critically. 'I don't know when I've seen ye look worse, but we're all getting on a bit, I suppose, and this has been a proper whoreson day.' He straightened. 'I shouldn't be surprised if you find a packet of tea over by the spring – real tea, not that wretched flowery stuff. Should fix us both up. Would you mind getting it? I've got to see what I can do about this bloody storm the Wild Feller has called up.'

Peewit got shakily to his feet, and the dwarf reached to steady him for a moment. 'What are you going to do?' the Littleman asked.

'I'm going to make a Weatherglass, of course.'

For some reason she could not fathom – because she knew nothing of the destruction of the Pipes – Ariadne suddenly felt as though a heavy weight had been lifted from her back. She took a deep breath of the cold air and tossed her head to the wind. A fluke rose before them, but she did not even have time to point and shout before the wizard had aimed his Fire at it. The creature sank beneath *Minnow*'s keel. Up on the pilot deck he scanned the dark waters through the streaming fog. His shoulders were hunched into his ice-rimed cloak.

'They're gone,' she called up to him.

'Can't be sure,' he shouted back.

'No, really, they're gone,' she insisted. 'You've scared them off. Come down now and get dry while I start bailing.'

She saw the swing of his head and knew he was looking down at her. 'Don't you mark it, Master Wizard?' Ariadne could hear the bubbling note in her own laugh. 'I don't know what it is, but I feel much better.'

Slowly his hands unclenched and he let the garnet wink out. 'You're right,' he said slowly as he descended the pilot ladder. She held the hatch for him, and he looked down into her woodsmoke eyes as he stepped through. For a moment he thought they'd taken another hit from a creature, and then he realized it was merely the bound of his own foolish heart.

Kursh drew the crystal from the fire, turning it this way and that in the tongs and examining it critically. Peewit sipped his bracing cup of tea – which was not exactly ordinary tea, having some richer taste that he could not identify – and watched. He had known that Kursh came from a long line of Glassmakers, but he had not suspected how much talent of his own the stalwart dwarf had. Ambassador Nissen Olafson had been right.

When the crystal was heated to his satisfaction, the dwarf took one of the blowtubes, transferred the glowing glass to the end of it, and began to blow the Weatherglass to its typical spherical shape. The truer the sphere, the more powerful the Glass. His hands spun the blowtube quickly and smoothly, and before Peewit's fascinated eyes, the glowing crystal ballooned.

Letting it set for a moment, Kursh deftly dropped the palm-sized ball into the bucket of hot spring water at his feet. He had told Peewit that if they heard a snap at this stage, the hot crystal would have shattered on contact with the quenching bath and his work would be ruined.

Steam rose, obscuring the glowing sphere, but there was no snap. The Littleman, hardly daring to breathe, went to the dwarf's elbow to peer down. A moment more and Kursh delicately reached in with one leather mitt and quickly transferred the cooling crystal to the second bucket, cold spring water. There were bubbles as the glass sank to the bottom of the bucket and slowly floated to the surface again. A pleased smile broke across Kursh's face. This was the sign of a good piece of Glass, he had told Peewit. The Littleman clapped him on the back with his good hand, and the dwarf straightened, tugging at his eyepatch. 'Hmm, yes, well, not bad.'

He left the crystal cooling and went to have some tea and the last of Thyla's biscuits. The next part of the process was far more difficult. So far, he had merely blown a piece of crystal. Now he had to etch and carve it into a multifaceted Weatherglass.

He frowned, munching the last of the biscuit. 'I'd like more light. Do you think we could fetch those silver torches in here and group them around the table?'

'I don't see why not,' Peewit answered and stood up to do it. There was a sudden sparkle of light around the walls, and both of them instinctively ducked, hands coming up to cover their ears. But there was no crashing concussion, and the light steadied and grew. The walls of the crystal cavern had lit from within with a shadowless silver light perfect for cutting Weatherglass. The Littleman and the dwarf exchanged a glance.

'That's fine,' Kursh murmured. 'Thanks.' Peewit knew the dwarf was not talking to him.

Kursh leaned to the bucket and fished out his piece of crystal. He set it in the soft leather that would protect it from mars, fastened it in the vise, and picked up the burring tool. 'Nothing like having an audience the first time you make Weatherglass,' he muttered. A quick look at Peewit. 'Sorry, I didn't mean you.'

The Littleman grinned and perched on the other stool. 'No offense taken. If Aashis lets you use his workroom, I suppose you have to expect him to take an interest.'

The dwarf gave him a look and settled himself on the cutter's stool. He bent to the crystal; flecks flew as he cut the first pattern. Intricate flowing channels banded the sphere when he put down the tool some time later. 'That's for the waters,' he said.

He rubbed his nose, rummaged through the tools, and picked a medium-pointed etching pen and a light leather-headed mallet. He began working a design in a thick band about the middle.

Minutely crosshatched, the etching picked out white shapes on the crystal's clear face. Two hours later he put down the tool and scanned the sphere with an eye-piece. He nodded and stretched. 'That's for clouds.'

They stopped for a cup of tea, and Kursh walked about a bit and flexed his shoulders and neck, peering up once through the roof window at the howling fog. He shook his head suddenly and strode back to the bench, as if he knew there was no more time to waste.

This time he chose the tiniest pipette. For a moment he held it in the furnace until the tip glowed red-hot, then he quickly heated the bottom of the crystal itself until it just warmed enough to work. While Peewit watched, he gently poked the pipette into the softened crystal and with the barest of breaths blew a tiny sphere no bigger than a firefly's eye within the crystal itself. He drew the pipette out, sealing the pinhole with heat, so the tiny bubble glowed.

Kursh held the Weatherglass up, and they both peered through it. Whether by his own art or by Aashis' benefaction, Kursh had captured a tiny point in the heart of his crystal that continued to glow after the rest of the Glass had cooled.

He set his masterpiece on the soft leather cloth and smiled over at the Littleman. 'And that,' he said, 'is for the stars.'

Peewit looked from the Weatherglass to his friend and was touched with awe.

Kursh drained his cold tea noisily, and stood up. 'Now let's see if it works.'

Alphonse had not thought it possible for the waves to get any higher, but they did. He had reattached the *Minnow*'s collar of ice and she was not taking on water, but he feared at any moment the mountains of water would crash down and split her in twain. He clung to the pilot deck rail and hoped his lifeline would hold.

When he first heard the bells, he thought the ice and cold and fear had finally gotten to him, but then Ariadne came on deck with Patience draped around her neck like a ruff, and he knew that if he was mad, he was not the only one. Tensely they peered through the blowing fog, hardly able to tell where the sea left off and the air began. For some moments the noise became clearer. 'I do believe we've found it,' Alphonse shouted above the jangling crystal.

He pointed.

Off the port bow the fog thinned. When they were lifted to the top of the next wave they could all see the island of the Crystal Keep. Then they slid down into the valley of a trough and waited for the wave to lift them again. Across the water they could begin to hear the boom of the mountainous surf against the island's shore and the crashing of breaking glass. At the apex of their wave, they could make out that the shining tower which stood on the high headland was shattering under the pounding of the waves and the scouring of the winds.

It was while they were in the trough, waves high around them on every side, that the queen looked up to him and said very calmly, 'We're going to miss it, aren't we?'

The wizard did not answer. The island was well to their left, and the merciless storm of the Unnamed was driving them straight on. When next they were at the top of a wave, he looked not at the island of the Crystal Keep, but straight ahead. He knew beyond doubt that the Falls at World's Edge lay right in front of them.

'Now, Aengus,' he murmured and brought up his ring.

One helping the other, they had shinnied up the rope that Kursh had cast up and out of the roof window. Now they sat on its edge with their legs hooked inside to keep them from being blown off. Peewit expected lightning any time now.

Kursh roared above the wind, 'Here's for luck!' and brought his fist to his chest in the Greenbriar salute. Peewit did not much like having to let go of the sill with one hand, but he answered it and then clung again.

From inside his tunic, the dwarf drew his Weatherglass and held it up. He began to chant above the storm, ancient words of dwarvish used now only for calming weather, and known only to the oldest families on Jarlshof.

On and on the chant went, until the Littleman wondered at it, for the dwarves were normally not so long-winded. He wondered, too, whether with so many verses, Kursh might have dropped any of the words. But out of good faith, he gripped the edge of the roof vent and fought his fear.

Korimson suddenly stopped chanting and thrust his crystal as high into the air as he could. A single word of command thundered into the streaming wind.

The star in the heart of the Weatherglass flared, growing brighter and brighter until it was as brilliant as sunlight in dew. The clouds etched around the middle band softened and puffed white and fluffy, and the channeled waters sparkled and flashed as though trout jumped there. Peewit was so mesmerized he forgot to clutch hard and be afraid.

Sunshine – the ordinary sun of a late-summer day – parted the fog, and the wind dropped to a good kite-flying breeze. They looked down through the breaking clouds and saw the city of Skejfalen far below, the crystal dome of the glass-blowers shining.

Kursh brought his Weatherglass down and regarded it. 'Oho!' he chuckled. 'This one's a corker!'

There was no point in going back into Olin's workroom, so they climbed down the outside of the cave to the landing. They found there the biggest kite Peewit had ever seen, and they both knew that Aashis had gifted them. Peewit whistled and walked around it. 'I'd like to see you fly this!'

Kursh was standing at the edge of the cliff face looking thoughtfully to the city far below. 'You don't fly it,' he said. 'It flies you.'

The Littleman looked puzzled until the dwarf tipped the kite a little and he saw the two leather harnesses folded neatly under the green silk canopy.

He went pale and backed a foot, all that there was room to. 'Oh, no,' he breathed.

Kursh was already buckling himself in. 'When a Power gives you a gift, Peewit, you don't refuse it. Oh, come on, don't be a nit. It's almost time for supper, and you don't want to have to climb down this sodding mountain in the dark, do you?' He turned his head to regard the white-faced Littleman. 'Come on, captain, I'll bet you a month's pay the thing works!'

It was clear that the dwarf intended to leave him behind if he refused, so Peewit shakily climbed into the other harness. Kursh finished lacing his tunic over the Weatherglass. 'Ready?' he asked.

'No,' the Littleman answered.

A bark of laughter echoed off the mountain, and the first few notes of Marian the Fair rolled down toward the unsuspecting good folk of Skejfalen. Then the brawny dwarf thrust them off the landing and they were falling.

The redhead took a breath and began to weave Aengus's Warding. Before he had even finished, the *Minnow* responded and began to tack across the bottom of a trough. He set her stern-on to the next wave, and then tacked again. Tack. Tack. Finally, there was crashing surf about the barque and the island lay dead on. If there are rocks, I'll rip out her keel, he thought, but there was no question of sailing around the island, looking for a good spot. From the roaring, he judged that the World's Edge must lie just behind the island. He gritted his teeth and set *Minnow* up for the final run, and the wave took the boat and hurled it like a dart into a wide estuary that cut the sloping rocks tumbling to the sea.

The smile Ariadne turned on him almost made the whole business worthwhile.

'Madam, your hand?' He helped her over the gunwales, and they clung together for a moment, looking up at the broken and jagged abutments and spires. Even as they watched, they were reminded that the Unnamed's wrath still raged: a towering wave broke on the headland, and the resulting shudder went through the cliff. One of the wide cracks already open in the Keep itself yawned even farther. Another such shock and the tower of the Winds would fall.

'It doesn't look too safe,' the wizard said.

The queen looked up at the ice beginning to drip off his ginger beard and laughed. To have come so far through such peril, nd now he was worried about cracks!

Alphonse began to grin, but a gasped thought came from Patience, still standing on the cabin roof. He swung to look, and a heavy rope of scaly green caught him around the ankles. 'Run!' he shouted in the queen's face, and then he hurled Fire at the swarming, suckered arms enveloping him.

The snap of his garnet threw her backward, farther up the strand.

'Run!' he repeated desperately.

She scrambled up and sprinted over the seaweeded rocks toward the chiming crystal tower. She looked back once and saw flares of garnet Fire and a mass of grasping tentacles. Knowing there was nothing she could do to help him, the queen raced to reach the Crystal Keep.

There was a path. She did not stop to question who could have made it, but followed it up and up, and then the jangling was all about her, so that she had to hold her ears as she plunged under the crystal portcullis. There was only one stairway, and she pounded up it, around and around the spirals.

Alphonse was covered with slime that oozed and burned, and still more arms of the thing wriggled toward him. He slashed his Fire at it, but then it had him around the arms and waist and he was dragged inexorably toward the roiling water of the estuary. He tried to grasp anything he could reach on *Minnow* as the water rose around his feet, but he was just too far away.

There was a spitting yowl and a blur of black-and-white went hurtling past his face to land on the scaly arm that pinioned his ring hand. Patience raked her claws across the tentacle, fighting to free her wizard. He nearly got the arm free as the loop that held him momentarily loosened, but then three other arms snared him and a fourth plucked Patience off and hurled her onto the rocks.

Alphonse cried out with rage, and a garnet-and-pearl web quickly formed around him and the creature that held him. His anger fed on the fear and exhaustion of the voyage and surged with a white and molten power to fry the tentacles to a crisp. There was a boiling from the depths, and then a vicious beak and malevolent eye surged through the water toward him.

Gold shot through his web.

Ariadne heard the shout of laughter from the strand in a voice she almost knew, then the crashing of the portcullis as it sealed the Crystal Keep behind her.

She clasped the small cloth-of-gold pouch and fought her way up the stairs. There was a place where a chunk of them had broken away and she had to leap up to bridge the distance. The crystal was slick beneath her hands, and she could find no purchase. Her kicking feet found nothing but air beneath her. There was an uplifting gust of wind and her fingers closed about the edge of the stair. She porpoised up the stairs until she could stand again. Every fiber of nerve was shaking, but she crawled on. How high is this thing? she mouthed with something between fear and desperation.

The chiming would surely deafen her. She knew now what it was like to be in a belltower when a carillon pealed forth. The whole tower was swaying in the wind, and she had no hand to spare to block her ears, so she put her head down and plowed on. Her mind became light and soared above the body that was only a speck on a glass stair. My, I've climbed a long way, she thought, and then her mind went winging out through one of the shattered crystal windows and swooped down to the *Minnow*. There was a green and scummy slick on the surface of the water, but the churning had stopped. Something black-and-white was broken on the rocks, and she realized with bitter grief that faithful Patience lay there. Of her wizard Ariadne could find no trace. Sorrow shot through her, and she turned from the sight of the broken-masted barque lolling in the greasy water.

Her mind spiraled away to Greenbriar. Very dimly, through the stained glass that a workman had finished soldering just that day, she saw the crowded hall below with servingfolk clearing the tables, while people leaned on an elbow and listened to Imris's sweet music. A little boy at the head table straightened his golden circlet with one sticky hand and licked the honey from his fingers. She smiled.

Then she spun over the water like a gull, and an island floated on the dark, star-reflecting water. Houses winking with candles came into view, and she saw a dark hillside. Something green and whispering like silk swooped by, and she could have sworn that it had four cross-gartered legs.

Before she could wonder more about it, the mote on the stairs cried out in terror and her mind flew back at all haste across the storm-tossed sea.

The crack opened right under her hands, and the queen felt herself begin to fall. The Keep was still shuddering, and she knew that another wave had hit. She hurled herself up the last few steps and fell on her face on the landing. The wind raged here, and she suddenly realized that she had reached the top and that there were no battlements or sheltering walls. Cowering from the force of the gale, she raised her head. Across the

smooth crystal floor to her left was the shattered remnant of
Aashis's Power on Earth: a wall which once had been of clearest
crystal, now webbed with cracks, had in the middle of it a single
large window. Beyond this, the queen could see stars piercing
bright against black firmament. She had come to the Window
Between the Worlds. While she lay gathering breath and courage to approach it, a stream of molten crystal, silver and eerily
beautiful, blew through the window in a bubble, like a child's
soap ring. She gazed in wonder as Aashis's crystal was etched
with clearest lines and strokes. Birds of all feather, leaping
porpoises, gliding gossamer-finned fish, moonglow and
starshine appeared on the Lord of the Winds' crystal.

But the Unnamed struck back, and now she saw why the stars
were disappearing from the sky and people's minds were
undone. With the force of a sledgehammer blow, the wind
summoned by Tydranth smashed Aashis's crystal and blew the
fragments back through the Window Between the Worlds.
Ariadne dropped her head to the slick floor of the landing. This
is what I did, she told herself, when I blew the Pipes. When she
opened her eyes again, the cloth-of-gold bag was right before
her, clutched in her hand.

How could the Lord of the Winds mend her Crystal if he
couldn't even protect his own creations? Despair swept her
under like a riptide.

The Crystal Keep began to vibrate like a struck glass. Below
her Ariadne could hear the final agony of the remaining spires
and buttresses as they exploded under the stress. Likely the
stair is gone, she thought very calmly.

She could not, could not, stand the gale of laughter that set the
crystal shivering.

So she dumped the fragments of her own Crystal of Healing
into her hand, making sure the seeds were there, and rose to her
feet. She had taken two stumbling steps when the rising of a
cloud of butterflies out of every cranny of the blasted tower
signaled the end. The ragged silk wings brushed her face. She
forced herself to go forward even as she saw out beyond the
headland the tidal wave that would overtop even this high
platform. Tydranth was coming for her Crystal.

The queen staggered to the Window Between the Worlds.
'Take it back then, Lord of the Winds, and do thou keep it safe
from the One We Do Not Name.' She cast the shining slivers and
the seeds toward the opening.

But her hand was shaking, and a sudden gentle puff came
through from the starry Realm, and the fragments of the Crystal
of Healing hit the window wall instead of going through the
opening. 'No!' the queen shrieked, diving toward the chips to
gather them feverishly and try again. The fragments were stuck
to the Keep, seeming to melt into the structure itself before her

horrified eyes. There was no time left. The raging monster wave strode over the headland, over the cliff, and smashed the Crystal Keep as a master smashes an apprentice's reject.

The Wizard of the Three felt smooth coolness under his bearded cheek and woke to gray light and gentle rocking.

He was clinging to a piece of crystal flotsam about a half mile off the island, and he could not remember how he had gotten there. Fighting back through a tangled web of memory, he saw a hooked beak, a kelp-crowned head. He kicked convulsively and spun in a slow circle in the dancing waves under a dawn sky. There was nothing entrapping his feet and he could sense no evil around him. When the new sunlight flashed into his eyes again on the next slow turn, he blinked and tried to focus. Wake up, wizard, he told himself. Something important has happened.

Lifting a head that seemed to weigh as much as a millstone, Alphonse saw the Crystal Keep sparkling on the headland. He peered and tried to blink the salt from his swollen eyes.

As he watched, the Keep grew new spires and battlements, like a city unfolding in a moment. His mouth fell open and he gulped seawater. He coughed wrackingly, but when he looked again, he saw that it was no hallucination. The Keep was healing itself.

Clear glass jumped for the lightening sky, and seawater streamed off the gutters and battlements, as though the whole thing had just risen dripping from the sea. Delicate tracery of spun crystal formed bridges and improbable promenades. To his ears was born the quiet tinkle of bells. Bright specks of color circled above the highest turret and coalesced into a cloud of butterflies that dipped and fluttered in the wind, a living pennon.

Somehow he knew Ariadne was responsible for the healing. He spat the salt water from his mouth and began to kick for the land.

After a time, Alphonse washed up on shore. He staggered out of the lapping water and braced his legs to keep from pitching on his face. 'Ariadne!' he tried to yell, but his throat was raw and his glad hail did not carry very far. He coughed and cleared his throat. 'Ariadne!' he shouted, and this was better; he could hear her name echoing off the Crystal Keep.

The glass chimes tinkled questioningly.

'My love!' the wizard called.

The sea sighed behind him.

'Ariadne?'

The lilac clouds floated in the carnation sky.

But from the Greenbriar Queen, there was no answer.

Sheila Gilluly

GREENBRIAR QUEEN

A GLORIOUS FANTASY EPIC

The runes surged at once into flame so that the whole
length of the wand was limned with a brilliant glow.
In the dim room they watched as a second, spell-image
staff materialised out of the thin air, seemingly, and
hovered there above the real wooden stave in Llodin's
hands. Two ghostly hands appeared, a mirror of the
wizard's own, and seized the light wand. With an
abruptness that startled them all, the magic hands
moved quickly in the manner of someone breaking a
twig, and the spell staff snapped in two. In the gap
between the two pieces a piercingly bright gem
shone like a star, caught and held there, distant
and unattainable.

The Dark Lord's reign is about to begin, for the age of doom
prophesied long ago is now upon the people of Ilyria. The
Greenbriar King is dead, his children vanished and his
treacherous bastard half-brother, Dendron, now holds the
throne. But more dangerous by far than Dendron is his
wizard adviser, the Fallen, who can free the dread Dark
Lord from exile and bring ruin to all the world.

The Fallen needs the blood of Princess Ariadne, the true
Greenbriar heir, to weave his spell. But a group of loyal
Watchmen would brave sorcerous evil and warriors' swords
to protect their future queen. For only she can wield the
magic Crystal, Ilyria's final weapon against the
Darkness to come . . .

FICTION/FANTASY   0 7472 3240 7   £6.95

More Fantasy Fiction from Headline:

ELF DEFENCE

A magical new fantasy by the
author of
NEW YORK BY KNIGHT

ESTHER M. FRIESNER

WHEN MAGIC MEETS MORTAL

**When Amanda Taylor and her stepson, the elf
prince Cassiodoron, fled Elfhame for the
mortal lands of Earth, Cass's father Kelerison,
Lord King of Elfhame Ultramar, swore he'd hunt
them down and bring them back.**

**Now he's found them . . . and their haven in
the peaceful town of Godwin's Corners faces
invasion by the not-so-peaceable Fair Folk.
But all is not well in Elfhame — and soon
Amanda, Cass and their unlikely allies find
themselves caught up in a struggle for the elfin
throne itself . . .**

ELF DEFENCE

**When magic meets reality anything can
happen.**

Also by Esther M. Friesner from Headline
NEW YORK BY KNIGHT

FICTION/FANTASY   0 7472 3243 1   £2.99

Headline books are available at your book-shop or newsagent, or can be ordered from the following address:

Headline Book Publishing PLC
Cash Sales Department
PO Box 11
Falmouth
Cornwall
TR10 9EN
England

UK customers please send cheque or postal order (no currency), allowing 60p for postage and packing for the first book, plus 25p for the second book and 15p for each additional book ordered up to a maximum charge of £1.90 in UK.

BFPO customers please allow 60p for postage and packing for the first book, plus 25p for the second book and 15p per copy for the next seven books, thereafter 9p per book.

Overseas and Eire customers please allow £1.25 for postage and packing for the first book, plus 75p for the second book and 28p for each subsequent book.